The Club Trilogy book three

THE REDEMPTION

Lauren Rowe

Chapter 1
Jonas

I don't want to stop holding on to her, but they peel my body off hers. I stumble backward, my eyes wide. I look down at my shirt. It's soaked in her blood. There's so much blood. It's everywhere.

"No pulse," one of the men says, holding her wrist. He moves his fingers to her throat. "Nothing." He frowns. "Damn. Her carotid's slashed clean through. Talk about belts and suspenders—Jesus." He shakes his head.

"What kind of animal...?" the other man says, but his voice goes quiet. He glances over at me. "Get him out of here. He shouldn't see this."

The men are dressed like firemen—but I don't think they're firemen because there's no fire.

"Body's already cool. I'd estimate a good fifteen, twenty minutes, at least."

I love you, Mommy, I said to her. But she didn't say it back to me. This is the very first time she didn't she say it back to me, ever. When I say it, she's supposed to say, "I love you, baby—my precious baby." That's what she always says, just like that. "I love you, baby—my precious baby." Why didn't she say it this time? And why won't she look at me? She just keeps staring out the window. I look out the window, too. An ambulance is parked in front of our house. The siren light on top is twirling around but it's not making any sound.

I hear faraway sirens. They're getting closer. I usually like hearing sirens—especially sirens that are getting closer. I like it when a police car chases after the bad guy or a big red fire truck zooms past our car. Mommy says when you hear a siren you have to pull over to

1

the side of the road. "There they go to save the day!" she always sings when they pass. But not today.

Today, I don't like hearing sirens.

I move to the corner of the room. I sit on the floor, rocking back and forth. I told her I love her, but she didn't say it back to me. And now she won't look at me, either. She just stares out the window. She doesn't even blink. She's mad at me for not saving her.

"Is this your mother, buddy?" the first man says. He bends down to me.

My voice doesn't work.

She's my mommy.

"Was there anyone else in the house with you two?"

I wanted to be alone with her. I wanted her all to myself. I wanted to take her pain away. I was a bad boy.

"We're here to help you, son. We're not going to hurt you. We're paramedics. The police are coming right now."

I swallow hard.

I stayed in the closet because I thought I could use the magic in my hands after the big man left, but then the magic didn't work. I don't know why the magic didn't work. I was bad.

"What's your name, son?" the other one asks.

"Get him out of here," the first man says again. "He shouldn't see this."

The man bending down to me waves the other man away. "You've got blood on you, buddy," he says softly. "I need to make sure it's not yours. Did anyone hurt you?"

He grabs for my hand, but I jerk free and run to her. I throw myself on top of her. I don't care if I get more blood on me. I hold on to her with all my might. They can't make me leave her. Maybe my magic hands will start working again if I try hard enough—maybe I didn't try hard enough before. Maybe she'll stop staring out the window if my magic starts working again. Maybe if I say, "I love you, Mommy," enough times, the magic will work again and she'll finally blink again and say, "I love you, too, baby—my precious baby."

I lie in my bed on top of my baseball sheets. Josh lies in his bed next to mine on top of his football sheets. Josh usually throws a fit if he can't have the baseball sheets, but this time, he let me have them without a fuss. "You can have the baseball sheets every night if you want," Josh said. "From now on, I'll give you first pick."

A week ago, I would have been happy he said that about the sheets. But now I don't care. I don't care about anything. I don't even care about talking ever again. It's been a week since Mommy went away forever and ever, and I haven't said a single word since then. The last words that came out of my mouth were, "I love you, Mommy" when I was hugging and kissing and touching her with my magic hands that aren't magic anymore—and I've decided to let those be the last words my mouth ever says.

Even when the policeman asked me what the big man looked like, I didn't say a word. Even when I heard Daddy crying behind the door of his study, I didn't say a word. Even when I dreamed about the big man cutting mommy up with a knife and then coming after me, I didn't say a word. Even when Daddy told us last night how the police figured out it was Mariela's sister's boyfriend who made Mommy go away forever and ever, and I heard Daddy say on the phone to Uncle William, "I'm gonna kill that motherfucker," I didn't say a word.

I sit up in my bed.

I hear Mariela's voice downstairs in the foyer. I know she's in the foyer because her voice is bouncing really loud and the foyer is the only place in our house where voices sound big and bouncy like that, especially a voice as soft as Mariela's.

I look at Josh. He's fast asleep. Maybe I should wake him up to say hi to Mariela? But no, Mariela's mine. I'm the one who sits and talks to her in the kitchen while she's cooking us Venezuelan food. I'm the one who helps her wash the pots and listens to her sing her pretty songs in Spanish. I like it when she dips her hands into the dishwater and her brown skin comes back up wet and shiny and looking like caramel sauce on an ice cream sundae. Mariela's skin is so soft and smooth and pretty, sometimes when she's singing, I touch her arm with my fingertips and close my eyes and rub softly up and down. And her eyes are pretty, too—the color of Tootsie Rolls. I like how Mariela's dark eyes twinkle at me when she hands me a pot to dry or when she sings me one of her songs.

"*Señor, por favor!*" Mariela shouts downstairs.

I jump out of bed and bolt out of my room. This is the first time I've left my bed since Mommy went away forever and ever. My legs

3

feel stiff and sore. My head hurts. I promised myself I'd never leave my bed again, but I want to see my Mariela. Even if I made that promise to myself about never leaving my bed ever again, maybe I can make a new rule that I'm allowed to leave my bed only if it's to see Mariela. I run down the steps as fast as I can. I can't wait to hear Mariela's voice calling me Jonasito or singing me one of her pretty songs.

But Daddy's voice stops me in the middle of the staircase.

"Get out of here," I hear Daddy say. He's using his mean voice. "Or I'm calling the police."

"*No, señor! Por favor,*" Mariela cries. "*Dios bendiga a la señora. Por favor, déjeme ver a mis bebes. Los quiero.*" *Let me see my babies. I love them.*

"You're the one who told that motherfucker we were going to the football game—you might as well have killed her yourself."

Mariela cries really loud. "*No, señor! Ay, Dios mio, señor. No sabía! Lo juro por Dios.*" Mariela switches to half-English. "Please, *señor*, I love my babies—*son como mis hijos.*" *They're like my sons.* "*Señor, por favor. Esta es mi familia.*" *This is my family.*

"Get out," Daddy yells. "Get the fuck out."

When Daddy's voice is angry like this, especially when he's yelling at Mommy or Mariela, I know I should stay out of his way. But I don't care. I want to see my Mariela.

I run down the steps and across the foyer and jump straight into her arms.

She screams the minute she sees me and hugs me to her. She's squeezing me so tight, I can't breathe.

For the first time since Mommy went away, I speak. "*Te quiero, Mariela.*" My voice sounds scratchy.

"*Ay, mi hijo,*" she says. "*Pobrecito, Jonasito. Te quiero.*"

I wanted the last words I ever said for the rest of my life to be "I love you, Mommy"—but I figure speaking Spanish to Mariela doesn't really count as talking, even if I tell her I love her, because Spanish isn't real. It's just my secret language with Mariela, like make-believe. Even Daddy doesn't understand our secret language, and he's the smartest man there is, so talking to Mariela, even telling her I love her—as long as I'm speaking Spanish—doesn't count as breaking my rule.

Daddy screams at Mariela and tells her to leave.

I grab ahold of Mariela's skirt. *"No me dejes, Mariela."* Don't leave me.

"Te quiero, Jonasito." Mariela's crying really hard. *"Te quiero siempre, pobrecito bebe."* I love you forever.

"No me dejes, Mariela."

"Mariela?" It's Josh. He must have heard her voice and woken up. He runs to her and hugs her.

Mariela kneels down and hugs him while I continue grabbing onto her shoulders.

"Te quiero," she says to Josh. *"Te quiero, bebe."*

Josh understands my secret language with Mariela, but he doesn't speak it very well. "I love you, too," Josh cries.

"It's time to leave," Daddy yells at Mariela. He picks up the phone. "I'm calling the police."

Mariela holds Josh's face in her hands (which makes me a little bit angry because I wish she'd do that to me) and she cries really hard. *"Cuida a su hermanito,"* Mariela says to Josh. *"Sabes que él es lo sensitivo."* Take care of your brother. You know he's the sensitive one.

"Okay, Mariela," Josh says. "I will."

"Te quiero, Mariela," I say, holding onto her skirt. *"No me dejes."* Don't leave me.

"Oh, Jonasito," Mariela says. *"Te quiero, bebe."*

Mariela tries to hug me, but Daddy pulls her away from me and drags her toward the front door. I beg Daddy to please let my Mariela stay with me. I scream her name. I tell her I love her. I cry and cry. But no matter what I say or do, Daddy makes my Mariela leave and never come back again.

Chapter 2
Jonas

She looks so pale.

"Blood pressure ninety over fifty," the EMT says. They're crowding around her, edging me out. Space is limited in the back of the ambulance, so I'm sitting down by her feet, clutching her ankle.

"What's her name?" the paramedic asks me.

I see his mouth moving—hear his words. But I can't speak. I promised to protect her. I promised her I'd never let harm come to her. And then I sat in that classroom and listened to fucking music on my laptop while she stood in that bathroom fighting for her life. My entire body shakes.

One EMT holds something down on her neck and the back of her head. Another holds something down on her ribs. An IV is attached to her arm.

"What's her name?" the guy asks me again.

I want to answer him, but my voice doesn't work.

"What's her age?"

I swallow hard. I won't let The Lunacy take over again. I'm stronger now. I'm different now. Sarah needs me.

"Sarah Cruz. Twenty-four."

She moans. Her eyes flutter open.

The EMT repositions himself, making room for me to lean into her. I shove my face into hers.

Her eyes are wide. Scared. A tear falls out the corner of her eye and down her temple.

"Jonas?" she says. Her voice is nothing but the faintest of whispers—but with that one barely audible word from her, my teetering mind lurches sharply away from the brink of darkness and

6

leans toward the light, toward Sarah, toward my precious baby. With that one faint utterance from her, The Lunacy retracts and skitters away like a cockroach after the kitchen light has come on. With that one word from Sarah, my mind reenters my body.

"I'm here, baby. We're on our way to the hospital. You're going to be fine."

"Class starts in five minutes," she says. "I have to go."

"Do you know your name?" the EMT asks.

She looks at the EMT blankly. "Jonas?"

"I'm right here."

"Sit back a little, sir."

I sit back. "I'm right here, baby. Let them work on you." I choke back a sob.

"Do you know your name?" the EMT asks her.

Her eyes are wide.

"Do you know your name?"

She doesn't answer. Her face is pale.

My heart is pounding violently against my chest wall.

"Do you know what today is?" the EMT asks.

"Con law."

"Do you know where you are?"

"Who are you?" she asks the EMT.

"I'm Michael, an emergency medical technician. I'm taking you to the hospital. Do you remember what happened to you?"

She moans. "Class starts in five minutes. You have to let me go." She's strapped to the stretcher.

"Stay still, Sarah. You're hurt. You have to stay still. We're going to the hospital. Tell them your name."

She stares at me blankly. "Jonas?"

"I'm right here, baby."

She bursts into tears. "Don't leave me."

"I'll never leave you. I'm right here." I choke back another sob. I promised to protect her. I promised no harm would come to her. "I'll never leave you, baby. I promise."

The ambulance stops. The back doors swing open.

Doctors surround her and whisk her away. I jog alongside her stretcher through the hallway until someone stops me outside the swinging doors.

"What's her name?"

"Sarah Cruz. C-R-U-Z."

"Age?"

"Twenty-four."

"Any known allergies to medication?"

"She's never mentioned any."

"Do you know if she's taken any medication today? Anything at all?"

I shake my head. "Nothing."

"Does she have any medical conditions?"

I shake my head. "No."

"Are you her husband?"

My entire body quivers. "Yes."

Five minutes later—or is it five hours?— someone finally approaches me in the waiting room. "We're running tests," the guy says. He's wearing scrubs. His eyes drift down to my shirt.

I look down, too. There's blood all over me.

"Were you injured?"

I shake my head.

"That blood is hers?"

I nod.

"She's conscious and speaking. Are you Jonas?"

I nod.

"She keeps asking for you." He grins sympathetically. "The minute we can, we'll bring you back to hold her hand. Just sit tight. We're running a bunch of tests to figure out the extent of her injuries."

I nod again.

"Just sit tight."

The doctor leaves and I sit back down. I'm shaking. My mind is not my own. The longer I sit here, the more my mind hurtles into space. I promised to keep her safe and I failed her. I'm losing it. I need Josh.

I reach for my phone in my pocket but it's not there. Where is it? I don't know Josh's phone number by heart. When I want to talk to Josh, all I ever do is press the button on my phone that says Josh.

My mind is not my own—it's bobbing and weaving and careening through space, trying its damnedest to outrun The Lunacy. And failing miserably.

Chapter 3
Jonas

"You wanna go climb the tree?" Josh asks.

I don't speak, as usual. I haven't spoken since Mommy left two months ago—not even when they sent me away to that mean place right after Daddy made Mariela leave. I never want to go back to that mean place again—I missed Josh and Mommy and Mariela and Daddy and my soft bed and I wanted to go home—and all those doctors cared about was trying to make me talk even though I can't ever talk again.

I knew the whole time I was at the mean place if I did what they wanted me to do, if I said anything at all, they'd let me go home to be with Josh and Daddy again. But they didn't understand my mouth isn't allowed to say anything ever again, not since my mouth said, "I love you, Mommy" and she didn't say it back.

"Let's go climb the tree like we used to," Josh says.

Back when Mommy lived at our house with us, Josh and I used to climb the big tree every day—but now that Mommy's gone I don't care about climbing the tree. I don't care about doing anything anymore. All I want to do is go to heaven with Mommy.

"Come on," Josh says. Josh grabs my hand and pulls me out of my bed.

When I just stand there and don't crawl back into bed, he smiles and grabs my hand again and drags me all the way downstairs, through the kitchen, out the back door, into the backyard, across the field, and to the big climbing tree.

"Come on, Jonas," Josh says. "Let's climb."

Josh starts climbing, but I stand at the bottom of the tree and watch him for a couple minutes. He's so much slower at climbing

9

than me—he's doing it all wrong. Oh my God, it's killing me to watch Josh climb the big tree like he's a fish. Mommy always used to say, "If you judge a fish by how well he climbs a tree, he'll always fail—so why not let the poor little fishy swim, instead?" Well, I'm sorry but it's true—Josh is a dang fish trying to climb a tree. I start climbing after him, but only because I can't stand watching Josh the Fish be so bad at it anymore.

In no time at all, I pass Josh on my way up the tree. When I get up as high as I'm allowed to climb, I sit and look up at the sky, waiting for my brother. When he finally reaches me, he sits and looks up at the sky, just like I'm doing. I don't know what Josh is thinking about, but I'm making pictures in my head with the puffy white clouds.

"You know what I figured out?" Josh says.

I don't reply.

"Mommy's floating in the clouds in the daytime, and at night, she's in the stars. When you see a star twinkle at night, it's Mommy winking at us, telling us it's time for bed."

I don't want to talk about this so I start climbing down. I thought my magic hands would make Mommy all better, and they didn't.

Almost every night since Mommy left, I've dreamed about the big man with the hairy butt cutting Mommy up into little tiny pieces. Sometimes, I dream he's coming after me, too. Once, after I dreamed about the big man cutting Mommy up, I woke up to find Mariela hugging me and singing one of her songs in Spanish—and that made me cry really hard because I was so happy to see her and I've missed her so much. But then I woke up again for real and Mariela wasn't there. No one was there except for stupid Josh, sleeping next to me in his bed, drooling. No Mommy. No Mariela. Just Josh with spit on his chin.

I keep climbing down the tree. The magic in my hands didn't work. And I don't understand why it didn't.

I can hear Josh climbing down after me, still talking about Mommy. But I don't want to talk about Mommy ever again, even with Josh. It makes me think of the blood—so much blood like an ocean of it—and that man's butt when he pulled his pants down. It makes me think about how Mommy looked afraid, but I didn't come out of the closet to help her. Because I was bad.

Josh hops down to the grass next to me.

"Let's get the football and throw it around," he says. He grabs my hand like he's going to pull me toward the shed where we keep all the sports stuff.

I pull my hand away.

"Come on, Jonas," he says, but I stomp away. He follows me. "We can throw a baseball, instead, if you want—we can do whatever you want. You can pick."

This is new. Josh never lets me pick. He's usually so bossy. I kind of want to pick, but I keep marching away, anyway.

Out of nowhere, Josh tackles me. I fall to the grass with him on top of me and he punches me in the stomach and then in the arm and then in the face. I don't fight back. I want him to punch me. Everyone should punch me. I was bad. It's my fault Mommy had to go away. If he punches me hard enough, maybe I can go to heaven with her. I don't want to be here anymore. I want to be with Mommy.

"Why don't you fight back?" Josh says. "Come on!" he screams.

I just lie there and let him hit me. I start to cry and so does he. He's crying and punching. I'm crying and getting punched. After a minute, Josh stops. He sits on top of me, breathing hard. Tears and snot run down his face.

I don't move. I wish he'd punch me some more.

We stare at each other. We don't know what to do. This is weird. We're both crying really hard.

Josh takes a big breath and then he slaps himself in the face. Really hard.

I smile, even though I'm crying. Why'd he do that? That was a dumb thing to do.

Josh smiles really big when I smile. This is the first time I've smiled since Mommy went away. He slaps himself again, even harder, and that makes me laugh.

"If you aren't going to fight back, I guess I'll have to do it for you," Josh says.

I slap myself, too—really hard—and that makes Josh laugh.

"Now doesn't that make you feel better, Jonas?"

It does.

Josh leans down and lies on top of me and we pretend to wrestle, but what we're really doing is hugging and crying for a really long time.

"What the hell?" It's Daddy. "Get up."

Oh man, I know that voice. That's the voice that tells me we're in big trouble. We get up really fast and wipe at our eyes.

"What the hell's going on? I come out here and this is what I see—you boys rolling around in the grass together, crying your eyes out?"

Oh boy, we're in such big trouble.

Daddy covers his face with his hands for a minute. He looks really sad. "If you boys want to cry, okay, but you can't do it where everyone's going to see you and you most certainly can't do it around me. I understand you might sometimes have to cry—but I don't want to see you do it, boys. I'm doing my best to get out of bed each day and I can't be around anyone, even you two, who can't keep his shit together. It's time for all three of us to pull ourselves together and stop fucking around." He shakes his head and makes a weird sound. "If you two boys need to talk about your feelings and cry your little eyes out, then I'll send you to a shrink and you can do it behind closed doors 'til you're blue in the face. But when you're home and in my presence, you boys are gonna start acting like men from here on out. Do you understand me?"

"Yes, sir," Josh says.

I stare at my father, but I don't answer him. I want Mommy.

Daddy's eyes flash at me. "Jonas Patrick, I've had it with you. I've been patient with you up 'til now, thinking you just needed to get it out of your system, but your time's up. It's time to quit fucking around and start talking again. You think you're the only one who feels like the world's crashing down around him?" His voice sounds funny, like he's going to cry. "Your mother was a fucking saint. She was my savior. And now she's gone and who's gonna save me now?"

Josh and I look at each other. We don't know what that means.

"Why don't you think about how someone else is feeling for a fucking change, huh? You're not the only one wanting to lie down and die. Maybe you should stop and think how other people might be feeling—especially considering you're the reason she was here at the house in the first place. If it wasn't for you..." Daddy makes a mean face at me and marches away.

I bolt to the big tree again, as fast as I can, and this time I climb higher than I've ever climbed, higher than Mommy lets me climb—

straight up to the very highest branch, the one Mommy says might break if I stand on it. But I don't care if it breaks. Maybe I want it to break.

Once I'm on the very highest branch, I reach my hands up over my head and try my hardest to touch the clouds. But even the highest branch isn't high enough for me to reach Mommy. I need to bring a ladder up here next time. Or better yet, I should climb a mountain—yeah, forget about this stupid tree, I'm going to climb a mountain, the tallest mountain in the whole world. And then I'll go to the tippy-top of it and reach my hands way up in the air and touch the clouds and Mommy will lean down and pull me up. And then we'll lie together in her cloud like it's that blue hammock at Uncle William's lake house and Mommy will smile at me and kiss me all over my face like she always does and we'll be together again forever and ever.

Chapter 4
Jonas

My mind bounces maniacally from one bizarre thought to another as I await word from the doctor. My knee keeps jiggling wildly. I can't make it stop. I'm having all kinds of crazy thoughts—thoughts about things I haven't thought about in years and years. Maybe I'm having some kind of nervous breakdown again. Why hasn't the doctor come out here to tell me what's going on?

I look down. My shirt is drenched in Sarah's blood. I head into the restroom to clean myself.

As I watch Sarah's blood swirl down the sink, I have the intense feeling I've lived this exact moment before.

The yarn bracelet tied to my wrist, the one that matches Sarah's, is covered in blood. I stand frozen for a minute, trying to figure out what to do. I don't want to take off the bracelet, but my sanity won't withstand having her blood on me, either. I pull off the bracelet and run it under the faucet. It's no use. I shove it into my pocket, my hands shaking.

I try to wring the blood out of my wet shirt, but it's a lost cause, so I throw it in the trash and head shirtless out of the bathroom. The hospital gift shop is just a short ways down the hall. Maybe they sell T-shirts for family members stuck at the hospital for long stretches of time.

A nurse makes a kind of yelping noise as I pass her in the hallway. I cross my arms over my bare chest and she looks away, blushing. I stare at her blankly. My mind can't process human interaction right now.

Yep. The gift shop sells shirts—Seattle Seahawks T-shirts. Kind of a non sequitur, considering the situation. But, hey, I need a clean shirt.

I return to the waiting room in my new shirt and sit in a chair in the corner.

I wait.

I've got the worst fucking headache right now. No, that's not true. Sarah's got the worst fucking headache right now, not me. The thought makes tears spring into my eyes, but I push them down. My mind keeps conjuring images of Sarah with lifeless blue eyes, her wrists tied up and her torso slashed with countless bleeding gashes. Holy fuck. It's official. I'm going crazy.

Some kids from Sarah's constitutional law class bound into the waiting room, and when they see me, they instantly swarm me and ask me how she's doing. *What did the doctor say? How are you holding up?*

They've brought Sarah's computer and mine, her book bag and purse, and my phone. I'm so grateful I could cry. It's not the stuff—I don't give a shit about the stuff—I guess it's just nice to feel like I'm not alone. I thank them profusely and quickly excuse myself to call Josh.

When I hear Josh's voice, I lose it. I can't stop myself.

"Hey, man, everything's gonna be okay," he says. "Take a deep breath."

I do what he tells me to do.

"I'll hop a plane right now, Jonas. Hang in there. Don't do anything stupid."

"I won't. But hurry. I can't think straight, Josh. I'm thinking all kinds of crazy shit."

"I'm coming. Just do your visualizations, bro. Breathe. Stay calm."

"Okay. Hurry."

Josh says he'll call Kat and tell her to call Sarah's mom.

Oh shit. Sarah's mom. This is not the way I envisioned meeting Sarah's mother for the first time. *Oh, hi, Mrs. Cruz, lovely to meet you. Sorry I almost got your daughter killed today.* Fuck me. This is all my fault. *Again.* I'm a fucking cancer. Everything I touch turns to blood.

As I return to the waiting room, my heart leaps into my throat. The doctor's standing there, looking around. When he sees me, he beelines right to me, but I'm paralyzed. I can't breathe. I clutch my chest. I can't think. I can't lose her. I won't survive losing her. No amount of deep breathing or visualizations will save me if she dies.

The doctor's mouth is moving. Words are coming out of his mouth.

He's sorry, he says, so very sorry, but there was nothing they could do. She's gone. But no, wait—that's not what he's saying. That's what I'm *expecting* him to say. If my ears are working and I'm not crazy, if I haven't gone totally, completely, batshit crazy, if I'm not just imagining his words and willing them out of his mouth, he's saying Sarah's going to be just fine—and quickly, too. I can't believe what I'm hearing. Am I hallucinating? Having another psychotic break?

"... and if her vital signs remain strong overnight, we'll release her tomorrow," he says.

I can't believe my ears. Blood on the floor has never worked out this way for me. "Tomorrow?" I ask, incredulous. "But there was so much blood." My legs give way.

The doctor grabs my arm and leads me to a chair. "Do you need some water?" he asks me.

I shake my head. "But there was so much blood." I'm still not sure if I'm imagining this.

"Yeah, she lost a lot of blood. The knife grazed her external jugular vein. That's the vein that stands out on the outside of your neck when you hold your breath." He touches a specific spot on his own neck by way of demonstration. "The external jugular bleeds like crazy when it gets cut—as you saw. There's a real danger of the patient bleeding out if direct pressure isn't applied right away—but in her case, luckily, it was. Our searchable exploration down the throat indicated there was no involvement of the carotid, trachea, or esophagus—just a nick to that one external vein. Despite all the blood, the wound itself was fairly superficial, so we stitched it up and that was that."

I feel like I'm waiting for the other shoe to drop. "What about the rest of her?" My heart pounds in my chest. I brace myself.

"Looks like she fell backwards and hit her head on something pretty hard—"

"The sink—the bathroom sink. There was blood on the edge of it."

16

"Yeah, that's consistent with the injury. Whacked the base of her skull pretty good. Pretty sizeable scalp laceration, mild concussion. Gonna have a doozy of a headache for a couple days, but she'll be fine. Scalp lacerations bleed profusely, as you saw—but again, not life threatening when direct pressure is applied right away, which it was. I'm sure the combination of the external jugular wound and the scalp laceration looked like something out of *Carrie*, but we've got her put back together now and she's gonna be just fine."

"Does she need surgery?"

He smiles. "Nope. We stapled her scalp laceration right up. And the stab wound to the ribcage didn't hit the major blood vessels, the breathing tube, heart or lungs—she got really lucky there—so we stitched that up and she's good to go. If all goes well overnight—vital signs remain strong, no signs of infection—we'll release her tomorrow. She'll be on strict bed rest for two or three days, and after that, I'd say in about a week, she'll be feeling close to her old self."

I'm elated. Shocked. Disbelieving. "She seemed really confused in the ambulance," I say. "Does she have"—I almost can't finish the sentence—"brain damage?"

"A CAT scan of the brain came back normal. Her confusion could have been the result of shock or the concussion—probably a little bit of both. Post-traumatic confusion is common. She seems pretty clear now. A police officer just went in to talk to her."

I let out the longest exhale of my life. "Can I see her now?"

"Right after she's done talking with the police officer, we'll come get you."

I physically shudder with relief, and he makes a sympathetic face.

"She's gonna be fine," he says. He squeezes my shoulder.

"Thank you, Doctor." I sit back down, my head in my hands, trying to focus my spiraling thoughts—but it's no use. My mind is a horse galloping away from the barn, and there's no way it's coming back until I see my baby alive with my own two eyes.

Chapter 5
Jonas

"Miss Westbrook, can Jonas go to the bathroom?" Josh asks, raising his hand.

All I did was look at Josh a little funny and he knew right away what I wanted. Josh has been doing my talking for me for so long, it's like he's inside my brain.

"*May* Jonas go to the bathroom, *please*," Miss Westbrook corrects him.

"*May* Jonas go to the bathroom, *please*?" Josh repeats.

Miss Westbrook looks at me. "Do you need to use the restroom, Jonas?"

I nod.

I don't know why Miss Westbrook always bothers to check with me when Josh speaks for me—he's always right about what I want. I don't mind, though—I like it when Miss Westbrook talks to me. She's pretty. Really, really pretty. Her dark hair is super shiny. I wish I could touch it. And I like how, when she talks to the class, she smiles, even when she's telling someone to say "may" instead of "can" or warning one of the kids to stop talking to his neighbor. Of course, she never has to warn *me* to stop talking to my neighbor—I haven't said a word since before I turned eight, since that day when I was seven when I said, "I love you, Mommy," and Mommy didn't say it back. (That one time I spoke to Mariela in Spanish doesn't count because Spanish isn't even real.)

When I get back from the bathroom, everyone in class is working on the math worksheet. I already finished that one. In fact, I've already finished the entire workbook. I walk toward my desk, but Miss Westbrook calls me over.

"Jonas," she says softly. Her dark eyes are twinkling at me. Man, oh man, Miss Westbrook has the prettiest eyes. They look kind of like chocolate and they sparkle whenever she smiles. "I could really use a classroom helper every afternoon for about an hour," she says. "Someone to help me get everything ready for the next day. Do you think you could be my helper?"

I nod. I don't even have to think about it.

Miss Westbrook flashes me her sparkly smile. Her smile is so pretty it almost makes me want to smile, too. "Wonderful," she says. "When your nanny comes to pick you up today, I'll talk to her about it. Maybe she can take Josh after school for a bit every day while you stay here with me."

I nod again. I'm excited.

After school, Miss Westbrook talks to Mrs. Jefferson about her idea just like she said she would, and she makes it sound like she really needs my help—like I'd be doing her a big favor. I look at Mrs. Jefferson's face, trying to figure out what she might be thinking about the idea, but I can't tell. My stomach hurts, I want to do this so bad.

"The thing is," Mrs. Jefferson says, "Josh and Jonas have a standing doctor's appointment twice a week after school." She lowers her voice. "The therapist."

At that last part, Josh rolls his eyes at me, but I'm too excited about this whole helper-thing with Miss Westbrook to pay any attention to Josh. But, yes, I know what he means. I hate seeing Dr. Silverman, too. Mostly. All we ever do at Dr. Silverman's is color pictures in that stupid coloring book about different kinds of feelings. Or we read from that stupid book, *Let's Talk About Our Feelings*. "Talking lets the feelings out," one of the pages says. "Talking about how we feel makes us feel better," another page says. "Someone might not feel the same way we do—and that's okay," another page explains. "Talking about it doesn't mean we're disagreeing." The last one makes Josh laugh the most. "Talking about it doesn't mean we're *disagreeing*," Josh always says. "It means I'm going to punch you in your stupid, frickin' face."

Every time Josh and I see Dr. Silverman, Josh does all the talking for me. Well, for me and for himself. Josh talks and talks to Dr. Silverman about everything—what he had for breakfast, how he wants to be a baseball player when he grows up, about a dream he might have had the night before—whatever. Sometimes, he even talks about Mommy and how he misses her and how he wishes she could be here with us instead of in the clouds and stars. Josh always cries when he talks about Mommy, but I don't cry. No matter what Josh talks about, even if it's Mommy, I just sit there, coloring in that stupid coloring book, flipping through the frickin' *Let's Talk About Our Feelings* book.

I'd say I hate going to see Dr. Silverman except for one thing. He always plays the best music—the kind of music that makes me feel like my mind is floating in the clouds or riding on a roller coaster. Sometimes, Dr. Silverman's music even makes me forget about feeling sad for a little while.

Dr. Silverman tells me I should listen to music whenever I feel like I have too many feelings inside me. "Music can be like opening a window for your feelings to fly through," he explained to me one time. And when he said it, I got goose bumps on my arms. *Music can be like opening a window for your feelings to fly through.* It was the first thing he'd said to me that made perfect sense. Ever since he told me that, I've been listening to music a lot, especially when I feel like banging my head against the wall. The music calms me down and helps me think straight. So, even though I *mostly* hate going to Dr. Silverman's office, I guess I don't *completely* hate it.

After a visit with Dr. Silverman, Josh always used to say to me, "You don't have to talk if you don't want to, Jonas. I'll talk for you forever if you want." But yesterday, out of nowhere, Josh tried to make me start talking just like everybody else does. "Maybe if you talk—just a little bit—Dad won't make us go to Dr. Silverman's anymore. Come on, Jonas, just make something up—I make stuff up every frickin' time."

At first, I was mad when Josh tried to get me to talk. But today, I think I understand how Josh feels. He's not the one who needs the music, after all.

The more I think about it, the more I'm sure Josh is right—if I said something, anything at all, we wouldn't have to go to Dr. Silverman's anymore. But the thing Josh doesn't understand, the thing no one understands, is that I can't talk ever again. Because talking is against the rules. And there's nothing I can do about that, whether I like it or not.

Miss Westbrook continues whispering with Mrs. Jefferson about what a big favor I'd be doing for her if I became her helper. I feel like my head's gonna explode, I want to do it so bad. Finally, Mrs. Jefferson nods and says, "Well, I guess there's no harm in giving it a shot."

When we get home, Mrs. Jefferson talks to Daddy about what Miss Westbrook said, and, much to my shock, he says I can do it. "Josh doesn't need Dr. Silverman anymore, anyway," Daddy says. "And I suppose Jonas can take a couple weeks off to give this a try. But if it doesn't work, Jonas will have to go back to Dr. Silverman— or, hell, maybe I'll just send him back to the treatment center."

When I hear Daddy say I can help Miss Westbrook, I feel like shouting, "Woohoo!" really loud (but, of course, I don't). I'm so excited about getting to be with Miss Westbrook every day, I don't even freak out that Daddy said that thing about the treatment center.

Later that night, Josh jumps on his bed like it's a trampoline and laughs about how lucky he is and how stupid I am. "Mrs. Jefferson's gonna take me for ice cream every afternoon while you're sitting there with Miss Westbrook," he says. "Sucker."

I roll on my side away from Josh and smile, thinking about how pretty Miss Westbrook is and how her eyes sparkle when she smiles at me. Stupid Josh can laugh at me all he wants—I'll take an hour with Miss Westbrook over a dumb ice cream cone any day of the week.

Chapter 6
Jonas

The cop exits as I walk into Sarah's hospital room. I'm shaking like a leaf. Will she even be able to look me in the eye? Or will she want nothing to do with me?

I stop just inside the door to her room, barely able to breathe. She looks impossibly small. She's got a bandage around her head like she's a Civil War soldier and another one around her neck. She's wearing a hospital gown, but I'm sure she's bandaged under there, too. Oh God, she's pale—though, thankfully, not nearly as pale as she was on the floor of that bathroom. I never want to think about how she looked on the floor of that bathroom again. I bite my lip to suppress a sudden surge of emotion.

Her bracelet's gone. They must have cut it off her. For a moment, the symbolism of her naked wrist threatens to make me lose it, but I stay strong. I'm a fucking beast now. I'm not weak like I used to be.

"Go Seahawks," she says softly. Her voice is gravelly.

I'm confused.

"Interesting time to show your Seahawks pride."

I look down. Oh yeah, my new T-shirt. This woman is bandaged and bruised and literally just escaped death, and she's still got enough gas in the tank to kick my ass. God, I love her. I laugh and cry at the same time and lurch to her bedside. I hug her gingerly, not wanting to break her.

I've never been on the other side of a bloody floor before. Usually, a red-soaked floor simultaneously marks the end of one person's life and my sanity. I don't even know how I'm supposed to react if the story of a bloody floor doesn't have the usual ending.

"I'm so sorry, Sarah," I say, softly kissing her precious lips. "I'm so sorry, baby."

"*I'm* sorry," she mumbles into my lips.

I kiss her again. "You have nothing to be sorry for, you big dummy."

"Jonas," she says.

"I thought I'd lost you," I say, kissing every inch of her face. "Oh my God, baby. I thought I'd lost you."

"Jonas," she says, almost inaudibly.

"This is all my fault. I'm so, so sorry. I fucked up so bad."

"You saved my life," she whispers.

I have no idea what the fuck she's talking about.

"*You saved my life,*" she says again. Her voice is the faintest of whispers.

What? I'm the one who let her go into that bathroom by herself. What the hell is she saying? I have a thousand questions—but before I can ask a single one, Sarah's mom bursts into the room, sobbing and wailing and hijacking Sarah into a sudden whirlwind of rapid-fire Spanish and hysterical tears.

"In English, Mom," Sarah whispers. "Jonas is here."

I understand Spanish fairly well, actually, but Mrs. Cruz talks so fast, I can't understand a word she says.

"Jonas," Mrs. Cruz says, hugging me fiercely.

I'm so ashamed I allowed harm to come to Mrs. Cruz's daughter, I can't even look her in the eye.

"Sarah has told me so much about you, Jonas." Mrs. Cruz touches my cheek. "Thank you so much for your donation. It was delivered this morning—ten times the biggest donation we've ever had. I tried calling Sarah to get your number to thank you, but she didn't answer her phone—" Mrs. Cruz looks at Sarah and bursts into tears.

Sarah squints at me—this is the first she's hearing about my donation to her mom's charity.

Mrs. Cruz hunches over Sarah, bawling her eyes out. "*Qué pasó, mi hijita?*"

"English, Mom," Sarah says softly. "Some guy attacked me with a knife in the bathroom at school."

Mrs. Cruz lets out a pained sob. "Who? Why?"

"I didn't know him. He just wanted what was in my purse. I gave the police a description of the guy—I'm sure they'll catch him. Don't worry."

So, this is the version of events Sarah told the police? What on earth is going on inside that head of hers? I glare at Sarah and she looks away.

"I'm staying here with you all night," Mrs. Cruz says. She pulls up a chair right next to Sarah's bed and drapes herself over Sarah's prostrate body. "Sarah," she says, emotion overwhelming her. "*Mi hijita.*"

I want to be the one sitting next to Sarah, draping myself over her. But, clearly, a mother's love trumps a boyfriend's—especially when the boyfriend's the one who fucked up and let harm come to his girlfriend in the first place.

"Is there anything you need?" I ask. "Mrs. Cruz? Can I get you something to eat? Anything to drink?"

Mrs. Cruz doesn't respond. She's got her head on Sarah's stomach and she's crying her eyes out.

Yeah, I know the fucking feeling.

I wake up in a chair in the corner of the hospital room. When did I fall asleep? I was having a crazy-ass dream—a dream about Miss Westbrook. What the hell? I haven't thought about Miss Westbrook in probably fifteen years.

The room is silent except for the clicks and beeps of the medical equipment. Sarah's fast asleep with her mom still draped over her. Kat's asleep in a chair on the opposite side of the room. I didn't see her arrive. A nurse is changing Sarah's IV bag. I stare at Sarah's heart monitor for several minutes, making sure her pulse is steady and strong, and then I close my eyes again.

My head jerks up. How long was I asleep? Fuck, these crazy-ass dreams won't leave me alone. Am I losing my mind?

Sarah's mom is awake, holding Sarah's hand as she sleeps. Kat's gone. I get up and tiptoe over to Sarah and softly kiss her lips. My heart is heavy—I'm surprised it can beat at all with fifty-pound rocks weighing it down.

"I'm sorry," Sarah whispers when my lips leave hers.

I didn't mean to wake her—but I'm relieved to hear her voice. "I'm the one who's sorry."

"You saved my life," she whispers. She closes her eyes and a tear trickles down her cheek.

I don't know why Sarah keeps saying that. I can only assume it's the painkillers talking because what's happened to Sarah is all my fucking fault.

Chapter 7
Jonas

On the first day of me being Miss Westbrook's after-school helper, she doesn't talk to me all that much except to tell me what jobs she wants me to do. I clean the whiteboard, making sure to erase every little smudge, even off the corners. After that, I sharpen her pencils, making each one the exact same length, and then I staple thirty sets of worksheets, making sure to line up the staples in each and every corner in exactly the same spot.

Miss Westbrook says I'm doing a great job and that I "pay great attention to detail." No one has ever said that to me before. I smile at her—just a teeny-tiny bit—and when I do, she smiles so big at me, I almost laugh. Almost.

The second day is the same as the first, except I pay even more "attention to detail," hoping she'll say something nice to me again. And she does.

"Jonas, you do excellent work," she says. "Anyone can do a *good* job, but it's the special few who care enough to do an *excellent* job. Thank you for caring so much about *excellence.*"

I feel all warm and gushy inside. She's the prettiest lady I've ever seen and I like it when she's nice to me.

On the third day, I know all my jobs so well, I finish them in half the time—so Miss Westbrook gives me even more jobs to do. And on this day, yippee, while I'm doing my extra work, Miss Westbrook starts talking to me. She shows me a teeny-tiny diamond ring on her finger—the diamond's so small it's like a grain of sand—and she tells me the ring is how you know she's getting married. I've seen that ring on Miss Westbrook's hand before, but I just thought she wore it to look pretty.

Miss Westbrook tells me her name's going to be Mrs. Santorini in a few weeks and that the man she's going to marry is in the Navy. She explains how people in the Navy are fighting to protect our country and our freedoms. She says we couldn't do any of the stuff we get to do in America if people like Mr. Santorini didn't fight for us. I listen carefully to everything she says. I like the sound of her soft voice. She smells good, too. I especially like her neck. She wears a little gold cross around it and I can't stop looking at it—her neck, not the cross. But I pretend I'm looking at the cross just in case I'm not supposed to look at her neck so much.

On the fourth day, Miss Westbrook sits me down at one of the desks even before I get started with my work. "I have a little present for you," she says. She puts a gigantic cookie on the desk in front of me. "I baked it for you last night."

It's a huge chocolate chip cookie with M&Ms in it—the biggest cookie I've ever seen—and the M&Ms are in the shape of a heart.

For some reason, I feel my bottom lip shaking when I look at that M&M heart.

Miss Westbrook doesn't talk for a really long time. "Go ahead, Jonas," she finally says. "Try it."

I take a tiny bite. It's the best cookie I've ever had.

"Jonas," she says softly. "If you don't want to talk, that's fine. But sometimes I get kind of lonely in the classroom and I'd love a little conversation. Do you think maybe you could talk to me? You wouldn't have to talk outside this classroom if you didn't want to— and you wouldn't have to talk when the other kids are here. But when it's just the two of us here after school, maybe this could be our little cocoon—a cocoon built for two—a magical place where you're allowed to talk, just to me."

We've been learning about how caterpillars turn into butterflies for the last month—we've even got a whole bunch of chrysalises hanging in a big box and we're waiting for them to hatch any day now. We've been learning that a caterpillar has a special kind of magic inside him right from the beginning, but he has to go inside a cocoon for his magic to work.

Maybe talking to Miss Westbrook in our little cocoon-built-for-two could be another exception to the rule? Like how speaking to Mariela in Spanish didn't break the rule, either? Maybe, even if I talk to Miss Westbrook inside our magical cocoon, my last *official* words in the *real* world would still be "I love you, Mommy."

"Can I still call you Miss Westbrook after you get married?" I ask. They're the first words I've spoken since way before I turned eight—since the day Mommy went away all that time ago. I forgot how my voice sounds. I don't even sound like me anymore.

Miss Westbrook's face looks really surprised. She clears her throat. "Of course, you can, Jonas. I'd love that."

For the next week, I chat up a storm with my pretty Miss Westbrook every single day. I tell her about how much I hate seeing Dr. Silverman, except for the fact that he plays music that sometimes makes me feel better. I tell her about how Josh sometimes slaps his own face when I'm feeling sad, just to make me laugh, and that it always works. I tell her about a book on Greek mythology I just read and about how the Greek gods and goddesses are called the Twelve Olympians and they live on Mount Olympus. And, finally, on the tenth day of me being Miss Westbrook's special helper, I tell her about how I'm going to climb the highest mountain in the whole world one day.

"Really?" she asks. "That's exciting."

"Yeah, Mount Everest," I say, standing on a stool so I can reach the farthest corner of the whiteboard. "Because that's the highest one. I'm going to climb to the tippy-top of it and reach my hands up in the air and touch my mommy in the clouds. And she's going to reach down and pull me up and up and up, and then we'll lie down together on one of the puffy clouds like it's a hammock and I'll rub her temples and take all her pain away like I always used to do."

Miss Westbrook has been sitting at her desk while I've been erasing the whiteboard and talking nonstop, and when I look over at her, she's crying. Without even thinking about it, I climb down from the stool, put the eraser down, walk over to her, and brush her tears off her cheeks with my fingertips. Miss Westbrook wipes her eyes and smiles at me. And then she does something that makes me want to curl up in her lap—she touches my cheek with the palm of her hand. That's what Mommy and Mariela used to do all the time to me and it's my favorite thing.

Since Mommy went away, lots of adults have hugged me, or patted me on the head, or squeezed my shoulder, but not a single one of them has ever touched my cheek. Since Mommy went away, I've dreamed about her touching my cheek lots and lots of times—and about Mariela doing it, too—but then I always wake up and I'm all alone and I have to touch my own cheek, which doesn't feel nearly as good as someone else doing it for you, especially someone pretty like Miss Westbrook.

I close my eyes and put my hand over Miss Westbrook's to make sure she doesn't move her hand. Her skin is soft.

"You're a special little boy," Miss Westbrook says. "I hope one day I'll have a little boy just like you."

When Mrs. Jefferson and Josh come to pick me up, for some reason it seems like maybe I could say hello to Josh just this once without breaking the rules. I mean, Josh is really just me in another body, I figure, and talking to myself can't be against the rules, right?

"Hi, Josh," I say.

Josh seems really happy when I say those two little words to him, even happier than he was about getting ice cream with Mrs. Jefferson; so a few minutes later, when we're sitting in the backseat of the car and Josh is singing along to the radio at the top of his lungs, I talk again.

"Shut up, Josh," I say. "You're singing so goddamned loud, I can't hear the fucking music."

Mrs. Jefferson gasps in the front seat.

"Fuck you, Jonas. *You* shut up," Josh replies, but then he covers his mouth with both hands. "I mean, no, don't shut up, Jonas. Keep talking."

Josh telling me to shut up after I haven't talked for so long makes us both laugh really, really hard—or maybe we're just laughing because we're being really bad and cussing like Daddy.

"You big dummy," I say.

"You're the big dummy. What kind of idiot doesn't talk for a whole year? Jesus."

Not too long after Miss Westbrook becomes Mrs. Santorini, she tells the class she's moving to San Diego on account of Mr. Santorini being in the Navy. All the kids seem sad to see her go, but the way I feel about it is much worse than sad. I feel like I'm dying inside.

Miss Westbrook tells the class to work on page fifty-four from our math workbook and she calls me up to her desk.

"Jonas, honey, it's sunny in San Diego all the time. I hope you'll come visit me."

How can I come visit her? I'm just a kid. I don't have a car or an airplane. I have to look away from her pretty brown eyes or else I might cry.

"And I'll come visit you here in Seattle any chance I get." She starts crying. "I promise."

I don't think Miss Westbrook should promise to come back to me. Everybody leaves me—everybody—and they never, ever come back. I wish she would just tell me the truth: She's leaving me just like everybody does and I'll never see her again. Even as I stand here looking at her pretty face, I feel like a big black scarf is floating down from the sky and covering my entire body.

"I like you, Miss Westbrook," I say, trying to keep the tears from coming. It's the first time I've spoken to her when the other kids are in the classroom, too, when we're outside our magical cocoon. But I can't help it—I have to tell her how I feel about her before she leaves me. Actually, I wish I could say the three words that match my true feelings about Miss Westbrook—but saying those three words to anyone besides Mommy would break the rules.

Miss Westbrook's eyes crinkle. "I like you, too, honey. I'll come back to visit you one day soon, Jonas. I promise."

29

Chapter 8
Jonas

I open my eyes. Sunshine streams through the window of Sarah's hospital room. A nurse stands next to Sarah's bed, checking Sarah's blood pressure.

"Looking good," the nurse says. "And no signs of infection. The doctor will be in soon to decide if you can go home today."

My phone vibrates with a text from Josh. He just landed in Seattle. Are we at UW Medical Center, he wants to know? I tell him not to come to the hospital, to meet me at home—and to please stop and pick up sick-person stuff like Saltines and Gatorade and Jello and chicken noodle soup on his way. Oh, and Oreo cookies. Sarah loves Oreo cookies.

He texts back, *I've got it covered.*

Thanks, I reply.

Hang in there, bro.

Thanks, I reply. *Will do.*

My phone buzzes again. I look down.

I love you, man.

Josh has never said that to me before, ever. Not in person, not in a text. Never. I stare at my phone for a long time, disbelieving my eyes.

Thanks, I text back. I don't know how else to respond.

I put the phone back in my pocket. If Josh were here, he'd surely slap his face right now, as he should.

The doctor arrives and confirms Sarah can go home and my heart leaps. Oh my God, I'm going to take such good care of my baby. No matter what it takes, we'll figure this out. Together.

Mrs. Cruz shrieks with joy at the doctor's news and starts asking

30

him about his discharge orders. Apparently, she thinks Sarah's coming home with her. I look at Sarah, expecting her to say she's coming home with me, but she doesn't. To the contrary, she nods at her mother. What the fuck? Sarah's not correcting her mother's misunderstanding. Sarah's not saying, "No, Mom. I live with Jonas now." Shit. I guess Mrs. Cruz isn't the one who misunderstands. I swallow my emotions. All that matters is what Sarah wants. What Sarah needs. And, clearly, it's not me.

"I can drive you there," I say. "And help with whatever's needed."

"My mom's got it," Sarah says. "I'm just going to sleep, anyway—take my pain meds and sleep. You should use this time to get caught up on whatever you need to do. I'm finally out of your hair." She grins, but there's no joy in it. "I'll be fine."

I can't speak.

"I think I just need a little mommy time," Sarah says softly. There's apology in her voice. But there's no need to apologize—I understand fully. Everything I touch turns to blood: bloody sheets, bloody carpets, bloody walls, bloody bathroom tiles. Sarah's right. For her own good, she should stay as far the fuck away from me as humanly possible.

A nurse loads Sarah into a wheelchair to transport her to the front of the hospital.

"I can walk," Sarah protests.

"Standard procedure," the nurse assures her.

When we arrive at the front of the hospital, Mrs. Cruz leaves Sarah in my care while she gets her car from the parking structure.

Sarah's quiet. I'm quiet. There's so much I want to say, but not here, not now. Maybe there's never going to be a time to say it. Maybe this is it. Sarah obviously needs a break from me. I just hope a break doesn't turn into forever.

My heart feels like a slab of cement inside my chest. "I'll hire a team to guard your mom's house," I say. "I can't let you go over there unprotected."

"No, I'm safe now, at least for a while," Sarah says. "They think I'm worth more to them alive than dead."

What does that mean?

She swallows hard. "Jonas, I have something to tell you." She

31

pauses, apparently getting up her nerve—but Mrs. Cruz returns with the car before Sarah can say another word.

Sarah looks at me with anxious eyes. Shit, the last time she looked at me like this was during our flight to Belize when she was summoning her courage to tell me the truth about The Club.

I open the passenger side of the car and gingerly load Sarah into the seat. My heart is breaking, aching, shattering. I might be dying, quite literally. Physical death couldn't feel any worse than this.

I lean down to her before I shut her door. "I can't let you go..." My brain intended to say, "I can't let you go there unprotected," but my mouth didn't finish the sentence. *I can't let you go.* Yeah, that about sums it up.

"It's just for a couple days," Sarah says. "My mom needs to be the one who takes care of me—and I need her right now. I'm just going to sleep the whole time, anyway." She shakes her head, stifling tears. "I'm not myself right now, Jonas. I'm overwhelmed. I'm in pain." She looks into my eyes and winces. "Don't worry, baby, I'll call you. I promise. It's just for a few days—just a little mommy time."

I nod as if I understand. But I don't understand. If she's leaving me for good, I wish she'd just tell me the truth instead of promising me something she doesn't plan to deliver. If she's not coming back to me, I wish she wouldn't tell me she is.

"Are you sure you're going to be safe?"

"I'm positive. There's no reason for them to come after me. They left me alive for a reason. I'll tell you about it later, I promise."

"I'll put guards at your mom's house anyway, just to be sure."

"No, don't, Jonas. My mom will freak out. Just trust me. Leave it alone."

I'm dumbfounded. They just tried to kill her and almost succeeded and I'm supposed to "leave it alone"? What the fuck am I missing here?

"*Lista?*" Mrs. Cruz asks.

"*Sí, Mama.*"

"I'll bring your clothes to you—whatever you need," I say lamely. I don't understand what's happening. Is this the end for us?

"I've got a bunch of old stuff at my mom's house. I'll be fine."

I'm speechless. She doesn't even want me to drop off a bag for her?

"I'll call you," Sarah says. But what my brain hears her say is, *Don't call me, I'll call you.*

I shut her door. She reclines in her seat and closes her eyes as the car drives away. I stare at the car until it's out of sight. And then I grab at my hair and swallow my tears.

Chapter 9
Jonas

Almost everyone in my seventh grade class is hard at work on today's stupid assignment. Mrs. Dinsdale said those few of us who've already finished, including me, can read whatever we want while waiting for the rest of the class to catch up. I'm reading a book about mountain climbing and there's an entire chapter about Mount Everest. I guess climbing Mount Everest is kind of a big deal—plenty of people have even died trying to do it. They don't let kids climb it, so it looks like I'll just have to climb rocks and trees and ropes and do sit-ups and push-ups and pull-ups in my room to get myself ready for when I'm older. Oh, and I just heard about an *indoor* rock climbing gym opening in Bellevue. Wow, rock climbing *indoors* sounds so cool I can barely sleep at night just thinking about it. Maybe Dad will let our driver take Josh and me there this weekend.

The door to the classroom opens and—holy shit—oh my God—holy fuck—I can't believe my eyes—Miss Westbrook walks in. She's right out of a dream—even more beautiful than I remembered her from four years ago. Wow.

Until just now, I couldn't even remember exactly what Miss Westbrook looked like, to be honest. She'd become nothing but a hazy fantasy in my mind that I sometimes like to think about late at night when I'm alone in my bed—but the minute she walks through the door, every memory comes rushing back into my head and heart and body. Especially my body.

Wow, Miss Westbrook is as pretty as ever. Even prettier than pretty, actually—she's *beautiful*. Her hair is shinier and a bit darker than I remembered it (which I like a lot). And her lips are much fuller than I remembered them, too. Man, oh man, I'd love to kiss Miss

34

Westbrook's lips. I feel a jolt between my legs just thinking about doing it. Should I go over to her? Or maybe wave to her? I don't move a muscle. Maybe this is just a coincidence. Maybe she's not here to see me. Yeah, I'm sure she's forgotten all about me.

Miss Westbrook scans the room and when her eyes lock onto mine, she smiles. Holy fuck, she's smiling right at me, I'm sure of it. I wave and she waves back. Oh my God.

Miss Westbrook turns slightly to the side and—holy shit—now I can plainly see that Miss Westbrook's gonna have a baby. When Miss Westbrook first walked in, I guess I was so busy looking at her beautiful face and imagining myself kissing her lips, I didn't notice her baby bump. Wow. The beautiful Miss Westbrook came back—I can't believe it—and she's gonna have a baby.

"Jonas," Mrs. Dinsdale says. "You have a visitor. Why don't you two go outside for a little bit? Take your time."

When we sit down on a bench outside, Miss Westbrook hugs me and kisses the top of my head. "Jonas! You're so big! Look at you! Wow!"

My cheeks hurt from smiling. My entire body is tingling. "You came back."

"Of course, I did. I came back to see *you*." She winks. "I never break a promise."

I can't believe she's here. I feel like there's electricity zapping my skin. I wish she would touch my cheek like she did that one time all those years ago. Or kiss the top of my head again like she just did a minute ago. Or, even better, kiss my lips. I'd give anything to get a kiss from her—a real kiss with tongue and everything. Oh my God. The thought makes me tingle everywhere, but especially between my legs.

We talk for twenty minutes. She asks me about school and my brother and what sports I'm playing. She tells me that San Diego is as sunny and beautiful as she thought it'd be, that she's a third grade teacher there, and that she and Mr. Santorini are happy and excited about meeting their new baby in a couple months.

"Oh," she says suddenly, touching her belly. "The baby just kicked. You want to feel?"

I'm not really sure. The whole idea of touching her belly kind of freaks me out. But she doesn't wait for my response. She grabs my hand and places it on the side of her hard stomach and two seconds later something inside of her karate chops my hand.

"Oh my God," I say, laughing. I've never felt anything like that before.

"It's a boy," she says, smiling at me really big.

"Wow. That's cool, Miss Westbrook."

"Do you know what I'm going to name him?"

I shrug. How on earth would I know that?

"Jonas," she says.

There's a long, awkward silence. Is she saying my name to make sure I listen carefully to whatever name she's about to say? Or is she telling me, "I'm naming my kid Jonas"? If she's telling me she's naming the baby Jonas, that's quite a coincidence, isn't it? It's not that common a name—not like Josh.

She rolls her eyes and sighs. "I'm naming the baby after *you*, Jonas."

I can't believe my ears.

She smiles. "Because I hope he'll grow up to be just like you one day. Sweet and smart and kind."

I can't remember the last time my heart has raced quite like this, if ever.

At dinner that night, I tell Dad and Josh about Miss Westbrook's surprise visit and how she's naming her baby after me. I'm floating on air when I tell my story, but the minute I'm done talking, I regret saying a damned thing. Clearly, Dad's been drinking—a lot—and that's never a good time to say a goddamned thing to him about anything at all, especially something you care about.

I grind my teeth, waiting for whatever mean thing Dad's going to say to me to make me feel like shit. I don't have to wait long.

"She wants her baby to grow up to be just like you?" he asks. He takes a long swig of his drink. "I guess she's hoping for a lifetime of fucking misery and pain, then."

Josh shoots me his usual look of sympathy. It means, *Ignore him—he's an asshole.* But ignoring him is easier said than done.

"If she gets her wish and her kid turns out to be just like you," Dad continues, "then she'd better watch Mr. Santorini's back." He laughs and swigs his drink. "That's all I'm fucking saying."

Chapter 10
Sarah

Jonas was right all along—the Ukrainian John Travolta was indeed stalking me in broad daylight. But rather than believe my gorgeous hunky-monkey boyfriend when he said he was "one hundred ten percent" sure of something, I decided the more likely scenario was that he was being overprotective and hypersensitive and maybe even a tad bit crazy. Shame on me.

And, now, thanks to my utter lack of good judgment and my inability to trust him, not only did I get relieved of a good portion of my blood supply, I've also put the love of my life through hell. I've made him relive the worst horror of his childhood—and not only that, I've put him in danger, too. Good God, what have I done? I've promised The Club I can get more money from Jonas—and also from a bunch of other guys, too. But, wait, there's more! Just in case all that wasn't bad enough, I gave the bastards Jonas' money—and it was a helluva lot of money, too.

Of course, Jonas will say the money doesn't matter to him— he'll say he'd pay any amount to keep me safe—but that money wasn't mine to give. The whole situation is just a colossal mess—a cluster fuck, as Jonas would say.

I crawl out of bed, pull back the curtains on the window, and peek across the street. Yup. Still there. Two guys sitting in a car. They've been there for the past four hours. I grab my phone off the nightstand and type out a text to Jonas. "Please tell me those two guys sitting across from my mom's place are yours. Or else I'm going to crap my pants."

"Yes. Sorry to worry you. I should have mentioned it. They're mine."

I'm about to tell him the bodyguards aren't necessary, that Jonas' check surely bought me a little wiggle room in the they're-coming-to-get-me department—but detailing yesterday's run-in with the Ukrainian Travolta is a conversation I want to have with Jonas in person. "Thank you," I type. "You always take such good care of me."

"You're welcome, baby. I miss you so much. How are you feeling?"

"High as a kite. Painkillers are an awesome perk of being stabbed."

There's a long pause. "I miss you so much," he finally texts.

"I miss you, too."

We've been apart for maybe four hours and I already feel like I'm going through physical Jonas-withdrawal. "I hope you understand," I type. "My mom needs to be the one who nurses me back to health." I'm about to add, *It's a mom thing,* but then I remember Jonas' mom, so I refrain.

And, truth be told, my mom's desire to take care of me isn't the only thing motivating me to stay here with her for a few days. The truth is that I need a little space—time to pull myself together and figure out what I'm going to do, what I'm going to say. I'm overwhelmed. Ashamed. Racked with guilt. I'm in pain, both physical and emotional. And most of all, I can't believe what I've put Jonas through—all because I didn't believe him. I could barely look him in the eye when my mom drove me away earlier today—I just feel so effing guilty.

"I understand," Jonas types. "I'm so sorry," he adds.

Why does he keep saying that? I'm the one who owes *him* an apology. If I'd had faith in him, if I'd trusted his intuition, if I'd believed him when he told me he was sure they were coming to get me, none of this would have happened. There's no excuse for the way I disregarded him.

"You have nothing to be sorry for, Jonas. I'm the one who blew it. Big time."

"Can I call you right now? We need to talk. I want to hear your voice."

I'm not ready to have this conversation yet. I'm still not sure how to explain how I feel. Plus, I'm drowsy as hell. "I just took a pain pill," I write. "I'm pretty sleepy. Talk later?"

He pauses again. "Whatever you need," he finally replies. "I'm here for you."

"Thank you. Talk soon." After a minute, I add, "Madness." I'm overwhelmed and remorseful and groggy and in pain, sure—but nothing, not even powerful painkillers, not even guilt and remorse and emotional exhaustion, not even a couple stab wounds or a bump on the head, can change the fact that I love Jonas Faraday with all my heart.

"Madness," he replies quickly. "So, so much."

I close my eyes and fall asleep.

Chapter 11
Sarah

The doctor told me I'd feel like myself again by day three of bed rest, and, wow, holy moly, he was right. I definitely feel like me again—a slightly beaten up version of me, true, but undeniably me. I open my laptop. Yesterday, a guy from school texted to say he'd emailed me notes from all my missed classes, and I finally feel alert enough to take a look. I click into my emails and my heart drops into my toes. There's an email from The Club.

"Dear Miss Cruz,

"It appears there has been an unfortunate miscommunication between us. We regret any discomfort this might have caused you. Please rest assured we have now acquired full information and look forward to putting the past behind us.

"We are interested in your recent proposal and believe you would make a valuable addition to our organization in the expanded role you have suggested. However, the split shall be seventy-thirty in our favor, not fifty-fifty as originally proposed by you. This is a non-negotiable term and quite fair since we will be supplying the clients.

"We will confirm further details through a Dropbox account within the next few days. But first things first, promptly confirm that you have not released the report you've described to our female associate. Release of any such report to any third party, including but not limited to the agencies you've named, would, of course, preclude the possibility of an amicable working relationship between us.

"Sincerely,

"The Club."

I can barely read the text of the email through my rage. Motherfuckers! They call almost bleeding me dry an "unfortunate miscommunication"? Really? Gosh, how about we sit down and talk things through? *Talking about it doesn't mean we're disagreeing—it means I'm going to stab you.* If Jonas were here, he'd laugh at that. Well, maybe not. You never know with Jonas.

Jonas. God, I miss him. Three days here at my mom's house has felt like an eternity, even in my drug-induced haze. I feel like I'm missing an arm or a leg. No, that's not right—I feel like I'm missing my heart. I've never ached for another human being the way I do for Jonas right now. I physically *need* him.

Speak of the devil, my phone buzzes with a text.

"Hi, baby," he says.

"Hi, boyfriend," I write back. "I was just thinking about you." We've texted and spoken several times over the past three days, but always briefly. Each time, I've told him I miss him and can't wait to see him. Every time, he's told me he's sorry—for what, I don't know. "Been keeping yourself busy?" I type.

"Yeah, went climbing with Josh yesterday. Been working on a business plan for Climb and Conquer. Hard to concentrate. I miss you too much."

"I miss you, too," I write. Why am I doing this to him? To myself?

"Do you need anything?"

"No, my mom is taking great care of me." I pause. I can feel his heartbreak through the phone line. He just wants to be with me. I know he does.

"Can I call you later?" I write. "Just finishing something up."

"Sure."

I can feel the tightness of that word through cyberspace.

"You promise you'll call?"

"I promise."

I *feel* his torture. I know I'm causing him pain. Heck, I'm causing myself pain. But I don't know how to tell him what I'm feeling. I feel guilty, ashamed. Downright depressed. I've put the man I love through hell. I've gotten him involved in something horrible and huge. And now I have to fix things, all by myself—but I don't know how. A part of me just wants to bury my head in the sand and wish it all away.

My mom comes into the room with a steaming bowl of soup and a tall glass of ice water. I close my laptop as she approaches.

41

"The soup's hot, so give it a minute," she says in Spanish.

"Okay, thanks."

"It's time for your antibiotic," she says. She looks at her watch. "And you can take another pain pill, too, if you want one."

"No," I say. "I think I'm done with painkillers. Maybe just an ibuprofen or whatever."

"Are you sure?"

"Yeah, I'm feeling a million times better. Those pain meds make me sleep too much."

"Sleep is how your body heals," she says. She touches my hair. "You look much better today."

"I feel much better."

"Are you doing schoolwork?" she asks.

"No, just checking my emails."

"Don't do too much. You're supposed to rest."

"I've been resting nonstop for three days. I'm starting to go crazy."

"Do you want me to stay in here with you? We can watch a movie."

Gah. I love my mom with all my heart. She's the best mom in the whole world, she really is. And this whole situation has to be her worst nightmare, even worse than what my father put her through. But oh my God, I'm going frickin' crazy staying here with her. The woman is smothering me with motherly love. Or maybe I just want Jonas.

"Yeah, that'd be great," I say. "Give me twenty minutes to finish what I'm doing on my computer and then we'll pick a movie."

"Okay. Don't do too much. The doctor said you need to rest." She kisses my cheek and leaves.

I open my laptop again. What the hell am I going to reply to these bastards? I can't show weakness, that's for sure. I've got to buy myself more time—time to figure out a game plan. I place my hands on my keyboard again.

"To Whom It May Concern," I type, biting my lip.

My phone buzzes with an incoming call and I grab it. *Georgia.* Wow, I'm elated Georgia's calling me back so soon after our phone conversation yesterday. "Hi, Georgia," I say. I didn't expect her to get back to me so fast. "How are you?"

"I'm great," she says. "How are *you* feeling today? Better?"

"Much better. Each day the pain gets less and less."

She sighs with relief. "I'm so glad to hear it. So, I've got the information you asked for." She sounds excited. "It was easy to get."

Yesterday, when I called Georgia (allegedly to tell her about Belize), I asked if she'd be willing to gather a teeny-tiny bit of post-office-related information for me. When she asked me why I needed the information, I told her a watered-down version of the truth, but the truth, nonetheless: I used to work for an online dating service that I've recently discovered was engaged in illegal activity (the nature of which I didn't specify), and I fear the attack on me at school might have had something to do with my discovery. "So I'm doing a little investigation to see if I'm right."

Of course, Georgia agreed to help me, if she could, although she was understandably worried.

"Okay, here's what I've been able to find out," Georgia says. "There are twelve Oksanas with post office boxes registered in the greater Las Vegas area—Las Vegas, Henderson, Winchester, etcetera. I've got their full names plus the physical address each Oksana provided when she signed up for her post office box."

"I owe you big, Georgia. Thank you. Can you email me the list?"

"Of course," she says. "But, hey, maybe you should go to the police with all of this?"

"I gave the police a statement in the hospital." True. "They think my attack was a random mugging." Also true (because that's what I led them to believe). "Hopefully, this information will lead to something helpful for the investigation." Also true—but helpful to whom and for what investigation I'm not exactly sure.

"Okay, just be careful," Georgia says.

After thanking Georgia profusely and assuring her I'd be careful, we say our goodbyes—and then I sit and ponder the situation for a moment. *Twelve* Oksanas? How am I going to find the right one? Knock on each Oksana's door and say, "Hi! Are you the Oksana who tried to kill me?"

It looks like my strongest play right now is buying myself time. What else can I do? I need time to figure out what to do next and that money I gave them isn't going to protect me forever. I open my laptop and continue typing my reply:

"I sincerely regret any discomfort caused by our 'unfortunate miscommunication,' too—seeing as how it left me dying in a puddle of my own blood on a bathroom floor. To answer your question, I haven't submitted my report to anyone yet, though it took a Herculean effort to stop it from automatically releasing to several agencies, as I'd previously arranged. Luckily, I was able to put the brakes on things at the last minute this time, but I won't be able to stop its widespread and immediate dissemination next time—nor will I even try. *So there better not be a next time.*"

I stop for a moment and consider deleting that last sentence. It's pretty ballsy. Eh, screw it. I'll just go balls to the walls—big risk, big reward, just like Jonas always says.

I continue typing:

"Thank you for your interest in my business proposal. I look forward to finalizing our arrangement, too. A fifty-fifty split is what I'm willing to do. Yes, you supply the clients, but I'm the one who's going to make them pay up. You can lead a horse to your watering hole all you like, but it's me who's going to make him slurp up gallons and gallons of water. In fact, I've recently learned I'm uniquely talented at making horses drink. Fifty-fifty. Take it or leave it, people. But be advised: If you decide to 'leave it,' my report goes live—no second chances. I'm done fucking around.

"The emergency room doctors I've recently visited, thanks to you—did I mention our 'unfortunate miscommunication' left me bleeding out on a bathroom floor?—have told me to take a solid two weeks strict bed rest to recuperate from my injuries. When my health returns and I'm able to walk, let alone ride the horses you plan on bringing to our mutual watering hole, I will let you know. I want this new venture to be a success as much as you do, I assure you—our interests are completely aligned—but I'm only human after all, and having a stab wound on my torso and staples in my head isn't all that conducive to sexy time.

"Sincerely,

"Your Faithful Intake Agent, Sarah Cruz

"P.S. By the way, I've described our recent 'unfortunate miscommunication' to the police as a random mugging. (I'm not fucking stupid.)"

Before I can change my mind, I press send.

Holy crappola. What am I doing? I'm insane. I'm not James Bond.

I'm not a superhero. I can call myself Orgasma the All-Powerful all I like, but I'm still just me. A girl made of flesh and bones—and *blood*, as my body so recently proved in spades. I don't know what the heck I think I'm doing. Damn. I need help. *I need Jonas.*

Or maybe I should throw in the towel and just call the FBI already? If that means I won't pass the ethics review for my law license, then I guess I'll just have to live with that. But I don't want to give up on my legal career. Tears rise up in my eyes. I've worked too hard to get here. My mother is counting on me and so are the countless women my mom helps. I can't let them down. I've got to figure this out. I wipe my eyes.

I need Jonas.

I have a stomachache.

I need Jonas.

Jonas. Jonas, Jonas, Jonas. Oh my God, Jonas. My heart and body and soul ache for him. He looked so sad when my mom drove me away from the hospital. I wanted to hurl my body out of the car and leap into his arms right then. But I didn't. I just closed my eyes and cried as the car peeled away, too overwhelmed and in pain and jumbled and depressed and anxious to do anything else.

I need Jonas.

My heart pangs violently. I miss him. I can't be apart from him for another minute. I thought I needed time away to remind myself who I am when I'm not in his intoxicating presence—to battle my addiction to him and regain my sense of self, to get a handle on my studies and figure things out and let my body heal without distraction. I thought I needed to take a break from the madness for a little while. But I was wrong. Oh God, I was so wrong. I need him. My sweet Jonas. The man I love with all my heart and soul. For better or worse.

I pick up the phone and dial him. He answers immediately.

"Baby," he says softly. He sounds out of breath, like he gasped when he saw my name come up on his screen.

At the sound of his voice, I lose it. "Jonas," I bawl.

"What is it, Sarah? Tell me." He lets out a pained exhale. "Whatever it is, we'll handle it." He sounds like he wants to leap through the phone line.

"Come get me, Jonas. I want you. I need you. Please, Jonas. Bring me home."

Chapter 12
Sarah

"I can walk," I say. But Jonas ignores me, as usual. He scoops me up from his car and carries me into his house, straight to his bedroom, and lays me down on top of his white sheets like I'm a porcelain doll.

"Welcome home," he says softly. He's triumphant—the picture of pure elation.

I smile at him. "It's good to be home."

"Say that again," he says.

"Home."

"You're forbidden to leave ever again," he says. "I'm gonna install bars on the windows and doors."

"I'm so happy to be here, I'm not even creeped out by that statement."

He lies down next to me, on his side. "You're so beautiful," he says, softly tracing my eyebrow with his finger. "I missed you so much." He takes my face in his hands. "Never leave me again."

"I won't."

"Never, ever, ever."

"Got it."

"Ever."

"I've learned my lesson. It was physically painful being away from you—or, wait, maybe that pain came from the knife in my side." I smile, but he doesn't. Clearly, it's too soon for knock-knock-who's-there-I-got-stabbed humor.

"I—," he chokes out. He stuffs down whatever he was about to say. "When I saw you on the bathroom floor, I thought you were dead."

"Oh, Jonas, I'm so sorry." I can't even imagine how that must have affected him.

He kisses me gently. "I thought I'd lost you." He wraps his arm over me and kisses every inch of my face. His muscles are taut against my body.

I close my eyes. My fingers find his bicep. "I'm sorry."

"Stop apologizing," he murmurs. "I'm the one who's sorry." He sighs. "Sarah, I need to—"

"Jonas, wait. Listen to me."

He pulls back and stares at me. He waits.

"I know we have a ton of stuff to talk about. Like, tons and tons. But before we start talking and probably never stop, can I ask a favor?"

"You can have whatever you want, my beautiful, precious baby. Forever and ever and ever and ever, whatever you want." He strokes my cheek.

I pause. That was a big statement. Wow. He just made my heart leap out of my chest. I clear my throat.

"Name it, baby," he says, kissing my cheek. "Whatever it is, it's yours. *I'm* yours. Forever and ever and ever. Whatever you want, it shall be yours." He kisses my nose.

Wow, he's making me giddy. Not to mention turning me on. I can hardly speak.

"Tell me," he says.

"I want you to kiss all my booboos."

He smiles. "Your booboos?"

I grin broadly. It's hilarious hearing that silly word come out of his mouth. "Yeah. I want you to give me *besitos* on my booboos and make 'em all better."

"*Besitos*?" he repeats. Jonas always loves it when I speak Spanish to him.

"Mmm hmm. Little kisses. On my booboos."

"*Besitos* on your booboos, huh?"

"Mmm hmm."

He bites his lip. "Whatever you say, my precious, pretty baby. My Magnificent Sarah." His cheeks are flushed.

How did we survive these past three days apart? Why did I feel the need to pull away from him? I can't even remember why I thought I needed space.

47

I sit up and raise my arms over my head, and he takes off my tank top.

"Oh," he says, wincing at the sight of me.

I look down at myself and shrug. The wound on my ribcage looks way better than it did three days ago. But I imagine Jonas doesn't appreciate all the healing my body has done—all he sees is my current state of disrepair.

I lie back down on the bed, inviting him to kiss my body. "It looks worse than it feels, I assure you."

He leans down to my torso and softly kisses me. "This booboo right here?"

Goose bumps erupt all over my skin. "That's the one."

He runs his fingertip over my stitches and then over the black-and-blue-and-yellowish skin surrounding the gash. "Does it hurt?"

"Not too bad."

He kisses my wound again and I shudder as my skin comes alive under his touch. His lips move up from my ribcage to the stitched-up gash on my neck.

"And this booboo here, too?"

"Mmm hmm." I shiver. I'm aching for him.

"Does it hurt when I kiss it?" he asks.

"No, it feels really good," I say. "Your *besitos* are making me all better."

"Can I see the back of your head?" he asks.

I sit up and turn my head. He moves my hair and gasps.

"Am I Frankenstein?" I ask. I'm anxious. I haven't actually taken a peek back there.

"Holy shit. They *stapled* you back together, Sarah." He lets out a groan of sympathy. "It looks like they used a staple gun from Home Depot on your head."

I quickly lean back, intending to lie back on my pillow. "You don't have to kiss that booboo—I'm not a sadist."

He puts his hand on my shoulder to stop me from reclining. "Hey, sit back up, Frankenstein. I want to kiss all your booboos—*especially* that one."

I pause. My heart is racing. I don't know what it looks like back there, but it's got to be pretty nasty looking. "It's okay. I don't want to gross you out."

"You're not grossing me out," he says, turning my shoulders away from him. "I love every inch of you, Sarah Cruz, even the disgusting parts."

I swivel back around and stare at him. Did he just say he *loves* every inch of me?

He meets my gaze. "Come on," he says, his eyes smoldering. "Let me show you how much I love every inch of you."

I'm speechless.

He swivels my head away from him, moves my hair aside, and softly presses his lips against the stapled wound at the base of my skull. "Does that feel good?"

I shiver. "Mmm hmm." Feeling his lips on my stapled skin is turning me on too much to say anything else.

His soft lips migrate down my neck, all the way to my bare shoulder. His hand wraps around my torso and cups my breast.

I feel him shudder with desire behind me—and I'm right there with him. I lie down on my back, and he instantly begins licking my erect nipples—and then my neck. My ear. My lips. His tongue enters my mouth and his hand touches my face.

Oh my gosh, I'm on fire. When my life flashed before my eyes in that bathroom, when I thought I was a goner for sure, what did I think about? *I love you, Jonas.* Of all the thoughts my brain might have conjured in that most vulnerable, raw, life-defining moment, my love for Jonas was everything.

"Sarah," he breathes, kissing me. "I thought I'd lost you." He chokes back emotion. "Sarah," he says again.

"Make love to me," I breathe.

He pulls back, unsure.

"The doctor said sex is okay after three days," I assure him. Okay, technically, I didn't ask the doctor when I can have sex again—but Dr. Sarah is here and she says it's okay. I feel like me again and I want him inside me. Oh my God, do I ever. I want to be as close to him as humanly possible. For goodness sake, the man just said he loves every inch of me, and I'm suddenly desperate for him to prove it, from the inside out.

He touches my face. "I don't want to hurt you."

"Just take it slow."

"Are you sure?"

"I'm sure." I take off my pajama bottoms. I'm yearning for him.

He takes his clothes off and lies down against me, his erection insistent against my belly, his skin warm and smooth against mine.

I'm trembling.

He holds me for a moment, looking into my eyes. "When I saw you in the bathroom... ," he says. But he stops.

"I'm sorry," I say. "That must have been terrifying."

"I thought you were dead."

"I'm sorry, Jonas."

He pauses a really long time.

Something in the way he's looking at me makes me hold my breath.

He inhales deeply. "I love you, Sarah."

My breathing halts. I'm not sure I heard him correctly.

"I love you so much," he says. His eyes are moist.

I burst into tears.

"I love you," he says softly, wiping at my tears. He kisses me.

I know this is the part where I'm supposed to tell him I love him, too, but I'm mute. I can't believe my ears. I'm dumbfounded. I'm spellbound. I return his kiss passionately and throw my leg over him, eager for him to fill me up. When his body enters mine, we both moan loudly at the pleasure of it.

"I love you," he says, his voice husky.

I open my mouth to speak, but nothing comes out. I'm overwhelmed.

"Am I hurting you?" he asks.

I shake my head.

He kisses my lips as his body moves inside mine. His hands stroke my back and butt. I feel nothing but pleasure and love and elation as his body leads mine into synchronized movement. Any pain my wounded body might have been feeling a moment ago has been replaced by pleasure, sublime pleasure. I feel euphoric.

"I love you," he says, his body zealously emphasizing his words.

"Oh, Jonas," I gasp, finding my voice. "I love you, too."

"Oh God," he exhales, shuddering. His lips find mine again, and then he whispers in my ear. "I love you, baby."

I moan and press myself into him enthusiastically. I never knew it could feel so good to hear those three little words.

"I love you, Jonas," I whimper. I'm bursting with joy. I can't believe this is happening.

He pulls out of me, his chest heaving. "I love every inch of you, Sarah Cruz." He gently pushes me onto my back and proceeds to kiss every single inch of me, from the top of my head to the wound on my neck, down to my breasts and belly and the gash on my ribcage, to my hips, thighs, crotch, arms and fingers and thighs and legs and toes, and then he begins working his way back up my legs and slowly up the insides of my thighs, to the sensitive skin right between my legs. By the time he gets to my clit and licks me ever so gently with his warm, wet tongue, I can barely hold it together. I'm arching my back, gripping the sheet, shuddering violently. I'm not sure if I'm going to scream or burst into tears or flames—or if all my stitches are going to simultaneously pop out of my skin like tiny projectile missiles—but, certainly, something's got to give. I can't withstand this pressure building inside me for much longer.

I make a guttural sound. I can't take it anymore. This is too exquisitely pleasurable to bear. *He loves me.* I feel like he's enveloping me in his love, wrapping me in it from head to toe—delivering me into a dream. But this is way better than any dream, even the one where Jonas became a slithering, sensuous cloud. *He loves me.* And I love him.

His wet tongue leaves my sweet spot, making me cry out in protest, but he ignores me, kissing his way back up my torso, all the way up to my face. Finally, he arrives at my mouth and devours my lips, urgently pressing the tip of his erection against my throbbing clit. He kisses me voraciously, all the while grinding the tip of his penis desperately into the most sensitive spot on my body. Oh God, he's rubbing me, coaxing me, making me cry out, and whispering into my ear all the while.

"I love you, Sarah Cruz," he says, his voice and tip conspiring to push me over the edge. "I love you so much, baby." His voice is gruff as he rubs against me, making me writhe in ecstasy. "I love you with all my heart."

I scream his name as my body releases and shudders, an all-consuming orgasm rippling through me, and he slides his shaft into me, deep, deep inside me. After a brief moment, he finds his release, too.

"I love you," he whispers again, his body heaving one final time.

"I love you, Jonas," I say, shivering.

We lie together for several minutes, neither of us speaking.

Holy crap, that was delicious, even if my wounds have started pulsing angrily at me from the exertion. I don't care about a few throbbing stab wounds—I can take an ibuprofen for that, for Pete's sake. I just experienced unmitigated ecstasy—life-changing, earth-shattering, heart-swooning euphoria. Oh good Lord, this beautiful man *loves* me. And I love him. *We actually said it out loud to each other.* Oh my God.

Jonas kisses my cheek and rolls onto his back, sighing happily. "The culmination of human possibility," he says, flashing me a beaming smile. He's the picture of sheer exhilaration. I've never seen him smile quite so joyously before—never seen his eyes light up and dance without reservation quite like this. It's as if something dark and heavy has lifted off his soul, unburdening him and leaving him light as a feather. He's the most beautiful creature I've ever beheld. Oh, Jonas. My sweet Jonas. I love him with all my heart. And, Lord have mercy, he loves me right back.

Chapter 13
Sarah

Jonas and I are sitting on his balcony, looking out at the city, sipping wine (me) and beer (him), and finally having that heart to heart I've been avoiding for the past three days. I've just told him every single detail about my run-in with the Ukrainian John Travolta in the bathroom and I've also shown him my recent email exchange with The Club, too. He's listened intently to every word, barely breathing.

"You're so fucking smart," he says. "Thank God you had that check in your purse."

"Not thank *God*," I retort. "Thank *you*. I had that check in my purse only because *you* gave it to me, Jonas. You saved my life."

He shakes his head, unwilling to accept this simple but incontrovertible fact.

"Yes, Jonas. Listen to me. Two things saved my life—knowing Oksana's name and having that check—and I have you to thank for both. See? You saved my life."

Jonas takes a swig of his beer, mulling that over. I can almost see the gears inside his brain turning.

"Hey, maybe you can stop payment on that check," I say. "I don't know why I didn't think of that until just now. "

"Hell no. We *want* them to deposit that check—it's a homing device. Couldn't have worked out better if we'd planned it." He clinks his beer to my wine glass. "'Twas a stroke of brilliance, Sarah Cruz."

"I don't understand."

"Once they deposit the check, we'll know their bank of deposit—and we can use that information to find them."

"Oh, wow," I say. "I didn't think of that." I twist my mouth. "But that's assuming they deposit the check. My name's listed as the payee, don't forget."

He scoffs. "Any two-bit criminal can chemically lift the payee name off any check."

"Really? Jeez, that's scary. For a girl employed by a global crime syndicate, I'm not very knowledgeable about organized crime."

"Sarah."

"What?"

He's staring at me, his eyes moist. "I'm so proud of you."

I swat at the air like it was nothing. "All I did was buy myself a little time. I'm just worried about what's gonna happen when I don't deliver the oodles of cash I've promised them." I shake my head, thinking about all my big promises. "How long before they figure out I'm full of crap? How long before they decide to finish the job they started in the bathroom?" My stomach tightens.

"Oh, don't you worry, my pretty baby, we're gonna figure them out long before they figure us out." He puts his hand on my thigh and his palm is warm in the evening air. "You just keep making them think you've got me right where you want me, just like you did in that bathroom. Just like you did in your email to them. We'll use their greed against them and fuck them up the ass six ways from Sunday."

"I'm sorry I threw you under the bus, Jonas," I say. "I wish I could have figured out a way to save myself that didn't drag you into this."

"Are you serious? You were brilliant. You said exactly the right thing." He swallows hard, choking back emotion. "Whatever you had to do to stay alive, I'm glad you did it."

I put my wine glass down and move to his lap.

He puts his beer bottle down and wraps his arms around my back, nuzzling his nose into mine. "So what were the other horrible things you wanted to tell me, my precious baby?" he asks. At the beginning of this conversation, I'd warned Jonas I had five things to tell him, some of them not so great. "Whatever they are, I guarantee you, I won't be upset."

We'll see about that. I've only told him two out of the five things on my list of horribles: One, I gave the bad guys Jonas' two-hundred-fifty-thousand-dollar check. Two, I told the bad guys I've been scamming Jonas and can get them even more money. So far, so good—he seems to think I've handled things brilliantly. But now it's time for items three, four, and five.

"Item three," I say. "I've got a list of twelve different Oksanas who rent post office boxes in the greater Las Vegas area—plus the physical addresses each Oksana used when she registered for her box."

His mouth hangs open. "Wow, that's amazing. Why would I be upset about..." His face suddenly darkens. "Sarah, how'd you get that information?"

I take a deep breath. "I asked Georgia to help me."

His face reddens and his body jerks beneath me like he's trying to buck me off.

I stand, my cheeks instantly burning.

"How could you even think about getting Georgia involved in all this?" He runs his hand through his hair, trying to contain his anger. Oh man, he's pissed. "That's just... I can't believe you did that." He looks like he's restraining himself from saying more.

I knew he wouldn't like this particular item, but I thought he might just roll his eyes about it. I didn't think he'd be genuinely *angry* with me.

His jaw muscles are pulsing in and out. "I don't want Georgia and Trey involved in all this—what were you thinking?" His voice is controlled rage.

What was I thinking? Well, in a nutshell that I'm going to do whatever I have to do to track these motherfuckers down. That I'm not going to sit around waiting for them to come back and finish the job they started. That I really didn't think I was putting Georgia and Trey in harm's way or else I never would have asked for Georgia's help, for Pete's sake, give me some effing credit.

I'm sure my indignation is written all over my face.

He stands. "Well, Jesus. What did you tell her when you asked her?"

I tell Jonas exactly what I said to Georgia, my voice tight and contained.

He's quiet for a solid minute, leaning over the balcony railing and looking out at the city.

I cross my arms over my chest and wait for the supreme lord-god-master to grace me with his verdict. Does he want to get the bad guys or not? Because I do—and that's all I was trying to do, for goodness sake. I sit back in my chair in a huff and grab my wine. Blood is pulsing in my ears.

He turns around and leans his back against the railing. "You're so fucking snoopy, you know that?"

I'm trying to keep my lip from trembling. I nod. Yes, I'm snoopy. I know this about myself. If he doesn't like that part of me, he's in for a long and tortured ride.

"You just can't help yourself, can you?"

I nod again. It's true. So what? I've always been this way. I can't help it. If he has a problem with the way I am, the way I've always been, the way I'm inherently wired, maybe this thing between us isn't going to work after all. What does he want me to do? Sit around and wait for them to come back and finish the job they started—

"Come here," he says, his voice full of warmth. He holds out his arms.

But I don't move. My cheeks are blazing. I've worked myself into a bit of a tizzy inside my own head and now I need a minute. What did he expect me to do? Sit around and twiddle my thumbs? That's not my style.

He walks over to me and pulls me out of my chair. I resist him for a grand total of three seconds, and then I melt into his broad chest.

"From now on, we're a team." He kisses the top of my head. "No more Snoopy Sarah running around conquering the world all by herself, okay?"

I don't reply. I'm just enjoying the feeling of his arms wrapped around me in the cool night.

"We make decisions together on this thing. And that goes for me, too—two and a half heads are always better than one."

I look up at him. "Two and a *half* heads? Is Josh the half?"

He laughs. "No, though I'll tell him you said that. I'm spotting you an extra half a head because you're so fucking smart."

I nuzzle into his neck. He smells so good. "I'm sorry, Jonas."

He tilts my face up to look at him. "What am I gonna do with you, baby? Hmm?"

I purse my lips. "Kiss me?" I raise my eyebrows hopefully.

He smiles and kisses me.

"Okay. What else is on the list?" he asks. He sounds a helluva lot more wary now than he did a few minutes ago when he so confidently proclaimed I couldn't possibly upset him.

I sigh. "I didn't believe you about seeing the Ukrainian Travolta. I thought you were overprotective and hypersensitive—and maybe even paranoid. I was an idiot. I should have believed you."

He cocks his head to the side and looks at me for a long time. He opens his mouth to say something and then reconsiders. "I understand," he finally says. "It's okay."

I'm expecting more, but apparently that's it.

He shrugs. "What else you got?"

So we're done with that one? Because if we are, I have no idea how it just got resolved. "Um. Well, last but not least, I think it's important for us to talk about how all of this must have affected *you*."

He clenches his jaw but doesn't speak.

"I feel so horrible." My eyes suddenly brim with tears. "I've put you through yet another bloody trauma—the last thing in the world I ever wanted to do to you. It must have been beyond torture for you to find me like that—the whole scenario must have brought up all kinds of stuff about your mother's murder. I'm so, so sorry—"

"*I'm* the one who's sorry." His voice is pure anguish. He sits back down in his chair and puts his head in his hands. "I'm the one who promised to protect you and then let you go into that bathroom, unprotected, all alone, while I sat in that classroom, listening to fucking music—" He's choking up, becoming more and more emotional as he speaks.

"You were listening to music? Were you listening to the playlist I made for you?"

He stops and stares at me, his train of thought hijacked.

I sit on his lap and wrap my arms around his neck. "Were you able to decipher the super-secret coded message I sent you in those songs?" I smile, but he scowls.

Boom. It suddenly hits me like a ton of bricks—this right here is the exact moment I've been wanting to avoid for the past three days—the exact thing that made me retreat from Jonas and seek out a little space. *This.* I don't want to do this. I knew in my bones Jonas would view this entire situation as his frickin' fault—as yet another example of how he's miserably failed to protect the one he loves the most. I knew he'd blur the attack on me with the horror of his mother's murder and wrap the two incidents together into a giant ball of intractable self-blame—and, frankly, I can't handle it. I just don't have the emotional bandwidth to watch to him spiral into yet another tortured round of self-loathing.

This beautiful man has blamed himself for twenty-three frickin' years for his mother's murder. So is he going to blame himself for my attack for the *next* twenty-three years, too? And if so, at what cost to his soul? And to mine? At what cost to our relationship? I'm a compassionate person, but I'm not a frickin' saint. I don't want to deal with this. It's bullshit and I don't have time or patience for it.

"I don't know how you'll ever forgive me," he says, covering his face with his hands.

I leap off Jonas' lap and pace the balcony, my thoughts racing. "Jonas," I begin, adrenaline surging inside my veins. "No."

He looks up at me. He folds his arms over his chest, bracing himself.

I take a deep breath. "No, no, no. Your entire life, you've blamed yourself for your mom's death—*and it wasn't your fault.* Fuck your father, Jonas. It wasn't your frickin' fault. *No.*"

He looks surprised. This isn't what he expected me to say.

"If you and I are going to have a fighting chance, you can't blame yourself for what happened to me the way you've blamed yourself for your mother's death. I'm just telling you, straight up, if you blame yourself this time, with me, it'll poison you—it'll poison me—and then it'll poison *us.*"

Now he looks shocked. And hurt. But it's too bad. I'm on a roll.

"You saved my life, Jonas—get it through your thick, tortured head. You're my hero, baby—my savior. It's the objective truth, but it's also the truth I *choose.* Don't you understand? I *choose* to be with the man who saved my life, not the man who's forever trying to undo yet another 'horrible failure' that isn't his fault. Enough with that tormented guy—enough with that self-blaming, *mea culpa* bullshit. In this fairytale—*our* fairytale—you're the guy who rides in on a white horse and kicks ass and takes names and loves me like nobody ever has—because you *are* that guy, Jonas Faraday. This isn't going to work for me if you're going to seek my forgiveness forevermore for something you didn't frickin' do."

He swallows hard.

"If you insist on talking about blame, fine. Let's talk about it. *Once.*"

He opens his mouth to speak, but I hold up my index finger to stop him.

"If anyone's to blame here, it's me. *I'm* the one who broke the rules and contacted you in the first place. *I'm* the one who went to spy on you and the software engineer, making it so damned easy for Stacy to put two and two together and rat me out. And *I'm* the one who refused to let you follow me into that bathroom because *I'm* the one who thought my brilliant and sensitive boyfriend was just being *paranoid*—and maybe even hallucinating."

He winces at that last word. Yeah, Jonas, I just called you crazy-pants.

"And all that's on me. Shame on me, Jonas. *Shame on me.* I'm the one who gave you a hard time for not trusting me completely— not leaping off a waterfall for me—and then I turned around and didn't trust you."

He looks like he's going to cry.

"But I forgive myself for all that, Jonas, and I hope you will, too, because, otherwise, it's going to eat me alive and doom our relationship." The expression on his face is breaking my heart, but I barrel ahead, anyway. "Jonas, I get the whole self-blame-thing when you're seven years old and your dad does a number on you your whole effing life. But when it comes to you and me, moving forward as adults, as equals, the tortured-guy routine isn't gonna end well, I guarantee it." I pause. "I'm not going to be in a relationship with a man who thinks everything that happens is on him. I mean, I know you've got a God complex, but that's taking things too damned far."

His eyes flicker.

"No more blame, Jonas. No more 'I don't know how you'll ever forgive me' bullshit. We move forward without blame or we don't move forward." I jut my chin at him. "Because I'm ready to do this shit, man—kick some ass, baby."

His chest heaves in cadence with mine. His eyes blaze.

"Just as soon as I get the staples out of my head, that is."

His mouth tilts up into a crooked smile.

I raise my hands. "So what's it gonna be, boyfriend? Decide. Are you in or are you out?"

He rises from his chair, his eyes smoldering, and wraps his bulging arms around me. All it takes is one kiss and, in a flash, we're mauling each other, pulling our pants down, consumed by the sudden electricity coursing through our veins. Without hesitation or wind-up, he pushes my back up against the balcony railing, plunges his fingers inside my wetness to find his target, and then enters me deeply, whispering "I love you" and "so fucking hot" and "baby" in my ear as he does it. Oh. My. God. Divine.

I could be wrong—I could be way off-base here—but I'm pretty sure this man right here is telling me, emphatically, that, yes, he's in. *All in.* Inside me, that is, nice and deep and all the way. In, in, in, in, in, in, in.

Chapter 14
Sarah

A noise next to the bed wakes me with a jolt. I squint into the darkness of the bedroom, my eyes slowly adjusting to the surrounding shapes and colors. My heart lurches into my throat. Oh my God. John Travolta from *Pulp Fiction* stands in a far corner of the room, gripping a large knife. When our eyes meet, he grins. I open my mouth to scream, but nothing comes out. He walks slowly toward me, smiling wickedly, the blade glinting in his hand.

I find my voice. "Oksana!" I yell.

He shakes his head. "Not this time, bitch." He raises the knife high over his head, his eyes cold, and plunges the blade into my heart.

I sit up, screaming at the top of my lungs, clutching my chest.

"Shh," Jonas says, gripping my jerking body. "It's okay."

I thrash against his grasp, my throat burning.

"You're dreaming, Sarah. It was just a dream."

I burst into tears and go slack in his arms, my entire body shaking violently.

He pulls me close.

I hiccup, trying to control my sobs.

"It was just a bad dream," he says. "Shh."

A soft rain batters the roof. My heart is racing.

"I'm here," Jonas says. "I'm here, baby. It was just a bad dream. I've got you."

His body is warm against mine. He pulls me close to him and kisses my wet cheeks. I can't stop shaking.

"We have to go to Vegas," I blurt, my voice trembling. "It's time to kick some bad-guy butt. I have to *do* something."

He brushes a chunk of hair away from my face and kisses my cheek again.

"Tomorrow I get the staples out of my head—and then we go," I say.

He pauses a long time. The sound of rain pelting the window fills the silence. "What about your classes?" he finally asks.

"Finals are in five weeks," I say, sighing with resignation. "I'm so far behind, I'll never ace my classes like I wanted to, no matter what I do." I'm sure he can hear the disappointment in my voice. "But on the bright side, I've studied so hard all year long, I could take my finals tomorrow and at least pass every class." I breathe deeply, still trying to steady myself. "I guess finishing middle-of-the-pack is just going to have to be enough for me, whether I like it or not."

He exhales. "You know you don't need that scholarship, right? Whatever happens, I'm gonna take care of you."

I nuzzle into his neck. "I know. Thank you." I want so badly to tell him I love him again, but I bite my tongue. So far, we've only said those three little words to each other during sex—and I don't want to push him too hard. I know it was a big step for him to say those words to me at all, so I settle for my usual three little words. "My sweet Jonas," I say softly.

He squeezes me. "You sure you're feeling up to tackling this?"

"Yep, I'm ready. It's time to kick some butt."

"Well, okay, then." He exhales loudly. "Let's go kick some bad-guy ass. I'll call Josh in the morning and tell him to grab his hacker buddy and meet us in Sin City."

"Why do we need Josh?"

"Josh and I share one brain. Plus, he'll bring the hacker to the party, and we need the hacker."

He's right about that. Yesterday, we discovered the bad guys had deposited Jonas' two hundred fifty thousand dollars at a small bank in Henderson, a town just outside Las Vegas—and Jonas immediately put the hacker to work poking around the bank's mainframe. If we hit pay dirt—if it turns out one of the Oksanas on our post-office-box list has an account at that particular bank—we'll be in butt-kicking business.

"Okay, that sounds good. I'll call Kat and we'll go frickin' *Ocean's Eleven* on their ass."

"Why do we need Kat?"

"Kat always comes in handy in any situation. You'll see. We might not know why or how we're gonna need that girl, but we will."

"But why involve Kat in this stuff? I'm pretty sure I convinced Stacy that Kat's totally clueless about The Club—and odds are high Stacy passed that information along up the chain. Let's just keep Kat off the bad guys' radar from now on."

"No, you don't understand. Kat's the female version of you, baby—people fall all over themselves when she bats her eyelashes. That's a powerful weapon to have at your disposal. And, anyway, come on—we've gotta have a bunch of good-lookin' people on our team to pull off a Las Vegas heist. Haven't you seen *Ocean's Eleven*?"

He exhales in frustration. "We shouldn't get Kat involved."

"I need her, Jonas. You need your Joshie-Woshie—I need my Kitty Kat."

He sighs. "Okay. Fine. Josh, Hacker, Kat." He rolls his eyes with mock-annoyance. "Who else do I need to fly out to Vegas on a moment's notice for you, boss? George Clooney? Brad Pitt? Matt Damon?"

"Yes, please. All three. Oh, and Don Cheadle, too. I love that guy. How about Ben Affleck, too, just to keep Matt Damon company? If you and I get to have our besties with us, then it's only fair Matt should, too."

"Aw, how sweet," Jonas says.

"Yeah, that's me. I'm a giver." I shrug. "It's just how I'm wired."

He laughs. "Even when you're plotting world domination, you make me laugh."

I sigh. "Sometimes, laughing's the best way to keep from crying."

He squeezes me again. "There's no reason to cry, baby," he says tenderly. "We've got this. You and me. Well, you, me, and Clooney."

I squeeze him back. "And Brad Pitt."

"And Matt and Ben."

"And Don Cheadle," I say. "And Joshie-Woshie and Kitty Kat and Hacker-Guy."

"We're a motley crew," he says.

"And a frickin' good-lookin' one, too."

"We're unstoppable."

We listen to the rain battering the roof for a minute.

"God, I hate Vegas," Jonas mutters.

"Why?"

"*Why?*" He says it like I've just asked him why he hates the Ebola virus. "Crowds. Neon lights. Cigarette smoke. Club music everywhere you go. *Dancing.*" He grimaces like that last item is the worst offender of all. "Not to mention mindless zombies throwing their hard-earned money away on nothingness in a desperate attempt to *feel* something, if only for a fleeting moment, and then trudging back to the bleak reality of their real lives without their fucking rent money." He grunts. "I hate everything about that fucking place."

All this coming from a guy who recently threw his hard-earned money away on nothingness in a desperate attempt to *feel* something, if only for a fleeting moment? I love this boy, God knows I do, but he sometimes slays me with his lack of self-awareness. But I'm in a saintly mood today so I'll refrain from pointing out that bit of irony. "And here I thought Vegas sounded like fun," I say. "Silly me."

"You haven't been to Las Vegas?"

"Nope."

He's surprised.

"Not everyone has been everywhere like you, Mr. Money Bags."

"But Las Vegas isn't an 'oh, I've been everywhere' kind of place. Belize, yes, I understand that, but Vegas? Everyone's been to Vegas."

"Apparently not."

"Huh." He exhales. "Well, then. Hmm." He kisses my cheek. "I guess I'll just have to hold my nose and show my baby a good time in hell, won't I?"

"That's the spirit. Just 'cause a girl's busy taking down a global crime syndicate doesn't mean she doesn't want to have a good time while she's doing it."

"Okay, then. It's settled. Tomorrow we gather our motley but good-lookin' crew and figure out how to fuck these motherfuckers up the ass."

"Sounds like a motherfucking plan," I say.

He kisses my neck. "First things first, though, let's get those staples out of your head tomorrow morning."

"Yes, please. Thank God."

"Although I happen to think those staples of yours are kinda sexy."

I feel his erection against my thigh. "Ew. You're depraved, Jonas."

He nips at my ear. "Everything about you is sexy, even the gross stuff."

"What gross stuff? I don't have any gross stuff."

"Sure you do. Staples... and staples... The list goes on and on." He kisses me again. "And staples." His hand skims the curve of my hip. "And staples." He reaches around and grabs my ass. "How 'bout I get me one last piece of Frankenstein ass before those staples come out tomorrow?"

"You're a sick puppy," I say, laughing. "I like that about you."

Chapter 15
Jonas

Sarah's running through our Las Vegas hotel suite, shrieking and squealing.

"Did you see this?" she yells. "Look at the view! Woohoo!" She starts singing "Fancy" by Iggy Azalea at the top of her lungs.

I exchange a smile with the bellhop. "Over here, sir?" he asks me, motioning with our bags.

"This place is three times bigger than my entire apartment!" Sarah screams, laughing and twirling around. "It's unreal."

"That's fine," I say to the guy. "Thank you."

"Jonas!" Sarah yells from somewhere deep in the bowels of the suite. "Come here."

I tip the bellhop.

"Thank you, sir," he says, smiling broadly. "Would you like me to open the champagne for you, sir?"

"No, I've got it covered."

"Would you like me to describe the full panel of amenities at your disposal here in the penthouse suite or perhaps in the hotel in general?"

"No, thank you. We'll figure it out."

"Very good, sir. Enjoy your stay."

"Jonas Faraday!" she screams. "Get your booty in here."

Damn, I love this woman.

I follow Sarah's voice into the bathroom. She's sitting fully clothed and grinning like a Cheshire cat in an empty bathtub the size of a small Jacuzzi. "Can you believe this?" she says. "Who needs a bathtub this big?"

I can't suppress the leer that flickers across my face.

"Oh," she says, her face turning as lecherous as mine. "I guess *we* need a bathtub this big." Her eyes gleam. "You know, I should warn you, this city's already bringing out the dirty girl in me. I can feel it."

"Oh yeah? I like your dirty girl."

"She likes you, too." I smirk. "Yep, I most definitely feel another addendum item coming on."

"Just as long as it doesn't involve tying neckties around my limbs."

"I learned my lesson about that, don't worry."

I climb into the empty tub with her and she crawls all over me, kissing me. "I'm already having a ridiculously good time."

"We've driven from the airport to our hotel and sat in an empty tub, fully clothed."

"I know—so much fun, right?"

I laugh. "Yep."

She kisses me again. "Hey, maybe there's enough time for a little fun and games before everyone else arrives?"

"Oh yeah, there's plenty of time," I say, kissing her.

"Why don't we fill this thing up and see who can hold their breath the longest?"

"Not exactly the kind of fun and games I was envisioning," I say.

"Ah, you must not understand what I'm planning to do to you while I'm holding my breath underwater."

My cock springs to life. "A breath-holding contest it is. You want some champagne?"

"You know I never say no to champagne."

"Coming right up." I hop out of the tub, my erection straining inside my jeans. Hey, maybe Vegas isn't so bad, after all.

"I feel s-e-e-e-xy, baby," she calls after me. "I'm tu-u-u-u-rned o-o-o-o-n, hunky-monkey bo-o-o-o-oyfriend. Get me that champagne and I guarantee my dirty, dirty girl's gonna come out to pla-a-a-a-ay."

Holy fuck. I pop the cork on the champagne bottle in record time and grab two glasses.

There's a knock on the door. "Hey!"

No, please, God, no. Not yet. Not now.

"Vegas, Baby!" It's Kat, yelling from behind the front door of our suite.

Fuck my life.

Sarah sprints out the bathroom and throws open the front door.

"Woohoo!" Kat shrieks. The two girls hug and scream like they just won the Showcase Showdown on *The Price is Right*.

Even in my current state of disappointment about not getting to be with Sarah in the tub, I laugh. They're pretty adorable right now.

"Wow, Jonas, you really knocked yourself out," Kat says, coming out of her clinch with Sarah. "I bet, like, rock stars and Prince Harry stay in this place, especially with that private elevator to get up here. It's amazing."

"I wanted to show my precious baby an extra good time, seeing as how this is her first trip to Sin City."

Kat and Sarah exchange a look of surprise when I call Sarah "my precious baby"—and, actually, I'm pretty shocked to hear myself use those words in Kat's presence. How did I let that slip out?

"Oh, Jonas," Sarah coos, blushing. "You're so sweet."

My cheeks burst into flames.

"Oh, and thank you for my room, Jonas," Kat says.

"You got checked in okay?"

"Yes, thank you."

Sarah beams at me and I flash her a look of pure longing. I don't want to be having a conversation with Kat right now—I want to be alone with Sarah, kicking her ass in an underwater-breath-holding contest.

"Did you see this view?" Kat squeals, grabbing Sarah's hand. They rush to the floor-to-ceiling windows at the far end of the room. "Just wait 'til you see The Strip at night," Kat says. "The lights are gonna blow you away." She sighs. "God, I love Vegas."

Why am I not surprised?

"I've seen The Strip in movies, but I bet it's really cool in person," Sarah says.

"Oh, champagne," Kat says, seeing the bottle on the bar.

"I'll get you a glass." I steal a pained look at Sarah and she laughs. Well, gosh, I'm glad she finds my agony so hilarious.

There's a loud knock at the door to the suite. "Open up, you beast!"

I open the door to find Josh standing next to a geek-turned-hipster guy with a goatee. After I bro-hug Josh, the hipster introduces himself as Hennessey. I'm not sure if that's his first or last name, but it's all he provides.

"But everyone just calls me Henn," he says, extending his hand.

"Or Fucking Genius," Josh adds.

"You're the only one who calls me that, Josh."

"Well, you are."

"Are you the genius who tracked down Sarah for me?" I ask.

"The one and only," Henn says.

"Then you're a fucking genius in my book, too."

Sarah and Kat bounce happily over to the group.

"Hey, Party Girl with a Hyphen," Josh says to Kat, his eyes sparkling.

"Well, hey yourself, Playboy. It's a crazy, fucked up world when a Playboy and a Party Girl cross paths in *Vegas*, huh?" They both burst out laughing. "It's good to see you again." Josh gives her an enthusiastic hug and she kisses him softly on the cheek—a noticeably warm greeting from both of them. Hmm. Interesting.

Kat introduces herself to Henn and the guy can't muster two coherent words. He might be a fucking genius with computers, but apparently not so much when it comes to pretty women.

After the girls refill their champagne glasses and the guys grab beer bottles from the fridge, we all make ourselves comfortable on black leather couches in the sitting area.

"I'm shocked you splurged on this place, bro," Josh says, glancing around at the grandeur. "So un-Jonas-like of you."

"Would you stop telling me what's Jonas- or un-Jonas-like of me already? Apparently, you have no idea what I'm like."

Josh laughs. "Apparently not."

The hacker flips open his laptop. "Okay, folks. I've got an update on the Oksana sitch you had me working on."

"Fantastic," I say, rubbing my hands together. Other than playing Underwater Oral Sex Olympics with my baby, there's nothing I want to do more than fuck these motherfuckers up the ass as soon as humanly possible. These fuckers almost took my baby away from me—which means they almost killed me, too—and now I don't only want to take them down, I want their blood.

We all crowd around Henn's laptop.

"I was able to hack into that bank in Henderson where your check was deposited—it was easy, actually—I'm constantly surprised how bad online security is at banks—I'd strongly advise keeping your money under a mattress, folks—and anyway, I got into the bank's mainframe and poked around a bit. I was able to cross-check account holders against the list of Oksanas you sent me, and Bingo-was-his-name-oh, I got a hit."

Sarah whoops.

"Our Oksana is Oksana Belenko—sounds like an Olympic ice skater, doesn't she? She's got an account at that Henderson bank *and* a P.O. box in Henderson. Boom shakalaka."

"See? Fucking genius," Josh says.

"You sure that's our girl?" Sarah asks.

"Yeah, it's her. I checked out the physical address she gave the post office, and, of course, it's total bullshit. But there's an Oksana Belenko registered with the State of Nevada as a member of an LLC that's been running a handful of legal whorehouses in Nevada for the past twenty years—and the address for the business license on the whorehouses matches the address given in the LLC filing."

"So that means we've got a confirmed physical address?" Sarah asks.

"Yep."

"Wow," Sarah says. She pauses, the gears turning inside her head. "So it sounds like Oksana supplies the girls for The Club—" She looks at Josh. "Or, if you'd prefer, the Mickey Mouse roller coasters."

Both Sarah and Kat burst out laughing, but Josh bristles.

"It was an *analogy*," Josh says.

"We know, Joshie, we know," Sarah says, winking at him. "But it's still funny."

I put my hand on Sarah's thigh. She turns me on no matter what she does, but especially when she's kicking someone's ass.

"Yeah, Oksana's like this frickin' old-school *madam*," Henn says. "Probably not the brains behind all the tech stuff."

"She's probably got a business partner who handles the tech side of things," I say.

"Definitely," Henn agrees. "And whoever that person is, he or she knows exactly what the hell they're doing. Because there's no finding these guys by accident."

Hmm. How the fuck did Josh get hooked up with The Club in the first place? All he said at the time was that some professional athlete buddy of his told him about it, but I never asked him for details. *Best money I've spent in my life*, he told me during our climb up Mount Rainier.

"And even then," Henn continues, sipping his beer, "their storefront is just a shell. Their real shit's gotta be buried way down in the Deep Web. And that's a scary place."

"What's the Deep Web?" Kat asks.

Henn grins broadly at her.

"Is that a stupid question?" Kat asks, blushing.

"Oh no, not stupid at all. I'm just so used to hanging out with computer geeks all day long, I forget normal people don't know about this stuff." He smiles at her again. "I'm glad you don't know what it is. It means you're probably a well adjusted, happy person."

Kat laughs. "I am, as a matter of fact."

"I can tell," Henn says. "Happiness is a very attractive quality in a person."

"Thank you," Kat says, her cheeks flushing.

Josh clears his throat. "So, guys, before Henn launches into The Grand Story of the Deep Web, how about we all do a shot of Patron? We're in Vegas, after all—when in Rome."

"Sounds like a fabulous idea to me," Kat says, her face lighting up. "Do we have Patron in the bar?"

"Of course," I say. "I made sure of it. My brother is nothing if not predictable."

Josh walks behind the bar to start pouring drinks and Kat bounds over to join him.

"I'll help you out, Playboy," she says.

"Why, thanks, Party Girl."

I lean into Sarah's ear. "What's the over-under on those two fucking?"

Sarah stifles a giggle. "I give it forty-eight hours at the absolute outside."

Chapter 16
Jonas

"The Deep Web," Henn begins, leaning back in his chair and rubbing his goatee like he's hosting an episode of *Masterpiece Theatre*. "It's a scary motherfucking place, fellas." He nods at Kat. "And very pretty ladies."

I've heard anecdotally about the Deep Web and I'm sure Josh has, too, but I don't have any practical experience with it. I look at Sarah to see if she knows about this already and she makes an "I have no idea" face.

"Let's start today's lesson with the *Surface Web*," Henn continues, speaking slowly, the consummate hipster-kindergarten teacher.

"The Surface Web," Sarah repeats slowly like she's a member of a cult.

"Yes, my child. Good," Henn says, instantly transforming into Sarah's cult leader.

Sarah and Henn share a smile.

"The Surface Web is the Internet we all know and love—the stuff that comes up when you ask Siri for movie show times or Google a sushi restaurant. But the Internet is much, much more than the Surface Web." Henn smiles devilishly.

"You're freaking me out, Henn," Kat says.

"You should be freaked out. The true Internet—and I mean the *entire* thing—is like an infinitely deep ocean—and the Surface Web is the mere surface of it. Everything below the surface floats around in the ink-black waters of the Deep Web."

"Holy shitballs," Kat says. "How have I never heard of this before? Have you heard about this, Sarah?"

Sarah shakes her head.

"Kinda freaks you out when you hear about it for the first time, huh?" Henn says.

"Totally," Kat agrees. "It reminds me of when I found out there are trillions of invisible microbes on my skin at all times." She shudders.

Josh groans. "Please don't talk about that whole microbes-on-your-skin thing. That always creeps me out."

The Playboy and the Party Girl share a hearty laugh.

Sarah leans into my ear. "Make that twenty-four hours, tops."

I smirk.

"So if normal search engines can't retrieve information that's in the Deep Web, how does anyone find what's there?" Henn asks himself. "Long story short, you gotta know exactly what you're looking for. *Exactly.* The only people you'll find trolling around the Deep Web besides upstanding guys like me are governments and criminals—and when I say 'criminals,' I'm talking jihadists and drug warlords and fucking human traffickers."

"You don't consider yourself a criminal?" Kat asks. There's no judgment in her tone, just curiosity.

"Hell no, I'm not a criminal—I wear a white hat all day long, sister," Henn says. "The only time I ever break the law is for the greater good or when I consider a law to be outdated." He pauses. "Or useless. Or stupid." He pauses again. "Or when breaking a particular law won't hurt anybody." He laughs. "So, yeah, hmm. Now that I think about it, I guess I break the law all the time." He laughs. "But I'm not a *criminal*—I'm one of the good guys."

I glance at Sarah. She doesn't seem at all bothered by Henn's lawlessness—actually, she seems amused. I suppose neither of us has any business being appalled by Henn's wild-west mentality—we already know the guy hacked into the University of Washington to find her for me and that certainly wasn't legal.

"My clients pay me to help them with a particular problem," Henn continues. "And I do. But I leave no trace, take nothing, do no harm—unless I'm being paid to leave a trace, take something, do harm, of course." Henn smirks. "But I only do that kind of thing when I'm positive I work for the good guys."

Sarah squeezes my arm, plainly telling me I'm one of the good guys Henn's talking about.

"For example," Henn continues, "when I poked around that bank looking for Oksana, I discovered a whole bunch of unsecured accounts. I could have taken a couple million bucks if I wanted, easy peasy, but I'd never do that. Why? Because I'm not a thief."

Josh smiles and nods his agreement. It's clear he trusts Henn completely.

"But you might *work* for thieves," Sarah says. "Ever think about that?"

"Nah. If my clients hire me to *take* something, it's always for a very good reason. Like I said, I only work for the good guys."

"But how do you know you're working for the good guys?" I ask. I'm beyond grateful to the guy for what he's done for me—asking him to find Sarah was the single best decision of my life—but hiring this quirky dude to help me take down The Club is an entirely different thing. Am I crazy to trust a guy in skinny jeans with the most important mission of my life? "Everyone thinks their cause is righteous," I say. "Hence, the concept of war."

"Well, yes, of course." Henn flashes a sideways smile at Kat like he's about to tell her a great joke. "But let me show you how I tell the good guys from the bad guys. It's foolproof." He looks right at Sarah. "Sarah, are you a good guy or a bad guy?"

"A good guy," Sarah says.

"And there you go."

Sarah shrugs like it makes perfect sense. "And there you go."

I scoff. "But who would ever say they're one of the bad guys? Who would even *think* that about themselves? People are brilliant at justifying their actions to themselves—trust me, I should know."

"Well, *yeah*," Henn concedes. "But I don't always *believe* people when they say they're one of the good guys. In fact, I rarely do. If I *believe* them, the way I just believed Miss Cruz here, then that's good enough for me."

"Aw, you believe me, Henn?" Sarah asks.

"I do. Indubitably."

"Why, thank you."

"Of course."

I shrug. It's hard to argue with that logic, actually. If I were to boil my own business philosophy down to its barest essence, I suppose I operate in exactly the same way. And, really, what other option do I have right now than to trust this guy? If Josh does, then I guess I do, too. *Indubitably.*

"Sometimes, it's a no-brainer," Henn continues. "Like when a job comes from Josh, for example, I always know I'm fighting for truth and justice and the American way, no questions asked. Because a guy can set his moral compass to Josh—he's *always* one of the good guys, through and through."

"Thanks, man," Josh says.

"Just speaking the truth."

"Well, well, well," Kat says. She shoots Josh an unmistakable smolder. "It turns out the Playboy's a good guy, after all—Mickey Mouse roller coasters notwithstanding."

I lean into Sarah. "Sixteen hours, absolute tops."

Sarah snickers. "Indubitably," she whispers.

"So, Henn," I say, feeling the need to herd cats here. "If The Club lives in the Deep Web, how the fuck do we find them and take them down?" I'm chomping at the bit to fuck these motherfuckers up the ass.

"We need a map," Henn says. "A precise map that gives us a pinpoint location. Once I have that, I can hack in and do a deep dive."

I put my hand on Sarah's bare thigh. I can't wait to do a deep dive with her later tonight in that Jacuzzi tub.

"How do we find this map?" Sarah asks. She puts her hand on top of mine and squeezes.

"We start with our friend, the pimpstress extraordinaire, Oksana Belenko. Whoever she's working with on the tech side of things, there's got to be communications. Or maybe she personally logs into their mainframe. Either way, she'll lead me right to them, one way or another."

"What do you need from us?" Sarah asks.

"A personal email address for Oksana—something you know links right to her."

Sarah shoots me a *mea culpa* look. That's what I was about to get from Stacy when Sarah interrupted my grand strategy at The Pine Box.

"We don't have an email address," Sarah says. "Thanks to me. Miss Bossy Boots." She smiles sheepishly, making me laugh.

"Well, that's what we need," Henn says. "I'll send Oksana

malware that'll give me access to her computer. Plus I'll install a good old-fashioned key log, too. But to do that, we need her to open an email."

"What's a key log?" I ask.

"It lets me remotely monitor every key she hits on her keyboard. Easy way to get all her passwords."

I rub my hands together villainously. "Excellent."

"So you'll need to do three things." He looks directly at Sarah. "First, get her email address. Second, obviously, send her an email. And, third, make sure she opens it, preferably in your presence so we don't leave anything up to chance. Do you think you can do all that?"

"Of course I can," Sarah says. "They think I'm scamming Jonas. I'll just find her and say I've come to negotiate my split on the scam."

"No fucking way," I say, probably much louder than required to make my point.

Sarah opens her mouth, shocked. "Jonas, yes. I'll meet her and negotiate my cut and then while I'm there I'll email her something to memorialize the deal. Done-zo."

"No fucking way," I say again, this time controlling the volume of my voice. "You're not gonna meet Oksana or anyone else from The Club all by yourself."

"Jonas, it'll be fine—"

"I'm going with you."

She rolls her eyes. "They think I'm *playing* you, remember? Why on earth would I bring you with me if I'm scamming you?"

"I don't know. Use that big-ass brain of yours to come up with something they'll believe."

She sighs in frustration.

"It's non-negotiable, Sarah. We're doing this together or we're not doing it at all."

She huffs. "Why would I bring you to meet her? It makes no sense."

I purse my lips, thinking. I can't think of anything off the top of my head.

The room is silent, everyone apparently pondering the same puzzle.

"They think I'm *playing* you," Sarah says slowly, like she's thinking out loud. "Why would I bring you with me?"

"I don't know, but it's non-negotiable."

"I heard you the first time, Lord-God-Master." She crosses her arms over her chest. After a moment, she picks up her champagne flute and ambles to the floor-to-ceiling window on the other side of the room. The sun has set as we've been talking and The Strip's frenetic neon lights are on dazzling display below us.

"Wow," Sarah says, staring out at the expanse of lights. "It's beautiful."

Everyone in the room gets up to take in the view alongside her, drinks in hand.

I put my arm around Sarah and she leans into me.

"Let's take a photo, Sarah," Kat says. The two girls smile for a selfie on Kat's phone with the iconic lights as their backdrop. "And one of you and Jonas, too," Kat commands, motioning for us to get together.

Sarah and I cuddle up and Kat takes our picture. It all feels so *normal*. I like it.

Kat looks at our photo. "You two look good together," she says to me, half-smiling. "*Really* good together."

My heart leaps. Sarah's fierce protector just told me she deems me worthy of her best friend?

"Don't post those pics anywhere, Kat," Henn warns. "We don't want the bad guys knowing we're on their turf."

"I won't post them, don't worry. I just want to remember being here in Vegas with my best friend for her first time." Kat suddenly wraps Sarah in an emotional hug. "Thank God you're okay. I was so worried about you. I love you so much."

"I love you, too." Sarah says, nuzzling into Kat's blonde hair. "I don't know what I would have done if you hadn't pulled through."

"I'm fine. 'Twas merely a flesh wound, Kitty Kat."

I watch them, fascinated. Their exchange is so affectionate and effortless and natural—it makes me envious somehow. I want to be the one hugging Sarah and declaring my love so easily and openly to her.

Sarah whips her head up and gasps. "I've got it," she says.

"You've got what?" Kat asks.

Sarah disengages from Kat. "We use their greed against them."

"That's my girl," I say. "I knew you'd think of something."

Sarah leaps over to me and hugs me. "This is gonna work."

"Of course, it will," I say. "We're an unstoppable team." I kiss her softly.

Henn looks at his watch. "Okay, get your plan figured out and we'll launch first thing tomorrow. I'm gonna work all night on my malware. I want to make sure whatever we send them is ironclad." He grabs his laptop, clearly excited to get to work.

Sarah and I exchange a look. There's a lot at stake here.

"Well," Kat says, her hands on her hips. "While Henn's hard at work cooking up a fancy virus, I guess the rest of us will have to have find *something* to do in Las Vegas. Hmm." She taps her index finger on her temple, pretending to think really hard. "What on earth could we possibly do in *Las Vegas*?"

I look at Sarah, hoping she's thinking what I am: that she's not the least bit interested in being part of a foursome tonight. But nope— one look at Sarah and it's abundantly clear she's thrilled at the idea of going out.

"You like to gamble, Kat?" Josh asks.

"I love it."

"What's your game?"

"Blackjack."

"Lame," Josh says.

"Excuse me?"

"The real fun is craps."

"I've never played," Kat says. "It seems complicated."

"Nah, it's easy. I'll spot you a grand and teach you how to play."

Kat's eyes pop out of her head. "I'm not gonna take your money. I'll just watch you."

"No, you've got to roll the dice for me, Party Girl. You've got first-timer's luck *and* lady-luck on your side, and they only let you roll when you've got a bet on the table."

"Well, then, I'll bet my own money."

"Kat," I interject. "Let my brother pay for your fun. There's nothing Josh Faraday loves more than throwing his hard-earned money away on mindless entertainment."

"That's your idea of helping me, bro?"

I laugh.

"You'd be doing me a favor, Kat. Betting on a first-time roller is the dream of every craps player—it's as exciting as it gets." He smiles. "And I love excitement." Even from here, I can see Josh's eyes flicker when he says that last word.

Kat grins. "Okay, Playboy. I'm in. You had me at 'excitement.' But we're all going out together, right?" She looks at Sarah for assurance.

"Of course," Sarah says.

Damn. I was hoping she'd say her dance card was already filled for tonight with the Underwater Rumba. I clear my throat, trying to catch Sarah's attention. One look at me and she'll know I'm not up for going out.

But the expression on Sarah's face melts me. Oh man, she's so fucking adorable—just bursting at the seams about painting the town red. What am I thinking? Sarah can have sex with me in a goddamned hotel room any time—I've got to nut up and show my baby a good time in the Seventh Circle of Hell.

"Where should we take these lovely ladies to dinner?" I ask Josh.

"It just so happens I know the perfect place."

"Of course you do," I reply.

"Do you ladies think you can handle a night out with the Faraday brothers?" Josh asks.

Both girls squeal with excitement in reply, and Sarah throws her arms around my neck. "Thank you, Jonas."

"You bet," I say softly, kissing her neck. "I'm gonna show you a good time in hell, baby, just like you deserve."

"And then we'll come back here and have an even better time in heaven—in that Jacuzzi tub, just the two of us."

Oh, how I love this woman.

"Henn, you wanna join us for dinner?" Josh calls to Henn across the room. "Yo, Henn?"

Henn looks up from his computer.

"You wanna join us for dinner, man?"

"Oh, Josh," Henn says, shaking his head. "How many times do I have to tell you? You can wine and dine me all you like, but you're never gonna get me into bed."

Chapter 17
Jonas

Okay, I admit it. I'm having fun. *In Las Vegas.* The Apocalypse is nigh. I guess I can count on having fun anywhere, anytime, even in hell, as long as Sarah's by my side.The restaurant Josh selected is superb—Sarah uses the word "ridiculous" at least ten times to describe her food—and the Cirque Du Soleil show we stumble into after dinner, totally on a whim, is spectacular. Every time I look over at Sarah during the show, her face is beaming with an almost childlike joy that makes my heart burst. *So this is what happiness feels like,* I think.

After the show, when the girls gallop off to the bathroom together, I use the opportunity to grill Josh about Henn.

"How well do you know the guy?" I ask. "You sure we can trust him?"

"One hundred percent sure."

"Sounds like we're messing with some pretty hairy shit," I say. "You sure he's *completely* trustworthy?"

"Jonas, I'm sure. He's been my guy since college. He's like a brother to me."

What the fuck does that mean? Henn's "like a brother" to him? Why does Josh need a *friend* who's *like* a brother when he's got an *actual* brother? And why have I never heard of Henn before now, if they're so damned close?

"When I first got to school, I kind of took Henn under my wing when he needed it most," Josh says. "At first, I thought I was the power player in the friendship, but I wound up relying on *him* far more than he ever did on *me*." He shrugs.

My stomach lurches. I know the exact timeframe he's referring to: right after Dad killed himself. *The Lunacy.* Josh went off to UCLA for his first year of college while I stayed behind, school deferred for a year, fighting to reclaim my mind from impenetrable darkness.

"I just needed someone to lean on back then," Josh adds. "And Henn turned out to be that guy."

"I get it," I say. But that doesn't mean I don't feel guilty as hell about it—and, if I'm being honest, jealous that Henn was there for Josh when I couldn't be. Henn is like a brother to Josh? Well, fuck me. The whole idea of Josh needing to lean on someone besides me surprises me—though it shouldn't, now that I think about it. Of course, Josh needed support after suddenly finding himself fatherless and brotherless all at once. Of course, he did.

But what about *after* The Lunacy? Did Josh continue to rely on Henn, even then? I guess I just assumed Josh has leaned on me through the years, despite all my weaknesses and flaws and fuckeduppedness, the way I've always leaned on him. But I should have known. A guy can't lean on someone who has broken legs, or they'll both come crashing down. I look at the ground, emotion threatening to rise up inside me.

"Hey," Josh says softly. "I've leaned on you, too, bro. More than you know. You're the man."

I look up at him. Now that I think about it, I can't remember a single time he's leaned on me. All I can recall are the countless times he's rushed to my aid when I've needed him so badly.

"And I still lean on you, all the time," he says. "All the time."

"You can, you know," I say. "Lean on me. Anytime."

"I know. And I do. You're half my brain, you know that—the better half, except when you're a dumbshit."

"I'm strong now," I say. "You don't have to take care of me anymore. I can take care of *you* sometimes, too. I'm strong now."

"I know you are," Josh says. "You're a beast, man."

"So are you," I say.

I suddenly remember the text Josh sent me as I sat vigil in Sarah's hospital room. *I love you, man,* he wrote. *Thanks,* I replied, emotionally stunted asshole that I am.

"Thanks for your text," I say. "When Sarah was in the hospital."

He knows the one. He nods.

My mouth twists. "It meant a lot."

There's a beat, neither of us knowing what to do.

Maybe I should say more, but that's all I've got.

Josh tries to grin at me, but he fails. His eyes are moist.

Fuck this. This is too weird. I slap my face and Josh laughs in surprise. I'm never the one who slaps first. Ever.

"Are we good, pussy-ass motherfucker?" I ask.

Josh laughs. "Yeah, we're good, motherfucking cocksucker."

I hear the sound of Sarah's laughter. I glance behind us and, sure enough, Sarah and Kat are traipsing noisily toward us from inside the theatre, big smiles plastered across both girls' faces.

"Hey," I say to Josh before the girls reach us, "if Henn's your brother, then he's mine, too. I'm glad he's been there for you."

Chapter 18
Jonas

The Playboy and The Party Girl have been making a killing together at the craps table for the past hour. Josh was right—he can't lose, not with Kat rolling the dice for him. For a ridiculously long time, Sarah and I have watched and cheered and high-fived and even bet more money than we should—but win or lose, my brain is utterly incapable of remaining interested for long in what numbers show up on a pair of dice.

When Sarah whispers to me, "You wanna get outta here?" every square inch of my skin tingles.

"You read my mind, baby," I reply, pushing all my chips over to Kat's mammoth stack and grabbing Sarah's hand. "See you guys later," I call out to Josh and Kat over my shoulder. "Let's go, baby." My cock is already hardening with delicious anticipation.

But, as it turns out, Sarah hasn't read my mind at all. She doesn't want to beeline back up to the suite for water sports like I do—she wants to race into the tattoo parlor on the other side of the casino to get inked with her first tattoo.

Sarah sits on the tattoo artist's table, explaining exactly what she wants him to do. I'm watching her, enraptured and turned on like a motherfucker. All I can think about is tasting her and making her come and then fucking her brains out in that Jacuzzi tub.

"Sounds simple enough," the guy says. "Show me exactly where you want it."

She lies back and without hesitation pulls up her dress to reveal her leopard-print G-string underneath. Wow, apparently modesty's not an issue for Sarah tonight—when in Rome, I guess. Or maybe

83

she's just a lot bit drunk. Or maybe she's finally come to peace with how fucking hot she is and doesn't give a damn who knows it— because, holy fuck, this woman is most definitely smokin' hot. I glance over at the tattoo artist and it's abundantly clear he appreciates the olive-toned canvas he'll be working on.

What the fuck is she doing now? She's peeling down the elastic of her itty-bitty panties, prompting me to lurch forward and reach for her hand to stop her—is she really *that* drunk?—but she stops on her own, just before she gives up the goods.

She points at a tiny swatch of olive skin normally covered by the front of her panties. "Right here," she says, her fingertip touching the exact spot she wants inked. "Boom."

I can't resist. I reach over and touch the spot, too, and she visibly shudders under my fingers. Oh man, what the fuck are we still doing here? Let's get into that fucking Jacuzzi tub already.

"You sure about this, baby?" I ask. The feel of her skin under my fingertips is making me rock hard.

"Hellz yeah," she replies. "The tattoo will be covered up when I'm wearing panties or a bikini—visible only when I'm buck naked— which means no one's ever gonna see it except me. And *you.*"

My blood pulses in my ears.

She licks her lips. "You're the only man who's ever gonna see this tattoo, Jonas."

My chest tightens. I nod.

She blinks slowly and grins. "The only one."

"Forever?" I ask.

Whoa. I can't believe I just said that. But, fuck it, I did, and I can't take it back now. *Forever.* Yeah. That's exactly what I want from her.

Her cheeks flush a beautiful shade of scarlet. She shrugs shyly and bites her lip.

"I want to be the only man who ever sees it," I say, my voice low. I motion to the tattoo artist. "Besides this guy."

She swallows hard and nods.

My skin is on fire. I wish I could consummate this pact of ours right now on top of the tattoo table, but since that's obviously not possible, even in a city as debauched as Vegas, I do the next best thing—I take her face in my hands and kiss her like I own her. Our kiss is so full of heat, so deliciously arousing, I can't muster the willpower needed to pull myself away from her. I know in my head the tattoo guy is sitting there waiting for us, but my body doesn't care. She's my crack. And, right now, I want my crack.

I make a big point of pulling Sarah's dress back down over her thighs—*I'm the only man who's allowed to see my baby's panties, motherfucker*—and then I scoop her up into my arms. *Mine.*

"Sorry man," I say to the tattoo guy. "We'll be back to do this another time." I look at Sarah in my arms. "I'll get you whatever tattoo you want before we leave this Godforsaken city, I promise, baby. But right now, I'm taking you straight to our room—straight to that Jacuzzi tub." I lean into her ear so the tattoo guy doesn't hear this next part. "And then I'm gonna dine on some delicious, par-boiled pussy."

Her face bursts into flames.

I reach to pull my wallet out of my pocket, but it's too hard to do while holding her in my arms. "Do me a favor and pay the nice man for me, baby—for his inconvenience."

She grabs my wallet and practically throws two hundred-dollar bills at the guy. She could have given him a thousand bucks and I wouldn't have cared—whatever I have to pay to get the fuck out of here so I can taste my baby's beautiful, sweet pussy underwater in a warm Jacuzzi tub is fine with me.

I kiss her again. "You are so fucking hot," I say.

She's panting.

I bound out of the tattoo parlor with my baby in my arms and beeline through the noisy casino toward the elevator bank on the far side of the lobby. When tight aisles and slot machines and crowds make it impractical to continue cradling her, she hops out of my arms and leaps onto my back, and I continue making my way past gaming tables and cocktail waitresses and drunk bachelorettes wearing tiaras, my hands grasping Sarah's smooth thighs, my cock aching with anticipation. I'm a man on a mission. My legs are pumping. My heart is racing. I hear her tipsy laughter from atop my back. Yeah, baby, I'm a horse racing back to the sweet-pussy barn. Nothing's gonna stop me from tasting my horny little pony as soon as humanly possible.

But my legs suddenly cease pumping. I stop dead in my tracks.

What the fuck? Apparently, my legs have a fucking mind of their own because I'm positive I didn't instruct them to stop moving. I look up.

I'm standing in front of a wedding chapel. It's an Elvis-themed chapel, a true Vegas absurdity—but a *bona fide* wedding chapel all the same.

I feel her heart beating against my back, but she doesn't speak. Neither do I.

Fuck. I shouldn't have stopped. Why did my legs stop? I didn't tell them to do that. Did I? They hijacked me and took over. Fuck. Her silence on top of me is as thick as molasses. I feel her chest heaving against my back. Why did I stop?

Because I want to marry this girl.

What?

I want to marry this girl.

Oh my God. I want to marry Sarah. I want her to be mine and only mine, and no one else's, ever again. *Forever.* I want to call her my wife.

But it's not possible.

I could never ask Sarah to pledge herself to me for eternity without first letting her see the non-traversable wasteland inside of me, the bastion of fuckeduppedness I've somehow managed to obscure from her thus far. I can't ask her to vow to love me forever without first telling her every last thing about The Lunacy—and that's something I'm just not willing to do.

Wordlessly, I start walking again, leaving the wedding chapel behind. As I gain speed, I feel the tension leave her body and melt away. She lays a soft kiss on the back of my neck.

I see the elevator bank, including the private elevator leading to our penthouse, off to the right—and I hang a sharp left.

"May I help you, sir?" the woman behind the jewelry counter asks.

"Yes, please. We're in the market for a couple of bracelets."

Sarah slides off my back and stands beside me, grasping my hand.

"There was blood all over my bracelet from Belize," I whisper to her. "I had to take it off."

She nods, her big brown eyes melting me. "They cut mine off at the hospital," she says softly. "I don't know where it is."

"See if you like any of these," the saleswoman says, placing two trays of bracelets on the counter in front of us. "These ones here are men's and those are women's."

I pick up a plain, platinum c-band off the men's tray. It's as basic as you can get. "Can I get this engraved across the face?" I ask.

"Of course," the saleswoman says.

"Sarah," I say, handing it back to her. "S-A-R-A-H."

"Very good." Now she looks at Sarah, her eyebrows raised. "And what about you, miss?"

Sarah peers at the tray of women's bracelets. Virtually all her options are much more elaborate than the simple one I've chosen for myself—full of diamonds and curlicues and chains and colorful gems.

"Do you see something you like, baby?" I ask.

She picks up the female version of mine—platinum, c-band, totally plain.

"No, baby, pick something pretty, something with diamonds. You can have whatever you like."

She grabs the simplest one and hands it to the saleswoman. "Jonas. J-O-N-A-S."

"No," I say. "Baby, listen. Pick one with diamonds on it." I grab a platinum bangle off the tray. It extends all the way around, unlike my c-band, and sparkling diamonds rim its edges. "This is pretty. Or how about this one?" I grab a dazzling diamond tennis bracelet off the tray. "This one is stunning."

The saleswoman puts my bracelet and the one Sarah handed her onto the counter, awaiting our final decision.

"I want the one that matches yours," Sarah says simply.

"Yeah, but—"

"Jonas, listen to me." The tone of her voice leaves zero room for argument. She picks up the matching bracelets off the counter and holds them up, side by side. "I'm the sole member of the Jonas Faraday Club—and you're the sole member of the Sarah Cruz Club. That's all that matters to me—not frickin' diamonds. Our bracelets have to be a perfect match because *we're* a perfect match." She juts her chin at me. "End of story."

Chapter 19
Sarah

I'm bursting out of my naked skin in the rising water, waiting for Jonas to return to the tub with our champagne. I run my fingertip over the engraved inscription on my new bracelet. *Jonas.* I should probably put it on the ledge of the tub so it doesn't get wet, but I don't want to take my new bracelet off. Ever.

I'm aching. Throbbing. Crazy. All I want to do is give this gorgeous man the blowjob of his life. Of course, I want to make love to him, too. And kiss him. And touch him. And feel him deep inside me. And, of course, I can't wait to tell him I love him using the actual, magic words again, too—sacred words it seems we're only allowed to exchange when we're making love—but, holy hell, that blowjob is my first priority. I'm going cuckoo for Cocoa Puffs wanting to take him into my mouth and pleasure him 'til he can't see straight. He gets crazy-turned-on pleasuring me? Well, I've discovered I get crazy-turned-on pleasuring him, too. So there.

I didn't know this about myself until recently, and I've never felt even remotely eager to perform oral sex on any other man, but with Jonas, I've discovered that if I open my mind and touch myself while I've got him in my mouth, sucking on him gets me so aroused, it almost makes me orgasm. I like having him at my mercy—literally and figuratively.

I wanted to drop to my knees and take his full length into my mouth the minute he said the word "forever" in that tattoo parlor, but since I'm a nice girl (and not a crack whore in a back alley), performing fellatio in public wasn't an option (even in a city as perverted as Las Vegas). And then, when he stopped in front of that wedding chapel, holy crappola, he "delivered me unto pure ecstasy" right then and there. I tried to whisper, "the culmination of human possibility" into his ear, but my voice wouldn't work. I knew in my bones Jonas was closing his eyes and pledging forever to me—and willing me to do the same. And so I did. I closed my eyes and thought, "I promise you forever, Jonas." It was every bit as magical as our kiss outside the cave in Belize—maybe even more so.

I touch my bracelet again and close my eyes.

We don't need to stand in front of our friends and family wearing traditional wedding clothes to make our love real and forever. We don't need a piece of paper. Today was our wedding day. And that's good enough for me.

Warm water is rising steadily in the tub around me, relaxing me and making me hella horny. I press my lower back into a blasting stream of hot water. "Aah," I sigh. "Come on, baby," I call to Jonas in the other room. "I'm w-a-a-a-a-i-t-i-n-g."

"I'm opening the bottle, baby," he calls back to me.

I don't blame Jonas for not being the marrying kind of guy because, frankly, I'm not the marrying kind of girl. I mean, seriously, what do I know about marriage? Nothing good. All I know about marriage is that it's when a man hits a woman, sometimes with his fist, sometimes with his belt, sometimes with a kick from his boot. I know it's when a man screams at a woman, seemingly out of nowhere, and sometimes calls her pleasant things like "whore" and "bitch."

I know it's when a man comes back the next day with flowers and tells his wife he's sorry, that he's going to change, that he's stopped drinking—and she cries with joy and relief and everything's good again for maybe six weeks. And then she inevitably says the wrong thing or looks at him the wrong way and he drinks a beer and another and another and then everything starts all over again—only the next time, everything's good again for maybe only four weeks, if you're lucky. One week if you're not.

What else do I know about marriage? I know it's when a nine-year-old little girl spends her nights cowering in a closet with a world map or, when things are really bad, lying in bed thinking of ways to kill her own father without getting caught. It's when, on a particularly bad night right after the girl's tenth birthday, a night when she's seen her mother beaten to within an inch of her life, the daughter calmly crushes up eight Tylenol PM tablets and slips them into her father's beer and

Lauren Rowe

waits for him to fall asleep like the worthless fuck he is. And when he does, it's when that little girl uses all her strength to drag her wobbly mother out of the house to an old, dilapidated shed she found only a few blocks away, a shed the girl's been stocking with provisions for the better part of a month. It's when the girl takes care of her mother in that shed and tells her everything's going to be all right, until, finally, after three days, the mother lifts her head and looks at her daughter with a previously unseen glint in her eye and says, "*No más. De hoy en adelante, renazco.*" *No more. From this day forward, I am reborn.*

The water level in the tub is finally at my shoulders and I turn off the gushing faucet. "The tub is filled, baby," I call out to Jonas. "It's s-e-e-e-x-y time, big boy!"

"Coming, baby," he calls from the other end of the suite.

So, yeah, Jonas isn't the marrying kind of guy, and that's just fine with me—because I'm not really the marrying kind of girl. I don't need marriage to give myself to Jonas Faraday. I've already done it. And he's given himself to me. *Forever.*

Ah, there he is. My sweet Jonas. Walking into the bathroom with two flutes of champagne and a gigantic woody. Good Lord, seeing this man naked never gets old. He smiles as he hands me my champagne glass and I down every last drop in one long, ravenous gulp.

"Take it easy, baby. This is the good stuff."

"Get in here, Jonas P. Faraday," I say, writhing like an eel. I'm so turned on I can't breathe.

Jonas lowers his glorious body into the warm water, his face glowing with excitement.

"You really like champagne, don't you?"

"You wanna know why?"

"Tell me."

I drift over to him in the tub and grip his delectable erection in my hand. "Because it brings out the dirty, *dirty* girl in me."

"I like your dirty girl."

"And she likes you." I lick my lips. "A whole lot."

With that, I lower myself slowly, slowly, slowly down toward the surface of the warm water—prolonging Jonas' delicious anticipation as long as humanly possible—until, finally, with great fanfare, I take a deep, long, dirty-girl breath, wink at Jonas' exuberant face, and submerge myself under the water.

90

Chapter 20
Sarah

"I still say it was a draw," Jonas says.

"Oh, please. I totally won," I say.

"I think it's just this next block up," Jonas says, looking at Google Maps on his phone.

"Damn, it's hot," I say.

"Welcome to Vegas."

"Henderson, actually," I correct him.

"Henderson, Vegas—wherever. Hotter than hell, either way. And you didn't *win,*" Jonas says. "If you add up all the minutes I was down there holding my breath in *aggregate,* I totally won. Hands down."

"Yeah but the only reason you were down there so damned long was you couldn't close the deal as efficiently as I could—that shouldn't be a reason to *win.*"

He laughs. "Oh my God. That's just men verses women—pure physiology—not a reflection of my skills. And the time it took me probably had a little something to do with all that champagne you drank—dulls the nerve endings."

"Excuses, excuses."

"No excuses—I still did it, didn't I?"

"You sure did. Amen to that."

"Just because you got me off faster than a pubescent boy doesn't mean you *won* a damned thing—the contest was who could hold their breath the *longest,* not who could get the job done *fastest.* "

"No, I changed the contest. It was who could be the most *efficient.*"

He laughs again. "You never said that. You're such a cheater."

"I only had to pop up for air once. You had to come up, like, four times. Ergo, I won."

He groans in fond remembrance of last night. "God, you were on fire last night. You are so fucking talented, you know that, Sarah Cruz? You're the goddess and the muse. Mmm mmm. Damn."

I shrug. "'Twas a labor of love."

"Yeah, well, still. You can't unilaterally change the rules of the contest at the last minute. It was never about who could get the job done the fastest and you know it."

"Most *efficiently*."

"Well, then, that's bullshit. I never stood a chance. Before your lips even touched my cock, I was already halfway gone."

"Excuses."

"Not excuses. Facts."

"Are you being a sore loser, Jonas?"

"Ha! No. I'm a very happy loser."

"Wait, is that the place?" I point to a nondescript building on the other side of the street.

Jonas double-checks the address again. "Yeah, that should be it. Fuck, it's hot. How does anyone live in this heat? I swear to God."

We keep walking until we're standing immediately across the street from the building and peeking at it from around the corner of a liquor store. The building is seventies-style cement with blinds covering all the windows and no signage. It's the kind of place you'd expect to see a chiropractor or real estate agent set up shop—just total blah. It most certainly does not scream "global crime syndicate."

"Not what I expected," I say.

"What'd you expect?"

"Like something out of *Diehard,* I guess? A high-rise steel building with mirrored windows filled with bad guys in couture suits wearing earpieces."

Jonas laughs. "Damn, that's quite specific. You expected all that from the fuckers who employ the Ukrainian Travolta?"

"Yeah, like John Travolta's boss in *Pulp Fiction.* He was kind of spiffy looking, wasn't he?"

"Marsellus Wallace."

"What?"

"That was the name of Travolta's boss in *Pulp Fiction*—Marsellus Wallace. And John Travolta was Vincent Vega."

I look at him blankly.

"And Uma Thurman was Mia Wallace—you sure you've seen *Pulp Fiction?* Because I'm beginning to doubt you about that."

I roll my eyes. "Of course, I've seen it. Best movie ever." I crinkle my nose at him. "I've never lied to you about a single thing, ever."

He smiles at me. "I know. You're cute when you get annoyed at me, you know that?"

I purse my lips and peek at the building again. I inhale, trying to steel myself.

"You ready to meet our friend, Oksana Belenko?" Jonas asks.

"Yup." I take a deep breath. "I think." I absentmindedly touch my wrist, but, of course, my bracelet isn't there—Jonas and I decided to go bracelet-free on this particular errand.

"You know what to do?" he asks.

"Yeah. I'm just nervous all of a sudden." I gasp. "What if the Ukrainian Travolta's in there?" I can't believe I haven't thought of that possibility before now.

"Well, then the plan is fucked because I'm killing the motherfucker with my bare hands."

My jaw drops. I wait for him to say, "Just kidding," but he doesn't. "Jonas, no. If he's in there, you have to figure out a way to keep your cool. Promise me you won't kill anyone."

"Nope. If that motherfucker's in there, he's a dead man, plan or no plan. If I tell you to run, you better run like hell."

My chest tightens. I feel a sudden panic coming on. Why didn't I consider what Jonas might do if he were to come face-to-face with my attacker? What might *I* do? I take a deep breath to steady myself. "Jonas, listen. If you do anything not according to plan, you could get us both killed. Or worse."

"What could be worse than getting us both killed?"

"You could get *yourself* killed and not me. Or you could go to prison. Both would be worse. I'd rather die than live without you."

"Well, then, let's pray that motherfucker's not inside that building right now." His eyes are hard. I've never seen him look like this.

My breathing is shaky. "Maybe we shouldn't go through with this. Maybe we should come up with another plan."

"Baby, listen to me." He grabs my shoulders and gazes at me

with those beautiful blue eyes of his. "We can't sit around the rest of our lives looking over our shoulders. You know that. It's time to take control."

I nod. Of course, he's right. Coming here to find Oksana was my idea, after all. I take another deep breath. I don't know why I'm suddenly freaking out.

"I refuse to sit around and wonder if they're coming after you again," Jonas continues. "I'm done letting shit happen to me. I'm taking charge."

I nod. I'm glad to hear it.

"So are you ready to fuck them up the ass with me or not?"

"Yeah, I'm ready." I shake it off. "That was just a momentary blip. I'm ready."

He grabs my hand and squeezes it. "All we have to do is get them to open an email. Easy as pie."

I nod. "Okay. You got your phone?"

He holds up his phone.

"And your checkbook?"

He pats his pocket. "Yup." He starts pulling me toward the street.

"Hang on." I drop his hand and step back.

He turns back around and stares at me, uncertain. "You okay?"

"I just had a sudden feeling—almost like a premonition."

Jonas looks at me expectantly.

"I'd kick myself if I ignored this feeling and then it turned out to be right."

Jonas waits.

"Do you think you could write me a check? Payable to me?"

"For what?"

"I don't know," I say. "I just feel like last time, having a check from you is what saved my life. I feel like I should go in there armed with the same protection as last time, just in case."

"Just in case what?"

"I don't know."

He looks concerned.

"I won't use it if I don't have to. But if our Plan A doesn't work out, I think I should have a check from you as our Plan B—"

"Baby, no. There is no Plan B. We're all about Plan A."

"What's the harm? If I don't need it, I'll rip it up afterwards." Adrenaline is suddenly surging throughout my body. The longer I stand here talking about this, the more certain I am that I need it. "Just humor me."

He studies my face. "I'm not gonna leave you alone with them—not even for a minute. You realize that? There's no Plan B."

"Of course. But what if they search my purse or something? That'd be a good thing for them to find, wouldn't it? It would confirm I've got you wrapped around my little finger, just like I've been telling them."

"You *do* have me wrapped around your little finger." He smiles.

I smile back at him. Damn, he's a good-looking man. "That check saved my life last time, Jonas. Maybe I'm being paranoid, but I don't want to walk in there without my good luck charm."

He slowly pulls out his checkbook. "This is not an invitation for you to go off plan. There's no Plan B."

"I know." I hand him a pen from my purse.

"How much? Two-fifty?"

"No, that's too much. A hundred, maybe."

He writes the check and hands it to me. "But we're sticking to the plan, no matter what. I'm only doing this because I trust your gut so damned much." He kisses the top of my head. "Because you're so fucking smart."

"Thank you. I feel better having it." I pat my purse.

He smiles reassuringly. "Just follow my lead. Our plan is foolproof."

"Let's do it."

"No going off plan."

"I know."

"Say it."

"No going off plan. I know."

"Okay. Let's do it."

Chapter 21
Jonas

"I'll tell Oksana you're here," the young woman in the front room says. She looks wary. "Can I get you something to drink?"

"No, thanks. We're good," I say.

"And tell me your names again?"

"Jonas Faraday and Sarah Cruz, here to see Oksana Belenko." I smile my most charming smile and the young woman's features noticeably soften.

"Okay. Just a minute."

She disappears into the next room and closes the door.

Sarah and I look at each other. My heart is beating like a steel drum.

Several minutes pass. I squeeze Sarah's hand. I didn't expect to feel this nervous.

The young woman comes out, followed by a guy of about my age, dressed in a designer suit, his dark blonde hair slicked back. I can almost feel Sarah smirking next to me—she just got her *Die Hard* villain.

"Can I help you?" he says, keeping his distance. He looks pointedly at Sarah.

"Hey there," I say, trying my best to come off like a bull in a china shop. "So great to meet you." I extend my hand like we're long-lost friends. "I'm Jonas Faraday—one of The Club's members." I look at Sarah and smile. "One of The Club's *very* satisfied members, I might add."

Sarah smiles back at me.

He shakes my hand, but he's not nearly as enthusiastic as I am. He pointedly doesn't give his name in reply to my self-introduction.

"I brought our girl Sarah to Vegas for a little fun, you know, and

96

I figured why not kill two birds with one stone while I'm here and do some business with you?"

The guy looks pointedly at Sarah again.

I glance at Sarah under his hard gaze, worried she's going to freak out, but she's cool as a cucumber. She smiles broadly at the guy and puts out her hand. "I'm Sarah Cruz," she says. "I don't think we've met yet." She looks at me. "I've always worked remotely from Seattle, so I haven't met everyone at headquarters yet."

The guy looks behind us toward the front door where we came in. "Is it just the two of you?"

"Yes," Sarah says evenly. "Absolutely. Just us."

"Yeah, Sarah told me to just email you guys, said that would be best, but she's not savvy in business like I am." I wink at her. "Are you, Sarah?"

"Nope."

"She just doesn't have practical experience yet, you know? Smart as hell but no real world experience. She doesn't understand you can get more done with a handshake and looking someone in the eye than with an email." I pull her to me and grab her ass. "What a girl this is, though, I'm telling you. What a girl."

At my rough touch, Sarah throws her head back and laughs. "Oh, Jonas."

"Stacy in Seattle told me Oksana's the one I've got to talk to about buying a block of a girl's time, so I figured, hey, I'll cut a deal with you aboveboard and come down here and buy Sarah from you."

"Jonas," Sarah says, swatting at me playfully.

"He knows what I mean. I'm buying your *time,* sweetheart— obviously, I'm not buying *you.*" I look back at the guy. "That is, unless she's for sale?" I laugh like I think I'm so funny.

Sarah laughs, too.

"Ah, but seriously. I'd like to buy a big block of this girl's time. She's so busy reviewing applications for you guys day and night, she won't give me all the time I want. And, believe me, I want *a lot.*"

I grope Sarah again and she giggles.

The guy looks wary. He doesn't speak. "I'll be right back."

He disappears through a door.

Sarah and I look at each other. We're playing our parts to a tee, just like we planned. But who the fuck is this guy? Where's Oksana?

Die Hard Fucker comes back out after a couple minutes. "Leave your phones and purse with Nina." He motions to the young woman who initially greeted us.

Sarah hands her purse to the woman without hesitation, but I stand immobilized.

"Mr. Faraday, we're more than happy to speak to you within the confines of this building, but we're not willing to risk our voices being recorded for all posterity."

Holy shit. This is the fucker who writes The Club's emails, there's no doubt about it—he talks just like he writes.

"Oh, sure. Yeah, no problem," I say, handing the woman my phone.

Die Hard Fucker pats us down, taking a lot more care frisking every inch of Sarah's body than mine, I notice. Does he trust her a whole lot less than he trusts me? Or is he just enjoying the pleasure of touching her body? I clench my jaw, trying to contain my murderous impulses.

When *Die Hard* Fucker is convinced we're both clean, he invites us into the office. A woman in maybe her late fifties or early sixties with dyed platinum blonde hair and severe eyeliner sits behind a large desk. Introductions all around reveal she's our friend Oksana and that *Die Hard* Fucker is her son, Maksim—though he instructs us to call him Max. Sarah and I take chairs opposite Oksana while Max sits off to the side and stares like a motherfucker at Sarah.

"Great to finally meet you, Oksana," I say breezily after everyone's taken their seats. "I've really enjoyed my Club experience so far—everything's been top notch."

Max clears his throat.

"I'm surprised to see you here," Oksana says evenly. Despite her thick Ukrainian accent, her English is perfect. "We don't take in-person meetings with clients. And our address is not advertised."

"Oh, sure, yeah. Sorry about that. Stacy in Seattle told me exactly where to find you." I feel an unexpected pang of guilt as I throw Stacy under the bus, but I can't think of another way to rationally explain how we've located Oksana. "I hope that's okay. I don't want to get Stacy into any trouble. She's a sweetheart. In fact, I'd originally planned to buy a bunch of *Stacy's* time—that girl is smokin' hot and really talented—"

Sarah stiffens in her seat, emulating barely contained jealousy.

"But then this one right here blew a gasket when I even *looked* at anyone else and my plans changed on a dime." I smirk at Sarah and she nods. "This girl's got a bit of a jealous streak it turns out—she's not too fond of sharing—so a threesome with Stacy was out of the question." I laugh.

Sarah clenches her jaw, playing her part exactly as planned.

"She's a handful this one. A stick of dynamite." I growl that last part.

Sarah flashes a wide smile at Oksana but gets nothing in return.

"Yes, she is," Oksana says. "That's our Sarah for you—quite a handful." Oksana squints at Sarah, apparently trying to figure out her game.

"Aw, I'm sweet, Jonas, you know that," Sarah purrs.

"That's true. As sweet as can be," I agree.

Max hasn't taken his eyes off Sarah the whole time we've been sitting here. I swear to God, if he touches her again like he did in the other room, I won't be able to control myself from strangling him.

"... and he always says I work too much," Sarah's saying. "Isn't that right, sweetheart?"

"Oh, yeah. This girl always has to work. Work, work, work. Poor thing's got school to pay for, plus this horrible thing with her mom's cancer—I'm sure you've heard all about that—" Oksana and her son exchange a look. "And now she tells me her dad just got laid off, too." I exhale loudly. "How much can one girl carry on her shoulders? Jesus. Even after some wacko hauled off and attacked her at school—Sarah, did you tell them about that?"

Sarah shakes her head. "No, I didn't mention it, sweetheart. It was no big deal."

"Are you kidding me? It was brutal," I say. "It's hard to believe there are sick fucks in the world who would want to hurt a sweet girl like this. I hope whoever did it burns in fucking hell." I glare at Max.

"Jonas," Sarah says, her voice tight.

Shit. I'm veering off plan. My heart is pounding mercilessly. I take a deep breath.

"Sorry to hear you were hurt, Sarah," Max says slowly. "Glad you've recovered." He leers at her. "So nicely."

I clear my throat. Motherfucker. I'm clenching my hands so tightly they physically hurt.

"Apparently, there's been a string of rapes at the university," Sarah says evenly. "The police are thinking the attack on me was a botched rape, or maybe just a mugging, they're not sure. But, either way, I'm fine now." She glares at me, warning me to stay on plan. "It was so sweet how Jonas doted on me when I was recovering, though."

"Yeah, the poor thing was hurt pretty bad. And that's what made me realize I want to take care of her, you know? Make life a little easier for her—take some of the weight off her if I can. How much can one girl take, you know? But even after the attack, nope, she just wanted to hop right back into school and work—said she has too many bills to pay, too many applications to review, couldn't afford to take any time off."

Sarah suddenly chokes up, or at least she appears to. Damn. She's good. I know she's acting—but, still, she's breaking my heart.

"Hey," I say gently. "It's okay." I grab her hand. "Everything's gonna be all right."

"I'm sorry," Sarah says. "I'm fine now." She swallows hard. "I've just had so much to deal with lately. It just means so much to me that you want to help me."

I kiss the top of her hand. "I do." I address Oksana. "Maybe I shouldn't admit this to you, but I keep telling her I'll pay her bills for her so she can just quit this intake agent job altogether and concentrate on me, twenty-four-seven, but she says it wouldn't be fair to you guys—that you depend on her too much."

Oksana and Max look at each other. They haven't sent Sarah an application to process since before she left for Belize.

"You know, it's funny. I signed up with The Club so I wouldn't have to deal with emotional attachments but, then, damn it to hell, I got *attached* to this girl right here." I grab her thigh. "No man could resist her. Look at her. She's gorgeous. But business is business, and I know that—I respect that. So that's why I'm here."

"What exactly can we do for you, Mr. Faraday?" Max asks.

"I was just hoping I could convince you to let me buy all Sarah's time for a maybe a month? She's always running out the door to process another application for you guys when I want to fly her somewhere or spend some alone time with her, she's so worried about paying her bills. So I thought maybe if I could convince her to take a paid leave of absence from the job, that would free up some of her time for me."

"I can't quit my job, Jonas," Sarah says, jutting out her chin. "I've got too many people depending on me."

"I know, sweetheart. But you've got to learn to accept my help. I just want to help you."

"Thank you, Jonas. You're so generous."

"I think we could accommodate you, Mr. Faraday," Oksana says. "Sarah's one of our very best intake agents, though, and we rely on her heavily on a daily basis. But, of course, we always want to make our clients happy, whenever possible."

"Fantastic. I'd like to buy her for a month to start with. I can't commit beyond that, at least not yet."

"Exactly the reason I won't quit my job," Sarah says to Oksana like they're best girlfriends. "He won't commit." Now she looks at me. "If you can't commit to me, Jonas Faraday, then I can't commit to you."

Oksana's eyes sparkle. She obviously appreciates Sarah's gamesmanship.

I roll my eyes. "This girl's tough, I'm not gonna lie. Keeps me on my toes." I smile at Sarah and she smiles back. "Obviously, I could have any other girl in The Club—or any girl in the world, for that matter, if you want to know the truth—but I can't seem to get enough of this particular girl. It's crazy. She's just... man, she's a pistol, I'm telling you."

Sarah smirks. "I'm just honest, that's all. I am who I am—take me or leave me."

"Yep, that's what she keeps saying—and I just keep taking her." I laugh like a total letch. "But she won't quit the job and she keeps insisting I have to pay you directly for her time if I want her undivided attention, and I respect that. She's loyal, this one. A straight shooter. I always say in business you've got to be aboveboard and lead with integrity."

Sarah shrugs. "I'd never leave these guys hanging." Sarah lowers her head and appears to become overwhelmed with emotion again. She takes a minute. "Sorry. I was just thinking about my mom and dad again. They've got so much to deal with."

Damn, if this show isn't convincing these fuckers that Sarah's the jewel in their crown, I don't know what will. Give this girl an Oscar.

"Don't you worry about anything, Sarah," I say. I peek at Oksana. Yeah, she's buying what Sarah's selling. "I'm going to help you with all your expenses, sweetheart, I promise. But first things first. What's it going to cost to release this beautiful girl for a month into my care? I want to *own* her—twenty-four-seven." I lick my lips.

"Oh, Jonas," Sarah says. "You're so sweet."

"Twenty-four-seven?" Oksana looks up at the ceiling, apparently calculating something. "Three thousand a day should suffice."

"Ninety thousand for a month?" I say, incredulous. "That seems high."

Sarah bristles and crosses her arms. "That seems *high* to you, Jonas Faraday? For a *month* with me, twenty-four-seven, whenever and wherever you want me? That seems awfully *low* to me."

I put my hands up defensively, trying to appease my impossible-to-please girlfriend, but she looks away, pissed.

Oksana smiles. Oh yeah, she loves Sarah. "We rely heavily on Sarah, that's why she's been so busy with her job. She's our brightest star. You understand she's not one of the girls in The Club, right? She's a highly specialized member of our team. You were never supposed to have her—she's not normally for sale. Someone like that comes at a high premium."

"Oh, yeah, I know that. By the way, sorry I broke The Club's rules to get with her—I just couldn't resist." I smile broadly. "She was just too tempting."

Sarah nods emphatically. *Damn straight.*

"If I understand what you're asking for," Oksana continues, "you'd like us to hold her job for her—guarantee her job will be waiting for her in a month—*and* you want us to continue paying her throughout the entire month she's gone, right? Like a paid leave?"

"Exactly."

"Which means we'll need to hire another intake agent to take her place, at least temporarily—and train that person, too. The whole situation is a huge inconvenience to us. We're running a for-profit organization here, you realize, not a charity."

I remain silent, acting like I'm thinking it over.

Sarah looks at me with pleading eyes. "What if I take a pay cut to make it work for you, Jonas? Because I'd really like to be available

for you, every minute of every day and *night,* for the next month."
She bats her eyelashes.

"I wouldn't ask you to take a pay cut, Sarah," I say. "Never. You
need the money." I sigh. "I wish you'd just let me pay you directly.
Wouldn't that be simpler?"

"We'll do it for eighty," Oksana blurts. "But not a penny less.
That's my final offer."

"Oh, thank you, Oksana," Sarah says brightly. "You see, Jonas?
Oksana's willing to work with you. So will you do the deal?" She
gets up from her chair and places her lips right on my ear. "I'll make
it worth your while, sweetheart," she whispers.

I know she's just play-acting, but she just turned me on. I turn
my head and kiss her mouth. She runs her hand through my hair.
Damn, even when we're faking it, she's my crack.

"You know I can't resist you," I say quietly. I pull out my
checkbook. "Eighty it is. Payable to The Club?" I ask.

"We'll fill in the payee name ourselves," Max answers.

I fill out the check and hand it to Oksana. I look at Sarah. "It's
official. I own you. Twenty-four seven. You're mine."

Sarah's eyes blaze. "For one month."

"Again, sorry I co-opted Sarah against your rules. I just couldn't
resist her—no man could have resisted her after what she wrote to me
in her email. And then when I found out about her jealous streak, too.
Man, that was just too much." I run my finger up Sarah's arm. "She's
a handful, this one. A tasty little handful."

Sarah smiles wickedly at me. "Thank you for your generosity,
Jonas. I think generosity is such an attractive trait in a man. It turns
me on."

I turn to them. "This has been the best money I've spent in my
life, hands down. I'm so glad I joined. In fact, I've been going on and
on about how awesome The Club is to all my friends. I was just at an
international finance convention with some heavy hitters, actually,
and I must have told at least twenty guys all about it one night over
Scotch—and they all want in, every last one of them. But these guys
are all, you know, big-time VIPs—accustomed to highly specialized
attention in all things."

"We'll be sure to give them a fantastic experience," Oksana
says.

"Some of these guys make me look like a pauper, seriously." I chuckle. "Just obscene amounts of money. I told them I'd ask you to contact them personally, sort of like a VIP concierge type thing, to answer questions, get them signed up, tell them what they'll be getting, assure them they'll be treated like kings. They don't want to sign up like everybody else—they want assurances they'll get the best of the best. These guys don't give a shit about romance, if you know what I mean, they just want premium *service*."

Oksana looks at Max, clearly asking for permission.

"We'll give them platinum service, I assure you," Max says. "Just give them the link to our application portal and we'll get the membership process going per our usual protocols."

"Why don't I just email you their contact info, and you can give them a quick call? I bet you could upsell each and every one of them to a VIP yearlong package for half a mil. Maybe more—maybe even create some sort of special VIP club within The Club, just for these guys? Seriously. Some of them make me look like a hobo." I laugh. "If you give me my phone from the other room, I'll pull up their contacts and send them to you in an email."

"No," Max says, his tone firm. "We don't make telephone contact and we don't solicit new members, ever. No exceptions. If they want to join, they'll have to do it through the appropriate channels, same as everyone else. I designed the protocols myself. We do it this way to ensure maximum protection and confidentiality for everyone involved in the transaction. I'm sure they'll understand that."

Oh, so this fucker designed the site, did he? His mom supplies the girls and he supplies everything else?

"I'm not sure they'll go for that," I persist.

"Jonas, please," Sarah says firmly. "Please respect what Max is telling you. Your friends can't ask The Club to do anything that might compromise confidentiality in any way, regardless of how much money they have. Don't forget, that confidentiality protects me as an employee as much as anyone."

I stare at Sarah. That's not part of the plan. What the fuck is she saying? The plan is for me to send them a fucking email about my rich friends who want to join. Why is she siding with Max?

"Can I be perfectly honest with you about something, Jonas?"

Sarah says, but she's looking at Max like they're sharing an inside joke.

"Of course." My heart is raging. What the fuck is she doing?

"If it gets out I've worked for The Club, I might not pass the ethics review for my law license. So it's really important to me that we follow whatever protocols The Club has in place to protect itself—because those protocols protect me, too. I mean, how well do you know these guys? Can you be sure of their absolute discretion?"

I'm speechless.

Sarah looks at Max, unflinching. He smiles at her, heat rising in his eyes. It's all I can do not to leap across the room and wring the fucker's neck the way he's looking at her right now.

"Sarah makes an excellent point," Max says. "Thank you, Sarah."

"Of course. Protecting The Club is in everyone's interest. Especially mine." She looks at me sweetly. "And so is protecting the privacy of members, too, of course." She smiles broadly, full of charm.

What the fuck is she doing? *This is not the fucking plan.*

"I agree," Max says. "Mr. Faraday, why don't you tell me the names of your friends so that when they contact us through appropriate channels, we'll be ready for them." He grabs a pad off Oksana's desk. "I promise, we'll make sure to show them the time of their lives."

"Sure thing," I say, thoroughly relieved. Looks like there was a method to Sarah's madness, after all—she was just gaining this fucker's trust. Good thinking. "Yeah, okay, the names are on my phone. Give me my phone and I'll email you the names."

"No, just tell me the names now, verbally." He positions his pen on the pad.

"Jonas, you can give the list to me later, and I'll make sure they get the names," Sarah says.

I'm speechless again. What the fuck is she doing? *This isn't the fucking plan.*

"Perfect," Max says. "Thank you, Sarah."

Sarah looks at me. "Hey, Jonas, would you mind giving me five minutes to speak to Max and Oksana in private?"

What the fuck? We both agreed I wouldn't leave her alone with these fuckers for a nanosecond. What the fuck is she doing?

"Just for five minutes," she says breezily. "I have some information about a member I need to give them—about the last application I processed—and the information's confidential, of course. This will be my last work-related task for a whole month, I promise. When we walk out that door, no more work." She winks.

I can't speak. This is insanity. No fucking way.

"Just five minutes, sweetheart," she says.

I don't move. No fucking way. *No fucking way.*

"Mr. Faraday, will you be so kind?" Max says, getting up and motioning to the door. "Just for a moment. Nina will get you some coffee." He opens the door leading out to the reception area.

I stare at Sarah. Fuck me. This is not happening. No fucking way.

"Thanks, Jonas," Sarah says. "It'll just take a minute. I promise."

I force my body to stand. I look at my watch. "Five minutes." My eyes are granite. "I'm timing you."

"Great, thanks. I'll be right out."

Chapter 22
Sarah

The minute the door closes behind Jonas, I whip around to face Oksana and Max, my eyes as hard as steel. "Fifty-fifty or I walk," I say evenly, clenching my jaw. "I've got this guy in the palm of my hand, as you can plainly see. He can't get enough of me. He's *addicted.* And now that I've given him my sob story about my mom having cancer and my dad losing his job—he's ready to throw money at me hand over fist. Fifty-fifty or I'm out of here."

Max snickers.

"Sixty-forty," Oksana says. "That's my final offer."

I sit back in my chair and cross my arms. "He's in the palm of my hand, I'm telling you."

Oksana's face has turned to stone. "Sixty-forty," she says. "Take it or leave it."

I wonder what she'd do to me if I leave it? "Fifty-fifty with this guy, and sixty-forty on future guys," I say. "I don't even need you anymore on Faraday—I could keep all this guy's money and you'd never even know it—but I'm keeping you in the loop because I want to work with you on future guys, too."

Oksana and Max look at each other.

"You could keep all this guy's money and we'd never know it?" Max says, chuckling to himself. "You think it'd be that simple?" His voice is pure menace.

"Shh, Maksim. *Dobre,*" Oksana says. "Fine, Sarah. You've obviously done a lot of work on Faraday already—so we'll do fifty-fifty on him and sixty-forty on everyone else."

"All right," I say. "Good. Now that we've got that settled—you'll be happy to know he gave me another check this morning. This time for a hundred thousand."

"That's all?" Max says.

I roll my eyes. "It was just 'fun money' to *gamble* with while we're here." I laugh. "I'm telling you, he's in the palm of my hand."

Oksana looks duly impressed. "Do you have the check with you?"

"Yeah, it's in my purse." I motion to the outside room.

Oksana motions to Max and he gets up to retrieve it.

"I'll squeeze everything I can out of Faraday for the next month, but after that I want more clients," I say to Oksana when Max is gone. "I'm actually enjoying this."

"Ah, you've discovered the power." Oksana laughs. "I always say, as long as a woman's got a pussy and a mouth, it's her own damned fault if she can't get whatever the hell she wants."

I smile through my sudden nausea. "Ain't that the truth. You'd think the man's never had sex before, the way he reacts to me."

"The power of the pussy," Oksana says with mock reverence.

We share a raucous laugh, though I'm seriously trying not to hurl. What a bitch.

Max comes back into the office with my purse, but as he tries to close the door behind him, I hear Jonas' anxious voice on the other side of the door.

"I've paid for her time," I hear Jonas say. "I'm coming back in."

"Just give us five minutes," Max says curtly. He slams the door and locks it and strides across the room, rummaging through my purse as he goes. He pulls out the check and holds it up for Oksana to see.

"Nice work," Oksana says.

"Next week, my mom's health will take a turn for the worse," I say. "And my dad will be in danger of losing his house—to the tune of five hundred thousand."

Oksana nods enthusiastically. "Good."

Max takes the seat vacated by Jonas and leans into my face, placing his hand firmly on my thigh.

I recoil under his touch.

"So did Faraday fix your little problem?"

I don't respond.

Max leans even closer and whispers. "Did he fix the little problem you wrote about in your email to him—your 'Mount Everest' problem,

I think you called it?" He licks his lips. "Because if not, I'm sure I can solve your problem in about five minutes."

I lean sharply away from Max's face. "I told the guy what he wanted to hear, that's all—the one thing I knew he couldn't resist."

Max chuckles. His face tells me he doesn't believe me. "You were very, very convincing."

"Maksim, *nemaye*," Oksana says. "Very clever, Sarah."

I grimace. I've only got one thing on my mind right now—getting Oksana to open an email, come hell or high water.

"So let's cut the crap," I say. "I'm willing to forgive our 'unfortunate miscommunication.' But I want to get paid within twenty-four hours, every time, or else I walk—and, believe me, I'll take you down when I go."

"You won't take us down," Max says.

I smash my mouth into a hard line.

"You just said so yourself—you won't pass the ethics review for your law license if it gets out you worked for us. You won't risk that."

I scowl like I'm pissed at myself for revealing my big secret to him. "Maybe I don't care about my law license," I say, trying my damnedest to sound like a terrible liar.

Max grins. "Oh yes you do. I've done my research on you. I'm quite confident you care more than anything about your law license—and that you therefore won't tell anyone about us."

I grit my teeth.

"But that's exactly why we can trust you, Miss Cruz. Our interests are obviously aligned. And that's good."

"If you piss me off enough, I'll send out that report, regardless of what might happen to my law career."

He smiles at me, not buying it.

"Fine," I huff, conceding his point. I cross my arms. "But if you send the Ukrainian John Travolta to hurt me again, all bets are off."

"The 'Ukrainian John Travolta'?" He bursts out laughing.

"Yeah. Like John Travolta in *Pulp Fiction*—only Ukrainian."

Max is highly amused. "I'll have to tell Yuri you said that." He says something to his mother in Ukrainian and she laughs. Max waves the air. "We're not going to harm you, Sarah. You've proved your value. You say you're not 'fucking stupid'? Well, neither are we."

I squint at him.

"You're an entertaining writer, by the way. A spitfire, just like your asshole boyfriend said."

"How do I know I can trust you? How do I know you won't send your hitman after me again?"

His eyes harden. "Because if I say you're safe, you're safe. And if I want you dead, you're dead."

A shiver runs up my spine—I'm six inches away from the man who personally ordered me dead.

"But the good news is I don't want you dead." He touches my arm and I shudder. "I do hope you weren't too inconvenienced by our unfortunate miscommunication."

"Oh no, not at all. I didn't need all that blood inside my body, anyway," I scoff.

"How bad are the scars?" Oksana asks. "I can't put you on the circuit if you're too scarred." Her tone is pure business.

There's a loud knock at the door. "Time's up," Jonas says loudly. He shakes the door, but it's locked. "Sarah? Time's up. Right now."

Max motions to the door. "Talk to him."

I walk to the door and open it. Jonas looks panicked. Or is that enraged?

"Everything's great, sweetheart," I say cheerily, poking my head out. "We're almost done talking business. We need just five more minutes and then we'll be all done—and I'll be all yours for a whole month."

He's bursting out of his skin.

"Come here," I say brightly.

He leans an inch from my face to whisper something to me, but I kiss him.

"Sarah," he whispers, pulling away, his eyes frantic. "Get out of there right now."

"Yeah, just a couple more minutes," I say at full voice. "And after that, I'm at your service, sweetheart."

"Sarah, now," he whispers fiercely. "*Right now.*"

"No," I whisper. "Trust me."

As I close the door on his face, he flashes white-hot anger. I turn back around, making sure to keep the door unlocked. "My wounds are healing surprisingly well," I say, sitting back down. "Thanks for your concern. This one on my neck is hardly anything." I tilt my head so they can get a good view of it.

"Yeah, not too bad," Oksana agrees.

"And the one on my ribcage isn't too bad, either—and it'll get better over time."

"Let's see it," Oksana says. "I need to see for myself."

"Actually, we have a little tradition here at The Club," Max says, his tone suddenly lecherous. "I audition every single girl before we send them out on the circuit—just to make sure they're worthy of our high standards." He looks at his mother and says something in Ukrainian.

My stomach drops into my toes. I glance at the door, suddenly feeling panicked. Holy crap.

"It won't take very long," Max says. "Five minutes." He stands and holds out his hand.

Holy shit. He expects to fuck me in the bathroom right now?

"Maksim," Oksana chastises. "*Ne zaraz.*"

My throat is closing up. "Faraday is right on the other side of the door," I sputter. "And he's already wondering what's going on—you saw him. He's freaking out. There's not enough time."

"Maksim, *nemaye*," Oksana says sharply. "*Ne s'ohodni.*"

Max scowls at his mother and exhales loudly. "Well, if not today, then before she leaves Las Vegas."

I try to smile, but I'm ninety-nine percent sure I'm failing at the attempt. I have to get out of here—I'm freaking out—but goddammit, I've got to get Oksana to open a frickin' email.

"When can you get away from him for an hour or so? I'll do it right." Max winks. "Tomorrow?"

"I don't know. He's high-maintenance—kind of intense."

"I'll drop whatever I'm doing at a moment's notice."

"Aw, how sweet—you'll take a break from stabbing me to fuck me?" My mind is racing. I've got to think of some reason to send Oksana an email. I'm running out of time.

Max laughs. "You *are* a little firecracker, aren't you? I see why he likes you. This is going to be fun."

"Maksim, *tysha*," Oksana says sharply. "Sarah, I need to see your scars before you leave here. I can't put you on the circuit unless

111

I know what the clients will see. I keep a private catalogue of pictures so I can assign girls to our client's specific preferences."

Think, Sarah, think.

"Faraday's right on the other side of the door waiting for me," I say. "I'm not going to get naked for you right here and now. You saw him—he's suspicious. He could knock down the door any second."

"Well, I need to see your body right now or there's no deal."

Lightning bolt. Hallelujah.

"Okay," I concede. "I'll go into the bathroom and take a naked selfie right now—for your *personal* catalogue only. Hand me my phone. But I'll tell you right now, I'm only gonna take the photo from the neck down and I'm keeping my undies on, too."

Max smiles. "You're just going to take a photo off the Internet."

I throw up my hands, exasperated. "How would I do that? I'll clearly be in *your* bathroom in the photo—and I'll be wearing *these*." I quickly lift up my skirt and flash my red G-string.

At the brief glimpse of my undies, Max's face lights up like a Christmas tree.

"I'll take the photo right now and email it to you. I'll even stand here while you open the photo to make sure it's acceptable to you." I grab a coffee mug decorated with cartoon-cats off Oksana's desk. "And, hey, I'll hold this cat-mug in the picture, too. I can't very well Photoshop a picture of me in *your* bathroom, wearing a red G-string, holding a cat-mug, now can I?"

"*Pravda*," Oksana says, satisfied. "Maksim?"

Max looks dubious for a moment, but then he nods.

I hold out my hand. "May I have my phone, please?"

Max rummages into my purse, pulls out my phone, and scrutinizes it for a long beat.

"It's not set to record," I say. I grab the phone from him and hold it against my mouth. "This is Sarah Cruz and I work for The Club. I've been bilking Jonas Faraday out of his money since day one and I'm about to embark on a fancy new career as a high-priced call girl." I smirk at Max. "Not recording."

He grins at me. "I'll come into the bathroom with you."

"Maksim, *bud' laska*," Oksana barks.

I hope to God that means "no." Without waiting to find out, I beeline into the bathroom with my cat-mug and quickly close the door behind me. The minute I'm alone, my knees buckle. I grab the sink ledge to steady myself. "Holy crap," I whisper, panting. "Pull yourself together, Cruz."

I pull my sundress over my head and quickly take a photo of myself in the mirror from the neck down, holding the mug; and then I stare at the photo of my almost-naked body, my pulse pounding in my ears. This feels wrong. So, so wrong. Then why am I so sure it's going to work?

I shake my hands and exhale, trying to calm myself. What's the worst that can happen here? They try to blackmail me with the photo? They post it to a porn site? I stare at the picture again, trying to imagine it posted on some skeezy porn site filled with topless women. Not the end of the world, right? My face isn't in the photo. There's nothing to identify this particular pair of boobs and torso as mine— other than the scar on my ribcage, I guess. In theory, someone could connect that scar to me—but not definitively. Not like they could with a tattoo. I could always deny the photo is of me, if I had to. I could say they Photoshopped that scar onto the photo.

Gah.

This feels like such a bad idea. What's my alternative, though? They're not going to open an email from Jonas—that much is clear. They don't fully trust him for some reason. But they trust me.

Yep, Plan A is officially done-zo. Now it's time to push ahead with Plan B or accept defeat. *And I refuse to accept defeat.* I embed my photo into the email template Henn gave me, throw my dress back on, and exit the bathroom.

"You want to make sure this isn't recording again?" I hold out my phone to Max with a shaky hand.

"I just won't say anything particularly interesting." He smirks.

"Fabulous." I look down at my phone. "What's your email address, Oksana?"

She tells it to me and my hands tremble as I type it into Henn's email template.

"Max? I'm assuming you want this photo, too?" His expression leaves no doubt his answer is yes. "What's your email address?"

He tells it to me and I quickly type it into my email header—and then I press send. *Oh. My. God.* I'm about to hyperventilate. I'm sure my cheeks are cherry red.

"Okay, I sent it," I say, trying to sound calm, but I can barely breathe. "Why don't you both make sure you got it."

It feels like time moves at glacial speed as Oksana logs onto her computer and opens her email account.

"Do I meet your high standards?" I ask, my voice quavering and my knees knocking.

"Oh yes, very nice," Oksana says, viewing the photo.

Oh my God. She opened my email. *She opened it!*

"You'll be a top favorite for the ones who like spicy," Oksana continues. "The scar is okay. You can blame it on a surgery. Your appendix, maybe, like Marilyn Monroe in the famous photos."

I smile politely at the Marilyn reference, though I have no idea what the hell she's talking about. "What do you think, Max?" I ask. "Do you like what you see?" I try to sound flirty and inviting, but I'm sure I just sound carsick.

Max taps the screen on his phone—*oh my God, he's opening the email!*—and I have to breathe through my mouth to keep myself from fainting.

He studies the picture. "I see why Mr. Faraday's such a big fan of yours." He looks up at me and licks his lips. "I look forward to sampling this tomorrow."

"How much are you planning to pay me for the pleasure?"

He scoffs.

"A smart prostitute never gives it away. Right, Oksana?"

Oksana chuckles. "To Maksim, she does—if she knows what's good for her."

"I always get my freebie," Max says. "But don't worry—I'll make sure you enjoy it, too. I'm very considerate in that way. Especially for a woman with your *problem.*"

My stomach churns. "I... I don't know if I can get away." I motion to the door. "Faraday is pretty possessive—"

"You'll figure out a way—if you know what's good for you."

There's an urgent pounding at the door.

"Sarah," Jonas yells. "It's time to go. Right now." He shakes on the door, but it's locked. When did they lock it?

I'm suddenly racked with panic. I've got to get out of this room.

"Sarah!" he shouts. "Time's up!"

"I'm coming," I call back, trying my damnedest to keep my

voice light and bright. I whisper to Oksana and Max, "He's really intense."

The door shakes again as Jonas tries to open it.

I turn to go, but Max grabs my arm with a vise-like grip.

"Just think. If Yuri had killed you like I'd told him to, I would have missed out on so much fun." Without warning, he swoops into my face and kisses me on the lips, thrusting his tongue to the back of my throat. I jerk back, utterly repulsed, and he twists my arm. "I guess things always work out for the best." He smiles like a shark. "I'll text you my phone number—and I'll expect your call *tomorrow*."

Chapter 23
Sarah

Just a tip. If you're ever planning on being in a relationship of any kind, but especially a monogamous, romantic relationship, with one Jonas P. Faraday, do not—I repeat, *do not*—do what I just did. Holy shitballs, as Kat always says, that did not go over well.

The minute Jonas and I were out of earshot from the bad guys, even before we'd reached our car, Jonas let me have it. To say he was angry with me is the understatement of the year. To say he ripped into me and created several new orifices in my body doesn't do it justice. For the first time ever, I got to see what Jonas' fury looks like when directed at me instead of his ever-patient brother—and I've got to say, it ain't pretty.

Of course, I cried my eyes out when Jonas started screaming at me, but his meltdown wasn't the only thing making me cry. The countless conflicting emotions simultaneously slamming into me probably had a lot to do with my tears, too. I felt relief, fury, anxiety, righteous indignation, apology, and shame, all at once—but, mostly, if I'm being honest, pure elation and pride that I'd figured out a way to get Oksana *and* Max to open Henn's malware email. And I was pissed as hell at Jonas for being so consumed with anger or anxiety or both that he couldn't appreciate and applaud my savage badassery.

After Jonas' verbal assault had died down and he was finally capable of speaking rationally again, he demanded I tell him every single thing that happened inside that room with Max and Oksana, from the minute he walked out until I joined him again—and I did. Well, almost everything. I didn't mention Max's disgusting demand for a "freebie" or the repulsive kiss he planted on me. What would have been the point of telling him about either wretched thing? I knew Jonas would only turn around, march right back over there, and try to kill the bastard with his bare hands—and I was deathly afraid he'd die in the process. I mean, jeez, I know better than anyone what kind of a monster Max truly is—and I wasn't about to let anything happen to Jonas.

I did, however, tell Jonas about the naked selfie I emailed to Oksana and Max, and that's when my hunky-monkey boyfriend went DEFCON-one ballistic on me. Understandably so, I guess, but, wow, the degree of horror and outrage he expressed about that one itty-bitty photo made me wonder if he'd heard the other thing I said, namely, "They opened the email."

He didn't react when I said it the first time, so I said it again. "They opened the email, Jonas—both of them. It worked. We did it." But he didn't frickin' care. Not in that moment, he didn't, anyway. Nope. He was just angry as hell and nothing—absolutely nothing— was going to distract him from his rage.

I felt empathetic about Jonas' anger to a point. Who would *want* their girlfriend to email a naked photo of herself to a murderous pimp? But come on. At the end of the day, what's the big effing deal? My face wasn't in the photo. It's a photo of a random, naked body, just like all the other bodies on this planet. A neck, two boobs, a belly button, a red-G-string, a pair of legs, and a cat-mug. Big effing deal.

Frankly, if you want to know the truth, I'm proud I did it. I'm Orgasma the All-Powerful, after all, and today I proved it. When Orgasma's on a mission for truth and justice, when she's hell-bent on decimating the bad guys and protecting the innocent, Orgasma stops at nothing to accomplish her mission. Hellz yeah! Orgasma. Will. Be. Victorious. Fuckers!

And, anyway, what the hell was I supposed to do? Go back to the hotel room and say, "Sorry, guys, we did our best—better luck next time?" No effing way. Before stepping foot into that office, I'd promised myself nothing would stop me. And nothing did. So I took a stupid picture of myself—so what? Considering the situation, it could have been worse. And, by the way, did I mention, it worked? Because, holy crappola, *both* of them opened the frickin' email. Boom.

It's been a solid fifteen minutes since Jonas and I have exchanged a single word. Both our chests are still heaving from our argument and my face still feels flushed. I glance at him. He's staring straight ahead, his jaw muscles pulsing in and out. I look out the passenger window of the car, fuming. I can't stop yelling at him inside my head. I'm certainly not going to be the first one to speak.

Jonas pulls our rental car up to the front of the hotel and we wait silently in line for the valet attendant behind several other cars. After a minute, Jonas pulls out his phone and taps out a text. "I'm telling the team to meet us in our suite in ten minutes," he mutters, breaking the silence.

But I don't reply. Screw him. He can't yell at me like he did and then expect me to act like everything's fine. Even before the valet guy opens my car door, I burst out of the car and march into our hotel, not looking back. Jonas is angry with me? Well, the more I think about it, I'm steaming mad at him, too.

Cold air from the air conditioning blasts me as I stride through the lobby toward the elevator bank, but it does nothing to cool my hot temper. He's overreacting, plain and simple. A little anger would have been okay. But a volcano erupting and spewing molten lava at me? Not okay. What he should have done was congratulate me and tell me I'm so fucking smart—that's what he *should* have said. That man needs to take a chill pill and celebrate our victory, no matter how we got it. Yeah, in fact, as far I'm concerned, Jonas can go to hell.

Chapter 24
Sarah

Everyone (besides Jonas) is hanging on my every word. Now *this* is the kind of reaction I'd hoped to elicit from Mr. Volcano. Jeez. When I get to the part about me taking a naked selfie in the bathroom, Kat shrieks, either with shock or glee, I'm not sure which. And when I regale the group with the part about Oksana and Max opening my email right on the spot, Josh whoops and high-fives me while Henn fist pumps the air and scrambles to his laptop to track the progress of his little malware-baby.

But Jonas? He sits in the corner, scowling, watching all of us but not saying a word. I feel like flipping Jonas the bird, to be honest, but I refrain because I'm a fancy lady.

"Bingo," Henn says after a brief moment of looking at his screen. "You did it. We're in. I've got Oksana's computer and that guy's phone. Holy shit, Sarah. Jackpot."

I look smugly at Jonas, but he looks away. Really, Jonas? You're pissed at me? Well, I'm pissed at you.

"Oh my God," Henn says, staring intently at his computer screen. "The bastard forwarded your email to another computer and opened your photo there, too." He chuckles. "Brilliant." He clicks a button on his keyboard and his entire face suddenly bursts into bright red flames.

Oh jeez. Why do I get the distinct feeling Henn just saw my boobs? I blush. "So, Henn?"

His head jerks up from his computer screen like a kid caught with his hand in the cookie jar. "Yes?"

"So now what?"

He swallows hard. "Well, um." His cheeks are still on fire. "I'll snoop around both computers and this Max guy's phone and see what I can find. And then we wait for them to hopefully access their mainframe and bank accounts. I imagine we won't have to wait too long."

"Can you delete that photo?" Jonas asks, his voice tight. "Can you find it and erase it everywhere?"

"Um, sure, no problem," Henn says quickly. "I can delete it right now, if you want me to. I've got total access."

"Yeah, but if you delete that photo off their computers now, won't that tip them off?" Kat asks.

"Yeah," Henn says. "If that photo magically disappears, this Max dude is gonna know something's up for sure—and if he designed their tech like he says, then he's a badass motherfucker of epic proportions and we don't want to do anything to tip him off."

"Well, then, don't delete it. I don't want to give them any reason whatsoever to be suspicious," I say.

"I agree," Henn says.

Jonas exhales and crosses his arms over his chest.

"God, Sarah," Kat laughs. "First the solo-boob shot and now this. You're quite the exhibitionist, aren't you?"

Oh jeez. Thanks, Kat. I steal a quick look at Jonas, just in time to see him clench his jaw. Yes, Jonas, I told my best friend about the left-boob picture I sent you when I was nothing but your anonymous intake agent. *So sue me.*

Kat sees the look on Jonas' face and she winces. "Sorry," she mouths to me.

I shrug and shoot her a "he can go fuck himself" look.

"A 'boob picture'?" Josh asks, raising his eyebrows. "Oh my goodness, tell us more, Sarah Cruz."

"Just a little sexting with this really hot guy I met online," I say, glancing at Jonas—only to find he's still pissed as hell. I roll my eyes. "A hot guy who *used* to have a sense of humor. It's no big deal—all the kids are doing it these days."

"And all the politicians," Josh says.

"And athletes," Henn says.

"And housewives," Kat adds.

"And grandmas," Josh says.

"And some priests, too," Henn says, and everyone (except Jonas) laughs.

"Sarah, you picked the perfect bait for your email," Kat says. "No matter how smart or powerful or rich a guy might be, he's got the same Kryptonite as every other man throughout history. Naked boobs."

"Are we really that simple?" Josh asks.

"Yes," Kat says. "You really are."

"Never underestimate the power of porn," Henn says.

"That's catchy," Kat says. "The porn industry should adopt that for a billboard campaign."

"I don't think the porn industry needs help with their marketing," Henn says.

Jonas hasn't stopped smoldering during this entire exchange. A vein in his neck—which I can now confidently identify as his external jugular vein—is throbbing.

"That was really quick thinking on your feet, Sarah," Josh says, but he's looking at his brother as he speaks. "You went in there hoping to harpoon a baby-whale, and you wound up landing Moby Dick. Great job." He raises his eyebrows at Jonas. "Right, bro? Aren't you proud of her?"

Jonas scowls at his brother.

"I was scared; I'm not gonna lie," I say. "My hands were shaking like crazy the whole time I was in there. But there was no way I was gonna leave that building without implanting that virus, no matter what. There was too much at stake."

"You're such a badass, Sarah," Kat says.

Jonas exhales and uncrosses his arms. I wrinkle my nose at him. I'm a badass and he's just going to have to deal with it. It's all I can do not to stick my tongue out at him.

"Hey, guys," Henn says, engrossed with something on his screen. "Holy shit. Oksana's going into her bank account right now—that Henderson Bank we were scouting out before." He stares at the screen for another ten seconds. "Sha-zam. She just typed in her password. Ha! I got it." He shakes his head. "Oh, man, I love technology."

"So what do we do?" I ask, my heart racing.

"We wait a few minutes for her to log off, and then we go in and snoop around."

"Sounds like the perfect time for me to fill drink orders," Josh says, heading to the bar.

Five minutes later, just as Josh is passing out the last of our drinks, Henn calls us over to his computer screen. "She's logged off," he announces. "Let's go in."

We all gather around Henn's computer like we're watching a Seahawks' game.

"Well, she's already deposited your checks—one hundred eighty thousand big ones," Henn says. "I bet that boils your blood, huh, Jonas?"

Jonas grunts.

"And she just transferred half of it into her savings account. Hmm," Henn says, sounding perplexed.

"What?" I ask. I'm practically breathless. This is all just too exciting to bear.

"Even after today's deposit, Oksana's got only about half a million total in these two accounts." He furrows his brow.

"Hmm," Josh says.

"Hmm, indeed," Henn agrees. "Chump change. These must be Oksana's personal accounts—definitely not The Club's main accounts."

"Damn," I say. "So how do we find the big money?"

Jonas ambles to the other side of the room, away from the group, apparently returning to his corner to sulk again.

"We just have to wait for them to log into their main bank accounts. It could be five minutes, five hours, five days—who knows?—but I guarantee they'll lead us there sooner or later. And in the meantime, I'll take a nice, long gander around their files and data, make copies of everything, see if there's anything of interest. Oh, and I'll listen to Max's voicemails, too. That's so cool you got Max's phone, Sarah." He sips his beer. "Dang, there's a lot to do."

Josh sighs. "Well, it looks like poor Henn's gonna be working through the night again, going through all this stuff." He looks at Kat. "What do you say, Party Girl with a Hyphen—you wanna paint Sin City red with me again?"

"I'd actually like to help Henn, if that's okay," Kat says. "I'm kind of excited about all this." She looks at me. "I have a strong motivation to want to bury these guys."

I grin at her. There's nothing like a best friend.

"Would that be okay with you, Henn?" Kat asks. "Or would I be in your way?"

"No, that'd be awesome. But only if you want to. I mean, Josh and Jonas are *paying* me to do this, so..." Henn sneaks a quick look at Josh, seemingly to make sure he's not stepping on any toes by accepting Kat's help.

But if Josh is disappointed about the unexpected agenda for the night, he doesn't show it. "Could you use my help, too?" he asks.

"Yeah," Henn says. "That'd be great."

"Okay, then. I'll order us room service and the three of us will get to work."

"Make that the four of us. I'll stick around and help, too," I say. "I'm pretty motivated to bury these guys, too." I glare at Jonas. If he's still pissed at me, that's not my problem.

Jonas raises his beer to his perfect lips and takes a long, sexy swig. Okay, I'm still mad at him, I swear I am—but, damn, his lips are luscious when he sips from a bottle like that. It makes me wish I were the bottle.

"Nah," Josh says. "You two kids should go out and celebrate." He looks at Jonas suggestively. "Or stay in and celebrate, whatever floats your boat. Either way, definitely celebrate—you both kicked ass today."

Jonas' eyes flicker at me, but I look away. If Jonas thinks he can yell at me the way he did today and then ravage me like nothing happened, then he's got another thing coming.

Josh grins at me. "The three of us will move our party down to my suite and let you two crazy kids swing on the chandeliers up here."

Jonas takes another long, slow sip of his beer, his eyes holding mine. I jut my chin at him and then look away. If he can't deal with the way today went down, I'm sorry, but that's just too bad for him. I didn't plan to desert him—I wanted Plan A to work out, but it didn't. I had to follow my gut—had to make a split-second decision in order to accomplish the mission. Big risk, big reward—isn't that what Jonas taught my contracts class?

Jonas drains the last drop of his beer, his eyes like lasers, and puts the bottle down. He crosses his arms over his muscled chest and stares at me. This time, I don't look away. Neither does he. I guess we're having a staring contest. Fine.

"What do you say, baby?" he finally says.

When he says the word *baby*, I feel my resolve instantly soften. Damn.

He licks his lips. Oh man, his eyes are a three-alarm fire. "You up for a little celebration tonight?"

I shrug. *No.*

"I think we should celebrate."

I shrug again. *No.* But I know I can't hold out forever. I'm addicted to him, after all.

"Aw, come on, baby." A side of his mouth tilts up, and just like that, heat flashes through my entire body. "You wanna have a little fun?"

"Maybe," I say. But then I remember I'm pissed at him and I steel myself again. "And maybe not." I purse my lips with indignation.

He purses his lips, too—but he's mocking me. "What if I said please?"

I look at Kat. She knows I'm a goner.

I twist my mouth. "Then I'd say *possibly*. But not *probably*."

"What if I said pretty please?" He flashes his full smile.

I smash my lips together, trying to resist him. Of course, I know my efforts are futile, but I'm giving it the ol' college try. I shrug again.

"What if I said pretty please *and* that we can do whatever you want, anything at all, you name it?"

Now he's got my attention. "Anything at all?"

"Anything at all."

"You'll be at my mercy completely?"

Jonas squints at me and bites his lip.

Out of the corner of my eye, I see Kat and Josh exchange a smile.

"Well? Will you be at my mercy or not?" I ask, tapping my toe. "What do you say?"

"Hmm." Jonas walks slowly toward me, his muscles taut. "What do I say?" When he reaches me, he takes my face in his hands. "I say, 'I'm an asshole.'"

Oh, those eyes. Those ridiculously beautiful eyes. "No, you're not. You're a cocky-bastard-asshole-motherfucker," I say softly.

He kisses me gently. His lips are cold and taste like beer. He's delicious.

"You did good today," he says. He kisses me again, this time slipping his tongue into my mouth.

My sweet Jonas.

Gah. I can't resist him. "I'm sorry I worried you," I say. And I am. I'm not at all sorry I did what I did today—it was effective and I totally kicked ass. But I regret the way my actions tortured him. I'm sure today took years off his life. I kiss his luscious lips, taking great care to suck on his lower lip as I depart his mouth. "We do whatever I want tonight—and you get absolutely no say in the matter," I whisper.

He looks wary for a moment, but I hold my ground. He leans into my ear. "No neckties," he whispers softly.

I smile. "Of course not."

"Then, okay, yes, you're in charge. Whatever you want to do."

"Okay, then," I say. "Count me in."

Chapter 25
Jonas

Of all the things we could be doing right now, of all the places we could have gone tonight, my baby drove us to a seedy strip club on the outskirts of downtown. What the hell? We're sitting in our rental car in the parking lot, staring at a flashing neon sign on the club's roof—"The Amsterdam Club." The place looks as seedy as hell—bargain-basement titty bar—definitely not one of the trendy hot spots on The Strip. This is where my baby wanted to come for her big night out? Jesus. I love my dirty, dirty girl, don't get me wrong—she's fucking hot as fuck and smart as hell and she turns me the fuck on, no matter what she does, even when she pisses me off like she did today—but, yeah, hot as she is, my dirty girl is also fucking crazy sometimes. There, I said it. She's batshit crazy.

"What the fuck is this skanky-ass place?" I say. "Why don't we just go back to the suite? I demand a rematch in our breath-holding contest. How about two out of three?"

"A deal's a deal," she says, putting up her hand. "As long as there are no neckties, you're required to do whatever I want tonight."

"How did you even find this place?"

"Google."

"No, I mean—yeah, Google." I roll my eyes. "I'm saying how did you even *think* to find this particular place out of all the strip clubs in Vegas? Why did you take us *here*?"

"Oh, you'll see."

"Why the fuck would I want to watch a dime-a-dozen stripper when I could glory in the exquisite pulchritude that is Sarah Cruz, the goddess and the muse?"

She laughs. "We're here to fulfill an item on my *addendum*. So hush."

Ah yes. Sarah's addendum. When she first hit me with that word, it sounded so sexy and exciting and mysterious. But ever since she tied me up like King Kong, I've become slightly less enthusiastic every time she pulls out that word. I have a sudden thought that makes me hopeful. "You're gonna strip for me?" Just the idea is making me tingle.

"Let's just go in and have a drink, shall we? Get a little loose. And then I'll tell you exactly what I have in mind."

Uh oh. She's got that crazy gleam in her eye. Shit. I can't resist her when she looks at me that way.

Four Scotches and I'm feeling fan-fucking-tastic right now. I'm not normally a Scotch drinker, but what the fuck—when in Vegas, you gotta act like a member of the Rat Pack, right? Fuck yeah. This place is so fucking old school tacky, four doses of Scotch was the only way I could stomach it. For the past hour, Sarah and I have been making out in the corner of the club like teenagers while naked women gyrate around poles a few yards away from us, and I'm bursting out of my skin wanting to lick her and get inside her. I've yet to see a single stripper who turns me on a fraction as much as Sarah does, though glimpsing an assortment of titties and asses while kissing and groping Sarah's titties and ass has been a certain kind of lowbrow entertainment. I guess it's the same thing as going to the county fair once a year and chowing down on disgusting crap like chicken-fried bacon. Wretched, yes—but kinda fun once every blue moon.

"I'll be right back, baby," she purrs, her cheeks flushed. "I'm gonna get everything set up for us. Don't go anywhere."

She disappears.

I'm hard as a rock. What the fuck is she up to? Is she gonna give me a little striptease? That'd be so fucking hot. Damn, this woman is something else. Never boring, that's for sure. I close my eyes. I can't feel my toes. Scotch will do that to you. I laugh. Where the fuck is she? I'm so worked up right now I might have to insist on a little bathroom action after her striptease. Or, hey, as long as we've been acting like teenagers all night, maybe we'll do it in the backseat of the car.

She's back. She grabs my hands. "Come on," she says. "My sweet Jonas. Come on." She pulls me to her and licks my face. "I'm losing my mind, baby." She drags me toward a dark hallway on the other side of the club.

"Where are we going?"

"The Red Light District." She points to a sign above our heads at the entrance to the hallway flashing "Red Light District."

We stop just inside the hallway, and a security guard trades our cell phones for claim checks. An imposing sign on the wall reads, "Video Taping Strictly Prohibited." After giving up our phones, we stumble into the darkened hallway, holding hands. We stop at a large, blackened pane of glass. "Pour Some Sugar on Me" blares at us from behind the glass.

"What the fuck is this?" I ask.

"A peep show. Like in Amsterdam," she says.

I laugh. "This is absolutely nothing like Amsterdam."

She frowns at me. "How would I possibly know that? Just play along, you snob." She begins feeding tokens into a slot until the black curtain on the other side of the glass rises. A naked woman in a tiny black room bathed in garish red light dances and touches herself for a grand total of about ten seconds. The curtain closes.

I shrug. "Whoop-de-doo. A naked girl. Now let's go back to the suite and fuck like animals."

She laughs and pulls me along to the next window, where we're treated to another naked, gyrating woman bathed in red light in a black box. This time, the song behind the glass is "Talk Dirty to Me."

"It's a porn juke box," I say. "Yippee."

She kisses me. "I can't stop thinking about my dream, Jonas. I want you to make my dream come true."

I stare at her. She can't possibly mean the dream with the Jonas poltergeists making love to her every which way, and the red wine pouring all over her, and the people in the restaurant watching us? Holy shit. *The people in the restaurant watching us.* Oh my God. She's insane. I knew she had some crazy in her—and in fact, I like my baby's crazy—but this is pure insanity.

"You said we'd do whatever I want tonight." She smiles. "This is a gonna get me off like crazy."

She tugs at me, smiling wickedly, and leads me to the end of the dark hallway to a door marked "Authorized Personnel Only." She opens the door to reveal a stripper who, seemingly, is expecting us.

"Baby, thank you, but I don't want a threesome," I say. "I only want you." I know most men have to beg their girlfriends or wives for this particular treat, but I've already done the threesome thing and I've discovered quite emphatically that the format diverts me from what I like best—and, regardless, I don't want to share Sarah with anyone, even another woman.

"No, you big dummy," she says. "This girl's here to help me get everything set up."

"Sarah, listen."

She licks my face. "I want to be a dirty girl tonight." She's panting. "With you. Let's do it, Jonas. Let's be crazy. I want to act out my dream."

"Baby, I'm all for fun and games, but this is really kinky."

Her eyes light up. "Kinky, yes. Good word. Let's be kinky."

I pull back, ready to tell her no—and yet I'm rock hard. Am I appalled or turned on by this whole thing? I can't tell which.

"I've arranged everything for us, baby. No one will know it's us. We'll be wearing masks. I've got bandages to wrap around your tattoos and my scars. You can wear your briefs if you want, I don't care. I'll wear my panties if you want me to—and you can just pull things down or push them aside, whatever we need to do—whatever you're comfortable with." She's talking so fast, I can barely follow what she's saying—or maybe she's talking normally and I'm just fucking drunk. "No one will even know it's us, Jonas," she continues. "We can do whatever we want in the window—anything at all—and no one will know it's us. Maybe people will see us, maybe they won't—it just depends if anyone happens to put tokens in the slot. But that's the turn-on—thinking someone *might* be watching the whole time."

"Why do you get so turned on by the idea of people watching us fuck?"

"Remember the library?" she purrs. "Wasn't that hot?" Her body is jerking and jolting with her arousal. She grabs at my cock through my jeans. "We'll be wearing masks—no one will know it's us. Come on, Jonas. You can lick me and no one will know it's us."

I shudder with anticipation. This is totally depraved.

"Sarah," I begin. This woman turns me on like nothing I've ever experienced before, but I have zero interest in becoming a porn star.

"Just this once," she says. "It's like a bucket list thing."

"Sarah—"

"Pretty please." She licks my face again.

I shiver. Fuck. I don't want to disappoint her. And she's awfully convincing. "I'll make out with you in the black box, but I'm not gonna lick your pussy—certain things are sacred." Truth be told, I might even fuck her in the window if things get too hot for me to resist, but I'm most certainly *not* going to church on her in a disgusting shithole like this.

She's instantly deflated. "Okay," she says. I've plainly taken the wind out of her sails.

I truly do not understand this crazy-ass woman. Aren't women supposed to want rainbows and unicorns and long walks on the beach? What the fuck is this? I can't believe out of the two of us *I'm* the voice of sexual reason in this relationship.

"Will you do me a big favor and pay this nice woman for me?" Sarah asks. "I promised her two hundred bucks to let us take her place in the window for twenty minutes."

I pull out the cash and hand it to the stripper.

"You've set up a table in there, right?" Sarah asks her.

"Yeah," the woman assures her.

"Oh, and there's a particular song I want playing."

"Sure. What is it?"

Sarah whispers to her.

"Never heard of it," the woman says. "You sure you don't want 'Baby Got Back' or 'Talk Dirty to Me' or something like that?"

"No—it's got to be that song."

My interest is piqued.

"Tell it to me again," the woman says, and Sarah leans in and whispers again.

"Okay, I got it. I'll do my best." She motions to a small cardboard box on the floor. "There's the stuff you asked for. I'll be right back."

Sarah laps at my mouth. "I'm so excited."

"Tell me again why you want people to watch us fuck? I don't get it."

"I guess I just... You're so frickin' gorgeous, Jonas. It turns me on to think of you making love to me in front of the entire world."

I study her face for a moment. "You know I'm not going anywhere, right?"

She crinkles her nose. "Even when I pull crazy stuff like this?"

"Even then."

"Even when I scare the bajeezus out of you and don't stick to the plan and piss you off?"

"Barely then—but, yes, even then." I grin. "I'm not going anywhere."

Her voice drops. "Even though there's clearly something wrong with me?" She motions to the cardboard box. "Even though I'm not normal?"

"Even then, baby." I kiss her. "There's no such thing as normal."

What the fuck have I agreed to do? We're standing in the black window box, naked except for our underpants and Lone Ranger masks, with all our respective identifying characteristics wrapped up in white gauze bandages.

"We look like horny mummies getting ready to rob a bank," I say.

At my comment, Sarah bursts out laughing, so hard she has to sit down on the edge of the table. I sit down next to her and she immediately leans into my shoulder, still laughing and holding her belly. Just as her laughter begins to die down and she leans in to kiss me, red lights suddenly shine in our eyes and "Baby Got Back" begins blaring through the speakers.

"What the hell?" Sarah mutters, clearly annoyed at the song selection.

"I think that's our cue," I say. I hold out my bandage-wrapped arms toward her. "It's Frankenstein versus the Mummy—who will prevail?"

Sarah throws her head back and laughs again, but this time she's laughing so hard tears stream down her cheeks from behind her Lone Ranger mask.

Without warning, the black curtain rises, and we suddenly see our reflections in the peep-show glass—which, we can now discern, is one-way glass—a mirror for us, a window for our high-class peeping Tom, whoever he may be. Sarah waves awkwardly at our masked reflections—sardonically greeting our unseen gawker on the other side of the glass—and then bursts out laughing yet again. As usual, Sarah's laughter gets me going, too, and I lose it along with her.

As we laugh together, as I watch this beautiful, sexy, insane but brilliant woman giggling from behind her ridiculous Lone Ranger mask, crazy-ass bandages tied around her neck and torso, Sir Mix-A-Lot serenading us about big butts, I suddenly realize with absolute clarity that I don't want to share my baby with anyone, anywhere, ever—and least of all with a bunch of losers peeping through a window in a rundown titty bar outside of Vegas. This beautiful woman is *my* treasure—not theirs. She wants the world to watch me make love to her? Too bad. I'm the only man who's ever witnessed her reach the highest heights of human pleasure, the culmination of human experience, the most truthful form of expression two people can share—and it's going to stay that way 'til the end of fucking time.

My heart's racing. I grab her hand. "Baby, you've got it all wrong."

She wipes her eyes. "What?"

"Your dream—you've got it all wrong."

She looks at me blankly.

"You think you need to act it out—but the dream's not literal, baby. It's a metaphor."

She still doesn't understand.

"Think about how the dream makes you *feel*—what it makes you *yearn* for. The dream's not literal, Sarah. It's means something different than all this. We could fuck each other's brains out in this window and a hundred people could watch us do it, and it still wouldn't satisfy your yearning."

She crosses her arms over her bare breasts, suddenly modest. Her laughter is gone.

Sir Mix-A-Lot asks the guys in the crowd if their girlfriends have bountiful butts of the variety he's been rapping about.

"Hell yeah," I answer, right on cue with the song, and Sarah's mouth twists adorably. "You do realize this song's making me want to take a big ol' juicy bite out of your delectable ass, right?"

She half-smiles at me, but I can tell she's deep in thought.

I touch her hair. "You ready to go?" I ask.

She nods.

"We'll go back to the suite and you can play whatever song you had in mind for tonight and I'll chomp your ass and lick your sweet pussy and fuck your brains out 'til you swear I'm your supreme lord-god-master—how does that sound?"

She smiles wistfully. "I'm sorry."

"You've got nothing to be sorry about." I push her hair behind her shoulder.

"About today. That I scared you."

"You did." I frown at her. "But you also kicked ass."

She shrugs.

Sir Mix-A-Lot once again proclaims his enthusiasm for large bottoms, in case we weren't clear on that by now.

"I'm sorry about all this." She motions to the black curtain.

"Don't be. It was fun. I mean, look at us right now. Jesus. What a great memory."

"I think I might be a wee bit crazy."

"Sarah, my precious baby, you never need to apologize to me about your crazy. I love every inch of you, inside and out—even your crazy parts."

Her breath catches sharply. She kisses me. "I love you, Jonas." She's trembling in my arms.

Without warning, the black curtain rises and we both stare at our masked reflections in the mirror again, red lights shining in our eyes. When the curtain drops again, I kiss her softly.

"You ready to go back to the hotel and let me make love to you?"

She nods. "Absolutely."

I sigh with relief.

Yet again, Sir Mix-A-Lot professes his abiding affection for ample behinds.

"Right after you take me dancing."

I throw up my hands. "Oh come on!"

She laughs. "I'm kidding." She shoots me a sideways smirk. "But I *do* want to swing by that tattoo parlor on our way back." She winks.

Chapter 26
Sarah

"I love it," he says, his lips an inch away from my new tattoo, his warm breath teasing my skin. "It's so fucking sexy." He kisses my tattoo gently, his soft lips sending a shiver up my spine, and then he licks it. "Is it too sensitive to lick?"

"No." I can barely talk. "Do it again."

He licks it again and goose bumps erupt over my entire body.

"God, it turns me on," he says, licking it again and again. "It's like a buried treasure—and I'm the only guy with the treasure map." His tongue begins sliding downward from my tattoo, making my clit tingle with anticipation.

"Press play on the music," I breathe. "I've got a song cued up for us." I'm already deliriously turned on.

When he gets up to play the song, I touch myself, aching for his return.

The song begins—the song I've been dying to play for him while making love to him. It's "Take me to Church" by the Irish musician, Hozier. The first time I heard the song, I instantly thought *Jonas.* Something about Hozier's combination of intelligence and vulnerability and passion and angst and masculinity perfectly captures Jonas' essence for me—so much so, I've tricked myself into thinking Jonas himself is singing the song. Surely, if Jonas were a songwriter, this is the song he'd write—not just about me but about everything he's been through in his life.

Jonas comes back and begins trailing kisses from my tattoo downward again, closing in on my sweet spot, making me writhe, but quickly, he's too enraptured by the song to continue his concentrated assault on me.

"What is this?" Jonas says after listening for a moment. "Holy fuck."

I smile at him. I know how much music means to him.

"I love it," he says softly. He closes his eyes for a moment, apparently moved by the unmistakable sound of his own soul singing to him, and then he leans down and begins gently kissing the insides of my thighs. When the song reaches its passionate conclusion—*amen*—and then begins again on a loop, Jonas lifts his head and assesses me with hungry eyes.

"Go to church, my love," I whisper, my breasts rising and falling with my arousal.

"Amen," he says.

He yanks my naked body all the way to the bottom edge of the bed and kneels down in front of me. After propping my thighs on the tops of his broad shoulders, he burrows his face between my legs and begins worshipping at my altar like a condemned man desperate to be saved.

Amen.

My orgasm comes fast and hard, and when it ends, Jonas wordlessly scoops up my sweaty body, carries me into the sitting area of the suite, and lays me down on a table. I don't ask what he's got in mind because it doesn't matter. My body is his to do with as he pleases, to manipulate into whatever position he desires, to cull from it whatever pleasure he craves. He's a classically trained cellist and I am but an inanimate slab of wood until my master enlivens me.

Standing at the edge of the table, he places my calves over his shoulders and stands to his full height, lifting my pelvis off the table as he goes and supporting my bottom with his strong hands. He pulls my pelvis into him and enters me, and I moan at the sensation of our bodies joining so effortlessly at this new and exotic angle.

"This is called the butterfly," Jonas says, his voice husky, his body moving magically inside mine. "Because you're my butterfly, baby."

Holy moly. This feels good. We can add this butterfly thing to the long list of sexual positions Jonas has introduced me to that are my new favorite thing.

I've loved every single freaktastic position Jonas has shown me—the ballerina, the seesaw, the "folded deck chair"—all of them.

Even the "folded deck chair" turned out to be a blast, even though we didn't actually perform it successfully (how anyone could make that one work, I have no idea)—because, thanks to that hilarious fiasco, I discovered that laughing hysterically with Jonas, especially naked, is every bit as arousing and intimate and pleasurable as having sex with him.

"Butterfly," Jonas groans. "My baby the hot-as-fuck butterfly."

He growls as he rocks his hips into mine, his eyes devouring me.

I arch my back into him, trying to relieve the pressure building inside me, and he pulls at my butt, drawing me into him even closer. I gaze across my torso to the spot where our bodies are fusing, eager to watch his glistening penis sliding in and out of me (a sight that always turns me on), and the unexpected sight of my brand new tattoo makes me moan.

From my vantage point, the tiny lettering of my tattoo is upside-down—Jonas is the only person in the world who'll ever have a right-side-up view of those three little letters—but that doesn't matter. The mere *existence* of the letters is what makes me feel bold and naughty and sexy in a whole new way. *OAP,* my new badge of honor boldly proclaims. It's the short but sweet shorthand for the butt-kicking superhero-crime-fighter-sexual-badass I've become. I look down at my tattoo again. *OAP.*

I groan loudly and Jonas does, too.

The pressure inside me is rising, rising, rising, on the cusp of boiling over.

"You're a butterfly," Jonas groans. "So fucking beautiful."

My body jolts. I'm on the absolute edge. Jonas' proxy lyrically offers me his life through the speakers of my computer—and, thus, so does Jonas in my mind—and I'm gone—unraveling like a spool of yarn—Orgasma the All-Powerful, yet again. Every muscle even remotely connected to where Jonas is thrusting in and out of me seizes. I scream Jonas' name, or at least I think I do—who knows what jumble of sounds actually escapes me as those delicious warm waves undulate through me—and then I dissolve into a relieved puddle, my emotions from this long and exhausting and scary and exciting day too much for me to physically contain.

I expect Jonas to release along with me, but he doesn't. Instead, he pulls out of me, lays my pelvis back down flush onto the table, removes my calves from his shoulders and straightens them up toward the ceiling at a ninety-degree angle from my torso. He crisscrosses my legs into a tight, closed scissor, pulling my ankles over each other in opposite directions, and then enters me again, groaning loudly as he does. A zealous moan escapes my mouth as a whole new kind of outrageous pleasure bursts through my body. Oh God, there's absolutely nothing to impede Jonas' access into me and my tightly closed legs are creating an exceptionally taut fit between our bodies.

He grunts as he thrusts into me deeply, over and over, pressing my legs tightly together as he enters me. A shockwave of delirium careens through me, almost painfully, as yet another orgasm builds inside me. When my convulsing finally hits and my body releases in fitful waves, Jonas uncrosses my legs and spreads my thighs. He pulls my torso up to a sitting position and guides my legs to wrap around his waist.

"Sarah," he says, kissing me voraciously with each powerful thrust. "Sarah," he says again, the word catching in his throat. "Oh, baby, you feel so fucking good."

I've got nothing left to give. I can't even hold myself up anymore, so he cradles my back in his arms as he thrusts. How is he holding on so long? It's got to be the Scotch. Because, holy hell, I'm turning into Jello and he's still going, going, going. I'm melting, oozing, dripping off the table and landing in a giant, quivering puddle on the floor and he's still on fire. He nibbles my ear, kisses my neck, all the while continuing his body's urgent assault. I'm toast. I'm gone. This is too much of a good thing. Pleasure and pain are blurring. My body can't handle anymore. How has he lasted so long? Oh my God, I can't stand it. I've got to push him over the edge.

"I love you," I say. "I love you, Jonas." I bite his neck. "I love, you, baby, forever and ever." I reach down to the spot on his body just beneath our joined bodies and fondle him fervently.

He shudders and groans so loud, it makes me flutter.

"I love every inch of you, baby, inside and out," I growl, continuing to touch him. I bite his nipple. "I love you."

His groan is tortured.

"I love you, baby, every part." I caress him with increased fervor and his entire body spasms. "Even your darkness—even your crazy parts. I love all of you, Jonas." I bite his neck. "Oh God, baby, all of you, even the parts you're hiding from me—even the parts you think I won't love. *I. Love. It. All.*"

He cries out as his body shudders violently and I collapse back onto the table. I'm a marathon runner who's just crossed the finish line. I'm completely spent.

With a loud groan, he collapses on top of me in a muscled, sweaty heap.

"I love, you, Jonas," I whisper, and then I kiss his sweaty cheek. "Every last inch of you, no matter what lies beneath."

Chapter 27
Sarah

I wonder if it's normal to feel like you're physically addicted to another person, to crave a man's touch so rabidly it's like his flesh is a narcotic. To find yourself daydreaming about him like he's some hunk on a movie poster, only to realize he's sitting right next to you on the couch, working on his laptop and munching on an apple. To feel like you were born to interlock your body with his, and only his, like you're two puzzle pieces with no other matches in the whole world. To be certain that, if given a choice at any given moment on any given day between kissing his luscious lips and eating a piece of the finest chocolate, you'd pick his kiss every single time—even on the rare days when you're so mad at him you want to flip him the bird. I wonder if it's normal to love someone so much, you don't just forgive his flaws and mistakes and imperfections and darkness, you don't just overlook them, you adore them and wouldn't have him any other way. Is any of this normal? I really don't know. But if it's not, then I think normal is grossly overrated.

After our marathon lovemaking session, Jonas carries me back into the bedroom over his shoulder caveman-style and lays my prostrate body down on the bed, a cocky grin illuminating his handsome face.

"Order us something from room service, baby," he instructs, rolling me onto my side and slapping my ass.

There's no "please" attached to the end of his command. No "if you'd like." Just the instruction, the ass slap, and an accompanying hoot of glee to the ceiling, followed by him shaking his adorable ass like a proud peacock shaking his tail feathers and strutting into the bathroom.

139

Maybe I should try to knock him down a peg, remind him it takes two to tango, tell him he didn't accomplish this latest act of *sexcellence* all by himself? But no. I have no desire to dampen his self-congratulatory mood. The truth is, after the way he so masterfully commandeered my body tonight—and always does, for that matter—he deserves whatever praise he wants to heap upon himself 'til the end of time. *Amen.*

Of course, that doesn't mean I'm going to order food from room service any time soon as my lord-god-master has commanded—I can't move a frickin' muscle after what he just did to me. All I can do is lie here like a wet noodle, listening to the sound of him hooting with glee in the shower. To hear him in there, he might as well be standing on the bow of the Titanic, shouting, "I'm king of the world!" Oh, Jonas.

"Amen!" Jonas sings from the shower, obviously trying to deliver one of the lines from Hozier's song. I've never heard Jonas sing before. I smile broadly.

Oh God, he does it again, but this time drawing out his voice like a tone-deaf opera singer. "A-a-a-a-m-e-e-en."

I laugh out loud. Wow, he's terrible—absolutely devoid of any singing ability whatsoever. I'm oddly thrilled by this new discovery about him. It makes me love him even more, if that's possible.

I reach for the room service menu on the nightstand and grab my phone, too. I promised to call my mom every day while we're in Las Vegas to assure her I'm okay and I just realized I never called today. Obviously, I can't call now in the middle of the night, but I figure I'll send her a text for the morning.

I glance at my phone and gasp. I've received a text from an unknown number that makes every hair on my body stand on end: *"When I get my turn with you, I won't take you to a low-class strip club and ask you to cover your beguiling face with a mask. Call me today. I'm not a patient man. M."*

I drop the phone, shaking. My stomach lurches. Oh my God. No. *Max saw us.*

He must have followed us to the strip club. How much did he see? I throw my hands over my face, overwhelmed with anxiety and fear and shame and repulsion. I'm in over my head.

Jonas comes out of the bathroom, a white towel wrapped around his waist. "A-a-a-m-e-e-e-n!" he sings, holding out his arm theatrically. "Hey, did you order us some food?" His tone shifts to worry on a dime. "Sarah?"

I'm incapable of speaking. I feel like I'm going to throw up.

He sits down on the edge of the bed. "What happened?"

I hand him my phone, unable to speak.

He reads the text. "Who... ?"

"Max. Maksim."

"What the fuck is this?" He's instantly enraged.

I burst into tears.

"What the fuck's going on? Tell me right now."

I tell him every detail about Max demanding a "freebie" from me earlier today. I tell him how Max said he was glad Travolta didn't kill me like he'd personally ordered, or else he would have missed out on so much fun. And then I admit that Max shoved his tongue down my throat right before I walked out the door.

Jonas grabs at his hair and then gesticulates frantically. "Why didn't you tell me about all this?"

I shake my head.

"How could you not tell me any of this?"

"I was scared."

"To tell *me*? You were scared of *me*?"

"No, no." I exhale in frustration.

He's pacing the room like a maniac. "That fucker followed us tonight."

"I was scared you'd run back there and try to kill the guy."

He grunts. "You were right. That's exactly what I'm gonna do— I'm gonna fucking kill him."

My heart is in my throat. "Jonas, no."

Jonas is so angry he doesn't even look like himself. His entire body is shaking. Every single muscle on his body is tensed and bulging.

He sits on the bed next to me again, his eyes on fire. "Have you told me everything?"

"Yes."

"Everything?"

"Yes. I promise."

He exhales. "What a fucking asshole," he mutters. His lip curls. "He *kissed* you?"

I nod. "It was repulsive." I swallow hard. "And scary." I lose it. My tears come fast and furious. "I'm sorry, Jonas. Today was really, really scary."

He touches my hair. "Never keep anything from me again, do you understand?" His voice is an odd mixture of compassion and rage.

I nod.

"Never. No matter what it is. Ever."

"I wanted to tell you earlier, but you were so mad at me when we left their building, I didn't want to add fuel to your fire. I didn't want you to go back there and try to kill him—and die trying. You were so mad at me—you weren't thinking clearly."

He exhales and hugs me. "I was never mad at you, Sarah. Don't you understand?" He looks into my eyes. "I shouldn't have screamed at you. I didn't handle that right. I'm sorry." He's shaking with adrenaline. "I wasn't mad at you—I was scared at the thought of anything happening to you again. But I acted like an asshole."

I nod. He did act like an asshole. But I understand.

"You poor thing." He grips me tightly. "Jesus."

"I'm sorry I didn't tell you."

"Never keep anything from me, ever again."

"I won't." I lay my cheek on his shoulder.

He pulls back. "Sarah, I can't express this strongly enough to you. This is non-negotiable. Never keep anything from me, ever again."

I nod.

"Promise me."

"I promise. I'm sorry."

He squeezes me and kisses my bare shoulder. "I'm sorry I yelled at you. I shouldn't have done that. You didn't deserve that."

"I forgive you."

"I just freaked out."

"I know."

"Don't keep anything from me again."

"I won't. I promise."

"Good."

"And you promise, too?"

He doesn't respond.

"You promise not to keep anything from me, too?"

He remains silent.

I push on his chest, disengaging from our hug.

"Why are you not saying, 'I promise?'"

"Because I don't promise."

I open my mouth, in shock.

"I can't make that promise—not when it comes to these fuckers. Regarding anything and everyone else, yes, I promise—cross my heart and hope to die, I'll always tell you the truth and never, ever keep anything from you. But when it comes to these motherfuckers, I'm gonna protect you no matter what I have to do, without any limitation on that statement whatsoever, even if that means not telling you something that'd be better for you not to know."

Chapter 28
Jonas

Henn looks bloodshot and bleary-eyed, like he hasn't slept a wink all night. We're all gathered around the table in the suite—the table where my baby became a butterfly so delectably last night—to hear what Henn and his two elves have uncovered about The Club thus far. Kat and Josh don't look particularly well rested, either, but, clearly, those two have slept, unlike Henn—and, if I'm not mistaken, Josh and Kat are sitting awfully close together at the table, too.

"Well, to summarize," Henn begins, "we're dealing with some big shit here, fellas. Like, oh my fucking God." He cracks a huge smile. "Totally awesome."

Sarah and I look at each other with nervous anticipation.

"I've been dive-bombing down this rabbit hole all night, and every which way leads me down yet another rabbit hole chasing yet another Ukrainian rabbit—I'm running a whole shitload of stuff through translation software, by the way, which isn't nearly as good as a human translator, but at least it'll give us an idea—"

"Take a deep breath, Henn," I say. "Slow down and start from the beginning. You're like the Energizer Bunny on meth right now."

Henn stops short and shakes his head. "Sorry, man. I've had like three quadruple-shot Americanos in the past twelve hours, plus two red bulls—"

"Jesus, Henn. That shit'll kill you," I say.

"Occupational hazard." He smirks.

"Just summarize what you know so far."

"Yes. Okay." Henn takes a deep breath. "We got a pretty good lay of the land last night and it's cuh-razy-corn chowder."

I wait.

144

Henn takes another deep breath. "Almost everything of any interest is in Ukrainian, but there's also a bunch of stuff in Russian, too—Ukrainian and Russian are distinct languages, did you know that?"

I blink slowly, trying to remain patient. "Just tell me—were you able to get into The Club's system?"

"No, not yet. Wherever it is, it's buried deep, deep, deep in the web, way deep. But I'm getting close. I've got lots of breadcrumbs to follow. I'm hot on their trail, fellas. And very pretty ladies." He smiles adoringly at Kat and then as a seeming afterthought shoots a polite wink at Sarah, too.

"You should have seen how Henn figures things out," Kat says. "He's a techno-Sherlock Holmes."

"The man's a fucking genius," Josh adds.

Why is it always like herding fucking cats around here? "What do we know so far?" I ask.

"Okay," Henn says. "Let's start with their scope of operations. Gigantic. Massive. Huge. Colossal. Mammoth. Way beyond what I expected. This is not some podunk mom and pop prostitution ring—not that I have any basis of comparison with another prostitution ring, of course—but, I'm just saying what I've seen has surpassed anything I expected—and, get this, it turns out prostitution is only part of the business."

"What else do they do?" Sarah asks.

"Well, Oksana runs the prostitution side of things, but Max runs a bunch of other stuff—drugs and weapons, mainly."

Everyone's mouths hang open all at once. Holy shit.

"And he's got *a lot* of guys working for him, all over the country, but mostly Vegas, Miami, and New York."

Sarah can't stop shaking her head. She looks totally floored.

I'm reeling, too. "What kind of volume are we talking about?" I ask. "Like, in terms of dollars."

"I don't have access to the banking yet, but I'm guessing the numbers are gonna be big."

"Define big," I say.

"Well, extrapolating on a few things I saw in their records—and I'm only extrapolating at this point—I'm guessing half a billion dollars a year. Maybe more."

Everyone in the room expresses complete shock.

"What about a member list? Any luck on that?" Sarah asks.

"Not yet. The actual data is buried somewhere in The Club's system, which I'm working on getting, but Oksana's got this prized list of VIPs she personally handles herself. She doesn't use real names—it's all managed with codes and nicknames—but I've traced a few things and figured out a few of these guys' identities. So far there are a bunch of CEOs and corporate bigwigs, some high-profile athletes—you know that guy on the Yankees who just signed that huge deal?—and at least two congressmen have been pretty big clients for quite a while. And there's this one guy I think might be a really big deal, some sort of über VIP—but I haven't figured him out yet. But, just from that sampling alone, we're talking about some high-profile people who'd be pretty bummed to find out they've been funding the Russian mafia—or, I guess, the Ukrainian mafia. Although, more on that later."

Sarah and I exchange a look. I didn't think about them as "the mafia." Is that what they are? Shit. My stomach is churning. I've been sitting at the table, my knee jiggling wildly, but now I stand and pace the room.

"The identity of that über VIP guy seems like something we'd better nail down," Henn says. "His emails are double encrypted but I cracked an email from Oksana to Max forwarding one of the über VIP guy's emails—and the guy said shit like 'my security personnel will post outside the door.' He's got security personnel? And they 'post' outside doors? Like, who the fuck says that?"

Sarah looks at me, her eyes bugging out of her head, and I return the sentiment.

"A rock star?" Sarah suggests. "Guys like that always have bodyguards."

"No," Henn says. "Not based on what I've seen."

"Yeah, I know plenty of rock stars with bodyguards—and they don't talk like that," Josh says. He looks anxious.

"I'll keep working on it," Henn says. "Okay, so are you guys ready for your minds to be officially blown?"

"You mean there's *more*?" Sarah asks.

"Oh yeah. The next part is what makes this so much fun." He turns to Kat. "I figured this next part out right after you left last night."

Kat looks at the rest of us sheepishly. "I finally had to get some sleep."

"That's what happens when you don't subsist on a diet of caffeine and nicotine," Henn says.

I steal a quick glance at Josh. He doesn't know what Henn's about to say, either.

"Did you leave to get some sleep, too?" I ask Josh.

"Yeah, I couldn't keep up with Henn, either," Josh says. "I think I left around the time Kat left." He glances at Kat. "Maybe just a little bit later."

Holy shit. They're fucking. I look quickly at Sarah to see if she sees what I see, but she's pale-faced and anxious, not the least bit interested in whether Kat and Josh are having sex.

"So what is it?" Kat asks, on the edge of her seat.

"I'm still waiting to get a bunch of stuff translated—I'm kind of handicapped by all the Ukrainian and Russian, so I'm not finished yet, but you guys, oh my God—Oksana's like some kind of political activist. She's like the Ukrainian Ché Guevara, man. She's in constant communication with these Ukrainian guys about 'Donbas.' I didn't know what that was, so I looked it up, and it refers to some kind of Ukrainian revolution."

"The separatists," I say. This has been all over the news lately.

"Yeah, right? That's what I thought." Henn says. "There are all these messages back and forth with these dudes in Ukrainian and she's spewing propaganda shit, and talking about 'the cause' and they're talking about needed funding and weapons. Like, serious weaponry, guys. Crazy shit. And Oksana keeps saying shit like, 'Keep the faith.'" Henn says this last part in a cartoon-Russian accent.

"Oh my God," Josh mumbles.

"What?" Kat says.

"They're funding the Ukrainian separatists," Josh explains.

"Which means Oksana's funding Putin through the back door," I add.

Kat looks blank. "You guys, break it down for me. Sorry."

"Okay, back in the day, there was the U.S.S.R., right?" I say. "Then it got broken up into all these pieces—Russia and Ukraine and the Baltic states. Well, now Putin wants to put all the pieces of mother Russia back together again, to resurrect the former empire—and he wants the diamond of his new Soviet Union to be Ukraine."

Kat nods. "And is Ukraine down with that plan?"

"No, not the official government. But there's a faction within Ukraine—the separatists—and they want to separate from their government and go along with Putin's reunification plan. So the separatists have waged armed conflicts with their own government, funded by the Russians."

I look at Josh. We're both thinking the same thing: Holy fuck, we gave our money to these people.

Sarah looks the way I feel right now. Mortified.

"Holy shitballs," Kat says softly.

"Yeah, most definitely," Henn says. "Well said."

"We've got to find out who Mr. Bigwig VIP is," I blurt, my stomach lurching into my mouth. "We need to know who all the heavy-hitters are. You said congressmen are involved in this shit, right?"

"Yup," Henn says.

"That could be really, really bad," Josh says.

"Seriously. 'Oh, hi, constituents. Please re-elect me,'" Henn says, putting on his best congressman-voice. "'I added more police to our streets, got a library built, and voted to increase the minimum wage. Oh, *and,* I paid a whole bunch of money to a Ukrainian prostitution and weapons ring to fund the reunification of the Soviet Union. Can I count on your vote during the next election?'"

I can't even laugh. Shit. I didn't see this one coming at all.

"This is too big for us to handle on our own," Sarah declares emphatically. "We've got to hand this over to the FBI." Her eyes widen. "Or the CIA? I don't even know which one. I mean, jeez, I'm a first-year law student at U Dub." She shakes her head. "This is like, a matter of international significance—and that's not even an exaggeration."

She's right. That's no exaggeration. And she's also right—we've got to hand this over to the right authorities. But I don't have the first clue how to handle something of this magnitude any more than she does. "The question is how and when," I say. "We can't just waltz into the FBI and ask for Johnny the Next Available Special Agent and say, 'Hi. There's a prostitution ring in Las Vegas that's laundering arms and money for Putin. Now go on—go get 'em, guys!' Even if they take us seriously, which is doubtful, who knows how long it'll take them to investigate and take meaningful action, if ever? If they take too long, how long before Max and Oksana get paranoid and decide Sarah's not as valuable to them as they thought? The only thing I care about in all this is protecting Sarah."

Sarah groans. "This ain't no casino heist, guys. We're gonna need a helluva lot more than George Clooney to pull this off."

I exhale. "How much of this can we prove as of right now, Henn?"

"The 'Funding the Evil Empire' thing is all circumstantial right now because I don't have the banking records yet. I can prove quite a bit with lots of creativity, putting the pieces together, but to immediately convince anyone else about all this you'd have to have an audience with a long attention span that's willing to listen closely and make certain leaps in logic."

"We can't count on that."

"I know. Everything will be airtight and clear as a bell when I'm able to hack into The Club's actual mainframe—and I'm super close on that."

"We need to be able to show them the money," I say. "That's the key—the only way we're gonna get anyone's attention."

"I agree," Henn says. "I don't have all their accounts or passwords yet—but I'm working on it."

"How long 'til you've got everything you need to make this airtight?"

"A couple more days and I'll be solid. Maybe not airtight, but solid. I mean, I could do this for months and months and still be gathering new information. But as far as having something to use as an opening salvo, something that'll get the good guys' attention quickly and make them take immediate action, I can get you what you'll need in a couple days."

"Excellent," I say.

"Henn, I'm your new best friend," Sarah says. "I'm gonna start collecting and collating the information you find and synthesizing it into one concise document—like a legal brief. We have to have something to hand over to the good guys and get their attention quickly. I'll make it easy for them—outline the facts, The Club operations, all potential criminal counts—RICO, wire fraud, money laundering, racketeering, etcetera, etcetera—and summarize the evidence collected thus far in relation to each count." Sarah's mind is really clicking now. "Kat."

"Yes, ma'am."

"For each and every criminal count, I'm gonna need a piece of supporting evidence—something to show them we're not making this stuff up. I'll tell you exactly what kind of thing I'm looking for, and then you'll go digging through whatever Henn's been able to find so far to get it for me. You'll be my research assistant."

"I can do that," Kat says.

"That's good," I say. "And Josh and I will pow-wow and figure out our best strategy for the hand-off. I agree—we're going to have to turn this over to *someone*—but to whom, that's the question. If we put it in the wrong hands, we might just buy ourselves an even bigger enemy than The Club."

"What does that mean?" Kat asks, her eyes wide.

"It sounds like there are plenty of powerful people on that client list who wouldn't want this scandal to see the light of day."

There's a long beat while everyone lets that sink in. We're about to open a very large and dangerous can of worms.

"It's all gonna come down to the money," I say. "Money talks."

"I agree," Josh says.

"Henn, that's top priority, okay?" I say. "Track the money. Get access to it."

"Roger," Henn says. "Shouldn't take me more than a couple days."

"We can do this," Sarah says, but she doesn't sound convinced. "Look at the talent in this room. We don't need no stinkin' George Clooney and Brad Pitt and Matt Damon."

"Yeah, but I sure wish we had that Chinese acrobat guy," Henn says. "He was cool."

"The one they stuffed into the little box?" Kat asks. "I loved him."

"Yeah, he was rad," Henn agrees.

"Yen. Wasn't that his name?"

Henn laughs. "Oh *yeah*. Good memory, Kat." He taps his temple. "Brains *and* beauty."

"Hey, guys, sorry to interrupt your profound musings, but I'm kind of getting tunnel vision here," Sarah says. "There's a lot to do and I wanna get started right away."

"Sure thing," Kat says. "Whatever you need, boss."

"Hey, Sarah," Henn says. "One more thing. What do you wanna do about Dr. Evil's text to you?"

Sarah's face turns bright red.

"I'm monitoring his phone, remember? 'I'm not a patient man.' What was *that* all about?"

Sarah obviously can't speak at the moment, so I grab her hand and explain Max's demand for a "freebie" from Sarah and the gist of his follow-up text. (I don't mention the specifics of Max's text—as far as I'm concerned, no one needs to know about Max's reference to a 'low-class strip club' and 'masks'—and, thankfully, Henn has the good sense not to reveal those details, either.)

"What should I do?" Sarah asks the room, her voice small. "Ignore him? Answer him? Hide?"

"Ignore him and hide," I say. "I don't want you saying a fucking thing to that motherfucker."

"I agree," Josh says. "Ignore him and hide."

"No," Kat says flatly. "Answer him and hide. Ignoring him will piss him off, and we don't want to piss that guy off. We want to keep him calm and confident and predictable."

Everyone looks at her, considering.

"Dr. Evil's real boner isn't for Sarah—it's for Jonas."

I grimace. "Jesus, Kat. Please don't say it that way."

"Not sexually. He's got an alpha-male boner for you, Jonas. This is all about a beta silverback wanting to knock off the obvious alpha. He wants what you've got so he can *win*. Hence, his Jonas-boner."

"For Chrissakes, *please* stop saying that," I say.

"So how should I reply to him, then?"

"We have to keep him off your back and convince him you're motivated solely by greed and absolutely *not* by loyalty to Jonas," Kat says. "The more he thinks your interests are the same as his, the safer you'll be. You've got to keep him trusting you. If you ignore him, he'll start getting paranoid."

Sarah looks at me. I nod. Kat's making a lot of sense.

Kat sees my nonverbal exchange with Sarah and seems encouraged. "Tell him that right after your meeting with him, Jonas went totally ballistic—out of his mind with jealousy. Jonas saw the obvious chemistry between you and Dr. Evil and he accused you of lying about never having met him before. Jonas is convinced you two are an item, and he thinks you wanted to be alone with Max just so you two could have sex in the bathroom. And now, dang it, there's absolutely no way you can get away without arousing Jonas' suspicion even more. Jonas the Jealous Boyfriend is watching you like a hawk now, not letting you leave your room without him. Just make Jonas out to be a wacko. Tell Max not to text—Jonas is monitoring your phone—and he's just on the cusp of giving you another humongous check. That way, you play right into his egomania and also appeal to his greed. No matter how much he wants his little freebie to satisfy his Jonas-boner—"

"Okay, Kat, that's enough," I caution.

"—he won't insist on it at the risk of sabotaging the scam. We'll just make Jonas out to be the bad guy and let Sarah sound like she's doing her best to manage him and keep the money rolling in."

Everyone stares at Kat, speechless and impressed.

Kat shrugs. "What? There are two things I know well in this life—PR and men."

"Nice," Henn says, his admiration palpable.

"Hey, I might be dumb, but I'm not blonde," Kat says, and everyone laughs.

Josh flashes Kat an adoring smile. "Does everyone agree with Kat on this? Because I most certainly do."

Everyone expresses agreement.

"Especially the part about how you're not allowed to leave the suite without me," I say. "That part is true. I don't want you going out there without me."

"Trust me, I won't," Sarah says. "Now that I know that creep's out there watching me, I have no desire to leave the suite ever again. I've got to hunker down and write my report, anyway. This is going to be a huge job." Sarah shakes her head in disbelief. "This is so crazy."

"It's totally insane," Henn agrees, exhaling happily. "Isn't it *awesome?*"

Chapter 29
Sarah

It's been a long-ass day. But a productive one. For the better part of today, Kat and I shadowed Henn as he worked furiously on his three computers, and when Henn finally crashed and burned due to total sleep deprivation, Kat and I kept going, doing our best to categorize and prioritize the information he'd retrieved thus far. And as Kat and I worked, Jonas and Josh did, too, brainstorming, researching governmental agencies, and drafting a spreadsheet outlining potential strategies.

Occasionally, the boys bickered until one of them started laughing and the other joined in—and, once, out of nowhere, they got into a heated argument about who would top the list of the best NFL quarterbacks of all-time—and, admittedly, at one point, Kat and I got so punchy we sat fully clothed in the empty Jacuzzi tub to drink a glass of wine—but otherwise, it was a day filled with nonstop work and stress.

In the middle of writing a particularly frustrating section on my report, I looked at Jonas across the room to find him intensely studying something on his laptop, his brow furrowed, and I felt an overwhelming desire to crawl into his lap and say, "To hell with everything—let's go back to Belize." But instead, I suggested he take a break to work out in the hotel gym.

"There's no time for that," he said. "I'm on a mission from God here, baby."

I was about to say his mind might actually benefit from a break, when, without notice, he added, right in front of everybody, "Because I love my baby more than life itself." And then he looked back down at his computer as if that wasn't the most heart-stopping moment of my entire life.

And now, finally, everyone's gone and there's nothing to keep me from crawling into his lap now—or doing whatever else the heck I might want to do to my hunky-monkey boyfriend.

Jonas comes out of the bathroom after his shower, every single inch of his naked body as hard as a rock, and crawls into bed next to me. He flips me onto my back roughly and crawls over me, his erection grazing my belly and his eyes gleaming. "What shall we do first, my lady?" he says. "Shall I take a big bite out of your ass? Or perhaps nibble on your crumpets?" He leans down and nibbles one of my nipples.

"Hang on, sir," I say in a clipped accent, and he pauses—though it looks like it physically pains him to do it. "I happen to have a few very specific thoughts on this subject this fair evening." I pat the bed next to me and he reluctantly obeys, a questioning look in his eyes. "When I was Googling to find that strip club I took you to the other night, I initially searched the term 'peep show Las Vegas,' and you know what came up?"

He shakes his head.

"All kinds of crap about some now-defunct topless musical revue on The Strip starring Ice-T's wife."

Jonas glances at my crotch with pure longing in his eyes.

I smile wickedly. "So then I searched 'peep show sex club,' just to see what might come up, and gosh darn it, Google must have thought I wanted search results for 'peep show *sex.*' Huh. Talk about fascinating reading." I bite my lower lip.

A shadow of a smile flickers across Jonas' face, but he somehow manages to keep his excitement under wraps.

"It turns out there's a sexual position called The Peep Show. Are you familiar with that one, sir?'

He pauses. "Well, actually, that could refer to one of several different things, my dearest lady." He licks his lips. "You'll have to be more specific about your particular item of interest."

I grab my laptop off the nightstand and quickly find the graphic 3-D animation I stumbled upon by accident the other night—two attractive, animated avatars performing "peep show fellatio" with body-jerking enthusiasm.

Considering how many different and sometimes surprising ways Jonas has performed oral sex on me—who knew there were so many ways to do it?—the sight of that "peep show fellatio" animation really shouldn't have surprised me at all. But it did.

All this time, I'd accepted Jonas' paradigm that *my* pleasure was the elusive beast—the hard-earned prize he'd studied and practiced and trained specifically to vanquish—and all the while it never even occurred to me that there might be a thing or two I could learn to maximize *his* pleasure, too. It was like a light bulb went off in my head—and between my legs.

I turn the computer screen toward Jonas and his face lights up. "This," I say, showing him the avatars performing peep show fellatio. "Ring any bells, sir?"

His smile spreads across the entire width of his face. "Why, yes, my lady," he says, his voice edged with suppressed excitement, "it rings bells and whistles and buzzers and clappers and ding-dongs."

I laugh heartily.

"I have indeed heard tell of this 'peep show' sex act to which you refer," he says, his eyes ablaze, "but I've never been so fortunate as to have someone suggest performing it on me." He bites his lip. "*For* me."

I'm floored. I didn't see that one coming. I thought Jonas had done every conceivable sex act known to man. I can't believe my ears. "How is that possible?" I ask, dropping our playful politeness.

"I've never done it."

"But, I mean, I thought when it came to sex, you've already done everything there is to do—and then some."

He shrugs.

"But, I thought... " I shake my head. I'm utterly confused. How is this possible?

He blushes. "It's not the kind of thing I'd ask some random hook-up to do. And I've never had a..." He sighs. "I've never had a girlfriend like you before."

Heat spreads throughout my body. "What do you mean?"

He shrugs again but doesn't answer.

"Your girlfriends have never wanted to do this for you?"

He shakes his head.

"You're going to have to give me more than a headshake here, big boy. 'Fess up. Come on."

He exhales. "It's just never come up."

"Why not?"

"Why don't I lick you and make you come and then we'll talk about this afterwards?" He starts crawling on top of me again, grinning lasciviously.

I push him off me. "This is too fascinating. Tell me first and then I promise it's crazy-sexy-freaky time 'til the break of dawn."

He sighs. "You're such a pain in the ass, you know that, woman?"

"Yes."

He rolls his eyes. "A little over a year ago, I went on a date with this woman and she faked having an orgasm—"

"Yes, I know, the woman who inspired you to seek *redemption* the second time around. I really should buy that lady a bottle of the finest champagne to thank her, by the way, since I'm the one who's benefited more than anyone from the higher learning she inspired."

Jonas smiles. "How about I tell you this story after I lick you and make you come?" He reaches for my inner thigh.

I swat his hand way. "Nope."

He frowns like a little boy denied a cookie.

"Come on. Spill."

He exhales, resigned to his fate. "Thanks to that faker, I started reading up and studying and I realized for the first time what a gift it is to make a woman reach orgasm—how much effort it takes beyond just fucking her. Before then, I just thought, 'If it feels good to me, it must feel good to her.' I thought it was a crapshoot whether a woman comes or not, like out of my control—sometimes yes, sometimes no." He smiles. "I mean, don't get me wrong, my natural instincts were better than most, I'm not a complete Neanderthal—but the minute I started reading and learning, I realized there was so much more to it—so much technique to learn. I realized that if I wanted to make a woman come, I could, every single time. I just had to do it *right.*"

"Oh, God, you're turning me on, Jonas."

His face explodes with desire and his erection twitches. "Then let me lick you and make you scream."

"You'll have to finish your story first." I tease him by caressing my breast.

His chest heaves. "So-then-I-licked-a-bunch-of-women-between-their-legs-and-made-them-come-whenever-I-wanted. The End." He smiles and reaches for me.

I push him away again. "You're so gross."

He laughs.

"Seriously, though. I'm blown away I've finally discovered the one sex act you've never done before."

"Oh, there are *lots* of sex acts I've never done before—and a whole bunch I've only done with you."

Now I'm genuinely reeling. "What? I've been your *first* for some of this stuff?"

"For lots and lots of it."

I blink quickly like he's just given me mental whiplash. I sit up and look him in the eyes. "Babe. What are you talking about? I'm totally confused."

He puts his hand on my cheek and kisses me. "My Magnificent Sarah," he says, nipping at my jawline. "You turn me on, baby. Do you have any idea how much you turn me on?" His hand softly brushes my breast.

Blood rushes between my legs. "No, Jonas. Tell me."

"How 'bout you give me a little taste first—your pussy's calling to me like a siren, woman."

"No."

He pouts.

"Tell me."

He grunts and sighs. "Before I found religion, so to speak, I'd already had plenty of sex, of course, with hook-ups, girlfriends, flings, one-night stands. All the typical stuff—fucking, oral, threesomes—I did it all. But never, ever like it is with you. Never like, you know... " His eyes sparkle. "Going to *church*." His face lights up. "And then *after* I found religion, after I'd started studying and learning and seeking out women to practice on, sex for me was always about making a woman come harder than she ever had, making her *surrender* to me—becoming *God*." He rolls his eyes at that last part.

"Redemption," I say quietly, a light bulb suddenly going off in my head. How have I not understood before this moment how thoroughly Jonas' need for redemption has pervaded his entire life? "Everything you do, even sex, is about redeeming yourself, Jonas. Proving you're not worthless."

He stares at me for a long beat. "Yeah," he finally says. "I guess so." He flashes me those mournful eyes. "Huh." There's another long beat. "So, anyway, I've always wanted to make my sexual partners surrender to me, but I never... " He twists his mouth. "I never wanted to be the one who surrendered." He swallows hard. "So, you know, to answer your question, I haven't done a whole lot of stuff that puts me on the receiving end of things—stuff like The Peep Show. I've always steered things in the opposite direction."

I can barely contain my bodily impulses right now.

"But what about before this past year—before your 'quest for *sexcellence?*' You've had girlfriends before all that—what about receiving from them?"

"Occasionally, sure. But before you, my girlfriends were pretty uptight. I guess I picked girls who made it easy for me to *suppress* rather than *reveal*. Yeah, I've had girlfriends before you, but this is the first time I've been a true *boyfriend* in return—the first time I've *revealed*."

I'm electrified. "But what about all those one-night stands? I can't believe you didn't try sex every which way... ?"

"Think about it. When you fuck a different woman every night, and your only goal is making your partner come hard, you actually wind up being *less* experimental, not *more*. You've got one, maybe two, shots to make this stranger come like a rocket, so you wind up having certain go-to moves you fall back on again and again, just to be absolutely sure you succeed."

"So all those sexual positions we've been doing?"

"I'm trying most of them out with you."

My entire body flutters with excitement. "The butterfly?"

He looks shy. "Just you. My beautiful butterfly."

My clit zings like he's just licked me there. "The ballerina?"

"Who else but you could even stand like that, let alone get fucked like that?"

My head is spinning. "What about that upside-down sixty-nine thing we did the day we got back from Belize?"

"Just you."

"But right before we did it you said it turns you on and—"

"I was talking about sixty-nining in general. I've done *that* before, sure, but not that crazy-ass acrobatic thing. I've always wanted to try that—but who would I have done that with besides you?" He sighs, enraptured. "That was amazing."

I'm ridiculously turned on. "Oh, Jonas." I shake my head. "I thought you'd done everything there is to do with a thousand other women."

He shakes his head. "I licked 'em and made 'em come and then fucked 'em just to get myself off. Nothing like what we've been doing. You're my first on a ton of stuff I've always wanted to try— my sexy little guinea pig."

I feel like a cat in heat, like I want to rub myself against his thigh.

"You've got to be plenty comfortable with someone to do some of the more adventurous stuff we've been doing—there's got to be mutual *trust*."

I grab his face and kiss him and he leans into me, ready to crawl on top of me and mount me. I push him back again and he groans.

"Come on, baby. I'm dying here. I can't wait anymore," he whimpers.

"Too bad." I'm panting. I grab my laptop and call up the diagram labeled "peep show fellatio." I click the back button on the website—an entire site devoted to every sexual position known to man, complete with animated diagrams, detailed instructions, and message boards—and navigate to the website's home page. On the left-hand side of the page, there's a lengthy menu of generalized categories like "face-to-face" and "sixty-nine" and "rear entry," each category linking in turn to a series of more specific sub-options and demonstrative animations. I click the general link for "fellatio" and twelve animated blowjob diagrams fill the screen.

"What about these? Which of these have you already done?"

He looks through the images, his chest heaving. "Oh man," he says. "Wow. Look at that one." His erection twitches. "No. I've just had, you know, the basic blowjob—which is fucking awesome and I'm not complaining, believe me. Oh, and that one, of course, standing up like that, but I'd consider that pretty basic. Oh, and that one, too, sitting down like that."

"But what about this one?" I click on a link.

He shakes his head and laughs. "Nope."

"This one?"

"Uh, no. I don't even *want* to do that one. I'd crush you."

I look. "Yeah, agreed. Scratch that one. I wouldn't survive it. But how about this one? Have you done that?"

"Nope."

"Well, baby, it's your lucky day. Today begins the Twelve Days of Fellatio-Christmas. We're gonna do each and every one of these variations, right down the line—except ones that might literally crush me." I laugh. "I might not be able to pull them all off with particular skill..." I glance down at one particularly enigmatic diagram and make a face. "Some of these look really challenging—I don't even understand how some of these would work from a logistical standpoint—but I promise, I'll give 'em the ol' college try."

"Sarah, you don't have to—"

"I *want* to."

"Baby, listen, when I go down on you, it isn't a tit for tat kind of thing. I *love* eating you out. I get off on tasting you. You're delicious. I don't do it to get something in return—"

I bend down and lick the tip of his penis and he instantly stops talking.

I look up at him. "You like tasting me?"

He inhales deeply. "It's my favorite thing."

"Well, that's how I feel about sucking on you. It's a total turn-on. I fantasize about doing it. I crave it. I dream about it. I like the way you taste. I like the way you feel in my mouth. I like the way you grab at my hair when I'm down there. I like the sounds you make." I lick him again and he moans. "I feel powerful when I do it—like I own you."

"Oh fuck, baby, I'm gonna blow my load before you even get started."

I grip his shaft. "Well, then, I guess we'd better stop talking about it and start doing it. Look at that list again and tell me which one you wanna start with. I'm horny as hell right now."

He looks at the computer and scrolls urgently through the options, his breathing labored.

"Well?"

"I can't pick—asking me to pick is cruel."

"What about this one?"

"Yes, please."

"Or this one?"

"Yes, please."

I laugh. "Which one do you want to try the most?"

160

"That's like asking me to pick a favorite child. I love all my babies equally."

I laugh again and take another look through the diagrams.

He tilts the computer toward himself. "Hey, why don't we look at all the cunning options for you, too? That'd be fun."

I tilt the computer back to me. "No, this is about *me* becoming a sexual samurai—you've already earned your sword."

"Hang on." He commandeers the computer from me again and clicks on the word "cunnilingus" on the side of the screen. When the options come up, he groans like I've just taken him into my mouth. "Just these little cartoons get me off like a motherfucker. I want to do them all to you right now."

"Haven't we already done them all by now?" I peer at the screen.

"Not this one," Jonas says. He moans. "You've never lain on top of me like that. Oh, I want that. Oh, God, yes, that looks nice. Yes, please."

He's right. It looks incredible. But I shake it off. "This is supposed to be about me doing something for you."

"Yeah, but you *would* be doing something for me, I promise." He moans again. "I'd probably cream rinse your hair if you let me eat you like that one." He points at another diagram in which the woman's head dangles precariously close to the man's penis. He shivers. "Oh, I want to do that one, Sarah. *Please.*" He moans. "Please, please."

I shudder with desire. "That certainly does look delicious."

He quivers again. "Let's do it right now." He reaches between my legs and touches me. When he feels how wet I am, he moans loudly again. "Come on."

"Hang on," I gasp. "Wait, Jonas. *Wait.*"

He pulls his hand back, pouting.

"It's your turn to *receive* right now."

He sighs and looks back at the computer, ignoring me. He clicks on another link. "We've never done this one before, have we? With your leg in the air like that?"

He's missing my point here—I want to be the giver. But I can't resist sneaking a peek at whatever cunnilingus option he's talking about this time. Oh God, it's so tantalizing, it makes my clit flutter just looking at it. "Licking the Flagpole," I read. "Oh, that one looks lovely."

"I want that," Jonas says like a kid in a candy shop. "Me want," he adds, caveman-style. "Me. Want. Now."

I grab the computer. "We're way off track here. This is about me figuring out how to maximize *your* pleasure."

"You couldn't possibly maximize my pleasure any more than you already do, just by being your beautiful, tasty, delectable self."

I blush. "But I really want to try some new things."

He bites his lip. "Okay, fine. I've got a proposal for you, my little samurai in training."

"What is it?"

"We'll do this tit for tat style."

"You really like that expression, don't you?"

"Shh. Listen up."

I make a smart-ass show of giving him my undivided attention.

"This is gonna be Jonas and Sarah's Tit-for-Tat Adventure. Of course, you'll be the Tit—"

"As usual."

"And I'll be the Tat. You'll kick things off each time with whatever configuration of fellatio you desire and I'll humbly and gratefully receive your precious gift—and then it's my turn to do whatever the fuck I want to you, any way I please." He shudders with excitement.

"Isn't that what we do now—you do whatever you want to me, any way you please? What's gonna be different about this?"

"Shh. Now it's *official*—with rules and everything. Tit for tat. You give to me however you like—and then I'll turn around and give back to you, however I damn well please." He licks his lips.

"For twelve days," I add. "It'll be the Twelve Days of Blowjobs for you."

"And the Twelve Days of Tasty Treats for you."

"Jonas, you give me tasty treats every single day. You're not proposing anything new or different here—"

"Just play along, woman. Why on earth do you feel compelled to boss me around and spoil my fun? You're so goddamned bossy."

I roll my eyes. "I'm sorry. Okay." I click back on the fellatio options on the side of the page. "Let's pick your inaugural blowjob."

I click on an animated diagram labeled The Jackhammer. "Well, I don't even understand how this one would work. I'd have to pull your penis all the way down in the wrong direction to my mouth. Wouldn't that hurt you?"

"I don't know—I guess we'll find out." He grins broadly.

"And this one—Snake Charmer—can you even do a handstand?"

He laughs. "I'm willing to try."

"Now that's the kind of can-do attitude I like to hear, baby. I tell you what. Let's start with The Peep Show, since that's what got me so hot and bothered in the first place." I grab his shaft and caress it.

He trembles.

"Welcome to the Twelve Days of Blowjobs, baby," I say softly, fondling him.

He yelps with excitement.

"I love you, Jonas," I say.

"I love you more than life itself," he replies. "My Magnificent Sarah."

"Now quit stalling and lie down on your side. You're mine to do with as I please."

He lies on his side, grinning from ear to ear, his erection straining.

"Okay, good." I glance at the computer screen again, trying to understand how this particular game of Twister is supposed to work. "And now I'm supposed to thread my head and neck through your thighs from behind." I get myself into the correct position, singing as I do, "On the first day of Christmas, my true love gave to me, a blowjob in a pear tree." He laughs with unfettered glee, and so do I. "Deck the halls with boughs of blowjobs," I sing merrily from between his thighs, cracking up. "Fa la la la la la la la la." I give him an enthusiastic lick. "Mmmm," I say. "Even better than figgy pudding."

He throws his head back and laughs. "God, I love you, Sarah."

Chapter 30
Jonas

I wake up to Sarah jerking and shrieking in my arms.

"No!" she screams at the top of her lungs, her voice raspy. "No!" She thrashes wildly.

"Sarah, wake up. You're dreaming." I grip her. "Sarah. You're having another nightmare."

She jolts awake, her breathing ragged, her eyes wild.

"You were having another bad dream."

She clutches me and bursts into tears.

"Shh, baby. You're safe. I'm here. It was just a dream." I caress her hair. "Shh. You're okay. I'm right here." After she calms down a bit, I pull her into me and kiss her cheeks. "The Ukrainian Travolta again?"

She nods. She swallows hard and catches her breath. "Only this time, Max was there, too. He was raping me while Travolta held the knife to my throat. And Max kept saying, 'He's gonna kill you when I'm done fucking you,' and I screamed and tried to break free, but my arms wouldn't work and my legs were paralyzed and I couldn't move—"

"Baby, it's okay. It was just a bad dream."

She whimpers again.

"You're safe." I hold on to her fiercely. I swear to God, I'm going to kill those motherfuckers.

She takes a moment to gather herself before she continues. "And then..." She pauses, apparently visualizing something. "My father appeared, out of nowhere." She shivers. "And for a split second, I felt *relieved*, like I thought he was there to *save* me—but then he leaned into my ear while Max was pounding into me and he said, 'Paybacks are a fucking bitch, huh?'"

My blood runs cold.

She trembles. "God, I haven't had a nightmare about my dad in years. I guess all this stuff with The Club has opened up some old psychological wounds."

I stroke her arm. "You used to have nightmares about your father?"

"All the time. For like a year after my mom and I ran away from him, I used to look over my shoulder, afraid he was gonna come up behind me, throw a bag over my head, and drag me away." She inhales deeply and exhales loudly. "And now I keep having that exact same feeling about Max and Travolta—like they're right behind me." She stifles another whimper. "I keep thinking they're coming to get me."

I squeeze her tight. *I'm gonna fucking kill those motherfuckers.*

"Damn. I thought I was done with nightmares about my dad." She wipes her eyes.

"You saw your dad do some horrible things, huh?"

"Yeah," she says quietly. "He used to beat the crap out of my mom—and then he expected me to act like he was father of the year."

"Did he ever hurt you?" She once told me her father had never laid a hand on her, but I wonder if that was completely true.

"He never touched me. I was his princess."

I exhale. I'm hugely relieved to hear that.

"But Jonas."

I wait but she doesn't continue. "What is it?" For some reason, I'm nervous.

"There's something I haven't told you—something I've never told anybody."

The hairs on the back of my neck stand up.

"What did I tell you about my dad? About how we left?"

I think back to what little she's told me. "You said your dad hurt your mom and that the two of you escaped him when you were ten."

"Yeah, that's all true." She sits up onto her elbow and looks down at my face. Her hair falls around her shoulders. "But there's something I've kept secret my whole life. I didn't mean to keep a secret from you—it's just something I've kept hidden from everyone." She touches my face. "But I don't want there to be any secrets between us anymore, about anything, big or small."

My skin breaks out in goose bumps. Is she talking about my

secrets or hers? My heart suddenly pounds in my ears. Did Josh tell her everything about me? Is that what she's hinting at?

"When I told you my mom and I 'escaped' my dad, that was true. He used to beat her up all the time." She pauses. "And then came this one horrific night when he beat her unconscious—to a bloody pulp," she says. "She was in such bad shape, I truly thought she was dead."

I hold my breath. I have no idea what she's about to reveal to me.

"When I told you my mom and I 'escaped' my dad, I tried to make it sound like my mom grabbed me and we fled—as if she'd finally decided enough is enough and we ran away."

I nod. That's exactly the scenario I'd envisioned.

"That's the story I tell myself. That's how I make myself remember it. But that's not how it happened."

My blood pulses in my ears.

"The truth is that I did it."

I look at her quizzically.

"He beat the crap out of her one night, so bad I thought she was dead. And when I realized she was alive, I was so relieved, just so frickin' *relieved*, I thought, 'That's it. No more. I'm not letting him kill her next time—I'm not gonna let there *be* a next time.'" She exhales a shaky breath. "So I drugged him and took her someplace where he couldn't find us. She was too weak to fight me on it."

I'm confused—wasn't she *ten*?

"I'd been stashing supplies in this old abandoned toolshed a couple blocks away for weeks, just sort of dreaming about running away, I guess—but I didn't really have an actual plan or anything. And then that night came and all bets were off. So I crushed a bunch of sleeping pills into his beer, like, you know, Tylenol PMs or whatever, and when he passed out, I dragged my mom to that shed. We stayed there for a few days, not making a peep, while she got her strength back. And then one day she woke up and looked me in the eye and said, 'From this day forward, I am reborn.' And that was that. She was done."

"And you were how old?"

"Ten."

My mind is reeling. I knew Sarah was a badass of epic proportions, but this proves she was *born* that way. Jesus.

"For the longest time after that, I worried I'd killed him by accident, like, maybe I'd given him too many sleeping pills—and I kept having nightmares the police were at the door to arrest me. When my mom finally filed for divorce, I realized he must have lived, but then I started having horrible nightmares that he was coming after me to get his revenge."

"When did the nightmares stop?"

"When he remarried and had a son with his new wife, we never heard from him again." She sighs and wipes her eyes. "That's when I slowly started feeling safe."

"Wow, Sarah. That's a lot of stress for a little girl."

She looks at me, astonished. "Says the boy with the saddest eyes I've ever seen." She touches my cheek.

I blush. I didn't mean to make this about me.

She sighs. "I've never told anyone about how I drugged him—not even my mom. She was so out of it, she never asked me for details about that night. Later, I think she was so ashamed she'd taken so much shit from him for so long, she never wanted to talk about him or what happened. And once she'd started devoting her life to helping other women and counseling them to leave bad situations, I didn't want to reveal the scandalous truth that it was her ten-year-old daughter, not her, who'd actually gathered the courage to leave. Well, just at first. My mom was plenty courageous after that."

"You were so brave, Sarah. Wow."

"No."

"Yeah, you were."

"I was more like *determined*. Isn't brave when you know you're doing something scary but you do it anyway? It was more like nothing could stop me. I never stopped to be scared. I just put blinders on and did what had to be done."

I smirk. "I think I've witnessed your 'determination mode' a time or two."

Her mouth twists into a shy smile. She leans down and kisses me. "I've never told anyone that story."

"You have nothing to be ashamed of. You should be proud of that story."

"I'm not proud. I mean, I'm not sorry I did it—maybe my mom would have died the next time if I didn't—but the story kind of proves I'm terminally fucked up, doesn't it?" She smiles. "Or at the very least a wee bit crazy."

Is she trying to get me to tell her about how I'm a wee bit crazy, too? Did Josh tell her about me? Is that what she's hinting here?

"Do you still love me even though I drugged my father and stole my mother out from under him?" She grins at me.

I try to smile back at her, but I can't. I'm suddenly racked with panic. What does she know? Is she trying to tell me something?

She kisses me. "Wow, it feels so good to tell you that." Her hand strokes my bare chest. "I feel so incredibly close to you, Jonas." Her lips press against my neck. She grinds against me. "I've never told anyone that." She kisses my lips. She's obviously getting aroused.

But I'm distracted. Now that she's told me her secrets, do I have to tell her mine? If I don't tell her everything right now, right this very minute, is that the same thing as lying to her? Isn't that what she just implicitly told me? Shit.

Her hand caresses my bicep. Her naked body presses into mine. My erection springs to life.

If I don't come clean right now, isn't that just like when I checked in with Stacy at The Pine Box and didn't mention it to her? What did she say about that? "Secrets create dark spaces within a relationship," she said. "When one person keeps secrets, the other person fills in the dark spaces with their fears and insecurities." She said my silence about Stacy had created a dark space between us—a reason for her not to trust me. Fuck. Will my silence now about my secrets create another dark space?

Her hand caresses my cock and of course it responds to her touch like a champ, as usual.

She moans. "I love you," she says. She wraps her thigh around me, grinding into me.

A normal man would confess his secrets right now. This is the moment for me to come clean. She just told me her deep, dark secret and said it made her feel closer to me to confess it. There are no do-overs for this moment. My heart is pounding. Is not telling the same as lying? Yes, it is. Maybe not before this very moment, but something's changed. I can feel it. I have to reciprocate. That's what she needs from me—what she deserves. And it's what a normal man would do for the woman he loves.

"I feel so close to you," she mutters. "I want you deep inside me."

She kisses me voraciously, but I don't kiss back. I'm paralyzed with fear. I promised not to lie to her. I promised to tell her anything and everything, except maybe relating to The Club. But this doesn't have anything to do with The Club. Shit.

She grips my cock and pulls on my hips, inviting me to make love to her. "Come on, Jonas."

"Sarah, wait."

There's an awkward silence as she looks at me, her eyes wide. She releases me.

"There's something I've got to tell you—several things, actually. Things you need to know about me."

Chapter 31
Sarah

For the last hour, Jonas and I have sat in our PJs on the bed, talking about the aftermath of Jonas' mother's death. I'm afraid to ask too many questions—the man's opening his heart to me like never before and I don't want to break the spell.

When Jonas tells me about his beloved Mariela, I ask if he ever looked for her later in life. He shakes his head sadly. "I never even knew her last name. I was too young. She was just Mariela to me— my Mariela." The ache in his voice is unmistakable. "I don't even remember her face. The only things I remember are her brown eyes and beautiful brown skin." He sighs. "And the way she sang to me in Spanish."

I suppress a grin. The first woman Jonas ever loved besides his mother was a Spanish-speaking, dark-eyed Latina with 'beautiful brown skin'? Um. Hello.

When he explains how he didn't speak for a whole year after his mother's death because he'd wanted the last words his mouth ever said to be 'I love you, Mommy,' my heart smashes into a thousand pieces. It takes all my restraint not to burst into ugly tears at the realization that this gorgeous, sensitive, poetic man let those precious words escape his mouth again for *me*.

And when he tells me about his teacher Miss Westbrook, how she kindly and brilliantly lured him out of his painful silence, how she made him feel *loved* during the loneliest point in his young life, how she nurtured this poor, aching boy when he was so obviously grasping for a drop of kindness, how she so lovingly showed him the purest kind of love through naming her child after him, I thought my heart would physically burst and splatter the poor man with even

170

more blood than he's already withstood. It seems I'm not the only woman to have fallen deeply in love with Jonas' innate sweetness—his mother, Mariela, and Miss Westbrook did, too.

"Oh, Jonas. You poor, sweet baby," I say, moving to hug him.

He holds up his hand. "No. I haven't told you what I need to tell you yet." His face is etched with pure anxiety. "Everything I just told you is mere background—stuff you need to know to understand the context of what I'm about to tell you."

I sit back and shut my mouth. What could he possibly need to tell me that would make him look this anxious?

He takes a deep breath and looks at me with those mournful eyes of his. "At first, when I wouldn't talk, my dad sent me away. To a hospital. You know, a mental hospital. A 'children's treatment center,' they called it."

At *seven*? Right after the poor little guy lost his mother *and* his beloved nanny? That seems like a pretty heartless thing to do to a kid.

"But I wouldn't talk. I wouldn't do anything the doctors wanted me to do. I didn't want to get better. I just wanted to die so I could be with my mom. When they finally let me out despite me not talking, I figured my dad must have missed me too much to make me stay there. I found out later my dad finally broke down and brought me home because Josh had begged and pleaded and cried so much." He smiles ruefully.

I keep forgetting about poor Josh in all this. Good Lord. He didn't have it easy, either.

"And then, after that, through the years, I just always knew there was this threat that at any moment, my father might send me back to the treatment center again. If I didn't talk like I was supposed to. Or if I cried, God forbid. Or if I just wasn't 'man enough,' whatever that meant. It was always hanging over me—say or do the wrong thing, be the wrong thing, think the wrong thing, and he'd say it was because I was 'crazy' and needed the 'fucking doctors to get my head straightened out again.'

"But sometimes I couldn't help it—I just couldn't follow his rules. Maybe I was just too sad to get out of bed for a week. Or maybe I couldn't make myself care about his opinion of me on a particular day. Sometimes, I'd lose my temper and start screaming at him—which became a pretty big problem for him the bigger I got.

"So, anyway, I was in and out of that fucking place for years—in and out, over and over. For long stretches, I'd get to go to school, even make a friend or two. Start to feel like maybe I was normal, after all—and then, boom, I'd have to go back for whatever reason. As I got older, I started to feel angrier and angrier about the whole thing and think I'd rather die than go back there. And then in my early teens, I distinctly remember thinking, 'I'd rather kill him than go back there.'" He swallows hard.

My heart skips a beat.

"He hated me." He runs his hand through his hair. "He just plain *despised* me." His eyes turn moist. "All those years, it was just my father, Josh and me living in that huge house—just the three of us—and two out of the three of us hated my guts."

Tears flood my eyes. Where did Jonas eek out any kind of love in his young life? With Josh, surely—but where else? How the heck did Jonas retain all the goodness and kindness I see in him?

"And all the while, I swear to God, it was my father who was the crazy one, not me. He was the one getting shit-faced drunk all the time, not me. He was the one fucking prostitutes and bringing them to our house and buying Bentleys and Bugattis and Porsches and helicopters and jewelry for his 'girlfriends' and spending money like it was water." He shakes his head. "He was the one who screamed all the time, not me." His eyes suddenly flash like a light bulb just went off in his head. "I'm sorry I screamed at you after we left The Club, Sarah." He wipes his eyes. "I shouldn't have done that. I was just so freaked out at the idea of losing you that I took it out on you." He shakes his head again. "Which makes absolutely no sense." He rubs his face. "Maybe I am fucking crazy, I don't know."

I crawl across the bed to him and hug him. "It's okay. I knew where it was coming from."

He nuzzles into my neck. "There's no excuse to scream at you, ever—you're the gentlest, kindest person I've ever met. You don't deserve that, especially with the asshole-father you had. Please, please forgive me."

"I do. Of course, I do."

"Please don't think I'm like your father."

I scoff at the thought. Jonas is a raw beast in so many ways—physically imposing, daunting, tortured, tempestuous, primal, sexual beyond anyone I've ever encountered—but I've never for a nanosecond thought he'd harm a hair on my head.

"I understand," I say. I kiss his lips and my entire body explodes with outrageous yearning. Oh good Lord, I want to make love to him. I kiss every inch of his face and he melts under me. An outrageous throbbing slams into me, right between my legs. In a flash, I've got a maddening itch and Jonas is the only one who can scratch it. I press my body into his, hungry for him.

He groans, clearly itching the way I am. He runs his hands down my back and pulls on my tank top—but then he jerks away from me, pulling on his hair.

"I haven't told you everything yet," he says, his voice strained. "Sarah, listen. If I don't tell you everything right now, I never will." He clenches his jaw. "I have to tell you." His eyes are pure pain.

I want to kiss his agony away. I want to feel him inside me and make him feel good and make his hurt disappear and make myself feel damned good in the process. But instead I nod and take a deep breath. "You can tell me anything." I crawl back to my assigned corner of the bed and stare at him, waiting.

There it is again, right there on his face: *Fear.* Really? Does this boy really think there's something he could say that would make me run away? Does he really think there's anything in this world that would make me stop loving him?

"Josh and I call it The Lunacy," he says, exhaling like he's just said an abominable curse word.

I wait.

"I was seventeen. My dad had his usual tickets to the Seahawks game, but he didn't feel great, he said, so he gave the tickets to Josh—Josh always had a thousand friends he could invite to a game. And my dad shocked the hell out of me by asking me to stay home with him and watch the game on TV. 'Let Josh go with his friends,' he said. 'You and I will stay home and make a memory.'" Jonas shakes his head and scoffs. "I was so fucking dumb, I was actually *excited* to stay home with him. I actually thought, 'Wow he wants to spend time with *me*—just *me*? Not Josh, too?' I was like, 'Wow, Dad, that'd be *great*.' I was *giddy* about it—like he'd just offered me some kind of fresh start."

I know what's coming next. Tears pool in my eyes.

"I was in the kitchen, making us turkey burgers before the game. God, I was such an idiot—I was *garnishing* the fucking plates." He lets out a bitter laugh. "Just like I'd seen on a cooking show."

I bite my lip. I know I need to let him get through this, but I'm not sure I can stand to hear what's coming next.

"When I heard the gunshot upstairs, I knew—right then, I knew. I remember I looked down at the plates I was fixing for us, the plates I was *garnishing,* and I actually laughed out loud. I knew right then he'd suckered me." He rubs his eyes. "I should have just walked out of the kitchen, straight out the front door, and never looked back. But I couldn't stop my legs from climbing the stairs, just like he wanted me to do."

He glances out the window of the bedroom. We've been talking for so long, the sun is rising over The Strip. His features are as beautiful as ever, but he looks tired. Exhausted, I'd even say. He licks his lips. They're as luscious as ever. I try my damnedest to think of something to say, but I can't. All I can think about is how beautiful he is. And how sorry I am for all he's had to endure.

"Can we put on some music?" he asks suddenly. "I'd really like to listen to some music for a minute, please."

"Sure. What would you like to hear?"

"Anything. You pick." But he quickly adds, "As long as you don't try to create some poignant moment with some shit like 'Everybody Hurts.'"

I laugh. "Okay. No R.E.M."

"And for the love of God. No 'Hurt' by Nine Inch Nails, either."

"Well, duh. If I was going to be poignant, I'd play the Johnny Cash version of that song."

"Ah, torture. So fucking amazing."

"I know. Makes me cry every time."

"Me, too. His voice slays me."

"Oh, and 'Tears in Heaven,' too," I say. "Talk about a crier."

"Gah. Please, no. Just a little background music to relax me."

"Yeah, yeah, got it. No worries, baby." I get up and fiddle with my computer. "One order of 'Love Shack' coming right up."

Chapter 32
Jonas

"What is this?" I ask.

"'My Favourite Book,'" she says.

"Who is it?"

"Stars. They're Canadian indie pop."

"Where the hell do you find this stuff?"

She shrugs. "I dunno. Just listen."

I close my eyes and let the music wash over me. It's a simple, effortless love song. Soothing. Sexy. Joyful. It's so Sarah.

"It's nice," I say. The song relaxes me. My scrambled thoughts begin to collate and organize themselves. "Thank you."

She blinks slowly at me, like she's caressing my cheeks from across the bed with supernaturally long lashes. God, she's beautiful. A jolt of anxiety flashes through my veins. What if finding out about The Lunacy changes everything for her?

I take solace in her warm brown eyes. No one's ever looked at me the way she does. Her eyes are coaxing me to throw caution to the wind and tell her my secrets.

"Okay," I say softly, girding myself for what I'm about to do. "The Lunacy."

She nods. She's ready.

Fuck it. Here goes. I exhale. "I went into his study. The room looked like he'd stuck his head into a giant blender without a lid."

She winces, but I feel nothing. I might as well be giving her driving directions to the post office. *You turn left on Fifty-Seventh Street and make a right on Seventeenth Avenue Northwest and it's on the right-hand side of the street.*

"He'd hung her wedding dress on a coat rack right next to his

175

desk," I continue. "Wedding pictures were spread out everywhere. His blood and brains were on everything." I clear my throat. Shit. I can't believe I'm about to tell her all this. "I found out later that day would have been their twentieth wedding anniversary."

She bites her lip in anticipation.

"An envelope with my name on it sat on his desk. I knew opening it would be the end of my sanity—but I couldn't stop myself. I had to know—even though I already knew." I sigh. "I guess there's only so long you can outrun your crazy, and I was just sick and tired of running."

She frowns sympathetically, but she doesn't speak.

"'*Everything you touch turns to blood.*' That's what his note said." I laugh bitterly. "Nothing else. Just one final, simple 'fuck you.' No apology. No last fatherly advice or expression of regret or pride or love." I scoff at myself for even uttering that last word. "Not even a goodbye to poor Josh. That was probably the most unforgivable thing of all, what he did to poor Josh—sending him off to cheer at yet another Seahawks game while yet another parent stayed home and died."

She makes a soft moaning noise.

I pause, trying to gather my composure before continuing—but not because this next part makes me want to cry. Quite the opposite. To this day, what happened next makes me want to laugh maniacally. "He had this incredible car collection," I say. "A McLaren, a Lamborghini, a vintage Bugatti, a bunch of Porsches, a couple of Bentleys, even a Lotus. Man, he loved those cars." I shake my head. "I grabbed a couple gas cans from the shed and I doused every last one of them, except for his favorite one, his most prized possession— a vintage silver Porsche 959."

I sneak a cautious peek at her. Her face is neutral, but her eyes are sparkling. Fuck, maybe I'm imagining it, but it almost seems like she's suppressing a smirk.

"I tore out of there in the Porsche—which, of course, he never allowed me to *touch,* so it was particularly gratifying. I had a fantastic view of the bonfire in my rearview mirror as I peeled out, too. That was special."

She nods. Her body language is open, relaxed, fascinated. Maybe even amused? Definitely not freaked out. So far so good. But, surely, this next part won't be quite so easy for her to digest.

"At first, I was laughing, but then I could barely drive through my tears. I was just a fucking wreck. Totally out of my head. I was sideswiping parked cars, running over curbs, doing one hundred on the freeway—just a bat out of hell. It's a miracle I didn't kill someone, a total miracle. To this day, I'm tortured by the thought of what might have happened that day if I'd wound up hurting or killing someone. What if I'd killed some kid's mother? I would have been no better than the fucker who killed my own mother."

She looks at me sympathetically, but she doesn't say anything.

"A police car started chasing me when I got to the freeway and I was like, *Oh yeah? Try to catch me now, motherfucker!* I just floored it, laughing hysterically the whole time. The cops must have thought I was on LSD or something, I swear to God, I was a fucking after-school special—and then another and another cop car showed up behind me until there was a fucking armada on my ass. And I remember, I just started thinking, over and over, like on a running loop, *Kill me, kill me, kill me, kill me, kill me, kill me, kill me.*" I rub my hand over my face. "I just wanted someone to put an end to my fucking misery once and for all."

She bites her lip. That shadow of a smirk I saw earlier, if indeed it was ever there, is long gone.

"And then I thought about Josh and that made me bawl like a baby—to think I was doing this to him on the very day Dad had just blown his brains out. God, it was so heartless of me, but I didn't care. I thought only about ending my own torture and not about the torment I'd be inflicting on Josh. I still can't believe I was willing to fuck up Josh's life beyond repair just to make myself feel better." I twist my mouth, trying not to choke up. "I guess I'd convinced myself I was doing him a favor by finally setting him free."

"Oh, Jonas."

She looks so fucking sympathetic. But is that sympathy or *pity*? Am I transforming from the boyfriend she loves and respects into a pitiful charity case right before her eyes?

"So what happened next?" she asks. "Since you're sitting here right now, I'm assuming suicide-by-cop didn't pan out?"

"Not for lack of trying, though. You know the Montlake canal bridge?"

"Of course. Right by campus."

"I was racing down Montlake toward that bridge with all those cop cars chasing me—I was fucking O.J. in the white Bronco—and I was laughing and crying and totally freaking out the whole time. A total madman. It was just so bizarre, like an out of body experience. And the bridge started opening to let some barge go through in the canal below and the cops started making a perimeter around me, drawing their weapons, and I just... I didn't even think about it. I just gunned it."

Her eyes widen. "Oh my God."

"Yeah."

"You drove that fancy Porsche right off the frickin' bridge?"

"Yep." I make a movement with my hand, imitating the falling trajectory of the car. "Plink."

She winces. "Oh my God, Jonas. How are you even here right now?"

"Eh. It turns out that bridge is renowned for being the worst bridge in all of Seattle for committing suicide. Not high enough. And the car broke my fall in the water." I pause, trying to remember my free fall, but I can't. "By then, I wasn't in my body anymore. I'd *departed,* so to speak. I guess it's like how the drunk guy's always the one who survives a head-on collision."

"Huh," she says flatly, as if I've just told her some fascinating bit of trivia about the average IQ of a turtle.

She's not reacting the way I thought she would. I thought we'd both be crying. I imagined myself trying desperately to convince her I'm fine now, that I'm a beast, that I'm still the same Jonas she knows and loves. But she doesn't seem to be on the verge of tears right now, not like she was earlier when I talked about Mariela and Miss Westbrook. She doesn't seem even remotely tempted to turn her back on me. She just seems oddly *fascinated,* and sympathetic, of course, but not particularly emotional.

"So, yada, yada, yada," I continue, "I didn't die—couldn't even do that right. I was surprisingly uninjured, in fact. A couple of broken ribs. A concussion. And when they pulled me out of the wreckage, I was so uncooperative, so out of my mind, so violent, they threw me into a juvie-psych facility on suicide watch. I don't know how long I was there. Could have been a week. Could have been a month. I really don't know. I just remember being tied up like fucking King Kong and thrashing around."

"How'd you get out?"

"Uncle William eventually got his lawyers on it. I got off with probation and restitution and involuntary psychiatric containment until I was eighteen. I guess my dad's suicide that same day and my prior medical history were considered 'extenuating circumstances.'"

Sarah looks at me intently, studying my face. She's totally unreadable to me right now. I pause. I keep thinking she's about to say something, but she doesn't.

"So is that everything?" she finally asks, her face somber.

I nod, scared to death of what she's going to say next. Is she going to leave me? Is she going to say she doesn't respect me anymore? That I'm not the man she thought I was? "Yes." I swallow hard.

"That's 'The Lunacy'?"

I nod again. I can hardly breathe.

She exhales loudly and smiles. *"That's* the big reveal? The dark and horrible secret that's going to make me run away screaming and never come back?"

I don't understand the smile on her face. Is she laughing at me?

"Well, yeah."

"You torched your daddy's fancy car collection, went on a joy ride in the prized Porsche he never let you touch, and then drove his car off a bridge in a desperate attempt to stop the pain that had tortured you relentlessly for ten years?"

Well, fuck. That's a gross over-simplification if I've ever heard one.

"That about sums it up, right?"

"Well, yeah. But, I mean, Sarah, maybe you don't understand. I had some sort of psychotic break that landed me in fucking restraints in a psych ward. That's kind of a big deal."

She shakes her head like she's chastising herself and crawls over to me on the bed. She takes my face in her hands. "I'm so sorry I tied you up, Jonas. I had no idea—"

"How could you know? Any normal guy would have been counting his lucky stars to get tied up by sexy little you." I shrug apologetically. "I'm sorry I'm not a normal guy."

She kisses me.

We're both quiet for a minute. My stomach is churning. I'm freaking out about whatever she's going to say next, but I wait.

She seems deep in thought.

179

I want to argue my case, tell her I'm all better now, that she can trust me—that I haven't had a major problem since I was seventeen— unless you count joining The Club for a year as a major problem, I guess—that I love her and would never harm her. But I don't speak. My thoughts are spinning out of control. Is she going to leave me? Does this change everything? Does she still love me?

"I thought you were about to tell me you punched a nun or threw a puppy off a cliff. I'm so effing relieved."

Relieved? I can't believe my ears. Maybe she doesn't understand everything I just told her. "Sarah, did you hear me? I crashed into parked cars, drove on the sidewalk. I easily could have killed a kid, a mother, some sweet old lady... and then I *purposefully* drove my car off a fucking bridge, laughing like a maniac the whole time. Did you hear any of that? I came this close to killing some innocent kid who happened to be standing on the sidewalk eating an ice cream cone."

"But you didn't."

"Only because I got lucky."

"Aha! That's the first time I've ever heard you describe yourself as lucky." She smiles broadly. "You see what just happened there? Life is nothing but the story you tell yourself in your own head. So instead of constantly telling yourself The Story of How Jonas Went to the Insane Asylum and Was at Fault for Every Goddamned Thing That Ever Happened to His Entire Family on an endless, self-defeating loop, change your story to The Story of How Jonas Got Super-Duper Lucky One Really Sucky Day."

My mouth hangs open. Why is she being so difficult? This stuff is horrible. Why can't she see that? "Sarah, I'm not sure you understand. I tried to kill myself mere hours after my father killed himself—Josh be damned. How could I even think of doing that to Josh? I was heartless. Selfish. Despicable."

"I think everything you did was perfectly understandable. Sad. Regrettable. Heartbreaking. Outrageous. Yes, pretty fucking crazy. But totally and completely understandable."

Mind officially blown. I shake my head. "No, Sarah. You're taking the 'understanding girlfriend' thing too far." She's just not getting it. I'm damaged. I'm worthless. "Here's something else you don't know: I'm told I punched the first guy who tried to pull me out of the Porsche in the water. I mean, talk about an asshole."

"Oh well, out of everything you've told me, that's the last straw. Sorry, baby, I'm outta here." She smiles.

"How are you so jovial about all this?"

"I'm not *jovial*." She exhales with obvious frustration. "That's not the right word." She squints at me.

I squint back. Why doesn't she get it? I'm hopelessly defective. Horrible. Worthless. Doesn't she understand what she's getting into if she stays with me? I'm not normal. At some point, I'm going to fuck this up. *Everything I touch turns to blood.*

"Are you happy?" she asks.

I pause. Is this a trick question?

"I mean are you happy with me?"

"Oh." Well, that's an easy one. "Yeah, of course. I'm happier with you than I've ever been in my whole life." Actually, happy isn't the right word for how I feel when I'm with her. "I'm beyond happy," I say. "I'm *crazy* happy. It's like I've got a serious mental disease or something." I grin sheepishly.

She grins back at me. "Same here. It's madness, I tell you." She twists her mouth to avoid a smirk. "So, considering my current state of madness, why the heck would I purposefully buy myself a big ol' steaming pile of wretched unhappiness, especially about something that happened thirteen years ago? Why wouldn't I just continue to be happy?"

I'm dumbfounded. I can't answer that question.

"Hmm?"

The woman makes a good point.

"And more importantly, why would *you* want to be anything other than crazy-happy? Wouldn't you just rather enjoy your happiness?"

I feel my lower lip trembling, so I bite it.

She cups my cheeks in her hands again. God, I love it when she does that. "Do you foresee trying to kill yourself again in the near future, love?"

I shake my head. "No. Never."

"Well, okay, then. Good." She drops her hands.

I wait but she doesn't say anything else.

But I'm confused. What does "good" mean? Is that all she's going to say? "So that's it?" I ask. "*Good?*"

She sighs. "Yeah. Good."

I'm incredulous.

She leans in and kisses me softly. "Jonas, failure isn't falling down—it's not getting back up. And you've gotten back up more than anyone I've ever known. I'm proud of you. I see your triumphs, not your failures. I see your goodness. And sweetness. And generosity of spirit. The beautiful kindness that glows inside of you. And I love you for all of it. Just like Mariela did. Just like Miss Westbrook did. Just like your mother did."

That last one makes my eyes water, so I close them. I'm blown away. Is she really going to make this so easy on me? So poetic? So beautiful? She's making me out to be a fucking hero?

"I do have one question, though."

Ah, here it comes. I nod, bracing myself.

"How did you get from Lunatic-Driving-Off-a-Bridge Jonas to Hunky-Monkey-Ass-Kicking-Sexy-Beast Jonas? How'd you get from there to here? I'm fascinated."

Shit. I bite the inside of my cheek, trying to figure out whether to tell her or avoid the topic altogether.

Sarah's eyes are patient. Warm. Curious.

"You really want to know?"

"Duh."

I don't like this part. I've never told anyone about this, not even Josh. All he knows is that I had some "treatments." I've never told him what finally made a huge difference for me. I pause.

"Was there some kind of turning point?" she asks. "Did you have some kind of epiphany? Something specific that helped you turn things around?"

Damn, my baby's nothing if not persistent. I nod.

"Well, what was it?"

I twist my mouth.

"Come on, Jonas. You can tell me anything."

I exhale.

"Come on, baby. Trust me."

Chapter 33
Jonas

My pulse pounds in my ears. Shit. I really don't want to tell her this. I know how bad it sounds. I know how much stigma is associated with this. But I've told her everything else, haven't I? I can't stop now. Fuck it.

"I got a whole bunch of ECT treatments," I say quietly. "Do you know what that is?"

She shakes her head.

"Electro-shock therapy."

She pauses. "You mean they shocked your *brain?* With electricity?"

I nod.

"Wow. That sounds barbaric."

"No, it wasn't like you think. It's not like *One Flew Over the Cuckoo's Nest.* They drug you first. I don't even remember it. It helped me."

"They did this to you when you were *seventeen?*"

"Yeah. I guess ECT is what they do to you when they've tried everything else."

"And that helped?"

"A lot. I don't know why, but it did. And then there was one additional piece of the puzzle. Something life-changing that happened right after my treatments were completed."

She's utterly captivated.

"On my eighteenth birthday, Josh sent me *The Republic* by Plato. His note said, 'I was forced to read this instrument of torture for Philosophy 101. I'd rather pry my fingernails off with rusty pliers than read it ever again. You're gonna love it, bro. Enjoy.' And he was right. I loved it. It introduced me to philosophy for the first time and got me reading everything—Locke, Descartes, Aristotle, Heraclitis, Nietzsche, Sen, Camus, Santayana, whoever. But, in the end, I kept going back to Plato. He was the forefather of modern thought—the one who inspired me to visualize the divine originals and conquer myself. 'For a man to conquer himself is the first and noblest of all victories.'" I exhale. "Are you sure you want to hear all this?"

"Are you *crazy*?" She laughs. "Of course, I do. I'm hanging on your every word."

I pause.

"Come on, Jonas. Continue. I love hearing about this stuff."

I exhale. "All my treatments were over. All charges against me had been expunged from my record thanks to me being a minor. Josh was at UCLA and Uncle William was busy trying to keep the company afloat after my father's death. So I just said, *Fuck yeah, Plato, let's do this shit.* I threw on a backpack and went to visit Plato in Greece—which is where I got my tattoos, by the way—and from there, I traveled all over Europe, wherever the fuck I wanted, all by myself. I climbed, hiked, explored, whatever. I listened to music and read my books and just figured my shit out."

"Oh, come on, Jonas—that's all you did? Climbed, hiked, and read your books? I'm sure you did a little something else, too." She smirks. "I bet all the horny college girls backpacking through Europe went crazy for eighteen-year-old Jonas Faraday with the shy smile and sad eyes."

Leave it to Sarah. Nothing gets past her. Yes, she's exactly right—I've left one particular activity out of my narrative. That trip was when I first got the inkling women might be especially attracted to me compared to the next guy hiking the trail or sitting at the bar. As long as I didn't blow it by being Creepy Jonas or Intense Jonas or Antisocial Jonas or Philosophical Jonas or Asshole Jonas or, God forbid, Crazy-Eyes Jonas, girls actually seemed pretty interested in me—though not being one of those aforementioned Jonases almost always took a lot out of me.

And on those rare and fucking awesome days when Charming Jonas randomly decided to show up, or at least Shy Jonas or Awkward Jonas, I couldn't miss. On those occasions, as few and far between as they were, getting girls was like shooting ducks in a barrel—I had my pick of any young woman on the youth hostel circuit.

"Yeah," I say, blushing. "I learned how much I thoroughly enjoy sex on that trip. That was when I lost my virginity, actually." I can't help but smile broadly. Sex with that pretty Swedish girl wasn't objectively all that great, really, but a guy never forgets finally getting to use his cock as nature intended for the first time in his life.

"I feel like cheering for eighteen-year-old Jonas and throwing confetti on him. That poor boy deserved to have a little carefree fun, don't you think?"

"Yes, I do. And he did."

She laughs.

Why was I so nervous about telling her all of this? She's so damned easy to talk to, so nonjudgmental. The woman is flat-out *kind*. Why didn't I have faith in her?

"Interesting factoid discovered by eighteen-year-old Jonas, though. Most girls don't like dudes who are creepy and intense."

"Really?" She's aghast. "Wait a minute—are you sure?"

"It's true. They run away, their arms flailing."

She laughs. "Well, those girls were all idiots, then. I happen to know it's the creepy and intense guys who make the best lovers." She winks.

I feel like the weight of the world's been lifted off me. "Well, not necessarily. I hadn't quite figured out the *sexcellence* thing yet. Not by a long shot." I laugh again. "I was like a frantic dog with a bone."

"Well, you *were* just a puppy, after all."

"Yeah, a puppy with a big ol' hard-on."

She laughs.

"A big ol hard-on and huge paws and a big ol' tail that knocked drinks off coffee tables."

"Are you sure it was your *tail* knocking those drinks off coffee tables, big boy?"

I laugh. God, I love her.

"So, okay. You weren't quite the woman wizard at age eighteen."

"Not quite. I'm pretty sure I thought the female orgasm was a myth propagated by the porn industry."

Lauren Rowe

She smiles broadly.

"Now, Josh, on the other hand, he was fantastic with girls—or, at least, compared to me. When school got out for the summer, Josh met me in Thailand so we could climb Crazy Horse—which is so fucking awesome, by the way, I can't wait to take you there—and then we traveled together for like ten weeks, climbing and hiking and partying and, you know." I grin broadly. "Fishing."

She knows what kind of fishing I'm talking about. "So Josh taught you how to get the girls?"

I laugh heartily. "The guy was my Obi Wan Kenobi. Before Josh showed up, the only strategy I'd formulated for catching fish was sitting in my boat, all alone, without any gear—basically trying not to come off like a serial killer—and *praying* a pretty fish might by chance leap out of the water and flop right into my lap."

She laughs. "Oh, Jonas."

"And, occasionally, a fish did—lucky me. But Josh? That boy had skills. He could do this revolutionary thing—he could *lure* the fish into his boat with an actual fishing rod and *bait*."

Her face is glowing. "What was Josh's bait?"

"Check this out. He *talked* to the fish. Pretty good, huh?"

She laughs. "What? That's crazy. He should write a book."

"Oh, and he taught me the simple art of buying a girl a *drink*. You know, being a gentleman. Being attentive. *Smiling*. Insane stuff."

"He was a woman wizard in training, sounds like."

I laugh. "Definitely."

I'm amazed. I never in a million years thought Sarah and I would be laughing during a conversation about The Lunacy. I thought we'd be crying—or that I'd be begging, apologizing, reassuring. But laughing? Never.

"You should have seen Josh in action. He was Mr. Smooth—or at least eighteen-year-old Jonas thought so. Josh would always say, 'Jonas, just shut the fuck up and look pretty, okay? Your job is to be the dew-covered web that attracts the girls—*you're the something shiny*—and my job is to be the *spider* who lies in wait and bites their legs off before they know what hit 'em.'"

She bursts out laughing and I join her, yet again.

"So, to answer your initial question, that's when everything started turning around for me—when Josh dragged me all over

Kingdom Come in search of big rocks and pretty girls to climb.
That's when I started to glimpse the divine original form of Jonas
Faraday-ness for the first time in my life, however dim and blurry the
image might have been back then."

"Where'd you guys go besides Thailand?"

"Well, I'd already done pretty much all of Europe by myself. So
with Josh, it was Asia, Australia, New Zealand, and then a little bit of
Central America on the way home. Actually, that's the first time I
went to Belize—on that trip with Josh."

The mere mention of Belize is enough to make Sarah's face light
up. "Belize," she says, sighing dreamily.

It suddenly strikes me, full force, how much my little caterpillar
has transformed since we first huddled together in our Belizian
cocoon-built-for-two. I thought I loved her then, and I did, in my own
way, but my love was a shallow pool compared to the limitless ocean
I feel for her now.

"Belize was just the beginning, my precious baby. I'm gonna
show you the world."

Her face bursts with excitement.

"Wherever you want to go, we'll go. You name it."

She squeals. "Oh, Jonas. Thank you."

God, I love this woman. Why was I so afraid to talk to her about
this stuff? This entire conversation has felt so *right*. This woman
loves me. My skin feels electrified. *She loves me.*

"So, what happened once you got home?"

I'm reeling. I can't concentrate. She loves me, despite
everything—and maybe even *because* of everything. She's told me
she loves me many times by now, of course, but this is the first time
I've believed it. *She loves me.* All of me. The real me. Not the pretend
me. Not some ridiculous projection of me. *Me.* For better or worse.

"Jonas, what happened when you got home?"

"Um." I smile at her. Damn, she's beautiful.

She raises an eyebrow. "Are you okay?"

"Yeah, I'm great, baby. Never better. Uh, Josh went back for his
second year at UCLA. I went off to Gonzaga and later down to
Berkeley for my MBA, and when Josh and I finished all our fancy
degrees, I took over Faraday & Sons in Seattle, Josh started the L.A.
branch, and Uncle William moved to New York to start a satellite

office out there. And that's when the company took off like a fucking rocket, beyond anything we'd imagined." I pause. I can't think of anything else to say on this topic. "And-now-I'm-here-with-you-in-Las-Vegas-and-I'm-totally-normal-in-every-conceivable-way-and-I-want-to-be-inside-you-more-than-I-want-to-breathe. The End."

She smiles but doesn't speak, as if she expects me to continue.

"The End," I say again. I put up my hands like I'm saying *ta-da*. "Jazz hands."

She laughs.

Sunlight streams through the window and illuminates Sarah's face. She looks beautiful—sleepy, but beautiful. I glance out the window at The Strip below us and sigh. I hate this hellish place. I miss Seattle. I miss the rain. I miss my crisp white sheets and my home gym and my espresso machine. I want to go home and start building Climb and Conquer into the vision I've got in my head. And most of all, more than anything else, I want to start my life with Sarah.

"The dawn of a new day," she says, following my gaze out the window. "Darkness, be gone." She crawls across the bed and drapes her body around mine. "I know how you love your metaphors, baby, so let this beautiful dawn inspire you. Let there be light in your life from this day forward, filling the nooks and crannies you've previously kept shrouded in darkness."

She's speaking my language. "You're a poet," I say.

"Only with you."

"How are you not fazed by everything I've told you?"

She shrugs. "I dunno."

"But seriously," I say, blood rushing into my face. "If there's something you want to say to me—something you're thinking, anything at all—just say it now. Please. Rip off the Band-Aid. I can take it."

She shakes her head. "Oh, Jonas, come on. It was thirteen years ago. Give yourself a frickin' break already—and give me some credit."

"You're not worried I might be a total lunatic?"

"I already *know* you're a total lunatic."

I wait for her to smile, but she doesn't.

"Jonas, I've known from minute one, from the second I read

your application, that you're a wee bit crazy. Duh. But I like your crazy, baby. It makes you sexy."

I'm utterly speechless.

"What happened back then doesn't define you. Has it shaped you? Yes, of course. But that's all. You're my sweet Jonas, no matter what happened then. You're the Jonas who spoke in front of my contracts class—brilliant and charming and intelligent and charismatic. You're the Jonas who caught me after I leaped off a thirty-foot waterfall. You're the Jonas who looked shy and sweet and awkward as he tied a friendship bracelet around my wrist. The guy who sent me Oreos to welcome me into the Jonas Faraday Club. The divine original form of man-ness who makes me come every single time you touch me, baby, even in my dreams."

That last one makes my cock tingle.

She kisses me. "Baby, you're the Jonas who unleashed Orgasma the All-Powerful." She nips at my lips and straddles my lap. "You're the man who saved my life—who gave me everything I needed to save myself and then literally stopped my bleeding with his bare hands." She skims her lips on mine. "And you're the man who's gonna kick some bad-guy ass with me." She licks at my lips. "You'd have to strangle a kitten or kick a girl scout in the teeth for me to run away from *that* guy."

My smile stretches so big across my face, I can't even kiss her.

"It was thirteen frickin' years ago, love. Time to give it a rest. *No más. De hoy en adelante, renaces.*"

Damn. My Spanish is pretty good, but not perfect. I got most of that, I think, but I'm not positive.

"No more," she translates, reading my mind. "From today forward, you are reborn." She grinds herself into my hard-on. "*Renaces—*you are reborn. *Renazco—*I am reborn." She kisses my neck.

I shiver. I love it when Sarah speaks Spanish to me, especially when she says something badass like that. "*Renazco,*" I repeat after her.

She kisses my cheek. "*No más. De hoy en adelante, renazco.*"

"*No más. De hoy en adelante, renazco,*" I repeat—but when I say it, it sounds clunky compared to the beautiful way Sarah says it.

"That's right. Exactly right. You're reborn, baby. From this day forward."

I pull at her tank top and she rips it off, followed quickly by her pajama bottoms. I follow her lead, kicking off my boxers, and then I climb on top of her, my heart racing.

She holds my face in her hands. "There are no more dark spaces between us, Jonas, no more secrets. Can you feel the difference?"

I nod. I can. Oh God, I want to be inside her.

She kisses me. "This is how it feels to trust someone completely. Do you understand?"

I nod because, yes, I understand what she's saying. But if it were up to me, I'd have phrased it slightly differently: This is how it feels to be *loved* by someone completely.

Before now, I didn't know how to let Sarah love me, not completely. Before this very moment, I didn't understand how much I'd been holding back and pushing her away. *I* knew how to love *her*—God knows I've loved this woman with all my heart and soul since she leaped off that waterfall into my arms, and maybe even before then—but, as much as I've loved her, I haven't been willing to leap off a waterfall and let her love me back. Until now.

I reach between her legs, eager to touch the part of her that's only for me, and when I feel how wet she is, oh my God, I practically leap out of my skin. I bring my finger up to my mouth to sneak a taste of her deliciousness. There's no sweeter flavor in the world than my baby's wetness and no sweeter moment than right now.

I kiss her mouth and massage her clit with my fingertip, my cock throbbing at the slippery texture of her, the slickness, the delicious hardness, and she shudders and bucks. My hard-on strains mercilessly for her, but I force myself to take my time. We've got all the time in the world, after all—I'm not going anywhere, and neither is she.

I reach deep inside her and massage her G-spot, and she jolts.

"My precious baby," I whisper, touching that magic spot again, and she moans. She's my Stradivarius—and there's no greater pleasure in the world than making her strings quiver. My fingers find her clit again, and she writhes. I can't wait anymore. I slip inside her, all the way, groaning loudly, and she lets out a long, quavering sigh in return.

This is a new feeling for me, a new holy grail—making love to the woman I love with no secrets, no dark places, and no doubt. Standing on top of Mount Everest itself couldn't possibly feel this good. *She loves me.* All of me. Even the fucked up parts.

She gyrates her hips in rhythm with mine and wraps her legs around my back.

"The culmination of human possibility," I groan, my body thrusting in and out of hers.

"Yes," she breathes. "Jonas."

She *loves* me. She *enlightens* me. She *graces* me. She *redeems* me.

A wave of pleasure rises up inside me, threatening to push me over the edge.

"Get on top," I say suddenly. "I need to look at you."

We maneuver until she's riding me, licking her lips, touching herself. I sit back and enjoy the view of her breasts softly bouncing, the curve of her hips, the fall of her hair around her shoulders. I love watching her control how deep, how fast, what angle. It turns me on like a motherfucker when she leans forward and rubs my hard cock against her clit or positions herself so that my tip touches some precise spot deep inside her. It's glorious to witness how well she's learned herself by now, how beautifully she knows exactly what to do to get herself off. What a transformation since day one. Jesus.

I grab her ass and let my palms go along for the magnificent ride. "I love this ass," I groan, clutching her. My fingers migrate greedily to explore every crevice of her and she shudders.

I run my hands up her smooth back and around to her breasts and then let my thumb glide over her angry scar. It's healing quickly. I peek down at her tiny tattoo, her secret proclamation of badassery, and shiver. Holy fuck, I love her. Sheer joy washes over me, palpably, like I've been doused with it from a bucket over my head. *I'm going to marry this girl,* I think. I know this as surely as I know my own name. *I'm going to marry this gorgeous girl and make her my wife.*

I can't hold on much longer. I'm right on the edge.

"Jonas," she breathes, trying to catch her breath. "Oh, oh, oh."

"Love is the joy of the good, the wonder of the wise, the amazement of the gods," I whisper, my voice halting and straining, and she throws her head back.

She makes The Sound. It means I'm about to be the lucky, lucky boy who's going to feel her orgasm from the inside out if I can just hang on a tiny bit longer.

I touch her clit with supreme devotion and she gasps.

"You're gorgeous, baby," I say, stroking her, luring her, doing my damnedest to push her over the edge. Oh fuck, I crave her release as badly as she does. "You're Orgasma the fucking All-Powerful, baby," I say, trembling, and her entire body quivers. "You're the goddess and the muse, Sarah Cruz." I buck wildly underneath her, trying to hang on. *And I'm going to marry you.*

Chapter 34
Sarah

Fifteen minutes ago, Henn texted an "all hands on desk" message to everyone. "I hit the motherlode!" Henn wrote. And the whole group, except for Jonas, quickly congregated in our suite to hear Henn's news.

"Will Jonas be joining us?" Henn asks. "Should we wait for him?"

"No, don't wait. He went to the gym first thing this morning," I say. "I don't know when he'll be back."

Jonas practically leaped out of bed this morning after our marathon conversation and delicious lovemaking session, saying he wanted to "hit the gym and then run an errand"—but he wouldn't tell me anything more than that.

"You're not going to do something stupid, are you, Jonas?" I asked, looking at him sideways, my heart suddenly pounding in my ears.

"Of course not," he said, his face the picture of pure innocence.

"Seriously, Jonas. You need to tell me—you're not going to hunt down Max, are you?"

He pulled me to him. "No, although the idea of killing that fucker gives me a hard-on. I've got my eye on the prize, baby. Don't worry." He grabbed my ass and nibbled my neck. "Just running an errand."

But I wasn't convinced.

He cupped my face in his hands. "I won't go off plan."

"You promise?" I asked.

"I promise."

I breathed a huge sigh of relief. Jonas never, ever falsely promises anything.

He kissed me, making my entire body melt into his. "I'll tell you about the errand when I get back. See you in a couple hours, My Magnificent Sarah." He practically skipped out the front door.

And now, Kat, Josh and I are huddled on the leather couches in the living area of the suite, staring with nervous anticipation at Henn, who looks like his eyes might pop out of his head with excitement.

Henn lets out an excited breath. "Okay." He pauses for effect. "Are you sitting down?" It's a rhetorical question—we're all sitting down right in front of him.

We hold our collective breath.

"I found 'em—and I got in."

I gasp.

"Oh my God," Kat says.

"You're a fucking genius," Josh adds.

"I *am* a fucking genius," Henn says. "I've got the keys to their whole fucking kingdom—member lists, passwords, emails, code. I'm in."

We all express noisy excitement.

Just when Henn is about to tell us something further that's going to "melt our faces off," as he puts it, Jonas bursts into the suite in his workout clothes and a sweatshirt, his hair matted with sweat. "Hey, guys. I just got your text, Henn. Please tell me you did it."

"I did it."

Jonas bounds across the room, bro-hugs Henn, high-fives Josh and Kat, and then swoops me up into a celebratory hug.

"Did you get your errand done?"

He smiles broadly and nods. "I'll show you later."

Show me?

"What'd I miss?" Jonas asks.

"Nothing yet. Perfect timing," I say. "Henn was just about to tell us something that's going to 'melt our faces off.'"

"The money?" Jonas asks. "Please tell us you cracked the money."

"I cracked the money."

"Oh my God, Henn," Kat says. "You're a fucking genius." She flashes Henn a huge smile and he beams at her.

"I've tracked down twelve different bank accounts in five different banks," Henn begins. He pauses for dramatic effect. "Jonas, you're gonna want to sit down for this next part."

194

Jonas sits next to me and puts his hand on my thigh.

"Twelve different bank accounts and they've got *cash*—I'm talkin' *cash* just sitting in the bank—totaling, oh, about five hundred fifty-four *million* dollars."

The collective reaction of the group blows the roof off the suite.

I put my face in my hands. I can't wrap my head around this.

"And I've got all their account numbers and passwords," Henn says, smirking. "For several of the larger accounts, transfers are set up for in-person banking only—and most banks require a signature to make transfers over a million, anyway—so I don't think we should get our sights set on grabbing the actual money. We'll just plan on handing over all the account numbers and passwords."

I look over at Jonas. He's deep in thought. "Can you get me printouts showing all the accounts and the balances in each?"

"Sure thing," Henn says. "I can do anything."

"This is unbelievable," Josh says. He looks at Kat, incredulous, and she returns his amazement.

"What about the member list?" I ask.

"Oh, well, that's the second piece of big news," Henn says. "That's the part that's gonna blow your minds."

"Five hundred fifty-four million bucks isn't mind blowing?" I ask.

"Nope." He pauses yet again, a master storyteller. "I've confirmed, with documentary proof, no doubt about it, you can stake your life on it, the member list includes seven U.S. congressmen, two state governors, a Canadian mayor, and . . ." He pauses like he's waiting on a drumroll. "*The fucking Secretary of Defense.*"

Everyone expresses simultaneous shock.

"The dude in charge of the entire U.S. Department of Defense—like, the guy who runs the entire fucking military."

"And sits on the President's cabinet," Jonas adds, his face pale.

Intense panic overtakes me. I feel my heart skip a beat.

Jonas rubs his face. "Shit," he mutters softly.

"Shit is right. Holy fucking shit," Josh says.

We're all silent for a moment, processing this new bit of information.

My heart is quite literally palpitating. "This is gonna be a huge *scandal*," I say. I know that's obvious and I sound like a simpleton right now, but it's all I can muster.

Henn nods furiously. "Insanity, right? The *Secretary of Defense* pays money to a sex club that supplies money and weapons to aid Russian imperialism." He snorts. "Oopsies."

"Not great for the guy's future prospects in politics," Josh adds.

"Not something he'd want to get out," Jonas says darkly.

Holy Baby Jesus in a manger. We're about to unleash a scandal onto the world of epic proportions—information that will surely rock the highest levels of government, all the way to the White House itself. I have no interest in toppling the Secretary of Defense—not to mention various congressmen and governors—or, hell, athletes and CEOs and everyday software engineers, either. And I certainly have zero interest in splattering incidental mud onto the President of the United States. Holy hell.

"When this gets out about the Secretary of Defense, I wonder if it's gonna cause a problem for the President?" Kat asks, reading my mind.

"Of course. The Secretary of Defense sits on the President's cabinet," Josh says. "He's in the inner circle. A guy like that being involved in a large-scale prostitution ring is scandalous all by itself—the press is gonna have a holier-than-thou field day with that little nugget—but add the fact that the guy's been indirectly funding the Ukrainian separatists, and that's the kind of shit that explodes like a political grenade on anyone within spitting distance of the guy—including the President."

"I'm freaking out," I mumble. I look at Jonas and Josh. "What about you two? How bad is this gonna be for you when all of this comes out?"

Jonas and Josh look at each other. "I don't know," Josh answers. He shrugs. "It won't be a shining moment for either of us, I'm sure."

I look down, suddenly nauseated. Josh might suffer minor embarrassment, but Jonas is the one who'll take the lion's share of the heat. Josh joined The Club for a month, after all, while Jonas paid two hundred fifty thousand bucks for a full year's gluttonous membership. Will this scandal obliterate Jonas' reputation in the business community? Will it affect his ability to build Climb and Conquer into the global brand he envisions?

And what about me? In two years, when I graduate from school and the Washington bar processes my application for a law license, will I be able to pass the ethics review? Will they believe me when I swear I didn't know the true nature of my employer?

Jonas squeezes my hand. "We'll just have to figure this out one day at a time. Maybe we can come up with a solution where none of this gets out."

I'm doubtful about that. "How?"

"Leave that part to me and Josh," Jonas says. He looks at his brother for confirmation.

Josh nods decisively, but the look in Josh's eyes doesn't instill confidence.

After a lengthy discussion during which everyone in the room basically shits a brick and says this is way too big for us to handle on our own and oh my God how did we get here and what the fuck are we going to do, we finally decide on an immediate strategy: I'll finish my report *today* with as much supporting evidence as we can put together in such a short amount of time, including printouts showing the balances in The Club's many bank accounts, Josh and Jonas will put their heads together about our strategy for submitting my report to the proper authorities, and then first thing tomorrow morning, we'll all traipse down to the Las Vegas branch of the FBI and do our best to convince whoever the heck is in charge over there to arrange a meeting with his or her boss in Washington, D.C. What else can we do? This is too big for us to sit on any longer than absolutely necessary and way too big for us to handle without backup from some pretty big guns. Not to mention, we're all paranoid The Club might transfer some or all of their funds out of our reach at any moment.

Just as everyone begins hunkering down to get to work, Jonas pulls me aside.

"I'm all sweaty from the gym," he says, his hands in the pockets of his hoodie. "I'm gonna take a quick shower. Will you join me? I wanna show you something."

He wants to show me something, huh? I'm sure he does. I'm never one to turn down a shower with Jonas, God knows, but a shower right now seems like a waste of valuable time. I've got to get this report completed—and he's got to figure out what the heck we're going to do with it. "I'll take a rain check," I say. "That's how we'll celebrate getting the report done."

He looks disappointed.

"Something to look forward to," I add. Honestly, I'm surprised

197

he's chosen this moment to think about shower sex. I love it, too, but come on—we've got bigger fish to fry.

"Sarah," Kat calls. "Henn's got the bank printouts ready. What part of the exhibit log do you want to attach it to?"

"Yeah, just a sec." I look at Jonas again. He looks like a dorky kid not picked for dodge ball. "Later, baby," I assure him. And then I walk across the room to answer Kat's question.

Chapter 35
Sarah

It's three in the morning and everyone on the team looks half dead. We've been cooped up all day and night together in the suite, barely talking, barely stopping to eat. Every single one of us understands the magnitude of what we're trying to do here—and the potential stakes if we fail. The hard work and long hours have paid off, though, because my report is done. Hallelujah. And it's pretty damned good.

Sure, I could keep writing for another three weeks if I had the time to write my report as thoroughly as I'd like, but time is of the essence and this will have to do. I've outlined the facts, the law, and the evidence as best I can and attached a corresponding exhibit log with proof of every single fact I've proffered. Nothing is speculation. Nothing is guesswork. Nothing is subject to debate. If this report doesn't get the FBI's attention, then I don't know what will.

Josh and Kat leave the suite together, both saying they're off to "get some sleep," ostensibly in their respective hotel rooms (but I'm not so sure). I'm beginning to suspect those two have become more than friends while we've been here in Vegas. I'll have to ask Kat about that tomorrow. Today, I was too obsessed with our mission to veer off track into thinking about anything but that report.

After Josh and Kat have left, Henn calls me over to his computer. I'd asked him to search through The Club's system for one more piece of evidence—something establishing a nexus between the names used during the application process and the codes assigned to member files post-application.

"Will this work?" he asks, his voice weary.

I stand behind him and look at his screen over his shoulder.

He explains the information he's called to his screen.

"Yeah, that's perfect," I say. "Thanks, Henn. I just think we've got to be ultra-clear about everything. No assumptions—no leaps of logic required."

Henn agrees.

Jonas sits quietly in the corner of the room, watching me with burning eyes and tense muscles.

"Jonas, do you want to take a look at this?" I ask.

He shakes his head.

Oh. I know that look. I bite my lip. My hunky-monkey boyfriend is sitting there with a hard-on right now.

"Thanks, Henn. You're a fucking genius," I say.

"So I've been told," he says. He grins and closes his laptop ceremoniously. "Okay, well, if that's all you need, then I'll head out. I've got a sudden intuition I should pull the lever on the one-hundred-dollar slot machine exactly seven times before I go to beddy-bye."

"Good luck," I say. "See you at ten." That's when the whole group's reconvening to head over to the Las Vegas branch of the FBI.

The moment the door closes on Henn, I turn to Jonas. "Will you accept that shower-sex rain check now?" I ask.

He nods slowly. Damn, he's a good-lookin' man.

I stride over to him in the corner, exhausted but excited at everything we accomplished today, and sit on his lap. Oh, hello there. Yup. Jonas is as hard as a rock. I run my fingertips over the engraving on the face of his platinum bracelet. *Sarah.*

"Hi, boyfriend," I say softly.

He smiles and touches my bracelet in return. "Hi, girlfriend." He pulls my face to his and kisses me deeply.

I run my hands over the fabric of his long-sleeved knit shirt, reveling in the feel of his broad chest and sculpted shoulders. I'll never grow tired of touching him. He's a work of art. I move on to his powerful biceps and then to his forearms—and my fingertips detect a different texture underneath his shirt than skin. I poke at the thin fabric above his right forearm. Yes, there's definitely something underneath there besides skin.

"What's under there?"

"My errand," he says, smiling. "What I've been dying to show you." He pulls off his shirt to reveal his glorious chest and abs and sculpted shoulders and bulging biceps—as well as thick, rectangular swaths of medical gauze taped to the tops of his forearms.

"What happened to you?" I ask. But then it hits me. "You got new *tattoos*?"

He smiles broadly.

I'm intrigued. In Belize I asked him if he'd ever thought about getting more ink—especially since he got his sacred Platonic tattoos so long ago—and he said no. "I don't need to tat myself up just for the sake of it," he said. "I'm only interested in marking my skin with ideas that are life-changing and worthy of eternity. Whose ideas besides Plato's could ever live up to that?"

Well, well, well—famous last words. I wonder what new idea suddenly became "life-changing and worthy of eternity" enough for him now?

He picks at the corner of the tape on his right forearm and rips off the bandage with a loud "Ow."

I hold up his arm to get a good look, and when I gasp, his face lights up. I read aloud, tears springing into my eyes, "*No más. De hoy en adelante, renazco.*" These are the words I said to Jonas last night. Oh my God. *My* words are life-changing and worthy of eternity? Tears pool in my eyes.

"*Renazco,*" he says softly, staring into my eyes. "I am reborn, My Magnificent Sarah, thanks to you." He looks shy for a moment, mustering the courage to say whatever's on the tip of his tongue. "*Mi amor siempre,*" he whispers. *My love forever.*

Oh, Jonas. I can't believe he's given *my* words equal billing with Plato's on his body. For eternity. I rearrange myself on his lap and straddle him. "*Mi amor siempre,*" I whisper, kissing him softly.

He returns my kiss deeply, and, just like that, I'm crazy-pants hot and ready to go. But there's a bandage on his other arm, too, of course, and I've got to know what lies beneath. I force myself to pull away from our kiss, though the feeling of his erection poking against my panties is driving me crazy.

"What about that one?" I point to the bandage on his left arm.

He smiles mischievously and begins picking at the corner of the tape.

When the bandage is off, he holds up his arm across his chest to give me a right-side-up view. I can't believe my eyes. The phrase is in English and easily readable by anyone who happens to glance at it.

But that makes no sense—Jonas once told me he'd purposefully gotten his tattoos in ancient Greek because he emphatically did *not* want casual passersby to know what they said. "My tattoos are there to inspire *me*, not the masses," he said. Well, it looks like Jonas Faraday has had a change of heart—on a lot of things, actually.

I read the bold English lettering aloud, this time with a quavering voice. "Love is the joy of the good, the wonder of the wise, the amazement of the gods."

He nods emphatically.

I recall Jonas saying this phrase to me, twice, I think, but both times when we were making love and I was too busy having an orgasm to ask him about it.

"Is it Plato?" I ask, running my fingers over the letters.

He nods. "Plato attributes it to the poet Agathon. It's from Plato's *Symposium*—Plato's lengthy dialogue on the nature, purpose, and genesis of love. *Romantic* love, specifically."

I bite my lip.

"According to Plato, romantic love is initially *felt* with our physical senses, but with contemplation, it transforms into something greater: the soul's appreciation of the beauty within another person."

My heart skips a beat.

"Ultimately, it's through love that our souls are able to recognize the ideal form of beauty—the divine original form of beauty itself." His eyes are on fire. "Which, in turn, leads us to understand the *truth*."

I place my hand over my heart to steady myself. "But Jonas." I'm reeling. "Plato in *English*? Not ancient Greek?"

He nods.

"I thought you didn't want people to understand your tattoos."

"This one, I do."

I hold my breath.

"Plato might have written these wise and sacred words thousands of years ago—but Jonas Faraday is declaring them today."

"Oh, Jonas," I breathe.

"With this tattoo, I'm shouting about my love for you from the top of the highest mountaintop, Sarah. I want the whole world to read it and know the truth—*I love Sarah Cruz*."

I'm melting.

He cups my face in his large hands. "Love is the joy of the good, the wonder of the wise, the amazement of the gods." His eyes are fierce. "That means you, Sarah Cruz. You and me. You're my beauty. You're my truth."

My heart is racing.

"There's never been a love like ours and there never will be again. We're the greatest love story ever told."

I can't believe the man who once professed his disdain for "Valentine's Day bullshit" has turned out to be the most romantic man in the world. I bite my lip.

"We're epic," he says, his eyes burning. "Our love is so pure and true, we're the amazement of the gods."

Who talks like this? Jonas Faraday, that's who. God, I love this man.

He's got that look in his eye—his patented Jonas-is-a-great-white-shark-and-Sarah-is-a-defenseless-sea-lion look. It's the gleam that means he's about to swallow me whole. He kisses me deeply and that's all she wrote—we're both suddenly crazed. He tugs urgently on my shirt and I lift my arms over my head to help him out. He unlatches and removes my bra and sucks at my nipples voraciously the minute my breasts are freed.

"Shower," I gasp, my body writhing with arousal.

He stands, pulling me up with him by my ass. I throw my arms around his neck and my legs around his waist and kiss him fervently, grinding myself into him, attacking him, inhaling him, as he carries my writhing body into the bedroom. He throws me down on the bed and rips off my pants and G-string—holy shit, he *literally* rips my G-string off my body—and then he buries his face between my legs in a frenzy of ravenous animalistic greed. There's no buildup, no finesse, no slow burn. There's no such thing as *sexcellence* this time around, folks. This right here is nothing but a shark tearing into his prey—and it's turning me the fuck on.

When he stands back up licking his lips, he's Incredible Hulk Jonas. A beast. The poet is gone. The romantic is gone. He pulls down his pants and briefs, giving me the view of him that never gets old, and before I can do a damned thing, he scoops me up like a rag doll and carries me to the bathroom, kissing me hungrily all the while.

I grab fistfuls of his hair in both my hands as I kiss him, and he grunts like a gorilla. Oh God, I love that primal sound he makes. He turns the water on behind my back as I writhe around, kissing him and yanking on his hair. Hot water pelts me in the back and cascades down my breasts. I try in vain to slam myself onto his erection, but he evades me.

"Let me down," I say, but I don't wait for his reply to slide down his slick, wet skin to my feet.

"I'm in charge," he says, his voice firm.

But I'm not listening. I get down on my knees and take him into my mouth, sucking on him enthusiastically, as hot water pounds the back of my head. He grabs fistfuls of my hair and gyrates into my mouth, groaning like I'm causing him extreme pain. Oh God, it turns me on to do this. He makes a sound like he's dying—of happiness, of course—and I reach down and touch myself, thinking about the look on Jonas' face when he showed me his new tattoos.

He shudders and growls and grips my hair harder than he ever has—but I don't care about a little discomfort to my scalp, not when I'm making him feel this good. Oh God, I can barely breathe, I'm so turned on. I continue touching myself, sucking on him, visualizing his new tattoos. Jonas engraved *my* words alongside Plato's. He declared his eternal love for me permanently onto his skin, in English, for the whole world to see.

My eyes spring open. My dream. The ten poltergeist Jonases, the dripping wine, the noisy spectators—*and Jonas looking up and declaring his love for me to the entire world.* Oh my God. My dream wasn't about *sexual* exhibitionism—it was about *emotional* exhibitionism—about me wanting Jonas to claim me in front of the entire world. Oh my God, with his new tattoos, Jonas has done just that.

My entire body seizes with a powerful orgasm and I moan loudly (though the sound is stifled somewhat by the vast amounts of penis down my throat). I yelp, trying my damnedest to continue sucking on him as my body ripples from within, but I can't do it.

He pulls out of my mouth. "I'm gonna fuck you, baby," he says.

My orgasm finishes. What did he just say? Hot water pelts my face as I look up at him, in a daze of satisfaction.

"Me," he says, caveman-style, pulling me up off my knees. "Now." His voice is raw. He's in charge. "I'm gonna fuck you."

He pulls me roughly to him, his eyes blazing, and touches me between my legs. I buckle. Oh wow, I'm not done—not by a long shot—I'm still totally turned on. He turns my body around away from him and I passively follow his nonverbal command.

"Bend over," he grunts in my ear. "Bend over and grab your ankles."

I have no thought in my head but to do his bidding—my desire for control is totally gone. I bend over and grasp my ankles. Holy hell, I'm utterly exposed and at his mercy in this position. I shift my grip on my ankles and shudder with anticipation.

One of his hands rubs my back as his other one reaches between my legs from behind and works my clit. He's aiming for another orgasm from me, obviously, and, oh my God, he's gonna get it. Hot water cascades down my back and gushes over my dangling face. I tremble with anticipation. What's he waiting for? My legs buckle and he steadies me.

His fingers are working me too well. The sensation is too intense. I can't remain in this position anymore if he's going to keep touching me like this—I can't maintain my balance while feeling so much pleasure. I bend my legs. I'm too turned on to stay bent over like this. I need to gyrate my body, to rub myself against him, to kiss him. I can't take it anymore. I need a release.

He enters my wetness without warning—and so deeply, so forcefully, and with such unapologetic ownership of my body, I scream—and, much to my surprise, I come, too, instantly.

Jonas thrusts mercilessly in and out of me as I climax, roaring loudly as he does, and in under a minute, he climaxes too, from deep, deep, deep, deep inside me, bellowing as he does. I shriek in reply. Oh man, we're loud. I love us.

When he's done, he presses his palm firmly into my upper back, signaling me to stay put. I do as I'm told, yet again. He pulls out of me and places the showerhead between my legs.

My entire body vibrates along with the warm stream of water pelting my sweet spot. It feels so damned good, I wobble forward, losing my balance, but he steadies me with a sure hand on my hip. I place my palms on the shower floor and he continues cleaning me between my legs, slowly lathering me with shower gel and then letting warm, pulsing water batter me deliciously.

I'm on the cusp of yet another orgasm. Oh my God, I've got to stand. I can't do this anymore. Blood has rushed into my dangling head and now pulses relentlessly in my ears and eyes. And, jeez, I'm drowning, too, from water cascading down my back and into my nose.

But before I can stand, Jonas kneels down behind my bent-over body and begins lapping at me ferociously—indiscriminately tasting every square inch of real estate back there, his mouth and tongue devouring every part of me even remotely in the vicinity of his usual licking grounds. Holy mother. The sensation of his tongue in forbidden places sends me into overload. Just a couple deep licks of his tongue and I come again, with different muscles than ever before.

The second my orgasm ends, Jonas abruptly grabs my torso and lifts me to standing. I wobble. My legs are rubber.

"I can't," I mumble. "Jonas." I reach for the shower wall to steady myself, but Jonas turns me around to face him. I throw my arms around his neck and rest my cheek on his strong shoulder. I'm totally spent. His skin is slick and taut and delicious under the warm shower stream. His arms are strong around me. Complete satisfaction floods me.

After a few minutes of relaxed silence, Jonas finally speaks. "While I was sitting there getting my tattoos," he says softly, "all I could think about was coming back up to the suite to make love to you."

"Mmm," I say. I'm not functional yet.

"I imagined myself making love to you slowly and tenderly while whispering words of supreme devotion into your ear."

We both burst out laughing at the same time.

"I guess your precious strategy got blown to bits," I say.

"As usual."

"Are you complaining?"

"Fuck no."

"I hate Strategic Jonas, anyway," I say.

"I just wanted to do something worthy of the moment—worthy of you," he says. "I wanted to do something romantic."

"Oh, Jonas." I raise my cheek off his shoulder and look him in the eye. "What we just did *was* romantic. It was Valentine's Day bullshit *and* hot monkey-sex, all rolled into one." I smile broadly at him. "You always give me both."

His eyes sparkle at me. "You were made for me, Sarah Cruz," he says.

"You were made for me, Jonas Faraday." I lay my cheek back down on his broad shoulder and sigh with contentment as he pulls me close. "Thank you for finding me."

"Thank you for being findable."

"That's not a word."

"It is now." He beams a heart-stopping smile at me. "Let's dry off. There's something I want to talk to you about."

We're bundled up in the fluffy white bathrobes supplied by the hotel, sitting on the fluffy white bed. The clock on the nightstand reads twelve minutes before four o'clock. What the hell are we still doing up? We're scheduled to meet the team in six hours to march down to the Las Vegas branch of the FBI. Oh man, I'm fading fast.

Jonas looks nervous. He's plainly trying to figure out what to say.

"You're gonna have to spit it out, baby," I say, yawning. "I'm falling asleep sitting up."

He exhales. "After we're done here, I want to take you on a trip—to a place that's really special to me."

I'm instantly wide awake. "Where?"

"Does it matter?"

"Not at all." I grin.

"It's out of the country—I'll tell you that much."

Holy moly, I'm elated. I've dreamed of traveling the world my entire life, ever since I was little. Whenever my father used to start screaming at my mother, when I knew he was getting all amped up and violence was surely imminent, I used to crawl into my closet with a world map and tune out the bad stuff by imagining myself in faraway places. I never in a million years thought my childhood fantasies would actually come true one day—or that I'd be lucky enough to have a tour guide with luscious lips and abs of steel and sad eyes—not to mention a seemingly inexhaustible travel budget.

"Wow," I say, at a loss for words.

"So that's a yes?" He looks hopeful.

"When?"

"The minute we're done here." His face bursts with excitement.

"You mean before we even go back home?"

"Yeah. I'll have my assistant overnight our passports and I'll take you on a shopping spree to buy whatever you need for the trip and we'll just hop a flight and go." His face is precious. He's a kid on Santa's lap, asking for that one special gift.

I want nothing more than to zip off to some exotic, faraway land with Jonas. But it's not possible—not right now. I kiss his nose. "You're so sweet, Jonas," I say. "Have I ever told you that, my sweet Jonas?"

His face falls. He knows what's coming.

I look at him sideways. "Have you put out your press release yet? About you leaving Faraday & Sons?"

He shakes his head, a second-grader busted for throwing spitballs.

"Have you told your uncle about Climb and Conquer?"

"No." He looks down.

"Don't you think you'd better do all that?"

He sighs. "There was a complication."

"Mmm hmm."

"With Josh. And then you were hurt and in the hospital—"

"But I'm not in the hospital anymore. Why haven't you talked to your uncle yet?"

He twists his mouth. "Because Josh wants to leave Faraday & Sons, too." His face is a mixture of elation and apology. "He wants to do Climb and Conquer with me full-time."

"Oh my God, Jonas. That's fantastic. You must be ecstatic."

"But Faraday & Sons won't survive both of us leaving. Uncle William's semi-retired these days. Who's gonna run the show?"

"And you feel guilty about that? You feel responsible for that?"

He nods.

I grab his hand. "Is this what you want to do with your life, my love? Climb and Conquer—and with Josh?"

He nods. "When Josh said he wanted to join me, it was a dream come true."

"This is what Josh wants?"

He nods.

"Then it's the right thing to do," I say. "You're not responsible for the fate of Faraday & Sons, and neither is he. You didn't ask to be the guardians of it. That company isn't your life's calling—Climb and Conquer is. You're responsible for being true to yourself and your destiny. You have to live your truth. Always."

His eyes soften and warm.

"You've got one life to live, my sweet love. *One*. Make the most of it. Every single day. That's your most sacred job on this earth."

His face flushes. "Thank you."

"You're welcome."

"You're so wise, Sarah. You're smart, yes, but you're *wise,* too."

I love it when he says that. "Butter me up all you like, big boy," I say. "But we're not going on that trip until you've gotten your butt in gear and started your new life. Our trip won't be an *escape*—it'll be a *celebration*. We'll be celebrating the beginning of Climb and Conquer and the end of my first year of law school."

His face falls now that he understands my proposed timeline for the trip.

"Jonas, I can't go away before finals. I've got to study."

He looks utterly disappointed.

"Finals are in four short weeks," I say. "We'll go right after that. Between now and then, you'll get your life in order and I'll study like a banshee, all day, every day, without stopping."

He opens his mouth to protest.

"*Except* that I'll take breaks to have howling monkey-sex with you, of course. I've already told you, Jonas, sex with you is a physical necessity—no different than sleeping, eating and breathing." I roll my eyes. "Duh."

"You read my mind."

"We can leave on our trip the day after finals. How's that?"

He sticks out his bottom lip and pouts.

"You know I'm right," I say.

His pout intensifies.

"You know I am."

He shrugs. "I hate waiting."

"It's just a rain check, that's all, baby. One short month. You just have to be patient."

"I'm not good at patience."

I laugh. "Really?"

He exhales loudly. "Well, it looks like I've got no choice." He shrugs. "Another goddamned round of delicious anticipation, for fuck's sake." He shakes his head. "One month. You'll study and I'll put on my big-boy pants, and every spare minute in between, we'll crawl into our little cocoon built for two and fuck each other's brains out like the sex-crazed caterpillars we are."

I laugh. "Do caterpillars fuck?"

He shrugs. "They do now."

I laugh again.

"But first things first," he says, his eyes turning to granite. "You and me, baby—we're gonna fuck The Club up the ass."

I put my arms around his neck. "You bet, baby. Sounds like a plan."

Chapter 36
Jonas

"We really need to talk to your boss," I say to the newbie FBI agent sitting across the table from me. Fuck me, this rookie agent isn't going to be able to mobilize anyone to do a goddamned thing.

"Yeah, well, that's not gonna happen. I'm who you get."

"I'm Jonas Faraday," I say, sounding like a total douche. "And this is my brother, Josh. We run Faraday & Sons in Seattle, L.A. and New York. We'd like to talk to the head of this office."

The kid shrugs. "I'm the only one available to talk to you, sir. Sorry." But he's not at all sorry.

I look at Sarah. Her eyes are bugging out of her head. And rightfully so. This isn't going to work if her report gets thrown onto the pile on this newbie's desk. We need prompt action, and that means getting the immediate attention of someone with a hell of a lot more pull within the FBI than this guy.

"How long have you been an agent?" Kat asks.

When the kid's gaze falls on Kat, his entire demeanor visibly softens. Oh yeah, I keep forgetting that Kat is exceptionally attractive. To me, she's just Kat—Sarah's best friend—the Party Girl with a Heart of Gold. But witnessing reactions like this guy's reminds me she's objectively a knockout.

"Four months," he says.

"Did you go to Quantico for training like they show in the movies?"

"Yeah."

"Wow. That's cool. So what's your assignment? All I know about the FBI is what I saw in *Silence of the Lambs*." The way Kat's talking to the guy, it's as if the two of them are cozied up together in the corner of a bar, getting to know each other over drinks.

The guy must know Kat's trying to butter him up—and yet his

smile says he doesn't care. "Well, new agents are assigned to run background checks for the first year, mostly. And, of course, I'm the lucky guy who gets to talk to all the nice people such as yourselves who come in off the streets of Las Vegas to report the crime of the century."

"Everyone's gotta start somewhere," Kat says, flashing perfect teeth. She leans forward across the table. "So here's the thing, Agent Sheffield. I've come here today off the streets of Las Vegas to report the crime of the century."

He can't help but laugh.

Oh boy, this Kitty Kat just caught herself a fish.

Kat's face turns serious. "Actually, I'm not kidding. I'm here to report the crime of the century."

He sighs. "What's your name?"

"Katherine Morgan. But you can call me Kat." She says this like she's granting him a special favor, like the whole world doesn't already call her by that name.

Special Agent Sheffield's face turns earnest. "Kat," he repeats. "I tell you what. You guys file your report with me and I promise I'll take a long look at it within the next two weeks—maybe even a week. And, if I see something there, I'll most certainly investigate further."

I'm tempted to speak up, but Sarah puts her hand on my thigh.

"Thank you, Special Agent Sheffield," Kat says, smiling. "I really appreciate that. What's your first name?"

"Eric."

"Special Agent Eric." She pushes her long blonde hair behind her shoulder. "The thing is, this is an urgent matter." She leans completely forward across the table again, and the tops of her breasts ride up into her neckline. "This is a career-making kind of case for an agent such as yourself, I swear to God."

I glance at Sarah again. She's suppressing a smirk. I imagine she's seen Kat's charm in action a time or two before.

The young agent looks dubious. "Even if *I* believe you," Eric says, "I'd have to present this to my boss in due course, whenever I could get her undivided attention. And if she's convinced, which isn't a given, then she'd have to present your report to *her* boss in Washington to get anyone to move on this, if it's truly as big as you say. And all that takes time, Miss Morgan. Do you know how many conspiracy theorists walk into the FBI every day to tell us about the crime of the century?"

211

Kat laughs and shakes her head and her golden blonde hair falls around her shoulders. "I can only imagine," she says. "But you don't actually think we're a bunch of conspiracy theorists, do you?" Kat's eyes are sparkling. "We're just a computer nerd, a law student, a PR specialist . . ." She motions to herself with flourish on the last one. "And two ridiculously rich business dudes with plenty of other stuff they could be doing than filing a report with the FBI. These two guys have been on the cover of *Businessweek,* for crying out loud." She laughs. "Not a crazy among us—well, yeah, okay—I admit I'm a teeny-tiny bit crazy." She holds up her index finger and thumb, slightly apart, to emphasize her point. "But not the kind of crazy you're referring to."

Oh man, she's good. I have to restrain myself from chuckling.

Agent Eric exhales. "I'd be happy to take a look at your report in due course—"

"Agent Sheffield, I'm begging you. Please don't throw our report onto some pile—take a hard look at it right now. Let us explain everything to you, page by page. I guarantee you won't regret it."

Eric looks at his watch. I imagine he's got a huge stack of background checks waiting for him.

"Henn," Sarah interjects, "will you please play Special Agent Sheffield that voicemail we have cued up?"

"Yes, ma'am." Henn presses a button on his computer and the Ukrainian Travolta's gruff voice fills the room for about eight seconds.

When the voicemail ends, Sarah speaks calmly. "That was one of several voicemails our computer expert, Peter Hennessey, has retrieved from the cell phone of Maksim Belenko. He's the brains behind The Club's various operations. In that particular voicemail, a hitman named Yuri Navolska asks Mr. Belenko if he should go ahead and kill his intended target as previously instructed, or, instead, hold off due to newly discovered information."

Special Agent Eric's eyes widen. He's most definitely intrigued.

"That's what a certified Ukrainian translator will tell you in a sworn statement under penalty of perjury—and, of course, Mr. Hennessey will swear that voicemail came from Belenko's cell phone."

Henn nods curtly.

"And since Yuri Navolska was holding a knife to my throat in a bathroom at the University of Washington when he left that voicemail, I can personally vouch for its authenticity."

She's got his undivided attention now.

Sarah continues her assault. "About a minute after leaving that message, Yuri Navolska sliced the external jugular vein in my neck and stabbed me in the ribcage, causing me to fall back and crack my skull on a sink ledge." She tilts her head to the side to display the scar on her neck. "If you need to see the scars on my head and torso, I'll show you."

Agent Eric inhales sharply. "No, that's okay. I believe you."

"Please," Kat says, her voice brimming with genuine emotion. "These guys tried to kill my best friend." All trace of Flirty Kat is gone—she's Earnest Kat now. "Just give us a couple hours of your time." Even I can see how stunningly beautiful Kat looks right now— vulnerability suits her.

"You've got more voicemails besides this one?" Eric asks.

"Several," Henn says. "About all kinds of nasty stuff. Maksim Belenko's a really bad dude—prostitution, weapons, drugs, money laundering."

"This report outlines everything for you in meticulous detail," Sarah says, grabbing the hefty document off the table and holding it in the air. "Every single allegation in here is true and supported with solid, incontrovertible evidence." She lets the report fall back onto the table with a loud thud.

Agent Eric's demeanor has done a complete one-eighty since we first walked through his door. "Okay," he says, exhaling. "Let's dig in. We'll go through the report together, page by page, and if it's everything you say it is, I'll take this to my boss today." He looks up at the ceiling. "But please, for the love of God, don't bullshit me about a single goddamned thing. Okay?"

We all nod profusely.

"If I'm gonna stick my neck out, you've got to promise to tell me the God's truth."

"Thank you," Kat says. "We promise." She shoots him a look like she's just promised him a blowjob, signaling the official retreat of Vulnerable Kat.

"Let's do it," Agent Eric says, getting comfortable in his chair. He looks directly at Kat. "I'm all yours."

Chapter 37
Jonas

We've been here almost three hours walking Special Agent Eric through Sarah's report and accompanying exhibit log. Throughout our discussion, Eric has looked variously excited, overwhelmed, anxious, and ecstatic—but always *convinced*.

"So what do you want me to do?" Agent Eric asks, thumbing through the exhibit log. He's clearly trying to hide the fact that he's shitting his pants right now.

"We want a meeting in D.C. within the next two days with power players at the FBI, CIA, and Secret Service," I say.

Eric keeps a straight face, but I can tell he's losing his shit. "I'm pretty sure I'll be able to convince my boss about all this," Eric says, motioning to the report. "But I doubt she'll be able to pull in those other agencies."

"We're talking about the U.S. Secretary of Defense," I say. "We don't know who within the FBI might be in that guy's pocket."

Eric opens his mouth to protest, but I barrel ahead.

"It's not that I mistrust anyone at the FBI *per se*—I'd say the same thing about power players at the CIA and Secret Service, too. It's simple checks and balances—I'm just trying to increase my odds that this situation gets handled right."

Agent Eric rubs his eyes. "All three agencies within two days?"

I nod.

He shakes his head. "That's gonna be a tough sell."

"Tell me how we can make that happen."

"Deliver the money."

"Done," Sarah says. "A printout of all The Club's bank accounts is at Tab D of the exhibit log. The account numbers are blacked out on that version, but—"

"No, deliver the *actual* money—not a printout. You want the FBI, CIA *and* Secret Service to jump when you say jump? Then make this a turnkey operation for them."

"But we can't do that," Sarah says. "Those accounts require—"

"Yeah, we can," Henn cuts in.

Sarah shoots Henn a "what the fuck?" look, and I'm right there with her. Henn told us the bank accounts require in-person signatures for large transfers.

"We can do it," Henn insists.

"Okay," Sarah says slowly, looking at Henn quizzically. "Even if that's true, we have a problem. If we move the money before law enforcement is ready to pounce, Belenko will immediately guess who screwed him over and come after Jonas and me—and who knows what else they might do?"

"She's right," I say. "We can't move the money to convince you guys to take action—it's got to be the other way around."

Eric sighs and looks up at the ceiling. "You're not bullshitting me? You can do it?"

Everyone looks at Henn.

"We can do it."

"Then I'll vouch for you with my boss," Eric says. "I'll do everything in my power."

Everyone sighs with relief.

"Hey, Agent Sheffield," Sarah says. "I've got a favor to ask of you."

The entire room looks at Sarah in surprise. This isn't something we talked about in advance. What the fuck is she talking about?

Eric purses his lips, apparently waiting to hear her request.

"You do background checks, right?" Sarah asks.

"Yeah," Eric replies. "Every day."

"I'd like you to find two people for me."

Agent Eric raises his eyebrows and so do I. What is she talking about?

"This isn't a demand. It's just a personal favor. But it's really important."

My heart is racing.

"Who are the two people?" Eric asks.

"The first is a woman named Mariela from Venezuela."

I'm instantly short of breath.

Sarah doesn't look at me. "I don't know her last name, but she worked for Joseph and Grace Faraday in Seattle during the years from I'm guessing 1984 to around 1991."

I glance at Josh. His mouth is hanging open. I put my hands over my face, trying to look like I'm deep in thought, or tired, or fighting off a headache. But the truth is, I'm stuffing down tears.

"In 1991, Grace Faraday was murdered in her home, and the man who was convicted of the killing turned out to be the boyfriend of Mariela's sister. You should be able to figure out Mariela's last name by tracing back from the convicted murderer to his girlfriend—and then to her sister, Mariela. Maybe the sister visited the killer in prison? Maybe she was interviewed or gave a statement in the investigation or at trial? Surely, there's some record of the girlfriend somewhere, and that should lead you to Mariela's full name."

I let out a shaky breath and Sarah grabs my thigh under the table. I peek at Josh. His face is in his hands. I can't breathe.

"Hang on," Eric says, taking notes. "Could you repeat all that?"

Sarah repeats everything again slowly, her hand now gently rubbing my thigh. "We need you to find Mariela—and if she's not alive, then her children."

That last part stabs me in the heart. Could Mariela be dead? I do a quick calculation in my head. How old was she when Josh and I were seven? Late twenties? I had no concept of age at the time—everyone was uniformly just an adult to me—but I bet she was younger than I am right now. So how old would she be now? In her fifties, probably?

Eric looks up from his notepad. "Okay. That sounds doable."

My stomach flips over. This kid's going to find my Mariela? I look at Josh and he shakes his head at me, like he's in total shock. I shoot him a look that says, "I'm just as shocked as you are, man."

"Awesome, Eric," Sarah says. "Thank you. And there's one more woman, too. I don't know her first name—but her maiden name was Westbrook."

Holy shit. Josh and I exchange a look of astonishment. Miss Westbrook, too? What the fuck is Sarah doing?

"Miss Westbrook was a teacher in Seattle in probably 1992 and then she married a guy in the Navy named Santorini who was stationed in San Diego."

"What do these two women have to do with The Club?" Eric asks.

"Absolutely nothing," Sarah says. She glances at me with sparkling eyes. "This would be a personal favor to me. I don't have the resources to find these ladies by myself without having their full names, but I think you can do it."

Eric shrugs like that's an obvious statement. He's the FBI, after all. "Shouldn't be a problem." He smiles at her.

"Thank you. I'm gonna need this information as soon as possible, please."

"I'll do my best."

My entire body tingles with anxiety and excitement and a whole bunch of other emotions I can't pin down. What's Sarah planning? I look at Josh again and he's looking at me like I'm an alien, clearly shocked as hell I've told Sarah about Mariela and Miss Westbrook.

"Oh," Sarah says. "I almost forgot. The second woman, Westbrook Santorini, has a son named Jonas—and he's probably . . . " She looks up at the ceiling, calculating. "About seventeen years old by now. Maybe that'll help you somehow."

My heart skips a beat. Holy shit. *Jonas Santorini.* I never thought about Miss Westbrook's baby actually *existing*, and definitely not as a *teenager*. To me, he's always been a baby bump, frozen in time.

"Got it," Eric says, making a note on his pad.

"What's the name of the school where Miss Westbrook worked in Seattle, Jonas?" Sarah asks. "That might be helpful for Eric to know for his search."

My cheeks feel hot. I open my mouth but nothing comes out.

"St. Francis Academy," Josh says.

I look at Josh and he smiles broadly at me. Just like old times.

Sarah puts her arm around my back and squeezes me.

"Okay. I'll do my best," Eric says.

"Thank you," Sarah says.

"Shouldn't be too hard." Eric pushes his pad aside, brimming with excitement. "Okay. I think I've got everything I need." He's trying to play it cool, but he's geeking out. "Now, just to be clear, you're promising to give us full access to everything, right? No limitations? No exceptions? Their operating systems, membership lists, voicemails, code—and the money, too?"

Everyone looks at Henn. He's the only one in this room who knows if we can deliver on a promise that big.

"Yep," Henn says. "Everything."

"But we'll only hand it over to senior level reps from the FBI, CIA and Secret Service. And I want you there, too, Eric—tell your boss we said your presence is a non-negotiable condition of the deal. Tell her I'll pay your way to D.C. if need be, but you've got to be there."

Eric's face lights up. I imagine he hasn't been involved in too many high-powered meetings in his nascent career.

"Okay," Agent Eric says, steeling himself for battle. "I'll go talk to my boss right now. I'll give you guys a call later." He nods at Kat, reassuring her in particular. "I promise I'll give it my all."

"I know you will, Eric," Kat purrs. "I have full faith in you."

Chapter 38
Sarah

"Henn, pass the ketchup," Josh says.

The five of us are eating like gluttons in the Americana restaurant in our hotel. It's burgers, fries, and beers all around—even Jonas is eating a bacon cheeseburger and French fries, two things I've never seen him eat—and we're enthusiastically rehashing our meeting with Special Agent Eric like we're dissecting every play of a Seahawks' game. The general consensus, of course, is that Kat was our quarterback today—and she crushed it.

Henn passes the ketchup to Josh, but he's looking at Kat. "Who's the fucking genius now?" Henn says. "Damn, girl." He fist bumps her.

Kat beams.

"To Kat," I say, raising my beer. All three guys hold up their beers in Kat's honor, too. "You're the reason Eric started taking us seriously," I say. "No doubt about it."

"Aw, thanks," Kat says. "But it was definitely a team effort."

We all raise our glasses again and drink to "the team."

"So how are we gonna get the money, Henn?" Josh asks. "I thought you said most of those accounts are set up for in-person transfer only."

"They are," Henn says. "Which, obviously, means we're going to transfer the money in-person."

We're all silent, not catching his meaning.

Henn looks pointedly at Kat. "Hello, Oksana Belenko."

Kat looks like Henn just said she's been selected to sing the national anthem at the Super Bowl.

"You'll be fine," Henn says. "I'll set you up with a passport and a driver's license—"

219

"Oh, I don't know," Kat says, sputtering. "I don't know if I can—"

"You *can*," Henn says soothingly. "Today proved that. Indubitably." He smiles broadly. "Don't worry, Kitty Kat." He touches the top of her hand. "I'll hack into each account and shave thirty years off Oksana's age—they won't even question you're her for a second. And then I'll walk into each and every bank with you, right by your side." Henn smiles at Kat reassuringly. Oh, that boy absolutely adores her.

"But will Kat be safe?" I ask.

"I'll make sure of it," Henn says.

"So will I," Josh adds.

This is crazy. Can we really ask Kat to do this? Why are Henn and Josh acting like this is a reasonable request? I look at Jonas, expecting him to be as anxious as I am about all this, but he's nodding emphatically. Have they all gone mad?

A waitress walks by and Kat flags her. "Double Patron shots all around, please." When the waitress leaves, Kat lets out a long exhale. "Okay, I'll do it."

"Kat, are you sure?" I ask. "You don't have to do this."

"Yes, I do. This ain't no casino heist, fellas—and very pretty lady." She winks at me. "This is about taking these guys down so they can't hurt you ever again, Sarah. It's a no-brainer."

Everyone besides me raises a beer in salute to Kat. I'm too freaked out to celebrate. I know all too well the kind of criminals we're dealing with here.

"We'll create an offshore account," Jonas says, forging right ahead. "And funnel everything into it at the last possible moment."

"*Two* offshore accounts," Josh interjects. "I think we're gonna have to take a little finder's fee on the deal—don't you think, bro? Maybe one percent?"

"Fuck yeah," Jonas says. "Great idea. Yeah, five and a half mill sounds about right for our commission. Kat and Henn, you guys will each get a cool mill off the top. You've both earned it."

Kat and Henn look at each other, in total shock.

"Are you *serious*?" Kat squeals. "You're gonna give me a *million* dollars?"

"You deserve it."

Kat squeals again. She stands and hugs Jonas across the table and kisses his cheek in sheer elation like she's won the Miss America pageant. And then she grabs me and kisses me hard on the lips, laughing. She moves on to Josh, obviously intending to plant a chaste kiss on his cheek, but he swoops in and kisses her on the lips. Holy hell, that's quite a kiss—wowza—and Kat's responding like her panties are melting. Good Lord, those two are sizzling hot. I guess that answers the question of whether Kat and Josh are sleeping together.

Henn looks away from their make-out session, crestfallen.

When Kat and Josh finally disengage, Josh says, "I feel like I've been waiting a lifetime to do that."

"Why the hell did you wait so long, Playboy?" Kat breathes, her face blazing.

Wait. *What?* That was their *first* kiss?

Josh chuckles. "Gee, I wonder why."

"So does this mean you're finally gonna tell me?" Kat whispers.

Josh nods. Oh my gosh, his cheeks are on fire.

What the hell are these two talking about? Color me curious.

Kat sits back down, grinning devilishly, but when she sees Henn's face across the table, her face falls. "Oh, Henny. I'm sorry."

Henn shakes his head. "No, it's great. You're both the best." He swallows hard. "Indubitably." He tries to smile.

Josh looks apologetic. "Hey, Henn—"

"No, really." He waves Josh away. "I'm good."

But he's not good. Not at all. Aw, poor Henn.

Kat maneuvers around the table and grabs Henn's shoulders. "You're the best." She kisses him softly on the cheek. "I'm proud to call you my friend."

That's probably no consolation to the poor boy, but it will have to do.

The waitress arrives with the tequila Kat ordered and we all raise our drinks in the air.

"To the Party Girl with a Heart of Gold and the Hacker," I say. "A couple of *mill-ion-aires.*"

"Here, here," Josh adds, his eyes blazing at Kat, and we all knock back our shots.

"Yeah, well, let's not put the cart before the horse," Kat says. "There's still the little matter of actually getting the money."

"Oh, we'll get it—don't you worry," Henn says, trying to imitate light-heartedness. The expression on his face is killing me right now. I guess a million bucks isn't enough to stave off a broken heart.

"What about you, Jonas?" I ask, trying to deflect attention from poor Henn. "They owe you money, too."

"Fuck yeah, they do. Those fuckers took that two-fifty I gave to you—and I'm gonna get it back for you—plus I want the one-eighty I paid them to convince them I'm a fucking idiot."

"Well, plus the two-fifty in membership fees you paid in the first place," I add.

"Nah, I don't deserve that two-fifty back," Jonas says. "I shouldn't get a refund for being a dumbshit."

"Jonas, they took your money under false pretenses," I say.

"No, they didn't." He shrugs. "Regardless, it was my choice to join that place for a fucking *year*. Who *does* that?" He glances over at Josh and half-smiles. "And, anyway, it turned out to be the best money I've ever spent." He winks at me and I smile from ear to ear. I love it when he says that. "All I want is the money they legitimately stole from me, a payday for Kat and Henn, and then the rest of the pot is all yours, Sarah Cruz," he says.

"What?" I blurt.

"Those fuckers almost killed you, baby—they owe you a shitload more than three million bucks. Plus, you've been our fearless George Clooney through all this—you deserve it."

Everyone at the table agrees enthusiastically.

"No, I can't—"

"Sure you can," Josh says.

"Absolutely," Kat adds.

"But what about you, Josh? Don't you want some of the money?" I ask.

Josh laughs. "Hell no."

"But you've been helping us from minute one—"

"Of course, I have. I wouldn't have it any other way." He smiles at Jonas.

I exhale. Wow. Three million dollars? It's tempting, I admit, but it's too much. Don't get me wrong—I'm no saint—if Kat and Henn are willing to take a million bucks out of the pot, then so am I. But *three* million? No. With a million bucks, I'd be able to do everything

I've ever dreamed about—buy my mom a house, pay for all my schooling (because, clearly, that scholarship's a pipe dream at this point), maybe put a little money away for the uncertainties of life. But, other than that, I don't need a thing. I'll always be able to take care of myself with my law degree, one way or another. I've got a beautiful place to live with Jonas for the foreseeable future. And if I want to travel, anywhere in the whole wide world, my hunky-monkey boyfriend's already told me I can just name it. What more do I need than all that?

I suppose, since Jonas isn't the marrying kind, I should in theory put money away for the allegedly inevitable day when things go to hell in a handbasket between us and I've got no one in this world to rely on but myself—but the thing is I know that day will never come. For Pete's sake, the man permanently declared his love for me on his skin. He's promised me forever as clearly as he knows how—and I believe him. Yes, even if it proves I'm hopelessly brainwashed by Lifetime and Hallmark and Disney, I believe my sweet Jonas with all my heart.

"Just don't make a decision about the money yet," Jonas says, gently rubbing my thigh. "Think about it for a little while."

I nod. "Okay, I'll think about it." And, in fact, even as I sit here, I already have a pretty good idea of how to put that money to good use. "So, Henn, how quickly do you think you can—"

I'm interrupted by the arrival of a figure at the edge of our table.

Holy crappola. Oh my God. Holy shitballs. No effing way. This can't be happening. No, no, no. *It's Max.*

Chapter 39
Jonas

What the fuck is Max doing here?

Sarah's body jolts next to me in the restaurant booth like she's been zapped by a Taser gun.

Shit. Did he see us go to the FBI today? Holy fuck. No, there's no fucking way. I made us jump through ridiculous hoops to ensure we weren't followed and I'm one hundred percent sure it worked. Max must have a goon stationed in the hotel who called him when we finally turned up again.

"What do you want?" I ask, putting my arm around Sarah. Wow, she's noticeably trembling.

"Hello, Mr. Faraday," Max says. "Sarah." He glances at the rest of the table but doesn't acknowledge anyone but Sarah and me. "I hope you're still enjoying your stay here in Las Vegas?"

"What the fuck do you want?" I ask.

Sarah squeezes my thigh, probably signaling me to tread carefully. But this fucker thinks I'm a possessive asshole, right? Which I am, actually, so fuck him.

"I had some business in the hotel—what a coincidence to run into you," Max says.

I clench my jaw and glare at him. It's taking all of my self-control not to leap up, grab a fistful of his fucking slick-backed hair, and pummel his smug face. This fucker spilled my baby's sacred blood onto a bathroom floor and left her for dead. This cock-sucking motherfucking fucker of an asshole haunts my baby's fucking nightmares almost every night. I want to rip his head off. I want to slit his throat and watch the lifeblood spill out of him and onto the floor. *I want him fucking dead.*

Sarah can read my thoughts, obviously, because she puts her arm across my body, as if she's holding me at bay. "Hi, Max," she says, her voice quavering. "Yeah, that's one helluva coincidence. Hey, everybody, this is Max—a friend of mine. These are some friends of Jonas' who met us in Vegas to party—Jonas' brother Josh, Josh's girlfriend Kayley, and his roommate from college, Scott."

Max nods absently at everyone. "I just need to steal you for a couple minutes, Sarah." He puts his hand out like he actually expects her to take it.

"No," I say, crushing her into me. I'm a heartbeat away from grabbing a knife off the table and slashing this motherfucker's fucking throat.

Max snarls at me.

"Hey, guys," Sarah says to Josh, Kat and Henn. "Could you all excuse us for a few minutes?"

They all look at each other, at a loss.

"Um," Josh says, looking at me for a signal.

I nod.

"Sure," Josh says. "Come on, Kayley. Scott. Let's go roll some dice." They leave, looking back at us warily as they do.

Max takes one of the newly vacated seats at the table and my heart leaps into my throat. I could kill this fucker right now. I could reach across the table, grab his fucking head in both my hands and twist with all my might. But, fuck me, I can't. For Sarah's sake—for the sake of the mission—for the sake of the forest and not the trees—for the sake of never having to look over our shoulders again—I've got to control my urges. I clench my jaw like an epileptic on the verge of a seizure.

"This will only take a few minutes," Max says evenly. "Why don't you do a little gambling, Mr. Faraday?"

I lean forward. "Fuck you," I say. "Motherfucker."

Max narrows his eyes.

"I paid you eighty thousand bucks to *own* this woman every second of every day for the next month. And I do—every inch of her, inside and out—every single hair on her beautiful head. So fuck you."

Max smirks and sits back, blatantly surprised.

Sarah leans into me, shaking like a leaf.

"For the next month, this woman is *mine*, motherfucker. I don't want you calling her. I don't want you texting her. I don't want you 'stopping by our table' by so-called 'coincidence' to talk to her. I don't even want you *looking* at her." I wouldn't be surprised if actual steam were shooting out my ears right now. "She's *mine.*"

Max squints and grinds his teeth together. After a moment, he stands, staring at Sarah despite my explicit instructions. "Enjoy your month, Sarah."

"Are you fucking deaf, motherfucker? Don't talk to her. Don't fucking look at her," I growl. "I paid eighty thousand bucks to be the only man who enjoys those sublime pleasures."

Max ignores me and continues staring at Sarah. "I'll expect to see you in my office the minute your month is up. That very day."

"Of course," she says. "I look forward to it."

I whip my head to look at her, about to blow a fucking gasket.

Sarah squeezes my thigh under the table again. "When our month is up, Jonas, I'm gonna have to work again," she says, her entire body quivering against mine. "I've got tuition to pay, my mom's medical bills, my dad's house payment. You know that."

Oh, Sarah. My Magnificent Sarah. I don't know how she always manages to keep her head in the game, even when she's obviously scared to death. "We'll chat about all that later," I say. I glare at Max. "Why are you still here?" I wave at him condescendingly. "Time to shoo, motherfucker."

Max trembles with rage. "I'll look forward to seeing you in a month, Sarah." He shoots daggers at me. "Mr. Faraday, I'd recommend you take care whom you call a *motherfucker.*" He clenches his jaw. It's clear he wants to kill me as much I want to kill him. "That's a strong word."

"Mo-ther-fuck-er," I say, drawing out the word. "Yeah, I see what you mean. That *is* a strong word, motherfucker." I lean forward and glare at him. "And so is asshole. And douchebag. Shithead. Asshat." Oh fuck, I want to kill this motherfucker so bad. "*Cock-suck-er.* The list goes on and on, *mo-ther-fuck-er.*"

Max shakes his head slowly. "Watch yourself, Mr. Faraday."

"Thanks. I'll be sure to do that, *motherfucker.*"

Max stands. He looks at Sarah for a brief moment, his nostrils flaring, and then he turns on his heel and exits the restaurant in a blaze of white-hot fury.

The minute he's gone, Sarah's entire body begins twitching next to me in the booth. I take her face in my hands and she shakes beneath my palms.

"Are you okay, baby?"

She nods and swallows hard.

"You're safe now, baby—my precious baby." I pull her into me. "He's gone."

"Jonas," she breathes, quivering violently against my chest.

"He's gone. You're safe." I stroke her hair—but she continues trembling. Jesus. Her entire body is jolting against me like a fish on a line.

"Jonas," she says again.

"I'm right here." I pull back from her and look into her big brown eyes.

"Jonas." Her voice is strained.

Oh my God, she's a wreck. "Baby, you're okay." I kiss her gently.

"Jonas, please." She sounds like she's got hypothermia. She's practically stuttering.

"I'm listening, baby. What is it? Tell me."

She closes her eyes and tilts her face up to mine. "Take me back up to the suite, Jonas." Her cheeks flush. "Take me up to the suite and fuck my brains clean out of my head."

Chapter 40
Sarah

In addition to Special Agent Eric and his boss from Las Vegas, there are no less than fifteen people in dark suits crowded into this conference room with Jonas and me at FBI headquarters in Washington D.C., all of them with hard eyes and humorless expressions, variously identified as representing the FBI, CIA, Secret Service, DEA, ATF, Department of Justice, and, holy hell, the Department of Defense, too. And, in addition to that whole crowd, there are three scary looking dudes who curtly declined to identify themselves at the outset of the meeting four hours ago and haven't spoken since.

Special Agent Eric, who looks like a kindergartner on take-your-kid-to-work-day amongst this room full of seasoned agents, called us yesterday and told us to get our butts to Washington on the next plane, and that's exactly what we did. According to Eric, my report ignited a firestorm of attention within the FBI, beginning with his boss in Las Vegas and quickly ascending up the chain of command to the highest power-players in Washington D.C.

It seems when two wealthy and respected business moguls (who don't appear on a single government watch list) claim the U.S. Secretary of Defense is unwittingly involved in a billion-dollar crime syndicate that supplies money and weapons to aid Russian aggression—and when those two business moguls are willing to sacrifice their own reputations and maybe even incriminate themselves by coming forward—and when they outline their allegations in a rock-solid fifty-page report with a detailed exhibit log and promise to turn over an easy half-billion to back up their claims, the FBI takes fucking notice. And—holy crappola—so do lots of other scary looking people with fancy badges, too.

It's just Jonas and me sitting here on the proverbial hot seat—Henn, Josh, and Kat (a.k.a. "Oksana Belenko") stayed behind in Las Vegas to make the money transfers at our signal. To say I've been crapping my pants for the past four hours in this conference room would be the understatement of the year. I've tried to sound calm and collected, of course, but I think I've mostly come across as a total and complete spazzoid.

Jonas, on the other hand, has been as cool as a cucumber throughout the whole meeting (other than the few times his knee has jiggled under the table). Jonas been charming. Disarming. Forthcoming. Honest. I'm learning a lot about quiet confidence watching him. He's personable without bending over backwards to make people like him—and as a result, they obviously *respect* him. Watching Jonas handle the room like a boss for the past four hours has made it plain to me why he's been so successful in the business world.

Before walking into this room today, Jonas and I agreed we'd be completely honest at all times, no matter what—and we've stuck with our plan, even when our answers to questions have embarrassed or possibly even incriminated us. And I think we made the right call. Because although the meeting started out feeling distinctly adversarial, I'm beginning to feel like all these hardass people in dark suits actually believe every word we say.

My palms are sweaty. I wipe them on my skirt.

"Who else knows about this?" the Department of Defense guy asks, holding up my report. "Anyone at all besides you two and your three team members?" He looks at his notes. "Katherine Morgan, Josh Faraday, and Peter Hennessey?"

"No one at all besides us five has seen the report or knows anything about its contents," Jonas says, his voice strong and firm. "We sent a few isolated voicemails to a certified Ukrainian translator—but with no context or identifying information whatsoever."

"You're sure? No one else besides you five knows anything about this?" the Defense guy asks, scrutinizing Jonas' face.

I glance at one of the CIA guys, the one who seems most capable of chopping us up and stuffing us into the trunk of his car—and he's hanging on Jonas' every word.

"No one," Jonas says. "It turns out Sarah's unwittingly been employed by a large-scale prostitution ring—not exactly résumé fodder for an aspiring lawyer—and I unwittingly paid a quarter of a million bucks to a prostitution ring to buy unlimited sex for a year." He looks at me apologetically and I smile at him. "And if that weren't enough for either of us to prefer discretion here, it turns out we're dealing with drug and weapons traffickers whose higher agenda is aiding Russian imperialism. If that's not motivation to keep our report on a need-to-know basis, I don't know what is."

The Department of Justice guy snickers and a couple other seemingly senior guys smirk. Good sign.

"We know we're up to our eyeballs in this shit, excuse my language. Believe me, we're not eager to spread the word about any of this."

That seems to satisfy the Department of Defense guy, as well as everyone else in the room.

"As you can understand, my only concern is protecting this woman right here," Jonas says, touching my arm. "We aren't here to expose anyone, including ourselves—and would prefer not to, given our personal involvement. We don't care how you want to go about this, how you want to spin it, what information you might choose to disseminate or not. It's your strategy—your show—and you won't hear a peep from us on any of it. We're only here to give you the information, help in any way we can, and then get the hell out of your way."

That was well said. And not a single f-bomb in the whole speech, too. I guess Jonas is Polite Jonas today.

"At the end of the day, all I care about is fucking them up the ass so hard they can't even fucking hobble when we're done with them," Jonas adds, grabbing my hand.

So much for no f-bombs.

"Ditto," I say. "I have no interest in humiliating or exposing anyone." I look pointedly at the Department of Defense guy, trying to convey I'm talking about his boss, the Secretary of Defense. It must have crossed his mind we could be planning to blackmail his boss. "And also ditto on that whole f-bomb-laden last part." I smile sheepishly. I'm freaking out. I might be Orgasma the All-Powerful behind closed doors with Jonas, but being a superhero in a room like this is seriously testing my self-confidence.

All the big wigs in the room look around, gauging each other's reactions.

"We're the good guys," I say earnestly, looking at all of them. "We're not here to harm anyone—we're here to do the right thing. I just want to keep the bad guys from hurting me or anyone else again." My voice wobbles at that last part and Jonas puts a protective arm around me.

The most senior CIA guy is looking at me like he believes me. And so are the silver-haired Secret Service guy and the FBI woman who looks like she could eat me for breakfast. Oh my God, they *all* believe us. I know they do.

The bigwig FBI agent exchanges a particularly long look with the Department of Defense guy. "And you'll turn everything over to us?" he says.

"Yes," Jonas says. "Everything."

Everyone nods, satisfied.

"Now, with respect to the money," Jonas says. "My team is in Vegas, ready to make the transfers into an offshore account. I just have to give them the word." He holds up his phone. "I got a text from my guy five minutes ago, confirming all the money's still in place and they're ready to move. But time is of the essence, obviously—Belenko could transfer every dime out of the country any time."

Jonas' knee starts jiggling under the table. I put my hand on his thigh and it stops.

The bigwig FBI boss motions to the Las Vegas FBI woman, and they confer quietly for a solid three minutes, shielding their mouths with their hands to prevent the rest of us from reading their lips. Everyone else in the room sits patiently.

"Okay," Mr. FBI guy finally says, pulling back from his colleague.

I'm not sure what that means. Okay what? There's an awkward pause.

Jonas fills the silence. "We do have a few small conditions before we transfer the funds to you," he says flatly.

There's a collective sigh of wariness throughout the room.

The FBI ringleader glares at Jonas, blatantly mistrustful. If this were a cartoon, he'd be saying, "Dangnabbit!" right now.

Jonas isn't daunted at all. "I want immunity for everyone on my team regarding our various affiliations with The Club, and also with respect to our investigation."

Mr. FBI nods. It's not clear if he's agreeing to this condition or simply acknowledging the request has been made.

"We'll help you guys with anything and everything you need from us, answer any and all questions, give you whatever sworn statements you need to aid your investigation. I'll pay my hacker to fly out here and help you assimilate everything we hand off to you, and I'll make sure he assists you guys with your investigation, too, if you think you need him. But our five names will be completely expunged from all records. We were never involved with The Club or this investigation in any way. Accordingly, the files we'll be handing-off to you will not contain any reference to Sarah, my brother, or myself. We've wiped the files clean of all such references." He puts his hand on my thigh under the table.

The main CIA guy and the Department of Defense guy share a glance.

"But believe me, even without mention of us in the records, you'll have everything you need to nail them six ways from Sunday," Jonas says.

The FBI guy is about to speak, but the Defense guy cuts him off.

"Your computer guy altered the files you'd be handing off to us?" he asks.

"Correct. To delete record of Sarah's employment and my and my brother's Club activities."

Mr. Defense guy purses his lips. "Do you still have access to the unredacted data?"

Jonas hesitates, apparently considering his answer. "Yes," he finally says, honestly. I'm glad he answered truthfully.

"Does anyone but you have access to that original data?"

"No."

Defense guy nods. "And you'll provide us with your hacker's services, without limitation?"

"Of course. For as long as you want him."

Defense guy looks happy to hear that. Maybe Defense guy is thinking about erasing a certain someone else's name from all the records, too—wink, wink.

"I'll make sure Peter Hennessey's available to assist you. Trust me, you'll be thrilled to have him on your team—he loves wearing a white hat." Jonas smirks.

There's a long pause, as several sub-groups from different agencies confer quietly.

"We agree to all your conditions," Mr. Defense guy says flatly, without conferring with anyone.

The bigwig FBI guy looks peeved, but he doesn't contradict the Department of Defense guy.

"All right," Mr. FBI says, a brief scowl flickering across his face. "Any other *conditions,* Mr. Faraday?"

"Yes."

Mr. FBI guy bristles. Obviously, that wasn't what he was expecting to hear.

"I'll instruct my team to transfer all but one percent of The Club's funds into an offshore account for your exclusive access," Jonas says. "You'll be enabled to unilaterally change passwords and take immediate and sole custody of the funds."

"And what about the remaining one percent you don't plan on transferring to us?" Mr. FBI guy asks.

"Our finder's fee," Jonas replies. "Five and a half million and change."

Mr. FBI guy walks over to the corner of the room to confer with one of the Department of Justice guys in the back for a moment. "That's a reasonable finder's fee," he says, returning to his chair. "Capped at one percent of whatever funds you ultimately transfer to us."

"There will be several beneficiaries who'll share in that one percent fund," Jonas says. "And I want all of them to partake in their money without taxation—completely tax-free."

FBI guy glances across the room at Department of Justice guy. "No one in this room has jurisdiction regarding individual tax implications on receipts of funds," Mr. FBI guy says evenly.

"But I'm confident *someone* in this room can make it happen, just this once, since it's a non-negotiable condition here," Jonas says.

Indubitably, I think.

Bigwig FBI guy looks at the Department of Justice guy again and gets a nod. CIA guy walks across the room and leans in for a pow-wow with FBI guy.

"As long as you tell us *today* who's going to share in that money, and in what amounts, we will agree to the tax-free status of any amounts distributed from that fund," FBI guy finally says. He sounds annoyed. "But after we cut this deal with you today, it's final. No new names."

"No problem," Jonas says. "I can identify all beneficiaries right now. Jonas Faraday at five hundred thousand, Peter Hennessey at a million, and Katherine Morgan at a million—for an aggregate total of two and a half million—and the balance of the pot, approximately three million and change, will go to Miss Sarah Cruz."

"No, actually," I pipe in, "that's not accurate."

Jonas gapes at me, blindsided.

I've been thinking about the three-million-dollar thing quite a bit since Jonas first suggested it to me, and I'm certain I've got a better way to distribute that money than handing it all to me. "The team members Jonas just identified, including myself, will share an aggregate pot of three and a half million and change. *One* million and change, not three, will go to me. The remaining two million dollars flat will be distributed in equal shares to certain beneficiaries who aren't on our team."

Jonas is dumbfounded.

"In order to maintain the strictest levels of confidentiality about this whole situation, I think the two million dollars should be distributed by the U.S. Government to these beneficiaries instead of by us. Are you amenable to that?"

Mr. FBI guy is noncommittal. "It depends. Let's hear it."

Jonas looks totally confused.

"Okay. The first recipient is Mariela Rafaela León de Guajardo, Jonas' former nanny, currently living in Venezuela with her husband and three teenage children."

Jonas' face turns bright red. He looks down at the table.

"Special Agent Sheffield has tracked down Mariela's contact information. Will you be so kind as to provide that to everyone, Agent Sheffield?"

Eric's face lights up at the mention of his name. "Yes."

"Mariela was deported to Venezuela in 1994. From what I can see, it looks like Jonas' father, Joseph Faraday, pulled some strings with friends in high places to make that happen."

I look at Jonas. He's biting his lip, staring at the table, apparently trying to contain himself.

"I was thinking you might characterize Mariela's payment as some sort of compensation relating to her deportment."

"She'll get her money," the FBI guy says curtly, taking notes. "How the payment will be characterized, I make no promises."

"Okay, that's great. Thank you. The second beneficiary is Mrs. Renee Westbrook Santorini—mother of two and widow of Navy SEAL Robert Santorini."

Jonas shakes his head at me—but it's a "you never cease to amaze me" gesture, not a chastisement.

"Special Agent Sheffield has Renee Santorini's contact information, as well."

Eric nods. He's trying to look serious and professional, I can tell, but he looks like a kid blowing out his birthday candles.

"Mrs. Santorini was Jonas' grade-school teacher. Her deceased husband was Navy SEAL Robert Santorini, based in San Diego and killed in action in 1999. I was thinking you could characterize Renee Santorini's money as something connected to her deceased husband's naval service?"

Mr. FBI guy nods. "I'm sure we can do something along those lines."

I'm on a roll. "Georgia Marianne Walker of Seattle."

Jonas' face contorts with emotion. He clears his throat and looks down again.

"I'm not sure how you should characterize her payment. She's a single mother, a recent cancer survivor, works for the U.S. Postal Service." I pause, thinking. "I don't know what—"

"I think Ms. Walker is about to receive an inheritance as the only surviving kin of a third cousin removed she's never heard of," Mr. Bigwig FBI says, suppressing a smile.

I grin. "Perfect. Thank you."

"Okay, anyone else?" FBI man says, looking up from his notepad. He's noticeably warmed to me during this exchange. I guess he's decided he's not too annoyed with me for making these requests, after all.

"Nope, that's it," I say, smiling at my new best friend. "Mariela, Renee, and Georgia will each share equally in two million."

"No, wait," Jonas says firmly, and my stomach drops into my toes. Have I misread his reaction to all this? Is he upset with me?

"There's one more recipient," Jonas says. "Four beneficiaries will make it an even five hundred thousand per person—and that's a nice round number."

Oh, thank God. He's on board. But who's his fourth? I hold my breath.

"Gloria Cruz of Seattle," Jonas says.

I put my hand over my mouth.

Jonas flashes me the briefest of smiles, but then he's quickly all business again.

Oh, my sweet Jonas. He's already donated a ridiculous amount of money to my mom's charity—and now he wants to give her a piece of this pie, too? This is a huge kindness to my mother, but it's also a windfall for me, seeing as how I'd planned to use half my finder's fee money to buy my mom a house. I beam at Jonas and he plants a soft kiss on my cheek.

"Thank you," I whisper.

He smiles at me warmly but then flashes hard eyes at Mr. FBI guy.

"Gloria Cruz runs a nonprofit for abused women, but we want the money to go to her personally, tax-free. You'll have to figure out a reason for her windfall, too."

"We'll figure something out," Mr. FBI guy says. "Is that everyone?" He looks down at his notes. "Mariela, Renee, Georgia, and Gloria. Five hundred thousand each, tax-free, assuming you hand over all the data as promised and successfully transfer the full half-billion."

"Yes, that's everyone," Jonas says. "And we will."

"Any other conditions?" Mr. FBI guy asks, but his tone makes it clear the answer had better be no.

"That's it," I say, exhaling with relief, but Jonas speaks over me at the same time.

"Yeah, one more thing," Jonas says.

More? What more? Holy crap. Whatever it is, he's clearly pushing our luck.

Several of the more uptight guys in the room moan with exasperation and two guys share a "what an asshole" glance.

What the hell is Jonas talking about?

Jonas pauses. "But I'll reveal our final condition to the highest-ranking members in the room only," he says flatly.

What the hell is he talking about?

"This last demand is on a strictly need-to-know basis."

Everyone looks around, not knowing what to do. Stay? Go? Tell him to fuck off? After a bit of low murmuring and hushed conferring, several underlings stand and leave the room, including poor Eric, who looks none too happy about it.

As Eric walks past Jonas toward the door, he shoots him a long, pleading look, clearly hoping Jonas will exempt him from dismissal. But Jonas does no such thing.

I glare at Jonas with my arms crossed over my chest, tapping my toe under the table. Man, oh man, I can't wait to hear this.

After the door has closed behind the departed underlings, including poor Special Agent Eric, Jonas leans into me, his face an inch from mine. "Will you excuse us, too, baby?" he asks softly. He looks like he's asked me if I'd like one lump or two at teatime.

My jaw drops.

A low-frequency rumble erupts throughout the remaining crowd. Every man in this room just flinched with anxiety on Jonas' behalf—they know they're looking at a dead man.

"There's something I prefer to say to these guys out of your presence," Jonas adds politely.

I blink quickly. Did Jonas just say he *prefers* to say something to all these nice gentlemen (and one lady) *outside* of my presence? I touch my cheeks to prevent my head from spinning wildly on my neck in three-sixties. Jonas *prefers* to say something outside of my presence, does he? Well, what if I *prefer* to hear whatever the *fuck* my fucking boyfriend plans to say to these fucking men (and one woman) about *my* fucking life? After all, *I'm* the one with fucking scars on my body. *I'm* the one who almost bled to death in that fucking bathroom. *I'm* the one looking over my shoulder everywhere I go and waking up in a cold sweat almost every fucking night. And *I'm* the one they'll come after if this whole fucking strategy blows up in our faces.

I open my mouth to protest, but Jonas beats me to the punch.

"Remember that promise I wouldn't make to you?" His eyes are granite. "When I wouldn't say, 'I promise to always tell you everything?'"

I nod. Yes, of course, I remember that conversation. It pissed me off.

"This is why." He clenches his jaw. "Right now is exactly the reason I wouldn't make that promise to you."

A shiver runs down my spine. Jonas anticipated this exact moment?

Jonas' gaze is firm.

Someone in the room coughs. I'm not sure if the guy has a tickle in his throat or if he's just too damned uncomfortable at the exchange he's witnessing to contain himself—but either way, my face flushes. I look around. Well, this is awkward. Everyone in the room is waiting on me to make a decision—will I stay or will I go? I can feel them placing mental bets on whether I'm going to burst into tears, shriek like a banshee, or flip the goddamned table in the next five seconds.

I look at Jonas. His eyes are fierce. Unmovable. He's a savage beast. But he's also my sweet Jonas—the man who loves me like no one ever has. The man I love without condition or reservation. The man who'd lay down his life for me without a moment's hesitation. He's the man I trust with my life.

I sigh. If my sweet Jonas needs to say something out of my presence to protect me, if that's what it's going to take for him to do whatever he thinks needs to be done, then so be it. I'll just have to take yet another leap of faith.

I lean in and kiss him on the mouth. I'm not instigating a make-out session with this brief kiss—I'm demonstrating to everyone in the room, including Jonas, that, yes, I trust this man unconditionally. I pull back from our kiss and lean my forehead against his. He touches my cheek. After a brief moment, I look around the room, defiant. There'll be no crying, shrieking or table-flipping today, fellas (and one badass-looking lady).

"Gentlemen," I say, standing. "And lady." She grins at the acknowledgment. "I'm extremely grateful for all your time and attention today. Thank you. Please know that, whatever Jonas is about to say to you, whatever it is, I'm one hundred percent on board."

Chapter 41
Sarah

I'd wanted so much to see the Lincoln Memorial, the Capitol building, the Washington Monument, the Smithsonian, and the Vietnam Veterans' Memorial during our stay in D.C., a place I've wanted to visit my whole life, but it wasn't meant to be. After yesterday's marathon meeting with "the feds" (the term I prefer to use because it sounds so damned cool), Jonas and I were escorted to our hotel—yes, *escorted*—by two men wearing suits and guns and earpieces—yes, *earpieces*—and deposited into our suite and told in no uncertain terms to stay put.

And those two armed escorts (and, eventually, their two replacements) have remained outside our hotel suite ever since, for close to twenty hours. It's not clear if those nice officers have been assigned to guard our door to keep the bad guys *out* or to keep the good guys *in*—but either way, it's pretty darned clear we're not free to leave our room.

So, of course, Jonas and I have made the most of the situation.

Jonas belly laughs and one of the strawberries I've positioned on his stomach rolls off his naked body and onto the bed.

"Oh jeez," I say, quickly replacing the fallen berry. "Stay still." I continue building my strawberry pyramid with utmost care, squinting and biting my lip with concentration as I do.

Jonas laughs again and yet another strawberry rolls onto the white sheet beneath us.

"Jonas P. Faraday," I scold him. "Control yourself. This is serious effing business, man." I take a big bite of one of my building blocks.

He laughs again.

"A little respect, please. I'm building an edifice of epic importance here." I carefully replace the latest errant strawberry, lodging it into a deep groove in Jonas' abs. "I've got to get my foundation right or the whole structure will fail."

"You're *engineering* a strawberry pyramid?" Jonas asks, laughing uproariously—and another strawberry goes ker-plop at his sudden movement.

"Oh my God," I bellow. "You are the worst human strawberry shortcake ever."

Jonas squeals with laughter. I've never heard him laugh quite like this. He sounds like a toddler being tickled. "Sorry," he chokes out.

I replace the latest rogue strawberry and continue building my masterpiece. "Now, hold still, for the love of God," I command. "Or you'll ruin *everything*."

He bursts out laughing again but quickly composes himself at my icy glare. "Yes, Mistress," he says, trying his best to sound submissive—but when I grab the whipped cream canister off the nightstand, eager to top off my teetering creation with a towering *coup de grace*, he guffaws before I've even creamed him.

Oh my gosh, his laughter is divine. It's the sound of pure, uninhibited silliness—absolute and complete abandon—the sound of joy. And it sends me into fits of giggles, too. I put the whipped cream canister back on the nightstand, laughing hysterically, and begin picking the strawberries off him, one by one, tossing them into the nearby champagne bucket as I go.

"I can't do it, " I say, giggling. "You're hopeless."

"Oh no, don't say that, Mistress. Give me another chance. Have mercy on me." He puts his hands behind his head on the pillow and gazes up at me. "There's no such thing as hopelessness, remember?"

I don't know what he's referring to—but I sure love the way his biceps bulge when he bends his arms like that. I take a big bite of another strawberry.

"Oh come on, My Beautiful Intake Agent," he says, smiling up at me. "'We must accept infinite disappointment, but never lose infinite hope.' A really smart intake agent with a delectable ass once recited that quote from Martin Luther King Jr."

Ah yes. I remember now. I mentioned that quote during our first email exchange, before he even knew my name. I can't believe he remembers that.

I snuggle up to him and place a strawberry at his lips. He takes a big bite.

"I've got a quote for you, too, My Brutally Honest Mr. Faraday. 'Hope is the dream of a waking man.' A beautiful, generous, funny, smart, heroic man-whore with smokin' hot abs and luscious lips and, hey, wow—look at that!—*happy* eyes—"

"Yes, very, *very* happy eyes—"

"Huh. A beautiful man-whore with very, *very* happy eyes once recited that Aristotle quote to me."

Jonas' blue eyes crinkle as he smiles at me. He opens his mouth like a baby bird and I feed him another strawberry.

"So, we're agreed I'm not hopeless?" he asks between bites. "You once said there's no such thing as hopelessness. Do you still believe that?"

"Of course, I do. There's always hope—infinite hope."

"Infinite hope," he repeats with reverence. "Speaking of which, you ready for another round of Tit for Tat, My Magnificent Sarah?"

"How is 'infinite hope' a segue for oral sex, Jonas?"

He laughs. "Everything's a segue for oral sex. How do you not know that by now?"

I throw my head back and laugh.

"So, is that a yes?"

"Only if it involves whipped cream."

"Well, fuck. Is there another way to do it?"

I grab the whipped cream canister. "If there is, I don't want to know about it."

Jonas' phone rings on the nightstand and he scrambles to grab it. He looks at the screen. "Oh shit," he mutters.

I know exactly what that means: Eric's calling. We've known something was up since Eric called three hours ago to say it was time for Kat and the boys to start transferring all the money immediately. But exactly what the feds were planning to do, and when, we had no idea. I guess we're about to find out.

"Hello?" Jonas says, answering his phone. "Hey, Eric. Yes." I can hear his heartbeat from here. He listens for a moment. "All of it?" He rolls his eyes like he can't believe what he's hearing. "You're sure?" He nods at me with wide eyes. *All of it,* he mouths. He flashes thumbs up.

Oh my God. Kat and the boys did it—they got the whole five hundred fifty-four million. Holy crap, we're so effing *Ocean's Eleven.*

"Hang on a sec." Jonas puts the phone to his chest. "The final number's just over six hundred million," he whispers. "They must have made some more deposits." He puts the phone back to his ear. "Okay, sorry, what?"

My heart's beating like a hummingbird's wings.

"Right now?" Jonas motions frantically to the TV remote on my side of the bed and I toss it to him like it's a hot potato. "What channel?" Jonas asks. "*Any* channel?" Jonas turns on the TV and flips past *Sponge Bob Square Pants* to the next channel. Bingo. There it is—a major, live-breaking news event—the kind of national story that lands on every major station at once. "Yeah, we're watching. I'll call you back." He hangs up his phone. "Holy shit."

On screen, a female reporter talks into a microphone and presses an earpiece into her ear. "Breaking News: Terrorist Threat Foiled in Las Vegas" scrolls beneath her on the screen. "... a sophisticated terrorist plot uncovered here in Las Vegas," the reporter is in the midst of saying. Behind the reporter, law enforcement officers in Kevlar vests march in and out of a nondescript building, carrying boxes. Wait, holy crap, that's not just any nondescript building—that's The Club's crappy-ass building, the place where Jonas and I met Oksana and Max.

Jonas turns up the volume on the TV.

"Authorities have confirmed the terrorist organization has been plotting a large-scale attack on U.S. soil—possibly in Las Vegas. Details of the plot have not yet been released."

Jonas grabs my thigh and squeezes it, but I'm too freaked out to squeeze back.

"What we know for certain is that the plot was, indeed, 'sophisticated, imminent and massive,' according to authorities—*and* that the terrorist organization has ties to the Russian government."

"Oh shit," Jonas says. "I think she just declared the start of the second Cold War."

"No mention of the prostitution ring?" I ask.

"I guess not."

"I repeat," the reporter says, as if we didn't hear her the first time, "federal authorities have thwarted an imminent terrorist attack here in Las Vegas—and we're being told by reliable sources that the terrorist threat is somehow related to Russia's recent bid for control of Ukraine."

Oksana suddenly appears onscreen behind the reporter. She's being escorted in handcuffs toward an unmarked car.

"There's Oksana," I gasp. Oksana looks shell-shocked—a deer in headlights.

"So far, fourteen people have been arrested in Las Vegas, four more in New York, and eight in Miami, all with confirmed ties to what's being called the largest Russian terrorist cell ever discovered on U.S. soil."

"Wow," Jonas says. "That's an interesting spin. Do they not know the difference between Russia and Ukraine?"

I can't speak. This is surreal.

The reporter presses her earpiece into her ear. "I'm being told that two of the terrorists—excuse me, two of the *alleged* terrorists—are confirmed dead."

Jonas jerks toward the television screen, suddenly mesmerized.

"Both men were killed in a shoot-out with law enforcement during the raid on the compound earlier today."

Jonas makes a low sound I've only previously heard him make during sex.

"The two men reportedly brandished weapons at law enforcement officers . . ."

Jonas growls softly.

". . . and multiple officers fired shots. Both men died immediately at the scene. No law enforcement officers were injured." The reporter presses her earpiece into her ear. "We're being advised by federal authorities that both men were known sympathizers of the Ukrainian separatist movement, but authorities are not yet releasing their identities."

Jonas looks at me, his face aglow, his chest heaving with excitement. Holy moly, he looks positively euphoric. All of a sudden, he grabs my face and kisses me hard, like a mob boss ordering a hit, and when he pulls back from me, his eyes are on frickin' fire.

"My precious baby," he says. He makes an exuberant noise, his face flushed, and kisses me again. He pulls away again, his eyes sparkling. "Yes," he says. "*Yes.*"

I'm in shock—a wet noodle. This is a lot to take in. They're saying The Club is a terrorist organization? Max and Oksana are part of a "Russian terrorist cell" in Las Vegas? I'd expected to hear the words "prostitution ring" and maybe "organized crime" or "crime syndicate." But "terrorist cell"? I never expected to hear those words in a million years, and especially not "Russian terrorist cell."

Jonas flips through the channels quickly, confirming that, yes, this story is everywhere, and then he mutes the TV. He picks up his phone.

"Eric," Jonas mutters, his voice low and intense. "Yeah, I saw. Fuck yeah. You've got the names?" His mouth tilts up into a crooked smile at whatever Eric's saying on the other end of the line and his eyes flicker ferociously. "Thank you. Yeah, you, too. Absolutely." Jonas hangs up and his smile widens.

Wow, that's quite a grin on Jonas' face—if I were to see it in a snapshot totally out of context, I'd swear the photo was taken while Jonas was getting a blowjob; he looks just that turned on.

"Boom," Jonas says softly, his voice simmering with ferocity.

I pause, waiting for more. But apparently that's all he's going to say.

"Boom?" I ask.

He nods slowly, his eyes on fire.

I wait for more, but it doesn't come.

Should I pretend to be confused by Jonas' one-word proclamation of victory? Because I'm not. I'm not confused at all. The truth is I know exactly what names Eric just said to Jonas—no one needs to tell me which two alleged *terrorists* happened to die today. I continue staring at Jonas' blazing eyes and an overwhelming kind of warmth spreads throughout my body.

"Boom, motherfuckers," I say, my voice as sharp as the knife those fuckers used to slice my throat.

Jonas licks his lips slowly. "That's right, baby." He touches the inside of my thigh. "We fucked 'em up the ass real good, didn't we?"

I bite my lip. This just might be the sexiest moment of my entire life. "We sure did, love."

"I've got the biggest boner right now," Jonas says, lifting up the white sheet to prove it.

"Me, too," I say, motioning to the invisible lady-boner on my naked lap.

Jonas chuckles. "Let me take you away today. I don't want to wait another day to take you to my special place." He gently caresses the inside of my thigh and my skin ignites under his touch.

"In a month," I say. Oh God, I'm on fire.

"I don't want to wait."

"I know you don't."

"I want to go right now."

"I know you do. But you have to wait." I shudder as his fingers brush gently between my legs and drift over my sweet spot.

"I hate waiting."

His expression morphs into his patented Jonas-is-a-great-white-shark-and-Sarah-is-a-defenseless-sea-lion smolder. His fingers brush between my legs again, right over my tip, making me throb.

"We did it, baby," he says. "You're safe." His fingers begin caressing me in earnest. "We're free."

My breathing catches with excitement. He's right. We're free—free to begin our new life together. Free to do whatever the hell we want to do. And I know exactly where I want to start exercising my newfound freedom. Without warning, I crawl on top of him and take him into me, all the way, as deeply as I can, moaning softly as I do.

He exhales loudly. "You're safe," he says, closing his eyes. "My Magnificent Sarah."

I exhale, too, a long, shaky breath, and begin moving slowly, ever so slowly, up and down and around, enjoying every sensation of his body fusing with mine.

"Let me take you away, baby," he moans. "I've got something I want to show you."

"In a month," I breathe.

"Bossy," he says. He touches my breast and groans.

"We'll stop in New York before we go home," I say. "You can introduce me to your uncle and tell him about Climb and Conquer in person."

He gently touches the scar on my ribcage. "Whatever you say, my love," he says, moving his body with mine. "A quick stop in New York it is." His hands move to my hips.

The intensity of my movement increases. He did it. Jonas

protected me, just like he promised he would. Oh, yes, yes, yes, my *man* did whatever the *fuck* he had to do to protect me, his *woman*, from the bad guys. And I love him for it. I *fucking* love him for it. Oh, yes, yes, yes, I do. "Thank you, Jonas," I growl, riding him with enthusiasm. "You're my hero."

"You're my everything," he replies. He grabs my butt with zeal. "God, I love this ass." He slaps it.

"Mmm," I say, because that's all the conversation I've got left in me at this particular moment.

He did it. He protected me. We're free. I could cry with joy and relief. I lean down and kiss him, enjoying the feeling of my erect nipples rubbing against his chest. For the first time since those bastards sliced me and stabbed me and left me bleeding out on a bathroom floor, I feel completely safe—carefree, in fact.

"You did it, Jonas."

"*We* did it, baby," he says, his voice straining. He's on the verge of climax. He groans. "We did it together."

Chapter 42
Jonas

Sarah's been talking up a storm the whole time we've been hiking up Mount Olympus behind our guide. Well, actually, she's been Chatty Cathy ever since we boarded our flight for Greece three days ago, obviously relieved as hell to be done with her final exams.

I don't mind Sarah holding up both ends of our conversation during this hike, not at all, because, for the last three weeks, as I've planned and plotted and waited for this special day to arrive, as I've gotten boners in my sleep dreaming about getting down on my knee, as I've daydreamed about asking her the magic question and yearned for the moment when I'm going to slip that ring on her finger (and it's a fucking *epic* ring, by the way), I've increasingly lost my ability to function let alone speak with each slowly passing day. Jesus, by the time we boarded our flight three days ago, I was a total wreck.

I pat the pocket of my hiking pants. Yes, the little box is still there. I let out a long, shaky exhale. I'm ninety-nine percent sure she'll say yes, but it's that one percent chance I'm about to get crushed that's making me crazy. Yes, Sarah loves me, of course. But with Sarah, you never know what she might say or do in any situation. What if she's got some bizarre idea about marriage being the death of a relationship or some other intractable prejudice against holy matrimony, thanks to the shit she witnessed as a kid? It's entirely possible. I don't think it's likely, but she's never once even *hinted* at wanting to get married—and neither have I, for that matter—so you just never know.

I tune into Sarah's chatter for a moment. She's talking about Josh and Kat—about how Kat was headed to L.A. for a long weekend when we left on our trip.

247

"Mmm hmm," I say. I'm elated to hear things are going well for the Playboy and the Party Girl, I really am—and, actually, Josh hasn't stopped talking about Kat since we left Vegas, so I'm not surprised at all—but I can't concentrate on that right now.

When I planned our trip to Greece, I stupidly thought it'd be best for us to arrive, relax, get over our jetlag, explore Athens for a few days, and *then* climb Mount Olympus so I could ask her to be my wife. I truly didn't understand how anticipating this moment would utterly consume me—how eating, sleeping, and simply conversing naturally would become a fucking impossibility. If I'd known, I would have planned this excursion for the first day of our trip.

"So I *think* I answered the question pretty well," she's saying. "But the whole question was totally ambiguous, you know? I feel like you could argue either side of the issue and be right."

She must be talking about one of her final exams from last week—which one, I haven't a clue.

"Sounds like you kicked ass with your answer," I say. Hopefully, that's the right thing to say at this particular moment.

"You really think so?"

"Yeah, I do."

"Well, that calms me down, then. You certainly know your contracts backwards and forwards. But, hey, what about this question on the torts exam . . . ?"

I pat my pants pocket. The little box is still there.

After today, she'll be wearing my ring on her finger for the whole world to see and I'll finally be able to breathe again. Thank God I booked that villa in Mykonos for tomorrow night instead of at the beginning of the trip. If I'd have booked Mykonos for *before* Mount Olympus, I never would have been able to enjoy it, paradise or not. This way, we'll have four glorious days in Nirvana to celebrate our engagement—assuming we'll be celebrating. Oh my God. Fuck me. If she says anything other than yes, I'm going to curl up and die on the spot.

"It's almost like you can feel the ghosts from thousands of years ago, just floating around you, you know?" she says.

"Mmm hmm," I say. I pat my pocket again.

"Like, I dunno, you can feel their collective *wisdom,*" she says. "Like, it's a physical *thing,* just floating in the air."

"Mmm hmm."

248

The hiking trail isn't particularly demanding nor is it all that scenic on this side of the mountain. But this hike isn't what we're here for—it's just a means to an end. Oh my God, I can't wait to finally spill the beans and tell her why we're here.

"It also makes me think, 'Hey, these were real people,' you know? Like, it makes it so clear these weren't just *names* in an ancient history textbook. They were *people* just like you and me. They ate, slept, made love, cried, laughed, loved... You know what I mean?"

"Mmm hmm."

She stops short and I almost walk into her back. She wheels around to look at me. "Are you listening to me, Jonas?"

"Totally," I say. "Every word. I totally agree with everything you've said." But I don't know what the fuck she's just said. I can't think straight right now. All I can think about is asking this beautiful woman to be my wife—the mother of my future children.

She studies me briefly. "Are you okay?"

"Of course."

"You're acting weird."

My chest tightens. Does she know? "I am?"

"Yes."

"Well, I think I'm just . . . deep in thought."

"About what?"

"You."

She studies me. "Me?"

"Yes."

"Good thoughts?"

"The best thoughts. You're the goddess and the muse, Sarah Cruz. There's nothing but goodness when my thoughts are about you."

"Oh, Jonas." She smiles. "You're so sweet." She turns back around happily and catches up to the guide on the trail. "So, anyway, what part did you like best?"

What part of what did I like best? What the fuck was she just talking about? I try to recall what the fuck she just said. *Real people.* Yeah, that's right. She said they're not just names in a history book, they're real people. She must have been talking about our walking tour of Athens on our first full day here.

"The Acropolis," I answer. "There's nothing like seeing the ground where Plato and Aristotle actually walked. That's what captured my imagination when I was eighteen and it was even more magical to see it with you." Oh my God. Stringing together so many coherent words just took a lot out of me. There's only one thing I want to talk about right now—and it's not the Acropolis. I'm dying to finally let loose with the speech I've been practicing in my head, day and night, for a solid three weeks.

"Yeah, me, too," she says. "That was amazing—especially getting to see it with you." She swivels her head around and shoots me a lovely smile.

I smile back. Or, at least I think I do. Who knows what the fuck my face looks like right now—my facial muscles are not my own. Holy shit, I'm losing my mind. I've been dreaming of this moment nonstop since we left Uncle William's house a month ago.

Of course, Uncle William fell head-over-heels in love with Sarah the minute he met her. In fact, I'm positive Uncle William reacted so well to the news of my departure from Faraday & Sons because Sarah was there, casting some kind of spell on him. Sure, when Josh joined us on the second night and dropped the "I'm leaving the company, too" bomb on poor Uncle William, that made things a little harder for him to swallow. But, call me crazy, my uncle actually seemed relieved by Josh's news a little bit, almost like he'd been waiting for the Faraday brothers' simultaneous departure from the company for a long time and now he could exhale. All in all, the whole weekend went surprisingly well—and I'm sure Sarah was mostly to thank for that.

"You gonna marry this girl?" Uncle William asked me after dinner on the second night, the minute Sarah had left the dining room to use the bathroom.

"Absolutely," I answered, shocking myself with how easily the word came out. It felt enthralling to admit my intentions out loud—especially to my family. "As soon as humanly possible, in fact."

"That's awesome, bro," Josh said. "Does she know?"

That's when my knee started jiggling under the table. "No," I said, my chest constricting. "Am I supposed to *ask* her if I can *ask* her?" It was an honest question.

Josh laughed. "No, Jonas, you dumbshit. That's not what I meant. I'm just saying if you're gonna surprise the girl, then make sure you blow her socks off. This is the story she's gonna be telling her grandkids one day. So don't fuck it up."

Well, duh, as Sarah says. I already knew that. And yet, at Josh's words, I suddenly felt like I was gonna throw up, and I haven't stopped feeling that way since. All throughout the past month, even as I've been busy as fuck transitioning out of Faraday & Sons and into Climb and Conquer, I've grown increasingly anxious. I'm not nervous about making Sarah my wife—fuck no, that's the thing I'm least anxious about in my whole life—I'm just worried I won't be able to deliver the fairytale proposal my precious baby so richly deserves.

"So this is Mount Olympus?" Sarah says, looking around. "Huh. Not what I expected."

"What'd you expect?"

She pauses. "Oh, I dunno. I thought maybe there'd be an old guy with a long white beard holding lightning bolts up here."

I chuckle. "Actually, little known fact: Zeus is so old by now, he's sitting in a rocking chair at the top of the mountain, doing Sudoku."

She laughs. "It's super cool to think about the ancient Greeks looking up at this very mountaintop, imagining the gods up here."

The guide takes this as his cue (thankfully, because I've just exhausted my ability to converse for the foreseeable future) and he begins a lengthy explanation about Mount Olympus as the mythological home of the Twelve Olympians.

Sarah listens to him with rapt attention as I tune out.

I love how Sarah hasn't once asked me why we're hiking up Mount Olympus. I guess she thinks the mere existence of a mountain, anywhere in the world, is enough of a draw for me to suggest climbing it—which, normally, I suppose, would be true. But today isn't a normal day.

We turn a corner in the trail and traverse over a small crest, and, just like that, we arrive at our destination—a small plateau spanning just below one of the mountain's craggy peaks. I'm relieved to see that our next set of guides is already here, exactly as planned, awaiting us with all appropriate gear.

Sarah stops short on the trail, apparently seeing the crew awaiting us, too. She whips around to face me. "Are you effing kidding me right now?"

She must have seen the two colorful parachutes spread out on the ground.

I smile at her. "No, I am not effing kidding you right now."

She glares at me.

"We're going to jump off Mount Olympus, baby. And then we're gonna paraglide through the air, all the way to the beautiful, white-sand beaches of the Aegean Sea."

She smashes her lips together.

"And it's gonna be fucking awesome."

"Have I mentioned I *hate* heights?"

"Many times."

She blinks rapidly. "Are you trying to make me hate you?"

"Quite the opposite."

"Then you suck at whatever you're trying to do because I *hate* you right now."

I laugh. "Come on, baby. Let me show you what we're gonna do."

Chapter 43
Sarah

I'm shaking. I really, really hate heights. "Jonas, I don't know about this," I say. I'm stuffed into a thick flight suit and the guy who's going to pilot my paraglider is securing my harness and double-checking all his lines, getting ready to jump off the frickin' mountain with me strapped to his body like an infant in a papoose. I can't imagine what part of this idea made Jonas think: *Sarah.*

"Looks good, baby," Jonas says. He steps up really close to me and double-checks the strap on my helmet. "Now remember, all you have to do is sit back and relax and enjoy the panoramic views as they segue from mountains to fields to sparkling sea."

He's quite a salesman, I must admit. He makes torture sound almost lovely.

"Just sit back and enjoy the ride. That's all you ever have to do when you're with me."

"You've already proved that to me a thousand times over— every single night, in fact—and I've *surrendered* to you countless times and acknowledged you as my lord-god-master. Why do you need me to enact yet another metaphor to emphasize your point?"

He rolls his eyes. "Because for once in my life, I'm not talking about sex, baby. I'm talking about *life*. This is a metaphor for *life*— for our life together. I want you to know that when you're with me, all you ever have to do is sit back, relax, and enjoy the ride—because I'll always take care of you."

Well, that was actually a very sweet little speech. He obviously put a lot of thought into it. And yet, I can't help myself from being irritated. I really, really hate heights. "Yeah. You'll always take care of me, other than when you're pushing me off high places, even though I'm scared to death of heights."

He looks distressed.

I sigh. I'm so mean. "Oh, I'm sorry, Jonas." I grab his hand. "I'm sorry. Tell me what you wanted to say. This is all a grand metaphor for *life,* not sex—if I sit back and relax and enjoy the ride . . . Come on, baby. I'm mean and horrible. You put a lot of thought into this. I'm listening. Continue."

His cheeks flush.

"Please. Seriously. I'm listening."

He clears his throat. "Even when something scares you, if you're willing to take a leap of faith—with me—you might discover you enjoy the ride more than you ever imagined possible," he says softly.

"That's lovely. A fantastic metaphor. Thank you for that."

He's gaining confidence again. "Ah, but this is only one of *many* metaphors I've planned for you today."

"Oh yeah? Is today Metaphor Day, my sweet Jonas?"

"Yes, as a matter of fact, it is. Today is Jonas and Sarah's Metaphorical Adventure."

"Oh, how you love your metaphors, Jonas Faraday."

"I really do." He takes a step forward, right up into my face. "May I tell you about the metaphor you've already unknowingly enacted for me today?"

"Please do."

"Our hike up Mount Olympus. 'Twas a metaphor."

"'Twas?"

"'Twas. You'll recall I followed you the entire way up the trail. Do you know why I did that?"

I shake my head, grinning. He's so cute.

"Because I've always got your back, my love—and because I'd follow you to the ends of the earth. 'Twas a double metaphor. I get double points."

I tilt my head at him. He's thought quite a bit about all this, hasn't he?

"Next metaphor. We're standing on the highest peak in all of Greece—Mount Olympus—the home of the gods." He puts his hand on my cheek. "Do you know why I wanted to bring you here—to this particular mountaintop, specifically?"

"Because you're a sadist?" I say softly, but my tone is much friendlier than my actual words.

He takes a long, deep, steadying breath and moves his hand to my shoulder. "Sarah Cruz, I brought you here, to this specific spot on planet earth, for two reasons." He grins. "Double points *again.*"

I smile broadly.

"First, this is the highest peak in all of Greece—which means I am therefore compelled to climb it and shout to the world about my undying love for you."

Oh my God.

"But we're not here simply because Mount Olympus is the tallest peak," he continues. "We're also here because it's the home of the gods, Sarah, which means it's *your* rightful home." His eyes sparkle. "You're the goddess and the muse, Sarah Cruz. My precious baby, you are every Greek goddess, rolled into one."

"Oh, Jonas."

"You're Aphrodite," he says, "the goddess of love, beauty, pleasure, and sex—the hottest fucking sex the world has ever seen, oh my God."

I blush.

"You're Athena—the goddess of wisdom, courage, inspiration, law, justice, strength, and strategy. You're so fucking smart, baby— you blow me away."

I bite my lip.

"You're Artemis—the protector of women. Baby, your gigantic heart—the way you so genuinely care about helping women and making the world a better place—it's my favorite thing about you, by far."

I can't believe he's saying all this. I'm swooning.

"But, wait, there's more." His mouth twists into a crooked grin. "You're my Demeter, too—the goddess of the harvest, life, and sustenance. Baby, you're *my* sustenance. I physically *need* you like a flower needs sunshine and soil and water—you *feed* me, baby, right at my roots. *You give me life.*"

Holy crap—my knees just wobbled.

"And, of course, My Magnificent Sarah, let us not forget, you're also Hera." He pauses for dramatic effect. "The goddess of *marriage.*"

Come again?

He beams at me.

He's speaking metaphorically, right?

"My Magnificent Sarah, you're all of these powerful and revered and beautiful goddesses, all rolled into one."

He wasn't being literal just now when he used the word *marriage*, was he?

"But on top of all that, let's not forget, you're also the *muse*, Sarah Cruz—the inspiration for female beauty itself. You are *woman-ness* from the ideal realm."

Oh my God. This is all just so over-the-top—so beautiful—so *epic.* "Oh, Jonas," I sigh. For reasons I'll never fully understand, my beautiful hunky-monkey boyfriend is flat-out addicted to mustard and, thank the Lord, I just happen to be a big ol' vat of it.

"And that, my dearest love, is why we're standing atop Mount Olympus, the home of the gods and the highest peak in all of Greece." He sighs like he's greatly relieved, and then he takes another deep breath, apparently gearing up to say something more.

There's more?

"But none of that answers the question why we're about to jump *off* the highest peak in Greece, does it?" He looks like he's bursting to tell me a grand secret.

I shake my head, grinning. He's so damned cute. How on earth did his beautiful mind come up with all this? "Please, love. Tell me why, oh why, we're jumping off this mythical mountain? I'm hanging on your every word."

"Because, lovely Sarah, you and I are ready to leap to the next level. We first leaped off a thirty-foot waterfall together—because that's what we could handle at the time. But now we're ready to leap from heaven itself."

I feel like he just made love to me with his words. Is he making some sort of eternal commitment to me—right here and now? Is this all some elaborate, metaphorical commitment ceremony?

"Which brings me to our next metaphor. We're about to take a giant leap off a mountain, My Magnificent Sarah. And yet, you'll notice I've provided you with a parachute for your landing—well, a paraglider, technically, but for purposes of our metaphor, we'll call it a parachute—because, no matter what happens, no matter how we wind up leaping in life, we'll always do it together—and your safety and protection and comfort will always be my greatest priority."

This is insane. I'm melting here.

Jonas' face is adorable right now—he's euphoric. He's the most beautiful man in the world. And I'm the luckiest girl in the world.

Yes, he's metaphorically marrying me right now; I'm sure of it. I touch the bracelet around my wrist.

"I love you, Jonas," I say. Oh good Lord, I want to say so much more than that—but if I know my Jonas, he's been planning this speech for quite some time and I don't want to knock him off his game.

"So you'll jump off Mount Olympus with me, then?" he asks. He looks unsure of my answer.

"Of course, I will, baby. I'll jump off any mountain with you—not to mention any waterfall, tree, ladder, bridge, footstool, or curb—as long as I'm with you."

He practically jumps up and down with glee.

"Oh, Jonas."

"But wait—there's more," he says. He stops to think. He suppresses a humongous smile. "But not now. Later."

My stomach flips. More? My mind is spiraling out of control, having all kinds of crazy-ass thoughts—thoughts I absolutely shouldn't be having. Thoughts he couldn't possibly live up to.

"I'm only sorry I can't pilot you myself. You being strapped to some random Greek dude when you leap off Mount Olympus really fucks up my metaphor. But I figured leaping and dying wasn't really optimal in light of the metaphor I'm going for here."

I laugh. "I'll just imagine I'm strapped to you the whole time."

"Please do."

A pilot approaches. "Are you ready?" he asks us in a thick Greek accent.

"Yeah. I'll be going first," Jonas tells him. "Okay, baby?"

"Great."

"I want to be down there waiting for you when you arrive."

"Another metaphor I presume?"

"No. I just want to take pictures of your face during the landing. It's gonna be hilarious."

I laugh.

"But there *is* yet another metaphor awaiting us down at the bottom—the biggest metaphor of all, my precious baby—which I'll tell you about in great detail after we land."

My stomach flips. Electricity courses through my veins. "Can you give me a little hint?"

"Nope. I'll tell you after you land." Jonas leans in and kisses me.

His tongue parts my lips and jolts my entire body. "Enjoy your ride, my precious baby," he says. "Just sit back, relax, and take in the beautiful views."

I have the urge to applaud raucously—holy hell, I've just been treated to the most magnificent declaration of love ever bestowed upon a woman throughout the history of time—this was the *Iliad* of love declarations, people—but I somehow manage to control myself. "That was beautiful, Jonas," I say. "I'm swooning—literally, swooning."

"Really? I'm doing okay so far?" He grins shyly.

What the heck does that mean? "Of course. You're doing great *so far*," I say. "You're a poet—the most romantic man who ever lived. An absolute master of Valentine's Day bullshit."

He grins.

"I pity the poor fool who even *thinks* about declaring his love to a woman after what you just did—I just experienced the divine original form of declaring-love-ness."

Jonas flashes an exuberant smile that lights up his entire face. "It's easy to deliver the divine original form of declaring-love-ness to the divine original form of woman-ness."

A giggle escapes my throat.

He laughs. "So are you ready to leap?"

Well, that sure makes me stop giggling in a heartbeat. Holy crap. I'd kind of forgotten about the actual jumping part. "Sure," I squeak out.

He laughs and kisses me on the cheek. "Then I'll see you down on the glorious, white-sand beaches of the Aegean, my precious baby." He turns to his pilot and flashes him a thumbs-up. "Let's do it."

Chapter 44
Jonas

Here she comes, floating down from the sky like the beautiful butterfly she is. Oh my God, her face is gorgeous right now—bursting with excitement and accomplishment and awe. I can almost hear her squealing from my vantage point all the way down on the beach. I laugh out loud as I crane my neck up to watch her descend. Wow, she's *elated.* I take a million pictures of her with my phone as she waves and mugs for the camera. Oh God, she's adorable in her little helmet with her cute, flushed cheeks. She's positively glowing.

Her pilot yells something to her—I'm sure he's prepping her for landing, probably telling her to stand up in the harness and get ready to hit the ground running. As he speaks, her happy expression completely vanishes. If I had to caption her face right now, it'd be, *Holy shit.* I can't help but belly laugh.

They're coming in fast. There's no turning back. Oh, my poor baby. She looks scared to death—in a sudden and total panic. I feel an acute pang of guilt for forcing her to do this. Maybe there was a kinder way to impose this last, glorious metaphor upon her? Oh well. It's too late now. Here she comes.

Their landing is perfect, thank God—soft as a feather, a gentle touchdown followed by an adrenaline-fueled run. Sarah and her pilot run, run, run together—oh man, look at her go—she's like a pro—for a solid five steps, that is, and then she crumples to the ground in a relieved heap.

I bound toward her, shouting her name as I approach.

She's thrashing around on the ground like an overturned turtle. Her pilot releases her tethers and she springs up off the ground. She runs toward me, shouting at the top of her lungs, and leaps into my arms, squealing and screaming.

"Did you see me?" she shrieks. "I did it!" She wraps her legs around my waist and clutches me, closing her eyes as I pepper her ebullient face with zealous kisses.

"You were amazing," I say. "Incredible!" I kiss her and kiss her and kiss her.

"I did it," she screams. She throws her arms around my neck and squeezes me tight. "I jumped off a cliff! I ran *toward* a frickin' cliff—not away from it—and then I *jumped*. Oh my God, I was crapping my pants, Jonas, but I kept running anyway and then I *leaped*." She kisses me again, but then she abruptly pulls away and swats at my shoulder, a sudden scowl overtaking her face. "I almost had a heart attack, Jonas Faraday. What the hell were you trying to do to me?" She's trying to sound pissed, but her face is playful. "It's not normal to run *toward* a cliff and jump, you know that, right?"

I laugh. "But it sure is fun, isn't it?"

"So fun."

"You did it, baby."

"I did it. And so did you. *We* did it." She beams at me. "And the view. Jonas, oh my God."

"Gorgeous, right?"

"The most beautiful thing I've ever seen. Just heaven on earth."

"The color of the water—"

"To die for," she says. "I've never seen water that shade of turquoise before."

"And wasn't it relaxing once you were up there?"

"Yeah, once I stopped having a heart attack from the takeoff, I was like, 'Hey, this is really nice.'" She swats my shoulder again. "Until the *landing,* oh my God, you sadist."

I burst out laughing. "You should have seen your face. Priceless."

"Are you *trying* to torture me?"

I kiss her. "No, my precious baby. Quite the opposite." My heart suddenly leaps into my mouth. This is it. The moment I've been waiting for. Oh my God. I take a deep breath. "Lemme put you down."

She unwraps her legs from me and slides down to the ground.

My face feels hot. I can't breathe. This is it. Holy shit. My pulse pounds in my ears. "There's one more metaphor I want to tell you about—the biggest one of all."

She shifts her weight.

I pat my pocket. Yep, the box is still there. "Sarah," I warble. I clear my throat. "My Magnificent Sarah." Oh God, my throat is closing up.

She unlatches her helmet and takes it off. She looks anxious.

I take another deep breath. "Thank you," I begin. Shit. That's not how I practiced this. Where did that come from? I've got to pull myself together and do this right.

She presses her lips together, gazing at me intently.

I take yet another deep breath, trying to gather myself. What did I plan to say? Whatever it was, it feels all wrong now. The only thing I feel right now is gratitude—love and gratitude. Fuck my planned speech. I'll just say what's in my heart right this minute. "Thank you, Sarah," I say. "Thank you for loving me—for teaching me how to be *loved*. Your love is my savior." My lip trembles and I pause, steadying myself. "Your love has given me life."

"Oh, Jonas," she says, her voice brimming with emotion.

I cup her face in my hands. "I got it wrong when I called our love madness. I'm sorry about that. Our love's not madness, baby—our love is what's finally made me *sane*."

She smiles.

I rest my hands on her shoulders. "Sarah Cruz, when you crawled inside that cocoon-built-for-two with me, when you gave yourself to me, totally and completely, that's when I discovered true happiness for the first time in my life." I stuff down a sudden wave of emotion.

She blinks slowly, suppressing tears.

"And I thought . . ." My voice quavers, so I pause. "I thought there could be no greater happiness than that, than being inside that cocoon with you for the rest of my life." My palms are sweaty. I pat my pocket and feel the little box bulging there.

The pilots and some other people milling on the beach are chatting in Greek around us. Sarah looks like she's about to burst into tears. I feel light-headed.

"I thought our little cocoon built for two was the culmination of human possibility," I say.

Her big brown eyes are smiling at me.

"But somewhere along the line, I'm not sure precisely when, I discovered an even greater joy than being inside that cocoon with you. It was watching you burst *out* of that cocoon and become the beautiful butterfly you were always meant to be, right before my eyes."

261

Her face contorts with a thousand emotions all at once.

"When you became my beautiful, powerful, delicate, miraculous, glorious, iron butterfly, *that's* when I discovered the divine original form of happiness. *Pure ecstasy.*"

Tears pool in her eyes.

Oh my God. This is it. My heart is going to crack my sternum from the inside.

I take a deep, steadying breath, pull the box out of my pocket, and bend down on my knee. I look up into Sarah's beautiful face and . . . she explodes into tears.

Oh my God. I haven't even asked her yet—*I haven't even opened the box yet.* I'm down on my knee with a *closed* ring box and she's bawling like I just stole her lunch money. Should I stand and comfort her? No, I can't. I'm gonna have a heart attack if I wait another second to say these words to her. I'm a runaway train.

I open the box and she turns into a certifiable maniac—she's crying uncontrollably and laughing with glee at the same time. Oh, my baby. She's a hot mess—and I'm loving it.

She puts a shaking hand to her mouth. "Jonas," she breathes. "Oh my God."

Our pilots and a few other bystanders milling on the beach have gathered around us. I guess a guy on bended knee with a ring translates in any culture.

"You're the goddess and the muse, Sarah Cruz," I say, hoisting the rock up. "I love you more than any man has ever loved any woman in the history of time. Our love is the joy of the good, the wonder of the wise, the amazement of the gods." I pause, not because I'm scared, not because I'm unsure, but because I want to savor the moment. "Our love is the *envy* of the gods, my precious baby." I inhale deeply and look into her big, brown eyes. "Will you marry me, My Magnificent Sarah Cruz?"

She drops to her knees right in front of me, leveling her face with mine, throws her arms around my neck, and kisses me voraciously, almost snuffing the life out of me as she does.

Our small audience on the beach applauds.

"Yes?" I choke out. I can't breathe. Good God, the woman's suffocating me. "Yes?"

"Yes," she shrieks. "Yes!" I grab her shaking hand and begin slipping the ring onto her finger, but she pulls away. Oh God, I've got the wrong hand. She laughs and gives me her other one and I somehow manage to slide the ring onto the correct finger. Oh my God, I can't believe it. She's wearing my ring. It's official. Sarah Cruz is going to be my wife.

Sarah squeals, gazing at her hand. "Oh my God, Jonas. It's breathtaking!"

I hold up her hand and take a look. Wow, it looks even prettier on her hand than I imagined it would. "It's *magnificent*," I say. "Because nothing short of that would have been worthy of My Magnificent Sarah." I stand and pull her up with me, and then I kiss her like I'm reviving a drowning woman—or maybe she's reviving me.

Our small audience on the beach applauds again and someone shouts, "*Bravo!*"

"My future wife," I say to the crowd, pointing at her. "She said yes."

She laughs. "Oh, Jonas."

"I don't want to wait." I grip her shoulders with urgency. "Let's get married right away."

Her face bursts into flames of excitement. "Whatever you say— my future *husband*." She giggles.

"Baby, take a month to plan the wedding and—"

"Whoa, what?"

"—make it however you want it. Hire ten wedding planners if you want. I don't care what you do, as long as I get to call you my wife a month from now."

She puts her hands on her cheeks like she's the *Home Alone* kid. "Jonas, I can't plan a wedding in a *month*."

"Sure you can."

"No, you don't understand. I need a year—six months at least."

I groan. There's no fucking way I can wait six months to marry this girl. "*Please*, Sarah. *Please*." I'm manic. I'd marry her right this very second if she'd let me. "Spend whatever you want—hire whoever you need. I don't care what you do. Just don't make me wait. *Please*."

She laughs. "You're so effing demanding, you know that?"

I don't care if I'm demanding. Not about this. I absolutely can't wait. Waiting a whole month for this moment to arrive almost killed me—I can't wait more than a month to call her my wife. "Sarah, please, please, please."

She shakes her head, like she can't believe what she's gotten herself into with me, but then she shrugs with resignation. "Okay, baby, whatever you say."

"Anything's possible when you throw enough money at it. Trust me."

She grins and rolls her eyes. "You know what? I don't even care about the wedding. All I care about is being married to you."

"No, no, baby, make it however you want it. Hire whoever you need to make it perfect—pay five times as much as any sane person would pay. I don't care what you do—just please, please, please don't make me wait."

"Okeedokee," she says. She snaps her fingers. "Easy peasy."

I pull her close. I'm so fucking relieved I could scream. "Really?"

"Of course." She kisses me. "I told you—all I care about is being married to you. The wedding's just a party. I can put together a party in a month. No sweat."

I feel high. Adrenaline is flooding me. My cock is tingling. My skin is electrified. "Let's run down the beach to some secluded spot and go skinny-dipping," I whisper, my chest heaving with excitement.

She looks at the rock on her hand and grimaces. "I don't want my ring to come off in the ocean."

Motherfucker. The engagement ring I bought for my future bride is gonna keep me from making love to my future bride right now? Talk about irony.

She motions to the pilots. "Do either of you have an extra parachute we could bring with us on a little walk? We'll bring it right back." She turns to me and grins. "Where there's a will, there's a way."

I smile broadly. She's so fucking smart. And so fucking hot.

One of the pilots pulls a colorful parachute from his pack. "Is not for flying. Is for to practice on the ground," he says. "Is okay?" He hands it to her.

"Perfect. Thank you." Her eyes blaze wickedly at me. "What do you think, baby?"

"I think, fuck yeah."

I grab the parachute in one hand and her hand in the other and we sprint down the beach, laughing the whole time. We run and run, until there's no one around us as far as the eye can see, and when we're sure we've reached a stretch of beach that's ours alone, we lie down in the sand and throw the parachute over us. Filtered sunlight streams through the brightly colored fabric casting glorious swaths of reflected red, blue, and yellow onto the sand all around us.

We're savage animals, both of us, desperate for each other. She rips off her shirt, gasping—her face awash in a haze of reflected blue—and I rip off mine. She pulls frantically at my pants and my cock springs out.

"Jack in the box," she says, panting.

"Only if you're the box."

She laughs—she always laughs at that one.

"The future Mrs. Faraday," I mutter, slipping my hand inside her pants and cupping her bare ass in my palm. Oh shit, I'm hard as a rock. "The future Mrs. Faraday," I say again, just because it feels so fucking good to say it. "You're gonna be my wife."

She groans loudly and nibbles on my lip. Her hand grips my shaft. "My future *husband.*"

Her words release a surge of electricity through my veins. "Again," I moan, pulling her pants off.

"My future *husband.*" She works my shaft with authority, making me shudder, and then leans back into the sand, pulling my cock with her, inviting me inside her, a haze of red-filtered sunlight washing across her beautiful face.

She tugs on me, coaxing me to enter her, but it's not going to happen. I've just asked this glorious woman to become my *wife*—and nothing, not even the indomitable Sarah Cruz, not even Orgasma the All-Powerful, is going to prevent me from taking my future wife to church.

I kneel between her legs and open her thighs and begin worshipping at her altar like the zealot I am—oh God, the future Mrs. Faraday tastes so good—and she moans and quivers under my tongue.

"My future wife," I whisper, licking her again and again. "I'm gonna marry you, baby," I say hoarsely, tasting her the way I know she likes it best—until, finally, deliciously, she arches her back into me, and comes undone.

When her climax subsides, she opens her eyes and smiles at me. "Get inside me, future husband."

That's all the encouragement I need.

"This is the best day of my life," she whispers into my ear, tilting her hips up to greet mine, her face now awash in a haze of yellow.

"Mine too." I kiss her deeply.

She trembles. "Oh, Jonas." She wraps her legs around my back and moves her pelvis with mine. "That was the best proposal ever."

"I did okay?"

"Oh, baby, better than okay. You're a *beast*." She grunts. "Now fuck me like the beast you are."

Damn, this woman turns me on. I do exactly as I'm told.

"Just like that," she says. "*Yes.*" She bites my neck.

"Ow." I shudder.

She laughs and bites me again.

"Why so violent?"

She laughs again.

I shift myself so my cock rubs her at a new angle and her body ignites underneath me.

"Oh, God, just like that. Don't stop doing that." She gasps. "Oh, yes, baby—oh my God—yes, yes, yes."

There are no words for this kind of ecstasy because there's never been a love like ours. She's the divine original form of woman—and our love is the divine original form of love. "Sarah," I say, teetering on the edge of my own Nirvana, "I love you."

"Mmm."

The parachute casts magnificent colors around us in the sand, illumineting our cathedral as surely as any stained glass window ever could.

"I love you, baby," I groan, kissing her again and again.

"Jonas," she breathes, teetering right on the edge. "*Yes.*"

"And I'm gonna marry you," I say.

She begins to make The Sound.

"You're gonna be my *wife*."

She's hanging on by a thread.

"Mrs. Faraday."

That does it. She's gone.

And so am I.

She's my savior.

She's my religion.

She's my redemption.

I'm born again.

There's never been a love like ours.

And there never will be again.

Our love is the joy of the good, the wonder of the wise, the amazement of the gods—the culmination of human possibility.

Epilogue
Jonas

"Mrs. Faraday," I whisper softly.

She doesn't reply. She's lying on her belly, her face smashed into her pillow.

I run my fingertips slowly down her back over her tank top, softly singing the chorus from "I Melt With You" by Modern English. I'm a horrifically bad singer, I know this without a doubt— but, for some reason, she loves it when I sing, especially this song.

Still nothing.

"Oh, Mrs. Faraday?" I call out softly. I sing to her again.

"Mmm."

"Good morning, My Magnificent Mrs. Faraday," I whisper. "You awake?"

"I am now," she says, her voice extra gravelly. "How are you already back on Seattle time?"

"I'm not. My body's still on New Zealand time—it's just that my mind is too happy to sleep."

She buries her face in her pillow and groans. "I'm married to a madman."

I poke her ass cheek through her pajama bottoms. "Hey, wifey."

She swats at my hand. "Weirdo."

"Wife?"

"What time is it in New Zealand right now? Because that's what time my body thinks it is."

"Come on, sleepyhead. I've been awake for three hours. I've worked out, done all the laundry in both our suitcases, and answered a hundred emails. And now I'm lonely for my sexy wifey."

"How the hell do you sleep so little, you nutball?" She still

267

won't look at me—she's stubbornly got her face buried in her pillow. "I swear to God you're not even human. You're a frickin' droid."

I sit on the bed next to her and caress the curve of her beautiful ass. I can't help myself—I pull down her pajama pants and lay a soft kiss on her ass cheek. It's taking all my restraint not to yank her pants all the way down and do a whole lot more than that, but I know she's exhausted. "What if I were to tell you I brought you a cappuccino?"

She lifts her head. "Then I would say, 'Why, good morning, dear husband. So nice to see you.' You should have opened with that, you big dummy." She turns over and sits up.

I hand her the mug off the nightstand. "Here you go, dear wife."

"Thank you, dear husband, you're the best—even if you're a nutball and a droid and a weirdo." She takes a sip. "Mmm."

"Did you sleep well?"

"Like a baby. It was amazing to finally sleep in my own bed again."

"There's no place like home." Especially when it's *our* home.

Of course, I loved every minute of our honeymoon—a week in New Zealand (it's the adventure capital of the world, after all), followed by three days in Venezuela, joined by Josh and Kat (Sarah had arranged an emotional reunion for Josh and me with Mariela), and capped off by four magical nights for my baby and me (and our friends the howler monkeys) in our jungle tree house in Belize. It was amazing, all of it—and yet, when it was time to come home, I wasn't at all sorry. In fact, I was chomping at the bit to come home and start my new life with my baby, my wife, the goddess and the muse, Sarah Faraday.

Sarah looks dazed as she sips her cappuccino. "Oh my God, I can't move," she groans. "After all that bungee jumping and rappelling and hot monkey-sex, my body's in a perpetual state of wet-noodledom."

"I'm pretty wiped, too," I admit.

"Yeah, that's why you've already worked out this morning and done all our laundry, you weirdo."

"I told you—I'm too happy to sleep."

"That's sweet," she says, which means she thinks I'm being intense or creepy or both.

"There's a big stack of cards and gifts in the kitchen," I say. "Josh and Kat must have brought everything back for us after the wedding. Do you want to open all that stuff today?"

"Yeah, but later, when I can focus," she says. "I'm just so frickin' *tired*."

I push her hair away from her face. "Even when you're tired, you're beautiful. Do you know that, Mrs. Faraday?"

She sighs happily. "Wasn't the wedding lovely?"

"It was perfect."

Sarah and I have talked about our wedding countless times over the past two weeks, of course, but apparently, neither of us has tired of the topic.

"Didn't Georgia look great?" Sarah asks. "And Trey was so dapper in his suit."

"Your mom didn't stop smiling the whole time."

"Well, except for when she was bawling like a baby."

"No, even then she was smiling."

"And, oh my gosh, the look on Miss Westbrook's face when she saw you, Jonas—oh my God, I could sob just thinking about it. That was a beautiful thing."

I smile. That *was* a beautiful thing. But I could say that about every minute of our wedding day. Sarah planned the whole thing top to bottom—all I had to do was pay the bills and show up like any other guest—and it was glorious. When she walked down the aisle toward me, I truly thought I'd died and gone to heaven. And when she said, "I do"—when she officially became my wife in front of God and everyone—it was the happiest moment of my life.

And then there was the party. Holy fuck, what a fucking party. I mean, Jesus, I even *danced*. All night long. With Sarah, of course, but also with Georgia and her new boyfriend and Trey and Miss Westbrook and her kids (including my namesake himself, who turned out to be quite a strapping young lad) and Sarah's mom and Kat and Josh and Henn and a whole bunch of Sarah's awesome friends. I even danced with Uncle William after the Scotch started flowing, after the band had kicked things into high gear.

I've never had so much fun in my life—good old fashioned, silly *fun*. Well, yeah, I've had plenty of silly fun with Sarah, of course—and with Josh, too—but I've never let loose like that with anyone besides those two, and especially not with a whole room full of people, some of whom I honestly didn't even know. What a stroke of genius on Sarah's part to rent out Canlis for the occasion. What better place to celebrate than the site of our first date?

"Earth to Jonas."

I smile at her.

"What are you thinking about, baby?"

"Our amazing wedding."

"It was amazing, wasn't it? Did you see Uncle William dancing with Kat?" Sarah asks. "He was adorable."

"Yeah. And did you see Henn trying to do some kind of, like, weird break dancing thing?"

Sarah laughs. "I honestly didn't know what the heck Henn was trying to do. I was a bit concerned for his safety."

"And the safety of everyone around him on the dance floor."

She laughs.

"Let's do it again soon."

Sarah shoots me a look that says I'm a complete idiot. "Let me explain something kind of basic to you, love. The thing about having a wedding is that, if you're really lucky, you only do it *once*. The whole concept is specifically designed as a one-off." She smirks.

"Smart-ass. I mean we should throw another party. I've never thrown a party before. It was fun."

Her jaw drops. "Jonas Faraday wants to throw a party?"

"Wait, no. Correction. I want *you* to throw a party and I want to attend. Just like our wedding. You do all the work, make all the decisions, invite everyone, don't bother me with any of it—and then I come and drink and dance and have fun and act like an idiot."

She laughs. "Oh, Jonas. I'll throw you a party any time, baby. It would be my pleasure."

I scoot up against her on the bed and hug her. "Thank you." I kiss her nose. "Wife." I press myself against her body and snuggle close. We lie in silence for a few minutes as I rub her back.

"What's today's date?" she suddenly asks, sitting up, having some sort of epiphany.

I tell her.

"Holy crap. My grades should have posted by now." She grabs her laptop and logs onto some sort of student portal as I peek over her shoulder, holding my breath. "Ah," she says. "Damn."

"What?"

"The good news is I got A's on all my exams," she says, and yet she sounds disappointed.

"That's fantastic. Why do you sound bummed?"

She sticks out her lower lip. "Because the bad news is that I sank like a stone in the rankings." She sighs. "I fell to number twelve. I went down eight spots."

"Number twelve in your whole class? *That's* sinking like a stone?" I laugh. "It's terrific, baby."

"But I didn't get the scholarship." She looks down at her hands—and when she does, I can't help but smile at the sparkling wedding band gracing her slender finger, nestled against her dazzling rock. "I missed the scholarship by two spots."

"Baby, listen to me. Considering everything you went through right before finals, number twelve is fantastic."

She shrugs.

"Don't worry about the scholarship. I told you, you're the lucky recipient of the Jonas Faraday Scholarship Fund. Just be proud of yourself and don't sweat it."

"I don't need the Jonas Faraday Scholarship Fund. I can use my finder's fee money to pay my tuition."

"Nope. I'm your husband now. That means I take care of you. In all things. In all ways. End of story."

She raises her eyebrows at me.

Oh yeah. I forgot she's not a fan of the whole "end of story" thing. "I *want* to take care of you, Sarah—Mrs. Faraday. *Please.*"

She smiles.

"In every conceivable way. For the rest of your life."

"Oh, Jonas."

I kiss her. "I'm proud of you. Just be proud of yourself. Don't sweat it."

"Thank you."

I grab her ass with gusto. "So what do you want to do today, wife? Bungee jump off a bridge? Rappel down a cliff? Fuck like monkeys and imagine our brethren in Belize howling in the jungle all around us?"

"Oh my God, I can't handle any more excitement. For the next week 'til school starts, I'm just gonna lie here and drool and stare at the ceiling."

Well, fuck that. I hope she's not being literal about that no excitement thing—unless, of course, she's planning on letting me lick every inch of her while she lies in bed and stares at the ceiling—because this woman is my crack and I'm not planning to go to rehab any time soon.

She pauses. "Although..."

I perk up. "Yes?"

"There is one thing I'd really like to do today, my dearest husband, if you're up for it."

"Name it, spouse." My cock tingles.

"Well, I've noticed when I'm curled up in the leather armchair in the family room reading my textbooks, there's no end table for my drink."

I look at her funny. What the hell is she talking about?

"And I've also noticed you don't have any shot glasses in your cabinets—"

"*We* don't have any shot glasses in *our* cabinets. We. Our."

She smiles. "*We* don't have any shot glasses."

"Mmm hmm." I'm not quite sure where she's going with this.

"So I was thinking it might be nice to do a little shopping today." She flashes a smart-ass smile, and I suddenly know what game she's playing.

"Shopping, huh?"

"Correct."

"For an end table and shot glasses?"

"Correct. And maybe a few other household items, as well."

Jesus. I can't believe this is what my life has become—*and that I like it.* "And *where* were you thinking about shopping for an end table and shot glasses and various unspecified sundries, Mrs. Faraday?"

"Well, hunky-monkey husband, I know this place where we could miraculously get all of these things and more—maybe even a gigantic, lime-green bean bag chair, too, just for the hell of it—*and* at the same time stuff our faces with some tasty Swedish meatballs."

I exhale with mock anxiety. "Wow, I don't know, baby. Sounds like a big step in our relationship. You really think we're ready for this?"

She makes a big show of considering her options. "Well, it definitely would signify we're taking our relationship to the next level. But I think I'm ready for that, if you are." She grins.

"As long as there are meatballs involved, and as long as I'm with you, I can handle just about anything, even shopping at IKEA. I'll just leave my dick and balls at home, and I'll be fine."

"No, you big dummy. That's not gonna work."

"Why not?"

"Think, Jonas, think. How are we gonna have hot monkey-sex in one of those private family bathrooms if you've left your dick and balls at home?"

Hello, instant hard-on. "Ah, excellent point. I'm glad one of us is thinking."

"Oh, I'm always thinking, Jonas. I assure you."

"That's the understatement of the century, baby."

She laughs. "So it's a date? Mr. and Mrs. Faraday go shopping at IKEA today?"

"Absolutely. But now that you've got me thinking about my dick and balls and meatballs, I'm craving some tasty *albóndigas* before we go."

A look of sheer terror fills her eyes. "Oh no, Jonas. Please, no."

"There's no way to stop me."

"No!" She screams, laughing, but resistance is futile.

I turn her onto her belly, yank down her pajama bottoms, and take a big bite out of her ass—a big, ol' juicy bite. "Mmm. I love this ass," I growl, and then I slap it.

She squeals again.

Oh man, I'm hard as a rock, ready for some good old fashioned fuckery with my sweet wife, My Magnificent Mrs. Faraday.

And yet, on second thought, there's no rush, is there? We've got all the time in the world, my wife and I. I'm not going anywhere, and neither is she. Forevermore. She promised in front of God and everyone and she can't take it back. So why not hold off and let a little delicious anticipation build? It sure sounds like, if I'm a patient boy, I'm going to get to fuck my dirty, dirty girl in a bathroom at IKEA this afternoon, and that's most certainly worth the wait. I hop off the bed and hoot at the ceiling—and then I slap her ass one more time for good measure.

"Come on, Mrs. Faraday," I bellow. "Get your delectable ass in gear. Your husband's got a gigantic boner and he wants to take his hot little wife shopping at IKEA!"

Acknowledgments

Writing this trilogy has been one of the great joys of my life. Thank you to my beloved early readers for your feedback and encouragement, with a special shout-out to my shining star, Nicki Starr. Thank you to my family for always giving me space and support for my writing, even though we all know the process of writing renders me clinically insane (and never more so than when I'm writing three books back-to-back).

In relation to this third book, *The Redemption,* in particular, thank you to the "village" that helped me with inspiration: Thank you to my neighbor, Steve, a retired Secret Service Agent, for the countless hours you spent with me, teaching me about federal investigations, organized crime, and hacking. We were an unlikely pair in some ways, but we sure had fun talking this thing through, didn't we? Thank you to those awesome hacker guys I met in Las Vegas at Mandalay Bay. You happened to be in Vegas for a hacker convention while I was there partying with my girlfriends, and, lucky me, you dudes absolutely styled me with ideas. I'll likely never see you gentlemen again and you'll probably never read this message— but you were so helpful and hilarious, and the free drinks you generously supplied to me were so appreciated, I nonetheless feel compelled to thank you expressly here.

My entire extended family is amazing. Thank you to my mother, mother-in-law, and aunt for reading the books and loving them. I love you all so much. Thank you to my uncle the motorcycle man for reading the first chapter of *The Club* and saying, "Yep," when I asked if it rang true as a male voice—your vote of confidence really encouraged me to keep going and trust Jonas' voice inside my head. Thank you to my uncle the computer whiz for giving me that super-duper, grand idea over lunch one day. Thank you to my Baby Cuz for reading the first chapters to *The Club* and calling me immediately to say, "Cuz, you're a savage beast." Thank you to Cuz for teaching me about the Deep Web. Eek. You can't un-hear that shit, man.

Thank you to my dad for listening to me go on and on about the plotting of these books over lunch one day (sex scenes abbreviated to "and then they have sex," of course). I don't know why I keep creating bastard fathers in my writing when I have the best one on the planet. I love you, Pops. (And I don't even know why I just thanked you here because if you read these books, I don't want to know about it.)

Thank you to Scott, the ER doctor who took so much time out of his busy schedule to help me formulate Sarah's injuries, treatment, and recovery in as realistic a manner as possible. Thank you also to bestselling author (and former ER nurse) Catherine (Fucking) Bybee who also helped me injure poor Sarah in exactly the right way and made me belly laugh as she did.

Thank you to my agents Jill and Kevin—as always, your belief in me, regardless of the name I happen to be writing under or the genre I'm writing in, means so much to me. Thank you to the Author Whisperer for your invaluable feedback and assistance. Thank you to Lisa, Melissa, and Sharon. You ladies rock. Thank you to Alicia for your proofing and editing and to Judi for formatting. I am a lucky girl to have such a great team of people supporting me. And, finally, thank you to the greatest team member of all: my hunky-monkey husband. You are my rock and I love you.

About the Author

Lauren Rowe is the pen name of a USA Today best-selling author, performer, audio book narrator, songwriter and media host/personality who decided to unleash her alter ego to write The Club Trilogy to ensure she didn't hold back or self-censor in writing the story. Lauren Rowe lives in San Diego, California where she lives with her family, sings with her band, hosts a show, and writes at all hours of the night. Find out more about The Club Trilogy and Lauren Rowe at www.LaurenRoweBooks.com and be sure to sign up for her emails to find out about new releases and exclusive giveaways.

Additional Books by Lauren Rowe

All books by Lauren Rowe are available in ebook, paperback, and audiobook formats.

The Club Series (The Faraday Brothers Books)

The Club Series is seven books about two brothers, Jonas and Josh Faraday, and the feisty, fierce, smart, funny women who eventually take complete ownership of their hearts: Sarah Cruz and Kat Morgan. *The Club Series* books are to be read in order*, as follows:

-*The Club* #1 (Jonas and Sarah)

-*The Reclamation* #2 (Jonas and Sarah)

-*The Redemption* #3 (Jonas and Sarah)

-*The Culmination* #4 (Jonas and Sarah with Josh and Kat)*
    *Note Lauren intended *The Club Series* to be read in order, 1-7. However, some readers have preferred skipping over book four and heading straight to Josh and Kat's story in *The Infatuation* (Book #5) and then looping back around after Book 7 to read Book 4. This is perfectly fine because *The Culmination* is set three years after the end of the series. It's up to individual preference if you prefer chronological storytelling, go for it. If you wish to read the books as Lauren intended, then read in order 1-4.

-*The Infatuation* #5 (Josh and Kat, Part I)

-*The Revelation* #6 (Josh and Kat, Part II)

Lauren Rowe

-*The Consummation* #7 (Josh and Kat, Part III)

In *The Consummation* (The Club #7), we meet Kat Morgan's family, including her four brothers, Colby, Ryan, Keane, and Dax. If you wish to read more about the Morgans, check out The Morgan Brothers Books. A series of complete standalones, they are set in the same universe as *The Club Series* with numerous cross-over scenes and characters. You do *not* need to read *The Club Series* first to enjoy The Morgan Brothers Books. **And all Morgan Brothers books are standalones to be read in *any* order.**

The Morgan Brothers Books:

Enjoy the Morgan Brothers books before or after or alongside *The Club Series,* in any order:

1. *Hero.* Coming March 12, 2018! This is the epic love story of heroic firefighter, **Colby Morgan,** Kat Morgan's oldest brother. After the worst catastrophe of Colby Morgan's life, will physical therapist Lydia save him… or will he save her? This story takes place alongside Josh and Kat's love story from books 5 to 7 of *The Club Series* and also parallel to Ryan Morgan's love story in *Captain.*

2. *Captain.* A steamy, funny, heartfelt, heart-palpitating insta-love-to-enemies-to-lovers romance. This is the love story of tattooed sex god, **Ryan Morgan**, and the woman he'd move heaven and earth to claim. Note this story takes place alongside *Hero* and The Josh and Kat books from *The Club Series* (Books 5-7). For fans of *The Club Series,* this book brings back not only Josh Faraday and Kat Morgan and the entire Morgan family, but we also get to see in detail Jonas Faraday and Sarah Cruz, Henn and Hannah, and Josh's friend, the music mogul, Reed Rivers, too.

3. *Ball Peen Hammer.* A steamy, hilarious enemies-to-friends-to-lovers romantic comedy. This is the story of cocky as hell male stripper, **Keane Morgan**, and the sassy, smart young

woman who brings him to his knees on a road trip. The story begins after *Hero* and *Captain* in time but is intended to be read as a true standalone in *any* order.

4. *Rock Star.* Do you love rock star romances? Then you'll want to read the love story of the youngest Morgan brother, **Dax Morgan,** and the woman who rocked his world, coming in 2018 (TBA)! Note Dax's story is set in time after *Ball Peen Hammer.* Please sign up for Lauren's newsletter at www.laurenrowebooks.com to make sure you don't miss any news about this release and all other upcoming releases and giveaways and behind the scenes scoops!

5. If you've started Lauren's books with The Morgan Brothers Books and you're intrigued about the Morgan brothers' feisty and fabulous sister, **Kat Morgan** (aka The Party Girl) and the sexy billionaire who falls head over heels for her, then it's time to enter the addicting world of the internationally bestselling series, *The Club Series.* Seven books about two brothers (**Jonas Faraday** and **Josh Faraday**) and the witty, sassy women who bring them to their knees (**Sarah Cruz** and **Kat Morgan**), *The Club Series* has been translated all over the world and hit multiple bestseller lists. Find out why readers call it one of their favorite series of all time, addicting, and unforgettable! The series begins with the story of Jonas and Sarah and ends with the story of Josh and Kat.

Does Lauren have standalone books outside the Faraday-Morgan universe? Yes! They are:

1. *Countdown to Killing Kurtis* – This is a sexy psychological thriller with twists and turns, dark humor, and an unconventional love story (not a traditional romance). When a seemingly naive Marilyn-Monroe-wanna-be from Texas discovers her porno-king husband has thwarted her lifelong Hollywood dreams, she hatches a surefire plan to kill him in exactly one year, in order to fulfill what she swears is her sacred destiny.

2. *Misadventures on the Night Shift* – a sexy, funny, scorching bad-boy-rock-star romance with a hint of angst. This is a quick read and Lauren's steamiest book by far, but filled with Lauren's trademark heart, wit, and depth of emotion and character development. Part of Waterhouse Press's Misadventures series featuring standalone works by a roster of kick-ass authors. Look for the first round of Misadventures books, including Lauren's, in fall 2017. For more, visit misadventures.com.

3. *Misadventures of a College Girl* – a sexy, funny romance with tons of heart, wit, steam, and truly unforgettable characters. Part of Waterhouse Press's Misadventures series featuring standalone works by a roster of kick-ass authors. Look for the first second of Misadventures books, including Lauren's, in spring 2018. For more visit misadventures.com.

4. Look for Lauren's third *Misadventures* title, coming in 2018.

Be sure to sign up for Lauren's newsletter at www.laurenrowe books.com to make sure you don't miss any news about releases and giveaways. Also, join Lauren on Facebook on her page and in her group, Lauren Rowe Books! And if you're an audiobook lover, all of Lauren's books are available in that format, too, narrated or co-narrated by Lauren Rowe, so check them out!